Quitting Time

QUITTING TIME

A Novel
by Leonard Kriegel

Pantheon Books   New York

Library of Congress Cataloging in Publication Data

Kriegel, Leonard, 1933–
Quitting time.

I. Title.
PS3561.R55Q5   813'.54   81–16941
ISBN 0–394–50893–9   AACR2

For my friends
Elizabeth Pochoda, Clancy Sigal, and Arthur Zeiger

Quitting Time

Marty

1

"The forces of history wrestle with each other like drunken strangers in a Turkish bath." From memory. Like a man talking in his sleep. Forty-eight years, three hundred and fifty-nine days back. A beginning. Another world. Sixty-eight when he died, the last fifteen of them useless. Lisa wrote me about it. A heart attack. In Albuquerque, where I saw him a few months earlier. A city like a phlegmatic zoo, performing drifters working their angles like trained seals. No surprises in Albuquerque. What could a man like Barney have thought of out there? Everything out in the open, the way each of us learns to proclaim his faith here in America. The giant billboard I passed on 66. ALBUQUERQUE: CITY OF NOW. And smaller letters beneath: LET IT BE YOUR CITY OF TOMORROW. Afterthoughts. Who believes in tomorrow in America? Maybe what Barney Kadish never understood is that America may be beyond the forces of history. No beginning, no end. Nothing. Except now. And that was where Barney Kadish, who believed in the forces of history, died in the arms of his Jewish penitent.

What better end could a man like Barney anticipate? What else could a revolutionary want? My friend Barney was

no Trotsky. No ax in the head at the end, the mind still struggling to resurrect the purity of line, the original vision, while
the body surrenders. A single thought to right the balance for
the whole world? Not for Barney Kadish. History might have
been his god, but he wasn't really a thinker. "Listen," he says,
pulling me out of the shop of that same Leftwich who is groan-
ing on the floor, surrounded by his other workers, "no matter
what else, you can depend upon this: a boss is a boss. Sucks
your blood, then wipes his ass with your carcass. It's his nature.
That bastard there is no worse than the others. No brains, no
talent. So what made him in this world? Nothing but ambition.
And money. All the bastards have ambition and money."

And later, the two of us sitting in Dolkin's, drinking the
sweet hot coffee. "It won't be different until we're all bosses.
Which means there'll be no bosses. What man wants to eat
another man's shit? Leftwich thinks I should be grateful to him.
Why? Because I need work and he needs workers. And because
his father and my father, they knew each other in Odessa. So
the bastard is going to sew his patterns with my blood. And
wants me to be grateful. *Landsmanshaft*. To hell with them
all!"

I was fifteen then. Barney was nineteen. June 1919, one
day before the Germans signed at Versailles. Marty Altschuler
and his mother Tzeerel are now three weeks in America. But
not yet part of it. Smuggled in from Montreal, I have been sent
that very morning to Leftwich's shop. An upstairs neighbor in
the railroad flat on Stanton Street convinces my mother to send
me. "Five dollars a week, missus. And he'll teach him to be a
cutter. On the machines." Barney had already been there a
year. It was his first job, too. His father, Old Isaac, had urged
him on to study law when he graduated from high school.
"Turn their laws against them, Barney. Don't be another peasant. Like your brothers." Barney didn't listen. He already had
other plans.

He was right about Leftwich. I could see it that morning in the way Leftwich worked alongside us. Body and ambition. And a start in life. No talent. Not even real business sense. Just the rich smell of dyes and patterns and money in the nostrils. Dead two years ago. In Miami. Seventy-eight years old. And rich. On the first anniversary of his death they strung a huge banner with his picture on it from one side of Seventh Avenue to the other: NEW YORK PATTERN AND SILK MANUFACTURERS' ASSOCIATION—JACK LEFTWICH CANCER MEMORIAL COMMITTEE. He had been the voice of the association, the one among them who hated Barney most. Raw death in his eye even then. Cut patterns, sew linings, claim souls. What did it matter to Jack Leftwich? An ox of a man, six feet five inches tall, thick in the shoulders and chest. In Odessa, his father had been a butcher.

"You eat too slow, Kadish," Leftwich complains at lunch. "What the hell you think I'm running? A goddamn restaurant? Move your ass or I'll send you packing."

"An hour for lunch. In the agreement, Mr. Leftwich."

"Agreement!" Leftwich roars. "Up your ass, I'll give you agreements! You want contracts, get the hell out on the street with the rest of them bums. Bolsheviks and bums." He advances on Barney. Barney backs into a corner. He himself not small, but giving away a good eight inches and seventy-five pounds to Leftwich. The workers in the shop suspend movement and talk. Our eyes follow Leftwich as he corners Barney. There are seven of us. But no one tries to stop it. Old Lobnick bends over his machine, yarmulke glued to his dried-out scalp, pretending nothing is happening. Other than silk linings, to be cut and sewed. A man's soul torn from his grasp, even the yarmulke a stranger's patch. Lobnick prays, eyes glued to the pattern he maneuvers on the cutting table.

Barney feints with his left hand. Leftwich's hands go up and then Barney slams him hard in the stomach with his right. As Leftwich grabs his stomach and farts out the pain of the blow, Barney drives his entire body—not fist alone but muscle, sinew, bone, cartilage—into Leftwich's chin so that Leftwich must have been as surprised as we were that his entire face didn't simply shatter like a pane of glass. Even before Leftwich's body hit the floor, Barney had grabbed his jacket and turned to look at me. I had no jacket. But I dropped the broom I had been leaning on and followed him to the elevator. "You, Altschuler! Come back!" Leftwich bellows from the floor. I can hear his pain, his rage. "Follow that Bolshevik scum, he'll lead you to hell." I didn't go back. I followed Barney.

2

In Dolkin's Cafeteria, Barney Kadish talks. First he talks about Leftwich and then about the impending revolution and then about himself. Like Leftwich, he came out of Odessa. Which accounted for the way he handled himself. In Odessa, the Jews fought first with the Russians and then with the Bulgarians and then with the Ukrainians, and when there were neither Russians nor Bulgarians nor Ukrainians available they fought with each other. Barney grew up watching his two older brothers fight—short muscular men who turned their backs on both the radicalism of their father and on the emancipation promised by the rising Jewish businessmen of Odessa. They followed Old Isaac into the stonecutting trade, working at anything that came their way—tombstones for the Gentiles, statues of angels, gargoyles, hooded figures of death with stone scythes etched into stone doors that led to stone tombs. Old Isaac wailed, excoriated the god he refused to believe in for giving him sons who read neither *Kapital* nor Talmud, for whom books were just so much garbage in the way of what propelled them through the streets of Odessa. Not even gangsters. Just two young Jews who liked to hit. Hands. That was how Barney remembered them. Thick, calloused, sinewy hands, veined and ridged like the stone they worked.

Avram and Moishe wanted nothing—not from Jew, not from Gentile, not from God, not from man. They ignored the Russian socialists, they ignored the Jewish Bund. Wedded to a vision of their own destruction, they were never forced to resign from their aspirations because they never had any. How make the world better when you do not recognize its existence? So Old Isaac gave the books to Barney. At twelve, Barney had already memorized entire pages of the *Manifesto*, had read Tolstoy on the peasants, Chekhov, Sholom Aleichem, Mendele, Turgenev, Peretz, had read Russian, Yiddish, Ukrainian—words descending on him. He loved words. But he also loved to trail behind his brothers into the port, where the sailors and outcasts would buy their whores for the night. Follow Avram and Moishe into the house and watch as they bought the woman and each in his turn took her while she lay in bed crying, "I am not a horse, Jews! No price you will not demand." And then, finished, hand her over to Barney, standing behind them embarrassed, ashamed for the woman, yet aware of his brothers' need to inflict their presence on a world dividing Russians and Jews and Ukrainians and Bulgarians and socialists and *narodniki* and Old Believers and Talmud pilpul disputants. All the time thinking of what Old Isaac taught him. To choose a side, to take a position with your own. And then to hold on. The whore's body crumples into the mattress, the icon shadows her from above the bed. The whore rests, willing to service this youngest brother, too, because even worn down to the nub of her soul she still remembers that she has been bought and paid for. "You don't have to," Barney says, crying with shame. "It is wrong what my brothers do to you."

"Your brothers paid," the whore says. She lies on the dirty mattress, the icon god staring down at her high cheekbones.

"It's a crime to buy another human being!" Barney cries.

"An abomination. But do not be angry with them. Ignorant men."

I can see the whore now. Sitting up, pulling him to her. Wrapping him against her flesh, thin, he said it was, like Japanese lantern paper, so that what he felt was neither disgust nor passion but a simple purity of rage. And the smell of her, already the sweet sour of death. Jews, Russians, Greeks, Bulgars, Poles, Ukrainians, how many thousands of bodies had lain here before him, had paid and tasted and gone away? No anger in his voice as he drinks the hot coffee in Dolkin's and remembers how she undressed him, guiding his hands into her flesh, so that he was engulfed by the need to treat her—"Listen, Marty, only don't laugh, I want you to understand, listen"—gently, decently, like a woman bestowing her favors upon a young Jewish boy. And then, finished, running from her, the thin body sitting up in bed now, amazed, staring at him, knees pulled to her chin, Japanese lantern flesh flooded with color.

Outside, he turns on Avram and Moishe. Attacks them as I had just seen him attack Leftwich. And the brothers laugh, pick him up, one holding his feet, the other his shoulders, and carry him while he flails the Odessa air with his curses, crying all the time because he loves them so, even if they are traitors to their class. Didn't they realize that their task was to unite with their brethren everywhere? Like it said in the books. What were they but stonecutters? Hands like stone. Heads like stone. And the two of them laughing all the way home, dumping him, still laughing, at the feet of the amazed father. Barney sobs, too ashamed to tell Old Isaac what happened.

"The way the goyim go to their Bible and the old rabbis to their Talmud, that was how I went to Marx. Not to understand. All night long I lay in bed reciting the last two paragraphs of the *Manifesto*. I already knew them by heart, like old Jews in the synagogue know their prayers. For the same reason, too. At least that night. Ward off evil. Pray for forgiveness. You repeat and repeat and then the words, they're part of you. Like the color of your eyes or the shape of your nose. Something certain. Something you can depend upon."

Was it that Avram and Moishe were evil? The unforgivable sin. To turn on your class. Not that he asked them to be moral. "There's no such thing as character in a man, Marty. Even Lobnick. A smell in the nostrils. Even he is what he is because nothing else was possible for him. History rains its choices down on us. We move where the wind pushes us because we're afraid to change the world."

Three years later and the brothers are dead. Barney and Old Isaac and Barney's mother and two sisters prepare to embark for America. By 1915, Avram and Moishe have been called to serve Czar Nicholas. Isaac pleads, tries to bribe them into defiance. "Go to America. I'll give you the money. It's not our war. Not the workers' war." The brothers laugh and go off to fight. Avram died a hero. He killed three Austrian soldiers in hand-to-hand combat before he was shot in the neck and tumbled to his trench-cut grave. "All Russia," wrote his commander to Isaac, "is proud of such Jews as your son. We shall remember him as a Russian hero. I enclose his cigarette case, his regimental service badge, and a requisition for money which can be filled at the local police station. I join you in mourning for this brave soldier who died in the service of our Holy Mother Russia. I salute you." Once again, Isaac cursed the God he did not believe in, cursed the naked mockery of a child born of his loins dying for Holy Mother Russia. Cursed and wept, and then forced his weeping youngest to recite from the *Manifesto* the passages foretelling the future. And then Isaac went to his stonecutter's yard and cursed his Russian foreman, too.

Moishe died two months later. But Moishe was not a hero. He did not die for Holy Mother Russia. He had been sent to the Ukraine, where he drove a wagon for the cooks. An attack was underway a few kilometers north of where the Russian troops had bivouacked. The shells burst overhead and the men huddled against their horses, peering into the flat Ukrainian sky. Men and animals were screaming all around Moishe, who did not understand what he was doing sitting in a wagon waiting to be killed by an exploding shell.

"I'm going to the front," Moishe says to his sergeant.

"At the front, you'll get killed."

"I'll be killed here. I prefer to take my chances at the front."

"Here I give the orders," the sergeant cries. "And I've heard enough from you goddamn rabbis!"

Moishe hit him. The sergeant lay on the ground and when the lieutenant called for him all he found was Moishe swinging his horsewhip to cut his way through a crowd of Russian soldiers. The shells were exploding against the flat Ukrainian sky and the lieutenant took out his pistol and shot Moishe through the neck, exactly where Avram had been shot by the Austrians, cutting the jugular just as Avram's had been cut. The commander did not send back Moishe's regimental service badge. Instead, one of the local police officers descended upon Isaac to tell him that this was what had come of filling his dead Moishe's head with nonsense, radical nonsense, and look, the man could have prospered in the service of his Imperial Highness, Czar of all the Russias, Nicholas Romanov. To think that one old Jew like Isaac had two such different sons, the one a hero, the other not worth the dirt they had filled his grave with. In any case, he had been told to make certain that Isaac understood that the money due him for the one son's heroism was now to be confiscated for the other son's treachery. Isaac himself was to report to police headquarters every two weeks. They would be keeping their eyes on him from this time on. Did he understand? Isaac nodded. He understood.

So Isaac could now lie to himself about one of his sons, could pretend that Moishe had seen the light at the end, had died a hero of the revolution. The lie committed to memory, Isaac took Barney, his wife Bronya, and his two daughters, Rachel and Bathsheva, sold his stonecutter's tools, reported to the police as he had been instructed, packed his revolutionary tracts in a used seaman's bag filled with sawdust and apples, and with the clothes on his back and money in his pocket left Odessa. Even in wartime, the departure wasn't difficult. After a year of war in Europe, there were still enough way stations to serve fleeing revolutionaries.

He could have traveled from Odessa to Tibet just as easily as he now went from Odessa to Warsaw, from Warsaw to Vienna, from Vienna to Berlin. In Berlin he paused long enough to walk down Unter den Linden with the frightened but unquestioning Bronya and the two docile handsome daughters who smiled and blushed in response to the whistles and stares of German officers. Isaac himself was oblivious to the officers. The enemy's face never particularly interested him, as it was to interest his son. He spent three days in Berlin speaking to the railroad workers, anarchists most of them, but still revolutionaries. The railroad workers knew that Isaac was not the enemy. The real enemy owned everything—freight yards and trains and what the trains carried and the whores and soldiers ogling each other. The real enemy owned them, owned their fathers and brothers and mothers and sisters, owned the food they ate and the buildings they hid themselves in when it rained. The real enemy owned it all. And men ate other men. Money. Dog's bread.

Isaac and his wife and daughters were put up in one of the warehouses. Barney stayed in the house of a railroad fireman. The fireman could neither read nor write but he made Barney recite his incantations, just as Isaac had. Barney recited from the *Manifesto* in Russian. The fireman shook his head. "Jewish speech," he muttered in his clipped Bavarian accent. "No Russia. Do not understand." It turned out that he didn't really understand the language of the Jews either. Still, he kept on smiling until Barney finished. Then he gave him tea and cake and brought him to the freight car where he was to travel northeast to Travemünde. There he linked up again with Isaac and his mother and sisters. The five of them were taken aboard a fishing boat that dropped them on the Danish coast. From there to Liverpool. From Liverpool to New York. At Ellis Island, equipped with a false visa, Barney sits on a bench and waits for his father's interview to be concluded. He does not guard sisters and mother. Even at fifteen, his Tartar eyes are on the larger future.

3

He was vain enough. He admitted that. Still, he saw himself as he saw others. Individuals were mere instruments to the larger necessities. Talking to me in Yiddish, an occasional English or Russian phrase dropped into his speech, he establishes an intimacy between us, as if the two of us are the last people on earth in whom hope for change resides. I am fifteen and he is nineteen. But in his eyes, we are veterans of the revolution.

"Of course, there is the union. We must have the union."

"Are they corrupt?" I ask, taking my question from his tone.

"Old and tired and frightened, Kosoff was the only real man among them. And they shipped him back to the Soviet Union three weeks ago. The others. . . ." He shrugs. "Incompetent." He lights a cigarette, offers one to me. I refuse. I still did not smoke then. I was afraid to smoke. Barney blows smoke at the ceiling. Outside, groups of garment workers pass by, some of them peering through the window seeking their fellows. "Look at them," Barney says, waving his cigarette at the window. "That's what we have to work with. In Russia, Lenin took worse and seized a country. And those two they have now, Bilsky and Heinrich, they're afraid of a few small manufacturers. Like Leftwich. Only not as good."

"Shouldn't we buy more coffee?"

"You're embarrassed?" Barney laughs. I shrug. "Dolkin's father was a cutter for silk linings. Dolkin won't chase you."

"We're taking advantage."

"Of what? His good nature? Listen, he won't be bothered and you have no money anyway. Sit."

"No, I have no money." For the first time, I feel guilty about walking out. My father and sister are still in Hostov, waiting until my mother and I earn enough to send for them. My father is sick, consumptive. Ransom money. "No money at all."

"Does it frighten you?"

"It's a problem. We have to get enough to send for my father and sister."

"Isaac is my father. But he himself taught me that family is what you belong to. Your fellow workers."

"Like Lobnick?"

He crushes his cigarette in the saucer. "Lobnick is Lobnick. But even Lobnick doesn't want to be what he is." He stands up. "Come. We'll get you a union card and you'll help make the revolution."

We walk down Seventh Avenue to Twenty-fifth Street. Between tenement buildings, children dart like weasels in the Hostov woods. The air cool for June, the emergence of summer still hidden in the calendar. We stop in front of a red-brick four story tenement. The hinges on the iron door are broken and Barney braces against it with his body. We maneuver past a table and chair that block the entrance. I follow him up two flights of stairs until we stand before a gray door. Across its face yellow letters amateurishly proclaim:

JOINT COUNCIL

INTERNATIONAL PATTERN MAKERS,

DYERS, AND SILK WORKERS

UNITED GARMENT WORKERS OF AMERICA

NEW YORK: LOCAL ONE

Barney knocks at the door, waits a few seconds, then kicks until a voice inside calls out in Yiddish, "Take it easy, I'm coming."

"Bednarik," Barney mutters. "He was Kosoff's right hand. Their Czech. Another worker. He's against leprosy. But find me something he's still for." The door opens and a short, thick man, around forty-five, with a body just beginning to slide into fat, stands in front of us.

"It's you, young Kadish. What do you want?"

"Where's Bilsky?"

"Not here. He's organizing."

"He wouldn't know how to organize himself. And Heinrich?"

"Also not here. Listen, Barney, you shouldn't be so hard on them. They're good union men." Barney doesn't answer. Bednarik seems very tired, as if movement were difficult. His body blocks the entrance until Barney pushes past him, brushing his gut with his hand. I follow Barney inside. An old wooden desk that had once been a color natural to wood but was now painted a faded salmon-pink and a mahogany desk chair on casters with the leather seat slashed and gray stuffing strewn out. Notices tacked to the bulletin board behind the desk. Two lamps, one on each side of the desk, on heavy brass pedestals with curlicued brass stems leading to bulbs that throw a dim, unsatisfactory light throughout the entire office. A room that stinks of deadness at its center. Ambition wasted away and all the dead things in their places. No workers around. Just this Bednarik. Another Lobnick, I assume, waiting to be lied to, waiting to be lifted by the scruff of his neck and told he can stand.

"Shut the door," Barney orders. Bednarik goes to shut the door. "Where are the cards?"

"What cards?"

"The union cards, idiot. What do you run here? A health spa? You're lucky they took you from Prague."

"I'm not from Prague."

"So much the better for Prague. You're a worker, no? This is still a trade union, no? So I have here one Marty Altschuler, an apprentice lining cutter, who is determined to be a good union man." As he talks, Barney rummages in the desk drawers. "Bilsky and Heinrich, Heinrich and Bilsky. A Jew and a German and . . ." His eyes take Bednarik's measure. "And a Czech who used to be better than any of us. What happened to you, Bednarik?"

Bednarik's face droops into his body. "They led us in 1916."

"Kosoff and you led in 1916."

"Anyway, who are you to question me?"

"The man you once were. Not age. That's not what I mean. I don't kiss anyone's ass. I don't do the work of the manufacturers and pretend I'm a union leader."

"We got an agreement. It's their job to see that the agreements are followed."

Barney removes a cardboard file box from the bottom drawer. He flips through the cards, removes one. "Fill this out."

"I can't."

"Why? You're recording secretary, aren't you?"

Bednarik sighs, shuffles over to the desk, plops himself down on the chair like a seal about to give birth. He takes a pen from the drawer, dips it in the ink bottle on the desk. "Spell your name," he says. He doesn't look at me.

"M-a-r-t-y A-l-t-s-c-h-u-l-e-r."

"Address?"

"Stanton Street. Number 278. Fourth floor."

"Where were you born?"

"Hostov."

"Poland or Russia?"

"Russia is now the Soviet Union," Barney interrupts. "The day is going to come when you can join a union without this nonsense."

"I'm only doing what has to be done. It's not my union."

"It's not a worker's union either. Listen, Bednarik, you have any brains you'll throw in with the real workers. Be what you were. I remember 1916."

Bednarik's face lightens. "It's not that I don't want it should change," he pleads. "Some things even I won't do. Last week, they sent for those gangsters from the Lower East Side. Beryl Farkas wants they should take care of the Bolsheviks at Kramer's shop. I tried to talk to Bilsky. Only he's scared. He's got to do what they decide."

"The gangsters tell him?"

"He's afraid. You know how it works, Barney. They get a percentage from the local, a percentage from the association. They don't want trouble. Nobody wants trouble. Just calm."

"You were wrong," I say to Barney. "That's corruption."

"That's terror," Barney answers. "A union is like a body. No brain, no direction. Bilsky's not smart. But he didn't bring the gangsters in here. Stamp his card, Bednarik."

Bednarik hands me the stamped card. "A dollar twenty-five. And twenty-five cents a week out of your wages."

"He'll pay after he gets work."

"Bilsky'll be angry, Barney. They'll give him trouble."

"They've taken Bilsky's soul. That doesn't mean you have

to give them yours, too. You don't jump yet when they whistle. You just cringe. That's why they allow you to stay here. They're more afraid of little old ladies with umbrellas than they are of you. Bednarik, life didn't end in 1916. You, me, Altschuler here, we're part of something that's still coming."

"You're a Bolshevik," Bednarik sighs.

"Of course, I am. Who else will give us what's owed? Who else should we trust to run the world?"

"I'm a small man, Barney," Bednarik pleads.

"You're a worker, Bednarik." Barney examines my card. "When the time comes, you'll be with us."

4

"You lose patience and you sometimes wonder whether or not people can do what you expect of them. A man should be able to touch someone like himself. Even better. Only people are people. Working people, they keep coming back to themselves. First they learn they're wallowing in shit and then they learn that there are choices. A leader's job is to remind them what those choices cost."

Fifteen when he arrived in New York. As old as I was when I met him. His father apprenticing himself to a toymaker so that his only remaining son could go to high school. To prepare himself. Isaac's vengeance on God. Better yet, his revenge on what the idea of God had left him. Barney was smart. Isaac plotted Barney's future in America so that destiny could be claimed. It did no harm for Isaac to believe. Barney studied. And Barney fought. And Barney observed. On Allen Street, the whores were Jewish instead of Russian. Swallowing his shame of exploitation, he visits the whores, tells them about the coming world, listens to their laughter and recites the formulas in Yiddish, in Russian. Soon he recites in English. The whores laugh, pull him to their bodies. He learns to take what they offer. Even as he curses their Tammany landlords.

A few days later and Barney takes me home to meet Old Isaac. The apartment on Allen Street is a carbon of the apartment I live in with my mother. But I have never seen anyone like Old Isaac before. A man of seventy, he looks beyond ninety, so old as to be ageless. His skin is dry and yellowed, his face wrinkled into a map of betrayal. No longer does he ask Barney to recite from the revolution's holy books. The books stand between the world of the living and the world of the dead. What do they matter to this man with the wrinkled skin and sour breath, this man who querulously grunts commands at wife and daughters, who fades into arguments with his two dead sons? He is still trying to get them to listen. He no longer remembers to what.

"My friend, Marty," Barney introduces me.

Old Isaac ignores me. I am no child of his. "It's too cold for June," he announces. "Bernashe says he'll take me back next month. A new line of cheap watches. I can fix them good."

Barney shrugs. "Fine," he says. Then turns to me as if Old Isaac has disappeared. "He was very good to me. My first teacher. He wanted me to be a lawyer to get the workers out of prison. Now he talks about fixing watches." We leave Old Isaac arguing in Odessa with his dead sons. Barney takes me into the kitchen. His mother is cooking dinner. Neither of his sisters has come home yet. The younger is an aspiring Yiddish actress, the older sews hats in a Fifth Avenue millinery. Before dinnertime, they arrive. Handsome women, full-bodied, with the good Jewish cat's eyes of Odessa. For them, dreams are of another order. The revolution is already a failure. The promise is American now.

At dinner, Barney talks. The rest of us listen. It is a family

role to which I have fallen heir. The women serve in silence,
Old Isaac scrapes his plate while muttering imprecations to his
dead sons, to the dead Romanovs, to the cheap watches that
now command his vision. Barney's mother moves from table to
oven, silent, furtively eying her husband as he sits slumped over
his soup.

"You see Bednarik now and it's difficult to remember how
good he was in 1916. He and Kosoff, Marty, they played Bilsky
and Heinrich. Like violins. That's when I met them. A year in
this country. And one day I'm sitting in union headquarters.
Where we were today. Bednarik welcomes me. He gives me
leaflets to distribute. I make coffee. He explains the ways of
American labor. Bilsky and Heinrich sit in the office until Kosoff or Bednarik tell them to go out. 'Make a speech. Encourage
the people.' Contempt. Still, no one was frightened back then.
The war was on in Europe. Bednarik brought them together.
Cutters, pattern makers, dyers. Until then, they had separate
unions. The manufacturers didn't understand what Bednarik
and Kosoff were capable of. By the time they knocked Bednarik
around, it was too late. 'When they beat you,' he tells me, 'you
got to make yourself think of nothing. Nothing is what you are
and nothing is what you come out of.' Only he's forgotten. For
a leader, there's pain. There has to be pain.

"The people in the market trusted Bednarik. And Kosoff.
The only dumb thing they did was in not getting rid of Bilsky
and Heinrich. Unity. More sins are committed in the name of
unity than in the name of Christ. Kosoff thinks. Bednarik acts.
Bilsky and Heinrich smile like prima donnas and take the credit.
The orders for silk linings come in from England and France
and Germany and from the rich ladies whose husbands are
smart enough to understand that America is going in, too.
Nevermind what this Wilson says. Bednarik wasn't smart.
Kosoff was smart. Still, at sixteen I could've taught them both
more Marx than they'd ever thought existed. So what? Bednarik

was like this Debs, the one they have in prison now. No theoretician. But he knew by instinct what it took me years to recognize. In America, even the class war is gradual. Take more soup, Marty. My mother makes a good vegetable soup. Better than Dolkin's even.

"You learn to move one step at a time. Into the nothingness. Like a kid feeling how cold the water is with his big toe. Facts are the worker's poetry. A dollar raise here, a fifteen minute break there. Facts explain themselves. Bednarik and Kosoff knew what the price of garment linings would be. Bednarik went to Montreal, spoke to LaTour of the Canadian locals. He had to get rid of Heinrich so he sent him to convince the all-German local in Milwaukee. Then he pulled the people out and the manufacturers looked at each other and they were beaten. So they worked him over. What good did it do? Goons don't buy expensive coats. Rich ladies buy.

"So you watch Bednarik now. Who knows what it is? Maybe he lost heart when Kosoff was deported. But he's a man who doesn't know what he did. Bilsky's clerk. You want some more chicken, Marty? Okay, a man breaks. But why should he break himself?"

Barney speaks. Isaac stares into the white tablecloth that has been laid in honor of my fifteen-year-old presence. The sisters sit in silence. The mother serves. I listen.

5

Barney got both of us jobs in one of the last of the German silk-lining houses. Ulrich Westreich had survived because he had a good sense of what was coming in 1914. He made a small fortune selling cheap coat linings to the kaiser's general staff. He could have sold to the French and English, too, and emerged from the war one of the wealthiest coat-lining manufacturers around. But Westreich was a patriot, frozen to one view of the world. Old Isaac had his revolution and Westreich had his Fatherland, rooted to the promise of its own permanence.

I worked in Westreich's shop with Barney and I saved the money needed to send for my father and sister. My mother had gotten a job as a sewing-machine operator on women's dresses. Every two weeks, we would receive a letter from my sister Esther in Hostov. The letters spoke of the weather, of my father's failing health, of her longing to come to America—a longing so romantically phrased that I dreaded the day she would arrive on these dense, dirty streets. My father died on the first day of Passover, 1920. Two months later, my mother and I greeted Esther at the pier.

But even before she arrived, I rarely thought of Hostov or the life I had left there. I was becoming an American, the language entering the tight circle of my existence. We were weighed down with so much less here. No matter how hard Barney and I worked, the future beckoned. In America, even a revolutionary's horizons seemed limitless. The straight up-and-down angles of the New York streets drew me in. Sitting on the upper deck of the Fifth Avenue buses, Barney and I would examine the city with growing anticipation. In Washington Square Park, we watched as the Italians gathered in thick hordes, the children already chalking the streets with American games.

Barney was learning, too. Having been taught by the Allen Street whores that a revolutionary need not deny the body's demands, he soon came to understand that even politics might cut a path to the body's satisfaction. "You should have seen me with her, Marty. A body like the Russian serving girls in Odessa. Solid. Like a healthy animal." Or bringing Lisa that first time. No more than fifteen. But a face in which one could already see a peasant's skepticism mingling with beauty. Did she know then how Barney spoke of her? Lisa, who was to do so much for him. Did it matter? I doubt it. "On the foxes, the skins piled in the back. She works in fur. After work. I tell you, Marty, there is something to be said for animals." And laughs.

And Lisa running breathless alongside us, the three of us straining to catch a bus before it pulls away. Or else the three of us walking downtown in the warm spring twilight, laughing with the secrets we already knew. Our time.

Above all, Barney's time. By 1921, Lisa had more rivals than she wanted to know about. But even as he pursued women, Barney's eyes took in his destined kingdom. He was as aware of the workers greeting him in the streets as he was of women. He was interested in their lives. Especially in the Greeks. By that time, almost all of the silk linings were made by Jews, except for a sprinkling of Italians and a growing cluster of Greeks who worked in their own shops. Usually, they worked for even less than did workers in the unorganized Jewish shops. They worked for what they were offered, and they worried about being deported. Or else, as with the Jews, the communal pull of origins was even stronger than the need of workers to take their own. Organizing them was never far from Barney's mind.

"When he got to LaTour, Bednarik won in 1916." He memorizes the names as we pass the Greek shops on Twenty-fifth Street. Lardas, Palatianos, Vassilios. "We have to do the same thing."

"There aren't enough Greek shops to get through a season."

"Enough to give the association leverage," Barney insists. "So we can never be sure of how much strength we have."

At Twenty-sixth Street, Barney waves off the greetings of

a few stray workers. He is popular, known. Then the two of us turn into a building that houses a gym. We race up the four flights of stairs. Another of Barney's discoveries. He had become friendly with the janitor, Jimmy Callahan, who had bummed his way from one coast to another and whose left hand was twisted into a broken birdlike claw. Callahan had come out of the IWW. The hand was a present from a group of Seattle veterans. " 'Bolshie scum!' That's what they called us. They nailed Mulcahy and some kid he was traveling with in Portland. They beat that kid to shit, like a rag doll he was. Begs them not to kill him. Cries he's just a hobo. 'Hobo, my ass. You're Bolshie scum. You'd spit on your mother's grave, Paddy.' I crawled between the boxcars and I watched. I never seen Mulcahy or the kid again. I ride up to Seattle. A good Wobbly town, I figure I'm safe there. But in 1919, everyone's a patriot. They was waiting. 'We ain't taking chances. Who knows where you're from?' They put it in a vise and they tightened until the pain was jelly, Barney. That's what I remember. I don't remember nothing else."

You could see Callahan tremble with the humiliation of memory. And Barney talking to him quietly, telling him to have patience, his day, all of our days, would come. We started going to the gym at Callahan's invitation. By eight, the last of the small maufacturers and salesmen were gone. The gym was one of those places born unfashionable that go downhill as soon as they open. In a few years, it would be converted into a storeroom for Persian lamps and imitation Oriental rugs. But in 1921 it was still a gym and Jimmy Callahan with his crippled claw hand was the janitor and Barney and I would work out while Callahan swept the place up and put the towels away. After a hard day of sweating over linings at Westreich's, with the window fan doing little more than stirring the dead air, we would put on the gloves and swing away at the body bag. I liked the way you could hear the leather grunt with the full force of your own body hitting it. I liked Callahan pausing to watch us as he swept up. "Hit the bastard for me, Marty."

"Let's go a few rounds!" Barney shouts. We dance guardedly in the square ring. And then Barney is coming at me and I remember how he describes going after his brothers that day with the whore in Odessa. He comes straight at my body with the overweight gloves. I weave, clinch, watch him carefully. After the first few minutes, I know that he drops his left arm when he moves toward me. I already knew how they did that on Stanton Street. Every block on the Lower East Side had its streetcorner fighters. At sixteen, I had already studied them, fought them. On the East Side you learned to attack like the lightweights did, moving in sideways, almost shuffling, crouched low. We practiced what we observed. "Fight smart!" Callahan shouts, watching us. Barney was vulnerable. He fought straight up and coming. He never learned other ways. His right hand knocked me down and Callahan waved his crippled claw hand in the air, laughing. But I see now how easy it is going to be. I get up, maneuver him into the corner, spin him against the ropes, and catch him flush on the jaw with a hard right hand. He never touched me after that. He was strong. Muscles in his shoulders like rope knots. But if you could move, you could hit him almost at will. He's been lucky with Leftwich.

In the shower later, the three of us talk. Fighting, revolution, unions. Excited, Callahan swears vengeance. Barney talks softly to him, like a father to a child. Callahan is thirty-eight. Barney is twenty-one. I am not yet seventeen. Barney brings Callahan out of his moment into the gym again. Downstairs, we stop in an Italian speakeasy on Broadway for a round of beers. Callahan's face softens in the dim bar light. He talks memories of space. "Like sometimes you're walking and you begin to think crazy. I would pretend I'm the only person in the world. There's nothing around. Just sky and trees and all those miles." Later, we walk south, to the wooden boardinghouse just north of Houston Street where Callahan lives. By the time Barney and I are back on Allen Street, it is ten-thirty at night. The sidewalks are still jammed with people. Their voices jab against each other, just as our fists had done in the gym. Our eyes drink in the chaos, the need for space. Thrust an elbow against the empty air and it is a victory. Still, it has its sweetness. Thousands of people flowing into one another. Barney, too, senses it. "The forces of history," he says. And laughs, embarrassed. "Even here. On these stinking streets."

6

Ten of us work in Westreich's shop. Like Leftwich, Westreich works alongside of us. He grumbles about business as he cuts the silk linings. The war long over, Germany beaten, the mark collapsing. War is the health of the state. Versailles is the tomb of Westreich's aspirations. He believes in nothing now that Germany has died. But he remains in business. He cuts silk linings, cotton patterns. He cuts for rich and poor, shifting his merchandise from season to season. Now he talks about retiring, dreams of his youth in Breslau, grumbles.

Barney is elected shop steward three weeks after we are hired. He talks incessantly about union affairs. Too short a lunch break finds him seeking out his fellow workers. "Don't try to impress Westreich, Olinsky. He's not yours to worry over."

"What's the union ever done for me?"

"There'll be changes. If you want a union that'll do things for you, help us get rid of Bilsky and Heinrich." Olinsky listens. Even Kaufman, a sallow hunched-up man who sits bent over his machine as if all the skins he had sewn in his fifty-six years were pressing down on his back, listens to Barney talk about the union. "You know what you're making. You're not as well off as during the war. Is Bilsky going to change it?"

"He's got them Hats after him," Kaufman argues. "Them gangsters."

"He invited them in."

'The bosses invited them."

"What's a little protection for the manufacturers?"

"I'll tell you," Barney says. "They buy labor peace from the Hats. And the Hats buy it from Bilsky."

"Let's say you're right," Olinsky says. "What can we do?"

"Ask Marty here." Olinsky turns to me. So do the others. Westreich looks up from the bench of his machine where he is eating a roll packed with sausage and sauerkraut. He whistles softly between his teeth. The clock in the front tells us that there are ten minutes of lunchtime left. "Nevermind him. Ask Marty."

"He's a kid," Kaufman protests. "A baby."

"So tell us how to get rid of them Hats, Mr. Young Genius," Olinsky says. Olinsky is smirking. He does not like me. Nor I him. He smells, an odor of mud.

"Barney can change it," I answer. "Put Barney on the joint council."

"That's enough to get rid of them Hats?" Olinsky mocks.

"It's a beginning. An opening. To get rid of them, you have to fight them."

"Fighting?" Kaufman cries. "Yes, that's just what we need."

"So you'll fight." I am angry at myself. "If there's going to be a union that belongs to us, then you fight. It's ours. Not Bilsky's."

"And if the Hats come after us? If they fight, too?" Olinsky asks.

"Work!" Westreich shouts, the hand with a remnant of roll and sausage pointing to the clock. "To work now. Everyone."

To hell with Olinsky, I think, as I turn back to my machine. Barney wouldn't have allowed himself the thought. That was when he still had a faith in these people I lacked. And he believed that someone like Olinsky was capable of making abstractions real. Olinsky could act. It was the same faith that had sent him into the party. Problems were never more simple than their solutions. And part of each solution was faith in the working class, even in the Olinskys and Kaufmans.

By the time we had been working for Westreich for two years, Barney had become a well-known figure throughout the garment center. Even the furriers, the most radical of the Jewish workers, knew about him. He was a leader, a union man, independent. And I suppose it was that reputation that led to our being stopped as we walked down Seventh Avenue one early spring evening. We knew who Beryl Farkas was. A big-shouldered, tall man who was both Bilsky's brother-in-law and the person who took care of any disputes that arose between the union and the Hats. "We'd like to talk to you," Beryl says, his hand on Barney's shoulder. There are two others with him, dressed exactly as he is dressed—dark brown overcoats, wide-brimmed gray fedoras, brown business suits, white shirts, brown silk ties. Except for the way his shoulders seemed to push out of his coat, Beryl looked as if he could have been a clerk in an undertakers' benevolent association. He wore sunglasses even though it was almost dark. And there was always a nervous expectancy about everything he did.

"I'm listening," Barney says, removing Beryl's hand from his shoulder.

"You're making trouble for us, Kadish."

"I'm not making trouble for anyone who doesn't deserve trouble."

The three of them fall into step as we walk down Seventh Avenue. At the corner, Beryl alongside Barney and the other two flanking me, we trun around and begin walking up Seventh. We turn left on Twenty-seventh Street. From the shop doors, a few workers who are leaving late greet us. The braver ones, noting Beryl and his two accomplices, make it a point to greet Barney publically. Barney is twenty-two, but in their eyes he is older than any of us. Beryl acknowledges the greetings as if they were meant for him, too. A man among men is Beryl Farkas.

We head west toward Eighth Avenue. Neither Barney nor I ask where we are going. The two men flanking me stop before we reach the corner and one of them grabs my arm. I know enough, even at eighteen, not to resist. My body goes slack and I let him pin me to the window of a Greek bakery. He turns me around. In the window, baklava and sesame rolls. The other one lights a cigarette and hands the pack to his companion who lets go of my hand and removes two cigarettes from the pack. He offers one to me. Barney and Beryl have disappeared around the corner. "They got things to talk over," the one who gave me the cigarette says. "Let them be alone together."

By now, it is darker, past seven o'clock. I turn to see whether any workers I know are in sight. I see no one. Then the other one turns me to face him. His unsmiling thin lips are pressed together. "You people been saying things."

"What things?"

"About the union. We don't like what we hear."

"It's an all right union," says the one who gave me the cigarette. "We don't need your kind to tell us how to run things. Understand?" He punctuates the question by a short chop of his elbow into my ribs. I try to turn, exploding with pain. Then the other one spins me past the bakery window into the tenement entrance and the two of them work me over quickly. They jam me between the stairway railing and the dimly lit mailboxes. I remember the color of the walls, dead mocha, like the dried blood on the skin of a fox I once saw hanging in a window in Hostov. An old Irish woman opens the door, sees the two of them hitting me, closes the door. I crumple to the floor and the two men turn and leave. About a minute later the apartment door opens again and the old woman peers out cautiously at my body lying between stairwell and mailboxes. I force myself to sit up. I am in great pain but there is nothing broken. I remember Callahan's description of what the patriots did to him. I feel grateful to the men in the dark brown overcoats. They have done what they were instructed to do. No more. "Rough him up a bit," I can hear Bilsky tell them. "Don't make him terrible hurt. Just so he won't follow Barney so quick. He shouldn't make trouble for us. Teach him a little."

The old woman is still staring at me. Her stringy white hair is framed by the yellowing wall of her apartment. I try to smile, wince with pain, force the smile. "They hit you," she says. "I saw them."

"I'm all right."

"Did they hurt you bad? Can you walk?"

"I don't think they broke anything," I tell her. "Just let me catch my breath and I'll be going."

"Come in and rest. I'll make you coffee."

I am tempted, but I want to find Barney. "I have to go," I say. "Thank you anyway." I get slowly to my feet. She stands without moving in the doorway. I deliberately brush my clothes off so that she can see that I am all right. I force my movements to be as fluid as possible. I have to control the pain that tingles across every inch of my body. I hurt like a man of seventy. I have never been beaten up before. I have never been hit by men who know exactly where to hit you, so that the pain is greatest and the damage least. Years later, while organizing Harvester in South Bend, I am beaten even worse. But in 1922, at eighteen, pain is still humiliating. More memorable, too.

On Eighth Avenue, I take two measured deep breaths and then begin to walk slowly down the block. I fight to keep my hands from rubbing my kidneys. I am proud that I can master the pain, as only an eighteen-year-old can be proud. I turn east at Twenty-fifth and walk slowly down the street until I arrive in front of union headquarters. The crisp air is smoky against my body. I push the front door open. I walk up the dirty stairs. The same desk and chair that I remember from the time I got my union card stand near the entrance. The same door with the hand-painted yellow lettering. I hear voices. I open the door and step inside.

Barney is seated behind the desk. Bilsky, Heinrich, and Beryl Farkas surround him. They are standing. Bednarik straddles a chair in the corner, looking heavy and uncomfortable. I recognize Bilsky and Heinrich from the pictures of them splashed across every issue of the union paper, *Fighting Together*. I have been working for almost three years, but this is the first time I have seen them in person. Bilsky is bent over Barney, gesticulating with his hands. Barney sits with his hands folded together on the desk. He looks as if he is enjoying himself. His Tartar eyes are amused, as if he and I share some secret joke. Momentarily, my rage shifts to him. Bilsky interrupts whatever he is saying to Barney to look up at me as if I were something brought to his attention by a clerk.

"Who's he?" he asks.

"Who are you?" Heinrich echoes. "What do you want here?"

"He's Barney's friend," Bednarik explains, shifting his weight in the chair. "The one I told you about. I gave him a union card a few years back."

"Altschuler!" Bilsky announces triumphantly. Bilsky is a short fat man with thick arms and a face crowned by a full head of curly black hair. His features are squashed, as if someone had sat on his face as a baby. "Altschuler. That's the one." He is pleased that he remembers.

"Barney's commissar," Beryl Farkas snorts.

"Are you hurt, Marty?" Barney asks.

"I'm all right," I say. "What do they want?"

"Tell the commissar, too, Bilsky," Beryl says. "If you beg from the master, you better have enough to feed his dog, too."

Still trembling with pain, I walk up to Beryl and throw a right at his chin. The punch lands. Beryl sits down, stares up at me from the floor. Then he bellows and jumps to his feet. But Barney collars him, leaping from his seat, and pins him against the bulletin board.

"Stop it!" Bilsky roars. "What the hell are we, animals? Why do you think we asked you here?"

"You didn't ask," Barney says, still pressing Beryl Farkas against the bulletin board. "You sent Beryl and his friends to bring us here."

"We didn't know you was willing to come," Heinrich explains. "Barney, this is a peace offering."

"We want you with us, Barney," Bilsky says. "We want a united union. No more Left, no more Right." He is trying to be sincere. He puts his hand on Barney's shoulder. Barney lets go of Beryl, who brushes himself off angrily. "United, Barney."

Beryl mumbles something I do not catch. Bilsky's face reddens. "Beryl, maybe it's time for a walk?" Beryl takes his hat and coat and slides past me out the door. "He got a temper," Bilsky explains soothingly. "I know it may be hard for you to believe, but he's a good union man. Honest he is. Okay, he's a bit too free with his hands. But he wants what's best for the union."

"Why did you tell his goons to belt me around?" I ask.

"We never told them. Nothing." It is Heinrich who answers.

"Why, Bilsky?" Barney adds. "You wanted me, not Marty."

"Let it go, Barney," Bednarik offers.

Bilsky sighs, looks quizzically at Bednarik. Then his eyes turn to me and he takes me in like a clothing salesman measuring a customer for a suit. "Okay," he says, "I told them to get you, Altschuler. I'll tell you why. Nothing personal. Only you're Barney's friend. Everybody says you're his right hand. So the two of you louse the union. It's all through the market, what the two of you say. Talking against the union leadership. All right, if it was me alone, I would've let Beryl and his people take care of Barney here, too. Only Bednarik thinks Barney can be talked to. All right. So I sent them to bring you here."

"Who hit Marty?" Barney asks.

Bilsky shrugs. "I didn't tell them *what* to do to him. I only told Beryl he had to make you two understand that we're tired of your creating opposition. I don't want two young punks to destroy this union."

"I have no power," Barney says. "And Marty, how long has he been a member? Who's going to listen to us?"

"I want unity," Bilsky insists angrily. "No games, Barney."

"Don't antagonize him, Barney," Bednarik begs. He looks as if he is going to cry.

"In another six weeks, we're going out. The contract expires in a month, I got to give two weeks' notice to negogiate. I want this to be successful, like 1916. If we don't win, the union's finished. Understand?"

"Listen, Barney," Bednarik urges. "We're in a bad time."

Barney turns to face me. Heinrich smiles like an idiot child waiting for a reward. "What do they want from you?" I ask. Barney shrugs. "You're not even an official. You're not on the joint council. Farkas is on the joint council. Isn't he, Bilsky?"

Bilsky shrugs. "I'm sorry the boys hit you, Altschuler. You're young."

"Marty's right. I'm not an official."

Bilsky reaches into his inside jacket pocket and pulls out a piece of paper. He hands the paper to Barney. Barney reads it, passes it to me. The paper appoints Barney to the joint council. "You can only be elected," I insist.

"A formality," Bilsky says. "Who's going to vote against him. Barney's popular."

"It's not democratic," I insist.

"Let's not argue," Bilsky says impatiently. "No games. In or out. But no games. We're finished if this strike is lost."

"What about the Hats?" Barney asks.

Bilsky is embarrassed. "Beryl knows their ways. Some things it's better not to know too much about."

I watch Barney's face. Tartar eyes narrow, a smile tracing the corners of his mouth, dark brown hair combed straight back. Bilsky has him. If he doesn't accept, he has to get out. The story will be all over the market about how Barney turned down Bilsky's plea for unity. I frame Olinsky's face in my imagination and then I know what Barney will do. "Okay," he says. "I'll come in." Bilsky smiles, Heinrich laughs. Bednarik gets to his feet, obviously pleased. I am silent. Even in this dingy office, the forces of history are wrestling. "I accept the appointment to the joint council," Barney says, as if explaining to me. "But understand this, Bilsky. I don't belong to you or to Beryl's gangsters either. I want to be a section leader during the strike. And I don't want any of the Hats in my section. Understand?"

"Understood," Bilsky snorts. "Your first job is to talk to the younger workers. Prepare them for the strike."

"What'll you do about the Greek shops?"

"We'll take care of the Greeks." He offers Barney his hand. Barney shakes it. Then Bilsky walks over to me and offers me his hand. I take it as if I were picking up a sausage that has been lying on the kitchen floor for a long time. Bednarik removes a bottle of bootleg whiskey from a file cabinet behind the trash basket. He opens it and begins to pour, while Heinrich shakes Barney's hand and then mine. Bilsky brings the drink to Barney. "With an appointment to the joint council, there's also a position as business agent. A hundred a week and another twenty for expenses."

"Save it for Beryl," Barney says. "I'll take the twenty."

"To each his own," Bilsky says, downing the whiskey.

When we leave, the pain still throbs in my lower back,

only softer now, as if it were permanent. "They hurt you bad?" Barney asks.

"Bad enough."

"We'll make them pay." We walk to the subway on Seventh. "The strike doesn't stand a chance. I always figured Bilsky wasn't too smart. Now he's desperate. I just can't figure Bednarik. He's not dumb."

"If it doesn't stand a chance, why did we throw in with him?"

"We had no choice. You take what time allows you. That's what Lenin understood. How's it feel now?"

"Nevermind my back. I want to understand."

"Sometimes, you think like an oxcart driver. All you see is what's in front of your nose. What you don't see doesn't exist. Well, it's there, around the next turn. After a while, it's hard to see anything else. That's when you have to wonder about what's around the turn after that. And the next. You can't anticipate too much."

"And what'll you do about Farkas and the Hats?"

"What can we do? In the long run, take care of them. We have to. The manufacturers won't give in and the union isn't strong enough to force anything out of them. Bilsky wants only one thing: To stay in power. If you have a good job, you protect it. Bilsky has a good job."

"For you, it's a religion, not a job."

"Not by itself," he laughs.

7

"You want to know why I joined. And me, I want to understand why you don't. My father was right, Marty. In a world where one dog measures the next for his coat, the only salvation is when all have coats. All right, they tear each other down. When Lenin's dead, who knows what'll happen? But the idea, Marty. What else are we working for? Beginnings are always difficult. But look past this strike. It's a war. And this time either the working class wins or nobody wins."

Did I think then that it was my foresight that kept me out of the party? Or did I recognize that I could never give them what they demanded? Barney could. A man follows where he must. By 1922, I would've followed Barney to hell. But not into the party. Not where there was no control, where it all came down from outside. Not that joining the party changed Barney. They didn't test him about individuals. I once thought they did. But they didn't. I remember coming into the office one morning in 1928. Barney is standing by the window, crying. "Conrad's daughter died," he says. Conrad was a manufacturer of expensive silk linings for expensive mink coats. He hated Barney. It was only because of his brother-in-law, who held half the business, that he agreed to sign with the union rather than close down altogether. "A man like that. He becomes what he does. And all the time he's telling himself he's got to make it easier for his children. Then the children disappear. And the man is left with nothing. Nothing." As part of a class, Conrad was damned by history. As an individual, Conrad suffered.

It wasn't principle that kept me out of the party back then. It was never principle. Not alone. I remember an afternoon in 1936. I had come in from Detroit and was having lunch with Esther and her dentist husband on Eastern Parkway in Brooklyn. After lunch, Charley and I take their two boys for a walk. A warm Sunday in May. "You're a political person, Marty," Charley says, sweeping in the entire parkway with one wave of his hand. "Look. On the one side, socialists. On the other, Communists. Everybody has his virtue. In Europe, they already got Hitler and Mussolini. And now, Franco, too. And here," he shrugs, "they got their virtue. Their purity." By that time, I would've been sitting with the socialists—except that I could never tell whether it was what I wanted or a reaction to what Barney had done.

But in 1922, only the union mattered. Barney had called it correctly. Bilsky was desperate. He needed Barney to heal the split between Left and Right in the union. On the one side, men who had long since given up; on the other, people like us, who wanted a collective presence. Bilsky never understood our kind of people.

The price of silk linings had risen more than 40 percent during the war. But a year after the war, the market collapsed. Prices plunged. The manufacturers in New York—the dominant American market—cut wages. At first, Bilsky went along "for the good of the industry." But by 1922, wages had been cut more than 20 percent since the Armistice. Workers were grumbling. Bilsky had to do something, but he was uncertain of what. Minschin informed Bilsky that the Hats would be neutral, as long as he left the Greek shops alone—and until they understood which side would win. They could afford to wait. The Hats took their percentage from both Bilsky and the association.

That was when we first heard of Minschin. I recognized him the night I saw him at the Labor Lyceum. He was one of the younger men who watched the fights at the Alliance. Occasionally, he would get in the ring himself. A hard, decisive fighter, more careful than you would expect him to be. Always waiting for his opponent to come to him. He didn't hit as hard as some others I knew and he wasn't very fast. Not as fast as me. But he waited, he was patient. And he had a sense of timing, he recognized when his moment arrived. I never saw him lose. He was too patient, too resourceful.

He had taken the Hats over a year earlier. Minschin created a new system of percentages, one that favored the younger gangsters who were just starting out. Then he walked into the Hester Street headquarters of Marcus Bercovitch who was said to run everything. "You're out, Marcus," he announces. "It's not yours anymore."

Marcus Bercovitch, who is already close to sixty and who has high blood pressure, blinks against the morning light. He is trying to remember who the well-dressed young man across from his desk is. Maybe a new messenger from Chicago. They can't hold onto their messengers in Chicago. Then he notices the eight young hoods at Minschin's back. They stand behind him, nervous and jumpy in their Delancey Street suits. Minschin is not nervous. "What?" Marcus says. "Who the hell are you? Are you from Chicago?" And then eying the gun in the right hand of the hood standing next to Minschin and understanding that he no longer possesses what one minute earlier he had no reason to believe would ever be taken from him. "Don't kill me, for Christ's sake! Don't!" Minschin didn't. He didn't need to. At twenty-four, he had taken power on the Lower East Side. It was that simple. And everyone knew he was good to his mother.

"Do nothing. Until you see which way it goes, we keep our hands off." Minschin instructs Beryl Farkas. Beryl tells Bilsky, who interprets Minschin's message to mean that he has clear sailing against the manufacturers. Bilsky is besieged. Bednarik urges him to go to Montreal to make peace with LaTour. The Jews and French had come together in LaTour's Montreal local. And in 1916, when the New York manufacturers asked for help from their Canadian brethren, LaTour threatened to pull out every worker from any shop that shipped to New York. But when LaTour himself went out three years later, Bilsky sent him $2,000 and his good wishes. The war had ended and New York's clothing industry was beginning to feel it. This time, when Bilsky sent Bednarik to LaTour instead of going himself, he was courting failure. LaTour met Bednarik in a small restaurant in Drummondville. He was ashamed to be seen with anyone from New York. "Them gangsters your boss works for, they fixed us good in 1919. Don't talk to me about solidarity of the working class, Bednarik. If I called my people out for that bastard Bilsky, they'd lynch me. You can tell him from me that if the manufacturers ask us to work overtime, we'll do it. I don't give him solidarity with my ass."

"We'll win without LaTour," Bilsky responds when Bednarik returns.

Like most men who sense that the structures on which they have risen are beginning to crumble, Bilsky is convinced of his own virtue. Lying to themselves is the great virtue of men who never consider virtue. A week after the strike begins on the fifteenth of May, the manufacturers begin to contract work out to the Greek shops and to Montreal and Toronto. Bilsky sweats. He calls a rally in Union Square for Sunday. I stand in the park with thousands of other strikers and listen to Bilsky speak in English through a hand-held megaphone. He sweats, even though it is brisk for May. It is difficult for the crowd to understand him. Even by 1922, many of our people still have difficulty with English. But the workers at the rally watch Beryl Farkas and Heinrich standing on the wooden stage behind Bilsky. They applaud when Beryl and Heinrich applaud. They, too, have marked the presence of the Hats scattered throughout the crowd. When Bilsky finishes speaking, polite applause. Bilsky turns to Heinrich, who whispers into his ear. Bilsky once again picks up his megaphone. "And now we're going to hear from Brother Barney Kadish, a member of our joint council," Bilsky announces.

On the wooden stage, in front of Beryl Farkas, Barney seems smaller than he is. He speaks in Yiddish, deliberately. In his left hand he holds the megaphone. His right hand gestures against the sky. His rhetoric charges against the collective memory of his audience. He speaks *into* his audience. He exploits everything he knows about their lives. Barney is an atheist, a Communist. But he makes this strike a part of the harsh history of the Jews in their shtetls. He speaks of the prices men pay to be men, he speaks of what is happening in the Soviet Union, in Hungary, in China. He makes this audience feel that their strike is part of a worldwide struggle. Their world is not limited to the cuts imposed by the manufacturers. On stage, Bilsky's foot taps nervously as he stands smiling behind Barney. To my left, a group of forty or fifty Greeks stand in silence, their eyes fixed on Barney. They understand even less of Barney's Yiddish than they do of Bilsky's English. But they sense that Barney is on their side. "You are nothing," Barney cries to his audience. "You have nothing, you own nothing, and you can claim nothing from the association. Not until you can claim each other. This strike is yours. You must lead us. And make no mistake, brothers, this strike will be long and difficult and maybe even brutal. And if the blood is ours, then we deserve the victory."

It was for this they now wanted to believe they had come. They pushed forward, surrounding the wooden stage, ignoring Bilsky's gavel hammering down on the lectern. Beryl Farkas's face sulks in the crisp May air. His lips curl as he eyes Bilsky. Bednarik is on his feet, cheering. Heinrich has disappeared. The Hats in the audience, clearly identifiable in their Delancey Street suits, are puzzled. They are not men for words.

That night Barney and I walk over to the East River. We look out across to the Brooklyn side. "You saw Farkas?" Barney asks. I nod. "He'll go to Minschin. And Minschin will wonder which way he has to move. Even he doesn't know."

"At least he pretends he doesn't," I say.

Barney stares into the deepening city darkness across the river. The cranes in the navy yard loom like giant spiders in the clear moonlit sky. "So much power. Sometimes, I think they're even more stupid about what they possess than they actually are. That's trouble, Marty. Never underestimate the enemy." At first, I thought he was talking about the association. Then I saw his eyes narrow down to slits as he searched the Brooklyn shore. The ships outlined against the houses. The great bridge and the warehouses and the churches and the parks and the docks. And the ships. They owned it all, the clothes we wore and the machines we worked. Why, I wonder now, didn't I follow Barney into the party that night? Because that was what he was asking me to do. "The party is not demonic, Marty. It knows what it must fight. That's all. And what it must fight is the same in every corner of the globe."

"The situation of the union," he says suddenly, "is hopeless. It's the wrong time for a strike. The association won't give in. Bilsky will have to save his own neck. That's what he'll ask of the Hats. And how does he do it?"

"By offering them us?"

"Right now, Minschin hardly knows we exist. Bilsky thinks he can put pressure on Minschin to force a settlement. Only Minschin will look around. The association won't give an inch. And then Minschin comes in on their side."

"For a price."

Barney shrugs. "He's smart. He doesn't have to give up anything. It's easier to control the union. There's no Farkas with the manufacturers. And there's always the danger of the police if he moves against them. They have enough power to make it difficult if they can't depend upon him. Minschin knows that."

"Then he'll move against the union."

"Yes," he says. "Only not right away. Minschin will take the temperature of the strike and then he'll go down to the association and see what he can get out of them. When he learns that the association isn't going to give anything, he'll throw in against us. Bilsky will blame it on the Left. And they'll come after us."

"Any chance of beating them?"

"There's always a chance. With Bednarik, there might have been a better chance. Bilsky is suspicious of Bednarik now, Farkas doesn't trust him. And the people don't really know him any more. The Greek shops won't go out. Everyone is a cousin and half are illegals. It's Greek *landsmanshaft*. No one's fault. That's just the way it's always been."

"What will we do?" Barney doesn't answer. "We could train our own. You must've thought of that."

Barney nods. "You, too?"

"Callahan," I guess.

"Of course, Callahan. We'll organize through our section. In Montreal and Toronto and Milwaukee, they'll be working. But between Twenty-fourth Street and Twenty-sixth Street, not a shop will be open. Not even that Greek on Twenty-fifth. Everything closed. Like a fist."

"And when Minschin sends the Hats?"

"I wish he would wait a few years. But we have no choice. Sometimes, the world comes to you."

"They don't play, Barney. They have a lot at stake. People will get hurt."

"Worse than hurt. When Bilsky gets desperate enough, he'll panic. Minschin may have to kill someone. To show he's in control. And it won't be Bilsky."

"You expect them to try to kill you."

"To warn me. It was you they beat up. Remember?"

Somehow, the prospect exhilarates me. I laugh.

8

"It wasn't courage. You and Callahan taught them to fight in groups. That was smart. But it was Minschin's mistake. Killing Becker's son. Still, if they didn't win, neither did we. Not altogether. You teach your own, you teach your enemy. So the next time, you can ask for a little more. Everyone in the market looks at you, sees your nose, looks at me, sees what they did to the eye. And then they look at Bilsky. They smell his sweat. They smell themselves. And Bilsky goes to Minschin and Minschin smells him, too, and he wonders whether it isn't time to give the union to Beryl Farkas. Courage he can't expect, but this. . . . Still, he can't do anything until he takes care of us. Minschin waits for us."

If you're lucky, you remember *your* moments. But I remember that summer as Barney's time. Even at twenty-two, Barney knew what he was doing. It amazes me to remember how he maneuvered. Bilsky was in his fifties, Heinrich in his forties. Even Beryl Farkas was thirty-seven. But they couldn't keep up with Barney.

The Greek shops stayed open. Except for the one in Barney's section. Gus Constantinou closed that one. Gus didn't look like much, sallow face, fat body, his shoulders drooping as if the weight of the world were crushing him. It never would have occurred to me to cultivate Gus. But Barney could spot need in a man. And Gus needed.

I never liked Gus. But he always worked hard. And once he joined us, he would have given his life if Barney asked for it.

He and Barney are walking toward the subway together, drifting into each other's paths. Barney stops to listen to an argument about a fight scheduled for the Garden. Abe Attel and some Irishman. And one suggests the Irishman is going to win and the other accuses him of being an anti-Semite and the first says he wasn't knocking Attel because he was a Jew but because the Irishman was a better fighter and the other one says, okay, when the revolution comes your Irishman can be a better fighter only now it's got to be Attel, and the first one calls him a chauvinist bastard and then he tells him he and his revolution and his Jews can go to hell in a basket and then they start hitting each other.

They were switching back and forth between Yiddish and English and Gus didn't understand very much. But he shifts from one foot to the other alongside Barney. "It's nonsense," he says. "Isn't it?" Barney nods. "So why do we allow them to divide us this way?"

"And that's enough to make him a revolutionary?" I am skeptical. Barney had pointed Gus out to me the day before. He looked puffed to the borders of his soul, like clay that expands until it dries out and crumbles.

"It makes him conscious," Barney insists. "Give a man his chance, Marty."

Gus read Marx and Engels in Greek before he came to America in 1916. He was eighteen when he arrived here. He'd been working in silk linings ever since, the first four years for an uncle whose business collapsed right after the war, then for a series of small Greek shops, usually owned by men who knew his uncle or had known his father. "Sometimes, they didn't even actually know each other. I'll bet the only time my father and Mycenas Palatianos ever saw each other was when they threw stones as children. In this life, everything divides us." But he knew nothing about the union, was barely aware of who Bilsky and Heinrich were.

"Imagine, Marty, he reads *Kapital* in secret because he has a father who can't read anything at all and who beats him with a strap because he wants no books in the house."

"But why didn't he learn here?"

Barney shakes his head. "Not interested. In Marx, there is working class and bourgeoisie. Slaves and owners. 'I did not really know about this,' he says to me when I tell him what we're trying to do with the union." He pauses. "Callahan has one thing to contribute, Gus another."

"Callahan wants his hand back."

"And Gus wants to get even. Like me. And you."

After that, Gus worked with me and Callahan. He helped

us set things up. The gym had disappeared by then, but Barney found a foreman in a meat-processing plant on 125th Street who was a party member. The plant was right near the Hudson and we would travel up there at night, filing one by one through the huge lockers with their hanging carcasses to a large unused storeroom that hooked at a right angle away from the rest of the building. Young workers shiver, stare at the hanging meat, as if for the first time they realize it had once existed as a body encased in skin. Sometimes, Lisa came with us, the sole woman. By that time, Barney had gotten her a job at Westreich's. Gus had a friend, a fellow Greek, who worked in the warehouse of a sporting goods manufacturer. He stole body bags for us and Gus and I spent a few nights anchoring the bags into the old beams.

"Hit the bastards!" Callahan yells. Crippled claw of a hand waving back and forth, like a threshing hook. "The groin, the groin. Don't go for the face. Cripple them, so they can't hit back. Let *them* worry."

The friend steals baseball bats. Children's bats. Gus and I hollow out the tops and pour lead filler inside. Like the night-sticks the cops use. All spring, Callahan and I work with our people. By the time Minschin came against us, we had close to fifty men ready to take on his Hats.

It was Gus who closed Mycenas and Sons. He stood outside early one morning flanked by three of our people. Only two of Mycenas's seven workers follow him inside the shop. The others stand around outside, looking from Gus to the three pickets surrounding them. Gus says nothing. After an hour, they leave. At noon, Gus hands Labish Kottler his sign. The sign is in Greek. He does not tell us what it says. We do not ask. He goes inside Mycenas's shop with one of the baseball bats tied around his wrist with a leather thong. When he comes out fifteen minutes later one of the two workers follows him and goes directly to the subway. Fifteen minutes after that, the other comes out crying, "I got two kids. What's going to happen to my kids?" Then he says something else in Greek to Gus.

"There are others with kids. You don't want to spit on your brother."

Mycenas comes to the door, glares at Gus, goes back inside and draws the window shade. When he locks the door, Gus says to him, "It's safer that way, old man. Believe me."

The first two weeks of the strike had been warm and sunny. It was difficult to keep the minds of the people on what we were doing. Except for our section, picketing was undisciplined. Workers gathered together on the streets. They played cards, talked about baseball and fights. Bilsky and Heinrich would drift through the market like embarrassed tax collectors. They were greeted with affection. The strike was still popular. But by mid-June, when the strike showed no signs of being settled, the men began to grow tense. That was when Bilsky went to Minschin.

And so, on a hot afternoon toward the end of June, Beryl Farkas entered the empty storefront we had rented for the duration of the strike. He was flanked by two other men. Not the same men who had beaten me up in the tenement hallway. But they, too, were dressed as Beryl was dressed, in white poplin suits that would have been suitable for a New Orleans banker in July. I was sitting in the corner of the room next to the file cabinet. "Where's Barney?" Beryl asks.

"Who wants him?"

"That's not your business. You're just Barney's commissar."

I remember that I am alone. But the others will be returning soon. "I see you have some new members in your club."

"Union members," Beryl says. "Show the commissar your card, Mickey."

The taller of the two waves his card in front of my face. "A member," Beryl says. "Local one. Pattern makers and dyers local."

"A butcher," I say.

"And silk workers, Commissar," Beryl laughs. "Get me Barney."

"I'll tell him you came here looking for him. Now get out."

As Beryl comes at me, I jump for his shoulders and drive my knee into his groin. I hear him suck for air like a drowning man. Then he falls to his knees and vomits on my shoes. I stare down at the vomit and my head explodes with pinwheels of color and pain that spin me around. Then I black out.

Later, Gus tells me about it. Two of our people returned to the office just when Mickey broke my nose. One went for help and the other tackled Mickey from behind. The third Hat was trying to get Beryl to his feet when six of our people rushed through the door. Callahan and Becker's son shook Beryl loose and then Callahan went to work on the one who broke my nose. He finished by rapping him across each knee with one of the baseball bats. Hard enough to swell the knees but not to break anything. Then Callahan turned to Beryl who was still lying on the floor, edging away from the vomit, and drove his heel into Beryl's outstretched hand, grinding it down. Callahan didn't say a word. Gus pointed that out when he told me what happened. Beryl went limping off, howling, doubled over in pain and holding his broken hand in front of him. The one who hit me was half-carried half-dragged by the other one. Picketing workers stand in the street, astonished.

Gus tells Becker's son he had better get me to the union doctor. Blood is still streaming from my nose. "Forget him," Becker's son says. The first words I hear when I wake up. "He's Bilsky's man." So Abe Becker takes me by cab down to Delancey Street, to the offices of Louis Weinstock, who has already earned the name Dr. Red because he treats so many party members. He packs my nose and I see the pinwheels again. My face is swollen. "You'll live," the doctor says in Yiddish. "Don't aggravate yourself. The pain will be gone soon."

"And my nose?"

"It's broken. So what? A good Jewish nose made a little more Jewish. Are you a party member?"

"Just a union man," I say.

"Better you were a party member," he answers. "It's your nose."

I spend the rest of that week and part of the following one being taken care of by my sister Esther. By this time, my mother has become an ardent member of the millinery workers' union. She likes Barney, considers both of us misguided. "Your Barney is a prisoner of Moscow," she says She likes to say that. She says it often. But when she comes home that night she doesn't scold me about the nose. She sends Esther to the movies and then repacks it as Dr. Weinstock had instructed.

I search the papers for news of the strike. The English papers barely mention it. In the Yiddish papers it commands a good deal of attention. Both *Fraye Mentschn* and *Der Royter Morgn*, the party's Yiddish newspaper, give the strike a great deal of coverage. The articles in *Fraye Mentschn* sound like they were written by a tightrope walker struggling for balance at the very moment he is trying to decide in which direction to move. Bilsky's leadership is praised, the Greek shops are condemned, the garment industry workers are told that they are more united than ever before. At the same time, there are hints of impending betrayals. It is not quite clear who is to betray what, but the paper is taking no chances. On Thursday, a hint that Bilsky cannot rely on the Left. On Friday, praise for Barney Kadish for keeping the union's need for unity in the forefront.

Der Royter Morgn was not then what it became after years of unquestioned allegiance to every twist in the party line. Roginsky was running it then. And Roginsky when he was young was as fine a journalist as the party ever commanded. Roginsky decided that the strike could be won only if all sides in the union kept clear of gangsters. He praised Barney sparingly, had a few good words for Bilsky. It was only after what happened to Abe Becker that Roginsky mounted his attack. By that time, everyone knew that the Hats were out to break the Left.

While I was recuperating, Becker and Gus took care of the section. Barney made himself inconspicuous. But when July 4th came and went without a settlement, everyone in the market considered the strike lost. The only man on the joint council who could now walk through the silk lining shops was Barney. And he didn't. The picket lines had by now collapsed. It was too hot, the strikers complained. The general strike fund, which Bilsky claimed was guaranteed by loans from the AFL, turned out to be nonexistent. Facing decreasing union membership throughout the nation, other union leaders gave Bilsky what he had given LaTour—advice and token sums of money. In the middle of July, Bilsky went to see Sam Minschin. The next day Minschin went to the New York Pattern and Silk Manufacturers' Association.

He wanted to know exactly what it was the members of the association expected. Perhaps, if they were reasonable, he might be able to help persuade the workers to return to the shops. They wanted an open shop, a three-hour extension of the work week to forty-five hours, and a further ten percent reduction in wages. Minschin listened. He would be reasonable. Mr. Bilsky would be reasonable. Nonetheless, the members of the association must recognize that a completely discredited union would do none of them any good. Sam Minschin would personally guarantee five uninterrupted years of labor peace in exchange for the same hours, with, of course, shorter lunch breaks (which didn't, since the gentlemen had his personal guarantee, have to be mentioned in the written agreement), and what would be essentially the same pay scale with a review promised after a year and a half if there were a general upturn in the industry. The manufacturers huddled briefly among themselves, while Minschin and Bilsky left the room. Ten minutes later and Minschin and Bilsky were brought back. A few handshakes finished the agreement. Minschin told Bilsky to announce the settlement the very next night. Sweating, Bilsky promised that he would call a membership meeting to ratify the new contract.

It was then that Leftwich, who had already been appointed to a seat on the association's executive council, leaned across the table and said to Minschin, "What'll you do with Barney Kadish, Mr. Minschin? He's not like your friend here."

In his tailor-made blue businessman's suit, Minschin stands puzzled. He brushes at his lapel, a habit he has when he is thinking. His sculpted, clean-shaven face seeks reassurance from the finest imported English woolens. Leftwich is a big man. Minschin notes his size. "I don't know the man, Mr. Leftwich. Why should he give us trouble? I've never done him harm."

"Ask your Mr. Bilsky."

Nervously biting his lips, Bilsky leaves the meeting with Minschin.

Minschin rarely wasted time. The next night he shows up at the Labor Lyceum flanked by two bodyguards. Other Hats are scattered throughout the audience. Minschin is now dressed in a gray tailor-made business suit. He wears pearl cuff links and a silver and pearl tie clip holds his black woolen tie to his impeccably pressed starched white shirt. Our people drift toward the back of the auditorium, the way Gus and I have told them to do. We want to keep our eyes on the exits. Becker stands against the rear center exit. He is measuring the angle from where he is standing to where Barney sits on the stage. The auditorium is almost full. About half the people are ours. Perhaps one-quarter are with Bilsky and Minschin's Hats. The rest are the curious and members of Local One who are afraid not to attend. Roginsky is there from *Der Royter Morgn*. He nods to me. It is difficult to guess the number of Hats Minschin has brought with him; this time they aren't all wearing suits and ties.

At seven-thirty, Heinrich calls the meeting to order. Bilsky walks to the dais. A smattering of applause. Our people sit with their hands folded. Gus frowns, shakes his head when his eyes catch mine. Abe Becker paces the rear, noting where each man in the audience is sitting. Minschin surveys the audience. His eyes examine Becker's son. The Hat who gave me a cigarette and then beat me in the tenement hallway sits two rows behind Minschin. He leans over, taps Minschin on the shoulder, says something into his cupped hand. Minschin nods.

Bilsky assesses the strike. The struggle, he assures his audience, has established the union. He does not mention that the union has existed since 1898. But the union has not gotten the support it was promised by the AFL. They have been let down by the national leadership of the federation, they have been betrayed by Brother Simplon LaTour in Montreal, who had actually encouraged the Montreal and Toronto shops to work overtime in order to fill scab orders from New York. But the greatest of all betrayals had come from one in their own midst. A faction of the local, a small minority financed by foreign money, had sold out the interests of the union. They all knew the man he was speaking about.

A nervous stir in the audience. Barney sits on the stage, along with the other members of the joint council. His face is blank. He does not even lose composure when Bilsky mentions "foreign gold." Minschin looks at his watch and then frowns, like a man late for an appointment. He adjusts his pearl tiepin. Like the rest of the audience, he is waiting for Bilsky to finish. I turn to look at Abe Becker. He shifts his weight from one foot to the other. Gus nods in Minschin's direction. Abe Becker nods, too. Minschin continues to fidget with tiepin and cuff links, as if he were about to enter an exclusive restaurant for the first time and wanted to check on the propriety of his dress.

"And so, brothers, I tell you that *we* have not lost this strike!" Bilsky shouts hoarsely, his finger directed at his audience's heart. Bednarik rises to his feet, but Beryl Farkas taps his shoulder with his cast and forces him to sit down again. Bednarik's face is a mask of anguish. "*We* have not lost this strike because neither the association nor Comrade Kadish and his Moscow goons are going to control this union. We can say to the manufacturers that the day will come when this union shall cleanse its blood. And on that day, *we*, the working people of this industry, shall dictate terms." He had shifted from English to Yiddish halfway through his speech, but his Yiddish was even more formal than his English. He was no longer comfortable with the language. "I ask this meeting of the membership to ratify the decision of the joint council to accept the new contract that we have agreed to with the association. And I further ask that this meeting join with me, and with all loyal American trade unionists, to demand that the United Garment Workers of America instruct the joint council to suspend Barney Kadish and his followers from the union. *They* . . ." And Bilsky pauses, waves his hand in a circle, slicing the air with his passion, "*They* have stabbed us in the back in order to breed dissent and chaos. In order to ingratiate themselves with their Moscow masters."

Sweating profusely, Bilsky stops talking, turns to his seat on the stage. A ripple of applause from the Hats. No other sound until a voice from the rear cries out, "Barney Kadish didn't sell us out, Bilsky!"

Another voice: "You and that bastard, Heinrich! You sold us out!"

Heinrich grabs the gavel and bangs on the speaker's table. "Who said that?" A buzz in the audience. "Whoever said that is out of order. No disrespect here."

"One dog speaks, the other barks!" Nervous laughter. A swelter of voices in Yiddish and English. Minschin is imperturbable as he sits and plays with tiepin and cuff links. It was almost as if he were still deciding which side was to be his.

"Let Barney speak!" This voice is recognizable. Becker. The cry is taken up until "Let Barney speak!" Echoes in unison throughout the Lyceum. On stage, Bednarik sits with his head in his hands. Bilsky stands in front of the table, sporadically banging it with his gavel. For ten minutes the Lyceum rocks with the demand that Barney speak. Even some of Bilsky's supporters are shouting now. Seated next to Bednarik, Barney waits quietly. History can be created in moments such as this. History washes over him while he sits on the stage.

But Minschin, too, is a child of history. His destiny was to seize the power others wanted. When things went against Minschin, he fought. He understood force. Now it was the manufacturers who possessed power. And he had too much to give up. The percentage was profitable. The crowd's demand for Barney left Minschin with no chance to do what he would have preferred—arrange a settlement. Common sense dictated a settlement. But he must have already begun to suspect that he and Barney had few mutual interests. Minschin had never been much for politics.

Becker's son runs toward the stage. Minschin's hand goes up, like an orchestra leader about to begin a concert. He points, caged in the sudden illumination of what it is he has to do. Two of the Hats step in front of Becker. Two shots ring out, a space of perhaps five seconds between them. Becker slides gently down to the inclined floor, where he sits holding his stomach and rocking back and forth, as if he were praying.

The auditorium swells with that awful silence you see rather than hear. The shots freeze each man in place. On stage, Bilsky grins like a child caught with his hand in a cookie jar. Barney stands up, pushes Bilsky aside, grabs the megaphone. The silence erupts into fierce breaths of anguish. Each of us is tightened into his fear. "Help him!" Barney cries, pointing to

Becker. Then Barney points to Minschin, sitting in the audience, staring directly at him. "Take it back!" he cries. "Take it back from Bilsky's boss!"

It was a large auditorium, and there must've been a thousand workers sitting there. But Minschin no longer pretended indifference. He signaled again and the Hats swept down from the back in a wave, while another wave moved up from just a few rows in front of the stage. Maybe there were forty of them in all, but they clubbed heads as they moved up and down the aisles, guns drawn for use as blackjacks, moving through the auditorium methodically, the way men who have mastered a talent use it—with concentration and discipline. They looked as if they had rehearsed earlier in the day. They had been designated areas and they worked across them, two by two. I've never seen more efficient hitting. Broken arms and battered heads and eight or nine broken legs from trying to get out of their way. On stage, Barney staggers against the table, hand covering his blood-gashed right eye. I spin past the propped-up body of Abe Becker. One of our people, not knowing what else to do when the head-clubbing started, had forced the body against the wall and propped it up on a folding chair so that it watched lifelessly while all around Minschin's Hats beat workers over the head. The blood of Abe Becker mixed with even fresher blood. Suddenly, I find myself gripped by a misshapen hand. Callahan pulls me out of the door.

Outside, I push him away. I turn to go back into the Lyceum. I hear sirens. "Don't be a fool," Callahan yells at me. "The cops are here. What chance do we have?" For a moment I don't understand. "The goddamn cops are theirs, Marty. Theirs." And then I find myself running after him, until we both disappear into the subway at Fourteenth Street.

9

That week, Sam Minschin tried to kill Barney Kadish and destroy Barney's idea of the union. Barney was in Willard Parker Hospital, probably the safest place he could have been, guarded by those same cops who had a warrant for his arrest. Not knowing what else to do, we went to see John Hudson, honorary chairman of the League for the Education of Immigrants and a leading Republican party adviser. Hudson agreed to help us.

Gus and Becker's father took the subway with me down to Hudson's office on Pearl Street. Old Becker was a cutter and he had seen his son killed at the meeting the day before. He was very quiet and when the three of us emerged from the subway Old Becker looked up at the tall buildings that seemed to spring over these narrow cavernous streets and cast the world into permanent shade and then he said, "For this, they took my *kaddishel.* Property. Only property. Who made them, Marty? Who made them in this world?"

I shrug. Old Becker spoke Yiddish. I translated for Gus. "God made them," Gus snorts. "Then they made God. To return the favor."

Whatever had made John Hudson had made him the best of his kind. He knew the rules and he knew the people who had created the rules. Of course, he didn't want to know for whom the rules existed. But it was easy enough to forgive him that. Men like John Hudson want order. And they want the possibility of justice, too. A white-haired Anglican patrician, he listened to us, called for his secretary, and set the world to rights. The secretary didn't approve of us. Distant recognition in the bone. A dingy tenement, the accents of her mother and father, too many brothers and sisters—a harsh and grating conscience. She wanted to escape it here, in the quiet mahogany dignity of Mr. John Hudson's office on Pearl Street.

That afternoon, at the very moment Barney was under the surgeon's knife in the hospital, John Hudson confronted the judge who had indicted him. At the time, unknown to the judge, the remnants of Barney Kadish's right eye were being removed no more than two hundred yards from the spot Barney and I had stood upon to stare across the East River into the Brooklyn Navy Yard. It wouldn't have meant very much to the Tammany judge, who would have looked at Barney's bandaged face packed in ice with much the same curiosity he would have looked at a fish a fellow judge caught off Montauk. It certainly wouldn't have meant very much to the assistant district attorney who was looking forward to the day Tammany would appoint him to the bench.

The indictment named Barney Kadish, Martin Altschuler, Costa Navros Constantinou, and Abraham Becker—even a dead man being liable to indictment in the law's eyes—for conspiracy with criminal intent. John Hudson suggested the indictment be quashed. For it was patently illegal. And since John Hudson spoke with the authority of those who shared his clubs high above the city—above, possibly, the range even of Tammany—the assistant district attorney was willing to listen to what he said. John Hudson threatened to bring Minschin and Bilsky into court if the indictment were not quashed. The assistant district attorney suggested a compromise. He apologized for the weakness of his legal case. Mr. Hudson had to understand, he was simply following orders. He understood that the prosecution's case was weak, but he was quite certain that Mr. Hudson, on his part, understood that the case against Bilsky and Sam Minschin was equally weak. "We have witnesses," John Hudson says. "Hundreds." The assistant district attorney, a bright young Harvard Jew with the proper Irish benefactors, understands that in this New York few things are easier to come by than witnesses. He breathes easier, reverses roles and becomes Mr. John Hudson's teacher, respectfully explaining that witnesses in cases such as this one could easily be contradicted by other witnesses, that such disturbances, such horrible occurrences as the killing of Abe Becker, were of course to be regretted, but that they had their origins, as Mr. Hudson undoubtedly knew, in the eruption of a certain, how should he phrase it, brutal spontaneity. In any case, guns had been found on a number of Mr. Kadish's supporters, too, although they had not—he was willing to admit this between gentlemen —found the gun which possessed ballistics markings that matched the bullets removed from young Becker's stomach. Perhaps the fairest possible solution would be to drop all charges and to see to it that both sides were warned against further violence.

John Hudson examines the assistant district attorney. He has neither wit nor money. But he will have both in the future, John Hudson recognizes, and wonders by what strange twist of logic they are now pitted against one another. John Hudson prides himself on not being a bigot. "And what is to happen to Mr. Kadish?" he asks. The assistant district attorney would, of course, see to it that not only was Mr. Kadish freed but that a police guard on an around-the-clock basis would be supplied by the city during Mr. Kadish's stay at the hospital. Should Mr. Kadish's union people wish to supplement the police, they would be free to do so. "We insist upon police scrutinized by *our* people," John Hudson says, and wonders when he has ever voiced a possessive so personally. "If anything happens to Mr. Kadish, the police force of the City of New York is responsible. We want that clearly understood." The cool unctuous smile of the assistant district attorney irritates John Hudson. "You ought to pay more attention to ridding this city of gangsters and less attention to radicals."

Outside the courthouse, having been escorted to the door by both the assistant district attorney and a somewhat humbled Tammany judge, John Hudson shakes Old Becker by the hand. "I'm sorry, Mr. Becker," he apologizes. "I'm afraid we are not going to be able to indict the men who shot your son."

Old Becker smiles. He understood John Hudson. "Tell him," he says to me in Yiddish, "I never expected it to be different. Tell him it's a faith, the way my Abe had of looking at the world." His eyes cloud over, and for just one moment I think he is going to cry. But he doesn't cry. "Tell him I appreciate what he has done for us. He's a good man. Only he don't see where he won't look."

I told him. I left out the last line. It wouldn't have done any good. John Hudson shakes Old Becker's hand once again. Then he departs, to walk over to Wall Street and lunch at the Bankers Club high above the city. Becker and I and Gus take the subway back. When Gus and I get to strike headquarters, we discover Jimmy Callahan and Itzik Perlin. The office has been wrecked. The file cabinets, the desk, the chairs have been smashed. But it hadn't really hurt us. Barney had emptied strike headquarters of all important material two weeks earlier. He sent it home with people we trusted. The Hats had come early that morning. When they drove away, some of our people had worked up enough courage to throw their lunches at the car. Near the corner of Seventh Avenue, a tomato hit the windshield and the driver swerved and almost crashed into a lamppost. Our people cheered. I didn't. Minschin had decided to take care of us immediately and I didn't know how to stop him. At eighteen, I now knew fifty-year-old men who were seeking my approval. It embarrassed me. It frightened me, too. And so I did what I usually did. I went to see Barney.

He was in one of the few private rooms they had in Willard Parker, a hospital that had been built during the Civil War to take care of Union wounded. I found him sitting up in bed, while Lisa Grumbach read Trotsky to him. Lisa was reading in

Yiddish and the blue-coated cop in front of the door was sweating with the heat and with his obvious distaste for the assignment.

Barney was always to admire Trotsky, even after the party destroyed him. Just before I broke with him, we spoke about Trotsky. It was less than a year after he had been sent into exile. "When you consider what he came out of, Marty, he might have been the most remarkable general in history. Still, when a man makes himself an issue, he becomes dangerous. You can go against the party on a matter of policy. But once it is decided, one way or the other, then your disagreement ceases. The decision is no longer yours."

Bolstered by pillows, his face mummified by bandages, he sat up in bed. They had cut a hole for him to see through the left eye. The only other visible part of his face was his nostrils. "How are you, Marty?" he says.

"You're in the hospital," I answer. "And the Hats wrecked the office. I'm not certain of how to deal with them, Barney."

"This isn't the time," Lisa protests.

"It's never the time," Barney says. He pauses. "They don't like to die either." It was an effort for him to speak. The words seem to drop out of the corners of his mouth. "I thought of going to Minschin. But there's nothing we can offer him now. Not until we stop him. The thing we have to find out is how others feel. The members of the Joint Council, for instance."

"We know who's with us."

"No, we don't," Barney says. "Bednarik. Others, too. They're afraid. But they know the people are fed up with a union that simply takes and gives nothing in return. Pearlstein, the business agent of the dyers, I've spoken to him. He's afraid. But he wants to do what will benefit his people." Barney pauses. I can see him swallowing beneath the bandages. "And Lauder from the silk workers. He knows there's no future unless the union can get rid of Bilsky. Listen, they came into the labor movement for the same reasons we did."

I am skeptical. Lauder is a cautious, dry man, always expecting to be surprised by panic even if you mention the weather.

"Just convince them to keep out. None brave enough to come in now. But maybe they're brave enough to stay out. Until we've had our chance with Minschin."

"And in the meantime?"

Barney sighs. He is in great pain, even from this short conversation. "You and Gus have to take care. Understand one thing. You don't have to beat them. Just keep them from destroying us. One good thing: they can't afford to lose and we can afford to do anything. Except disappear." He closes his left eye. The lid is a patch of flesh pasted on a mummy's face. "I told the doctor I wouldn't stay for more than two weeks. In the meantime, it's you and Gus. I wish Abe Becker were still alive." I get up to leave. Lisa stays. As I pass the cop standing outside the door, I hear Barney say, "And the people. Don't forget them."

10

They hit us again two days after I visited Barney in the hospital. But we planned for them. And we planned well. They came from both avenues, four from one side, three from the other. All dressed like working people, except for the student who carried his briefcase. Gus opened the briefcase afterwards. He found a chicken sandwich and two books. We brought the books to Barney in the hospital: *Chambers' Cyclopaedia of English Literature* and Gustavus Myers's *History of the Great American Fortunes*.

The shops all through Twenty-fifth were controlled by our people. We had refused to sign, but the manufacturers, all of them small, let us alone as long as we didn't damage their property. Our people spent their days sitting at the windows watching the street below. The foreman of our building hated the Hats. Across the street from strike headquarters was a flower shop owned by a Greek Gus had cultivated. In the two silk lining places flanking it, we had fifteen men. If we needed to do it, we could muster fifty within a minute.

They had it timed so that they arrived together. "We're closing you up," the leader says. He surveys the headquarters. There isn't very much in the office. Gus and I and Itzik Perlin are sitting on wooden folding chairs we'd picked up from the Salvation Army. There is a deal folding table on rickety legs in front of us. The leader looks at the office dubiously. "Charlie! You, Heshie, and Noobie knock this place apart. Even the light bulbs. Understand. The toilet even."

Charlie nods. But he is suddenly overwhelmed by the rush of bodies pushing into the office. The two bodyguards they have stationed at the door are pushed inside. One tries to pull a gun from his pants, but Itzik slams him in the stomach and takes the gun from him. We search them, collect a total of five pistols, and bring them down to the cellar one at a time. Itzik and Leib Peretz work over the leader. Itzik says, "I'd like to kill you. Like you did Abe Becker. You ever come around here again, I will kill you." Itzik speaks in Yiddish. The Hat understands. But he says nothing.

I work on the one with the briefcase. "You're a student?"

He doesn't answer. He doesn't whimper either. I beat him. He doesn't acknowledge pain. I beat him harder. I'm not comfortable remembering it, but that's what I did. When I finished, he straightened up and spit a glob of blood in my face. Then Leib slammed him on the side of the head and he fell against the toilet door. We dragged him upstairs and threw him at the feet of the lead Hat. "Take your shit," Leib says. "And don't ever come back."

"Maybe you want to telephone Minschin," Gus laughs. "I'm sorry. They removed the telephone last week."

"There'll be other days," the one I had been hitting mumbles. "Tell your boss that."

"We don't have a boss," Leib answers. "This is a union."

"Shut up, Al!" the lead Hat says. He takes Al under one arm and helps him outside. The five others leave like members of a whipped high school football team.

During the rest of the two weeks Barney remained in the hospital, we discovered there wasn't too much we could count on. But the people were finished with Bilsky. After the contract was signed, Bilsky and Heinrich stayed away from the market. Between editorials excoriating Barney Kadish and his Moscow thugs, *Fighting Together* announced that Bilsky and Heinrich were in Milwaukee on important union business. Perlin, Gus, and I moved through the market urging workers to go back out. Old Becker came to see us, volunteered to work in his dead son's place. Old Becker was very effective. By mid-August, our position had improved. Expensive coats were again in demand. And expensive coats needed silk linings. There was an unexpected market in Europe, particularly from the Soviet Union whose own clothing industry had been destroyed by the post-revolutionary fighting. Patterns had to be cut and prepared now in order to be ready for the winter. One hot afternoon, an emissary from LaTour entered the basement, which we now used as our headquarters. Leib Peretz accompanies him. A tall heavy man who carries his weight well. "You're not Kadish," he says to me, surveying the cellar with obvious distaste. "Kadish is young, but you look like you just left school."

"Who're you?"

"I'm Barnet Bernstein, first vice-president of the Montreal local. Sent here to meet Barney Kadish by Simplon LaTour. He wants us to speak the same language."

"French or Yiddish?"

"Even English," Bernstein laughs. "In the country of the workers, all languages are equal."

"And all workers are linguists."

"So much wisdom in such a young man. Take me to Barney."

I took him. Barney was resting at home by that time. Bernstein had brought ten thousand dollars. In cash. The money was to be used only by our section. Barney was to be personally responsible for it. LaTour wanted it understood that for the time being he would keep his people working. But he would cut out overtime. He wasn't quite certain of how much more money he could spare. But he would try. In return, he wanted Barney's promise to support the Canadians if they went out in the future. Together, they could lead the International. "LaTour wants you as president, Barney. An American is necessary. And a Jew. But he wants to be heard."

"It's only fair," Barney says.

"Also, a question. "Are you a party man?"

"I joined the party as soon as I found out where to sign up. In 1919."

"LaTour is a practical man. So am I." Bernstein sighs.

"And your politics?"

"I also left Odessa, Barney. Like you, I didn't go back after the revolution."

"A man can work here as well."

"The Russians will eat us all." Bernstein shrugs. "The party in America is nonsense. Someday, dangerous nonsense."

"But you have no objections?"

"Not enough to tell LaTour he's doing the wrong thing. You know, Barney, I knew your brothers. They were smarter than you think. But they should have listened to Isaac. They should have come to America. Maybe they would have learned to be practical men. Here, practical men go far." He stands up. "How is Isaac, by the way?"

"He waits to die," Barney answers. "He no longer believes."

"He was a brave man," Bernstein says. "Smart, too."

"That's the way it is with the old sometimes. He's not brave enough apparently. Not smart enough either. The time came and he retreated into his dreams. That's not practical, is it, Bernstein?"

"Still," Bernstein says, "he got to America. I can tell LaTour?"

"A wedding. We have no choice. Neither does LaTour."

"The money shouldn't be talked about. LaTour can't take on our own Montreal gangsters right now. First you have to win here. You can let it be known we're sympathizers. But don't make it so loud they have to hit on us." He walks to the bed and touches Barney's hand. "And the party?"

"I'm not as practical as you. Or LaTour."

"They'll spit your bones for breakfast."

"We'll see."

"Take care then. With Minschin and his Hats, the best. Don't take too much of him on at once if you don't have to. Fortunately for us, he's got other interests. He's smart. If he wants to meet you halfway, that's no disgrace. From the parlor to the foyer. Next time, we'll show him the door."

Barney returned a week later. His face was still swathed in bandages and the missing eye was covered over by a black leather patch. His return was an indictment that even Bilsky's supporters had been waiting for. They wanted out. Having survived, Barney attracted everyone, Left and Right. His bandaged face and the black patch reminded every worker of what was being taken from him. "I never been for you, Barney," Kaufman confesses. "I don't approve no Bolsheviks. But Bilsky, he can drop dead. He sold us out."

When Bilsky's people came hesitantly down into the cellar, Barney was smart. He would invite them inside, as if he were exposing our guts to view. It wasn't a surrender, it was a joining of forces. "What can they learn? The Hats know the place anyhow. There's nothing here. Anyway, Bilsky has nothing to do with it. It's only Minschin now."

"Can we beat him?"

He shrugs. The shrug makes him look even more bizarre, as if the scrunched-up bandages were going to push the leather eyepatch off his face. "If we can keep on the way you and Gus have been going, we'll come close."

With the money from LaTour, Barney could act. He began by putting Callahan and Itzik Perlin on the payroll. Together with Gus and me, they helped organize a small army of tough, young union people. By the end of the strike, we had a nucleus of three hundred trained workers.

Barney decided to force Minschin to come to us. Minschin had to avoid shootings now. The newspapers had opened a crusade against shootings in the city's clothing and apparel industries. LaTour's money bought a few reporters. And both the *Times* and the *Sun*, two papers that weren't usually friendly to unions, particularly Jewish unions, editorialized against union gangsterism. It was one thing for a few immigrants to belt each other around. But murder was a serious affair. Even Minschin's fellow gangsters were nervous. The word was that he had been urged to keep his shootings to a minimum. Minschin sent Bilsky back into the market. More and more workers were defying the terms of the contract and remaining out. Bilsky went from man to man, urging a return to work. The contract had been signed. There was work for all. The manufacturers had agreed not to cut wages. But he was greeted by silence. Workers kept on going out. Manufacturers grew nervous. Bednarik resigned as recording secretary. A few days later, he showed up at our headquarters. He stood in the doorway, like a child who knows he deserves a scolding. "Hello, Barney," he says.

"So you've come home at last." Barney laughs. "Look, Marty, the Czechs have joined the revolution."

Barney sent Bednarik out the very next day to buttonhole every worker who was wavering. "Drop Bilsky," he urges, a convert given the freedom to preach. "We can still win. Like 1916." They listened. He was the only one in the old union leadership they had ever really trusted. Three days later, the Hats caught him under the clock that hung from the cigar store on Twenty-eighth and Seventh. They beat him until he was senseless. Our people took him to Bellevue, where they patched him up and let him go. But Bednarik was finished.

"He did what he had to do," Barney said. "It's not so terrible for us."

And yet, he really liked Bednarik. It was he who had insisted all along that Bednarik was no Bilsky. "Still, Marty. I've paid. So has Bednarik. But you—you're Marty Altschuler and you think you can choose prices. And when you pay? Bednarik has no more use for the party than you do. But he doesn't lie to himself. It takes more than loyalty and good instincts. So they beat Bednarik. Deep down, it fills him with pride. It's not the party that's demonic. It's people like you." And laughs. The one eye digs past me, the lone Tartar eye, what Minschin left him. Well, he always claimed he was willing to give the other eye, too. The world was a mere reflection of angles locking into each other. And if he could see himself as acting under the dictates of history, how else see Bednarik? "Sentiment, Marty. You don't know the man. Listen, this is the first thing he's done since 1916 that makes sense. He's like a Christian about to be fed to the lions. That's his vindication. You think it's natural for a man to look like a tired dog. He's been living on memory since 1916. Now he'll die, knowing that 1916 was real, that he was as good then as he's been telling himself he was. Everytime they hit him, his life gained in meaning." So that we had done him a favor, I protested. And he laughed again. He had no right to convert men into martyrs. Bednarik was a man. Didn't Barney understand that much without his theories? And the bandages and leather patch disappear into the laughter, and what I see again is the Tartar-eyed tough of three years earlier about to be cornered by Leftwich, about to change my life. "If he had remained with Bilsky, become Minschin's thing. *That* would have been a denial of being a man. A man is what he does. If I can forgive my own father's failure, can't I forgive Bednarik, too? I'm not his judge. Bednarik made his choice. Let him live with it. He deserves that much. Anyway, he gave us a way to win the strike."

11

Had he been beaten to death under the clock, Bednarik might have cost us. Killing him right there in the open might have frightened some of the less brave back to work. But beating him so that he looked like some bloodied vegetable mass when the ambulance came to take him to Bellevue left the men enraged. To go back now would be to confirm Minschin in his view of what they were. And they were no longer willing to be the thing they had been. They gathered throughout the market, in groups of four and five, discussing what had happened to Bednarik. They knew Bednarik from 1916—and if they knew he had lately been no more than Bilsky's clerk, that he had been too afraid to act on their behalf, they also recognized his fear in themselves. In forgiving Bednarik his cowardice, they forgave themselves their own. They created out of Bednarik a man who had once embraced their cowardice but who now embodied their courage. Two days after Bednarik was beaten, the shops were virtually deserted.

The following day, a special issue of *Fighting Together* appeared. Below a picture of Bilsky trying to look stern, an editorial denounced Barney Kadish and the wildcat strike. A contract was a contract. What future could the labor movement in America seek if it proved unable to agree to what its own elected representatives had signed? The violence and bloodshed that had recently plagued the entire clothing industry were the responsibility of Bolshevik agitators. Workers should immediately return to the shops to guarantee the integrity of the contract *their* elected representatives had signed. Legitimate grievances could be negotiated by those who had the workingman's best interests in mind.

Had we written it ourselves, the editorial couldn't have served us better. The beating of Bednarik had been witnessed by hundreds. They might believe a great deal about Barney. But they knew who brought violence to the clothing industry. By the week's end, even the Greek shops had been closed. Gus walked from one shop to the other with a small army of our people behind him.

"They fixed Bednarik," Barney says to me on Labor Day. "Maybe it's time we hit one of their people. I'll make the arrangements. You and Gus work out the details."

The Hats now openly operated out of the largest building in the market, the Carney Tower, which had been built in 1921. Leftwich, who had acquired a sense of style in the years since Barney and I left his shop, immediately moved in. He took the entire second floor. In the front, he had a large showroom; behind that, the shop. Leftwich had come a long way since Barney sent him crashing to the floor. He now specialized in expensive coats for both men and women—silks, Indian cottons of unusual weaves, British tweeds, even furs. He had the fur skins matched by two of the more expensive furriers on Twenty-seventh Street. He was one of the first men in the industry to understand the value of labels. And the silver and black silk crest with the words, "A Jack Leftwich Original" sewn into every garment that emerged from his shop, was as much his badge as it was the world of fashion's.

Leftwich had learned other things, too. Enough to offer
Minschin the use of his place. Leftwich remembered what the
issues were between him and Barney. Barney had to be handled
the way his furrier friends on Twenty-seventh Street handled
skins—cut, stretched, made part of something larger. Exactly
here, Leftwich sensed, he could be Minschin's teacher. He sent
for Bilsky and offered to house the Hats in the Carney Tower.
"Tell Minschin he can work from here." By this time, Minschin
knew who Barney Kadish was. He accepted Leftwich's offer.

Despite what had happened to them in the cellar, the Hats
still believed they could terrorize us. They never learned to look
at the world through Barney's eyes. Neither did Leftwich. Not
until the end. Small people fight small wars. But while they
fight, they remember that it's all part of something larger.

When we learned that the Hats were quartered in Leftwich's showrooms, we kept a man stationed in the kosher deli
on the other side of Seventh Avenue. I didn't assign anyone the
Hats might recognize. I chose older workers for that job. First,
I would describe to each of them the one I wanted—the student
with the briefcase. My first inclination had been to choose the
one who had tried to wreck our office. Then I remembered the
student Al. He interested me more than the others. And he
infuriated me, too. I created an identity for him that couldn't
have been more real if he had been my brother.

Our people wait patiently. They know how. Especially
during slack times. The deli opened at seven in the morning and
closed at nine at night. We had someone there all the time. A
few days of waiting and it paid off. At lunchtime, the student
Al emerged from the Carney Tower and crossed over to the
deli. Our man finished his corned beef sandwich, telephoned
Alex Brailowsky in the shop across the street from strike headquarters, then returned to the deli. I took Gus and Itzik Perlin
and one of the Shapiro twins—I could never tell who was who
—and ran over to Seventh Avenue. Gus and the Shapiro twin

got into a cab. I walked up to the deli with Itzik. We waited outside until the student Al left. As Al came out into the warm September air, I saw our man inside pick up a toothpick. "Remember me, student?"

He didn't even seem surprised. "I remember," he says. "I still owe you." Just like that. He glances up to the windows of JACK LEFTWICH, FINE COATS, SILKS, FURS. "You got more balls than brains coming here."

I walk alongside. He heads toward the corner. Itzik walks on his other side. Law-abiding. A law-abiding college student. Cross at the corner. As we pass the idling cab, Gus jumps out of the back. The student Al knows what is behind the blue handkerchief in Gus's hand. "Jesus, mister," I hear the cabbie say. The Shapiro twin smiles at him, puts his finger to his lips.

"Don't you worry," Itzik Perlin says. He pushes the jump seat down. The student Al takes a last look at Leftwich's window and enters the cab quietly. Gus and I get in behind him.

We sit facing him. The student Al is wedged in the back seat between the Shapiro twin and Itzik. Gus and I are on the jump seats. The cabbie's voice freezes us. "Where to?" he asks nervously. "Jesus, I don't want no trouble. They can have my license."

"To Brooklyn," Gus orders. "Across the Brooklyn Bridge."

Al feigns indifference. A mask for all dangers. Like Chekhov's dead people, who discover that they are dead. I wonder whether Al has read Chekhov. Suddenly, I want him to behave with dignity, to talk to me about Chekhov, books, Mozart's music. He is a student. I envy him. The cab darts through wide avenues and narrow streets propelled by the furtive hysteria of the driver. Fear is his time. Terror nests in doubt. He pictures what is to happen to him. What will we do to him when he swears on all that is holy (and we can name the god, the gun gives us that right, too) that he will keep quiet? And he will.

We know that. Al's unvoiced pleas drop like pennies in my mind. But the face in the jump seat stares out the window as if it belonged to a contemptuous aristocrat. Memories of Europe. A mother trapped in an East Side tenement, sisters who dream of Polish countesses descending curved staircases in the mind. This time, Al's Cossacks are Jewish.

My reverie is interrupted by Gus's voice. "You're the garbage our class throws up from its own guts."

"How far, mister?" the cabbie whimpers.

"Through Brownsville," Itzik Perlin says in Yiddish. "We'll tell you when to stop."

"Your name is Marvin Kaleb," the Shapiro twin says in English. He is staring at the hack license framed above the cabbie's head.

"On my mother's life, I won't say nothing."

"Why should you, Marvin?" Gus says, without turning around in his seat. He has come a long way over these past few months.

After the Lower East Side, Brownsville seems a distant territory. More American. Quiet. Gus tells the cabbie to stop and we get out. One step beyond. The streets are cleaner here. "Marvin Kaleb," Gus repeats, as he nestles the gun into the handkerchief and against Al's back. I pay. I tip the cabbie double the fare. He will say nothing. The people on the streets do not look up as we pass by. Old women sit in the sun on wooden milk crates. Brownsville lives within itself. It can ignore us.

After a ten minute walk through these unknown streets, we enter an apartment building that has not yet been finished. But there are no laborers around. In the apartment on the second floor, Al's face has begun to lose its haughtiness. I sit in the kitchen in the chair opposite his and watch as fear corners out on his lips and note how he takes a dry swallow when he thinks no one is watching. Gus stands at the kitchen door with the gun.

"Did Barney give you the address?" I ask.

"Yes," Gus answers. I wonder why Barney did not give the address to me. "He made the arrangements."

"What are you going to do with me?" Al asks, swallowing.

Itzik enters the kitchen. "He talks," Itzik says in Yiddish.

"Maybe you want a cigarette?" Gus says mockingly. "A glass of milk?"

Al shakes his head. He is afraid enough by now so that he does not even understand that Gus is mocking him. "If you kill me, you better keep on running," he says nervously. "Minschin don't like his men getting killed."

"And if we let you go?" I ask. "Do we get to kiss Mr. Minschin if we let you go?"

Al slides back into silence. He braces his shoulders, pulling his lean college boy body erect in the blue kitchen chair. Something in his soul has begun to turn. I think of Chekhov and I am disappointed. The fear spreads its edges now. I wonder whether he is going to break down and cry. I pretend I am a physician and the student Al is my patient. Itzik goes to the tap to get a glass of water. No water comes out. I watch, fascinated, as the student Al's body tenses. He is going to spring at Itzik. I do not cry out in warning. Before he can gather enough courage, Gus lurches forward and hits him with the gun on the back of the neck. Al is thrown off the chair. Itzik jumps aside, still cursing the useless water faucet, and kicks Al in the stomach. Then he turns around and walks out of the room. I follow him into the next room. There is a frayed brown couch in the center of the room. Two soiled stuffed armchairs face it. The armchairs are matted with age. Salvation Army furniture. Itzik sprawls in one of the chairs.

"You shouldn't have done that," I say in Yiddish. I sit on the couch facing him.

"I could kill the bastard. I'd like to kill them all. I keep remembering Abe Becker." His Yiddish is thick, guttural.

"This one's a boy. He didn't do it."

"A boy. He's older than you. Maybe as old as Gus. How old am I? Or any of us? What difference does age make?" Sweat tinges his brow, he leans back in the chair. I think he is going to cry with rage. "If it was up to me, I'd kill the son of a bitch."

"And Minschin? What will Minschin do?"

"He'll do it anyways. I'm not smart, Marty. Like you. And Barney. Only I know as good as you how it is with us. The Hats shit on us. The bosses buy the Hats and the Hats buy their Bilskys. And when anyone gets tired eating their shit, like Bednarik, then they fix him so he can't eat anything no more. 'It's their nature.' Barney tells me. All right. I'm not smart enough to argue. But tell me, what's *our* nature? That we eat their shit all the time. Not for me, Marty. If it was up to me, I'd kill all the bastards."

I return to the kitchen. There is nothing I can say to Itzik. The student Al is sitting in the chair again. His hands are tied behind him and his face is very pale and he is obviously in pain. Itzik follows me back into the kitchen. The student Al catches Itzik's eyes and turns his head away. His eyes are watery. He has been crying. His lips and forehead are beaded with sweat. I feel embarrassed for him. I am eighteen and he is twenty-two and Itzik is twenty-six. But I feel as if I were Al's father. And Itzik's father.

"He claims he's Minschin's nephew," Gus laughs. "Can you beat that? Minschin's nephew." He laughs again.

Itzik cups Al's chin in his huge right hand. "I spit on your family. Old Becker had a son. I spit on your uncle Minschin. Do you understand?" The student Al thinks Itzik is asking whether he understands Yiddish. He nods, pleased to please. Itzik spits in his face.

"Leave him alone!" I command. "Go downstairs. Telephone Barney."

Gus leaves with Itzik. Gus gives me the gun. I stick it in

my belt. The Shapiro twin is sitting on the other side of the kitchen, at a broken table, trying to read. He is reading a party pamphlet, a series of quotations from Lenin offering the essentials of Marxism. I watch the Shapiro twin read. He lives on Broome Street, surrounded by Italians, with his twin brother and stroke-paralyzed mother. He has lived there for twenty years. "I have no head for theories," the Shapiro twin sighs, and puts the pamphlet down on the kitchen table. A modest man.

Barney and Gus walk into the kitchen. Barney is dressed in dark black slacks and a light-blue summer jacket. "I was already on my way. I met Gus and Itzik downstairs." Gus carries a bag of groceries. He goes to the kitchen table and the Shapiro twin gets up and walks into the living room. Barney's black leather-patched eye contrasts stylishly with the summer-blue jacket, blends with the pants. He gestures. I follow him into the bedroom. The bedroom is empty of furniture. "You don't approve?" he asks.

I shrug. "For what purpose? Itzik wants to kill him."

"Why does it disturb you?"

Barney's voice is low and steady. I am not sure of exactly why I am against killing the student Al. "It's not practical."

"That's not what's bothering you."

"What's the purpose of it? If we kill him, Minschin has to kill at least two of us."

"Maybe," Barney admits. "And maybe it will simply finish him. LaTour says he'll try. I'm not certain."

"You spoke to LaTour?" LaTour will tell Barney to be careful.

"He sent Bernstein from Canada again."

"Isn't it enough to beat him? He's a student."

Barney laughs. "Gus says he's Minschin's nephew."

"He thinks that will frighten us."

"LaTour agrees with me, Marty. If Minschin doesn't quit, he thinks we should kill him." He measures me with the one eye. His eye commands the center. The bandages have been removed. His face seems pale, suspended. I have to focus on the eye in order to believe that Barney Kadish is here, in this room, his face blending into the shadows until I find it difficult to distinguish between Barney and the twilight.

"It makes no sense."

"It makes sense." His voice is coming out of the shadows now. "It's time to push against them. Even LaTour is convinced. The manufacturers are beginning to beg for a settlement. Leftwich alone is holding the association in line for Minschin. He keeps telling them Minschin will break us. Only they are beginning to suspect that maybe this time Minschin can't fix anything. Now the risks are as great for him as they are for us." I try to remember what he looked like without the eyepatch. The man is my closest friend and I cannot remember what he looked like six weeks ago. In one room, the face of a friend. In the other, the student Al waiting to die.

"Let me kill him then," I hear myself say. Barney shrugs.

12

Killing doesn't change very much. I remember it now and the things that come back are Barney's face floating into the twilight, the student Al going to piss with Gus and Itzik and me staring at him as he hangs over the toilet bowl, his legs untied now and the tears streaming down his face, so that when he turns around and zips his fly his face is streaming tears and he is laughing and hiccuping. And I remember him, hands and legs tied, thrown across the couch at night while Gus and I and Itzik and the Shapiro twin take turns sitting up just to make certain that he doesn't get away. There's nothing romantic about dying. He sleeps. The naked fact reduced to its future. Al sleeps.

The next morning Barney returns. He has left Callahan with instructions. "Minschin has twenty-four hours to quit," Callahan says to Leftwich over the phone. "Tell him that from us." Late that night a bomb goes off in the basement and destroys our strike headquarters. No one is hurt. Even the night watchman has been called away to the telephone. Minschin is being careful. Maybe he is also afraid. The next morning, Callahan surveys the damage, takes the Seventh Avenue to Fourteenth Street, walks over to Astor Place on Broadway, takes the Lexington back to Thirty-fourth, and from there takes the train to Brooklyn. At eleven o'clock, Callahan enters the apartment. It is our third day in the apartment. Callahan is going to kill him. First we all eat lunch in silence. Then Callahan steps behind the chair in which the student Al is bound and gagged and cuts his throat with a hunting knife he has brought for that very purpose. I do not try to stop Callahan. Nor do I look at the body as we leave the apartment. "He was a traitor to his class," Gus says, on the train going back to Manhattan. Like a rabbi at a funeral. One single sentence for a man's life.

We couldn't live with our eyes shut. In the days that followed, the student Al's death was not to be denied. Barney tried to pretend it had been a passionless pursuit. But he was like the rest of us, vultures circling around a wounded memory, waiting for it to die. To see a man murder another man is to teach yourself how not to see. Purposeful blindness. Barney's lone eye saw as much as ours. Death is never a simple strategy.

Barney had the revolution to lean on. Callahan had his revenge. And Gus and Itzik had their ferocious hatred of Minschin and the owners. Me? After we did it, the killing seemed justified. Only—something was missing. Maybe that's why I wanted to kill him myself, as if that way I could affirm his life. Anyway, what would the life have been if we had chosen to allow it to continue? As much our decision as their choosing to beat Bednarik into unconsciousness. Even LaTour had wanted to seize a certain equality from it, to pay them back for what union people had been taking all these years. You never lose it—the need to call the turn on them the way they've done to you.

The body was found a week after we killed him. He wasn't Sam Minschin's nephew. Just a bright City College boy who turned out to be not quite bright enough. The afternoon papers said the police had received a telephone call complaining about a smell from a new but uncompleted apartment building in Brownsville. The builders had been forced into bankruptcy during construction. No one in any of the adjoining buildings remembered seeing anything unusual. The body, its throat slashed, was on the floor, tied to an old blue kitchen chair. Blood stained the kitchen floor. A few other pieces of old furniture were found in the apartment along with some rotted fruit and an empty milk carton. The body was identified as that of Alvin Gerstetler, a student at the City College of New York who had transferred to night school last semester to help support his widowed mother and two sisters. The next day's *Daily News* added that Alvin Gerstetler had been working for the noted society clothing designer, Jack Leftwich. When interviewed, Mr. Leftwich had been in tears. "A good hard-working boy," Mr. Leftwich said. "Absolutely devoted to his mother and sisters." Mrs. Gerstetler had fainted upon learning her son had been found murdered. She was under the care of Mr. Jack Leftwich's personal physician. The case had been assigned to Deputy Inspector Thomas Shugrue.

A week later and the association signed a contract with the union. Although he was officially no more than a member of the joint council, it was Barney who signed for the union. The members of the association insisted on it. The new wage scale provided a ten percent raise for every union member, a reduction of work hours from forty-two to forty, and a firm guarantee of full hour lunch breaks. While our people celebrated their victory near the end of September, Callahan and I were arrested for the murder of Alvin Gerstetler.

13

The cops walked into the suite of rooms we had rented in the Hotel Philadelphia, on Twenty-ninth and Seventh, to serve as temporary union headquarters. Even Minschin wouldn't bomb a hotel. The young cop who entered first looked around as if he knew someone in the room. He was followed by four others. A tall, lean cop with sergeant's stripes, his face lined and rutted, stepped to the center. He pointed at Barney with his nightstick. "You? Are you Altschuler?" Despite the wear on his face, he was no more than thirty-five and he still had a slight brogue, the kind of note a man is left to decide whether he wants to give up. I liked his having kept it.

"I'm Altschuler," I say, stepping from behind the table. The table is strewn with papers. "What do you want?"

"And Callahan?" the sergeant says, still looking at Barney.

"What do you want with them?" Barney asks.

"I don't want nothing," the sergeant says. "But we got warrants from the City of New York. The City of New York wants Altschuler and Callahan." He shakes his head, smiles. "A strange combination."

"Does it bother you?"

"Nothing bothers me. Sooner or later, we all manage to get back to our own." He turns to me. "Will you come?"

"I'd like to see the warrant," Barney says.

"Let him ask for it," the sergeant says. "He's the one."

"And Callahan," Barney reminds him.

"And Callahan," the sergeant echoes. "Can't forget my own."

While I read the warrant, Barney waves toward the next room. Callahan walks inside. He taps the sergeant on the shoulder. The sergeant's eyes frame him, an insect mounted. "Do you want to see the warrant, too?"

"Not from one of my own," Callahan says.

"Who would believe it?" the sergeant says, almost tenderly.

"You'll tell me County Cork stories?"

"Never deny it. Only you'll do the telling. All there is."

"Like a zoo," Callahan says, turning to Barney. "Separate man from his brother man and look how willing he is to serve his master."

"But not you," the sergeant laughs.

"And not me either," I interrupt.

"Now from the Hebrew side. Come along, the both of you. To the bosom of mother church. Christ help us."

Barney sent two shop stewards with us to police headquarters. By the time we were booked, there must have been a dozen union people, workers and officials, milling around the station. The sergeant's face caricatured itself in its crude matter-of-factness. He, too, had chosen sides. The brogue was a minor defiance.

You could feel the hatred in the air. For Callahan most of all. They could dismiss the rest of us. We were foreigners. They expected us to be what we were. Our presence simply confirmed their expectations, the flotsam washed up by the current. But Callahan was theirs.

It was warm inside the station house. They took both Callahan and me into a back room to be fingerprinted. The desk sergeant at the front desk complained when we returned. Our people were still in the station house. The lieutenant threatened to arrest them, but by that time Roginsky had appeared and was scribbling away in his notebook. At that time, Roginsky was still running *Der Royter Morgn*. After Hungary, the party would reward him by making him editor of its English language paper. By 1957, Roginsky could be trusted in any language.

Roginsky is near the desk and the desk sergeant leans over and pulls his notebook from him. He examines it, curses the idea that anyone can write in that archaic script, curses the strange faces in front of him, then hands the notebook back to Roginsky. That desk sergeant knows that men should stand with the proper order behind them. Mother church, father clubhouse, this New York waiting to be kissed by whoever was willing to bend the knee and woo her. The cops were disgusted. They took both Callahan and me into the back room again, then separated us. No, I knew nothing about the murder of Alvin Gestetler, except what I had read in the papers. No, I didn't realize he was the same man we had beaten up in strike headquarters. Yes, we had beaten him. Defending ourselves. No, I had never been to the apartment house in Brownsville where he had been found. Yes, Callahan and I were friends, we worked together in the union. Sometimes, he would even teach me to box. Celebrating Callahan. As he would celebrate himself. Telling me about it later. "Brothers," he tells them, "my own. My sweet spirits of Cork." With that Bolshie scum, Callahan? "Brothers, fighters mine, come trot to the revolution. Look what they've made of you." And the sergeant's hand slashed back across his mouth. "Bastards. So eager they were to kiss the asses that shit on them," Callahan tells us later. And the other cops begging to work him over because Callahan had offended the natural order of things in their proper places. I hadn't.

Only John Hudson had already shown up at the front desk. I love the memory. John Hudson, impeccable proprietor of the law, Roginsky scribbling furiously in Yiddish in front of the desk sergeant's disbelieving eyes, Gus cursing softly under his breath, cursing strategically in Greek, because he had learned long ago not to take any unnecessary chances. In the background, our people like a chorus waiting to praise the justice of our gods. And then we were out on bail and Callahan and I and Barney and Gus are sitting in Dolkin's, laughing with the memory of it, and Callahan describing the faces of the cops peering down at him.

At that time, I thought it was the party that ordered Barney to kill Al. I should have known better. But I didn't want to acknowledge what should have been clear even then: the party had no life of its own. Barney was the party. Barney and the many thousands like him. And yet, I couldn't accept that—perhaps because I wanted something less prosaic. The party functioned in my imagination like a demon of the real, the patterns I created for it as symmetrical as the way jewelers match diamonds for an expensive bracelet. I wanted to believe that the demon existed, always lurking in the background, like Roginsky, recording sentences in his notebook with all the certainty of a judge appointed by the party, convinced the time had come. Roginsky's note-taking was the world's witness. And Barney was the time made visible. But the party hadn't given any orders. It would, for the time being anyway, steer clear of the Minschin's of the world.

The case was dropped. Lack of evidence, the police admitted. It turned out that the party did manage that, with the unknowing help of John Hudson, Esq. One day, as Callahan and Gus are walking along Seventh Avenue, the tall lean sergeant steps out of a passing patrol car. "You win this time," he says to Callahan. "Only be careful. This is not the future. Not for our kind."

"And what's our kind, sergeant?" Callahan mocks.

"I'll get you someday." The patrolman behind the wheel is nervous. He gestures to the sergeant but is ignored. "You're a traitor to your people."

"And you to your class." Before Gus can stop him, Callahan's withered claw of a hand rakes the sergeant's face like a razor. Gus steps between the sergeant and Callahan, grabs Callahan.

"I'm sorry, sergeant," Gus says. The sergeant glares at the two of them, gets back into the patrol car, and drives off. "Callahan, Callahan," Gus whistles, "when the hell you going to understand? You can't change the world all by yourself."

Callahan? For what they did to him, he could never get enough back.

14

In September 1925, three years after the strike has been settled and almost two years since the reorganized United Garment Workers of America had moved into their new headquarters on Twenty-seventh Street near the corner of Seventh Avenue, the telephone in my office rings. I am twenty-one. I am now first vice-president of the union. And I have my own telephone. "Bednarik's dead," the voice at the other end says. Barney and Gus are in my office. I repeat it aloud for them. "Bednarik's dead." The voice at the other end anticipates my question. "He collapsed on the street. Just like that. By the time the ambulance arrived from the hospital, he was already dead."

Outside, sun slants across the street lamps. Bright language of death. Abe Becker and then the student Al and now Bednarik. "We'll hold a rally. As a memorial," Barney says. "What's better for a good union man like Bednarik?"

The voice on the telephone says, "Hello. Hello. Are you still there?"

"I'm still here," I say. Then I hang up.

Good union men. Bednarik and Old Becker's son. The newspaper picture of Abe Becker bleeding to death inside the Labor Lyceum. Barney's description of Bednarik exhorting a crowd of striking cutters in 1916, looking like a Lenin with a full head of hair, still lean and hungry, before he took on that dead man's shuffle and hangdog look. "Ain't we men, too?" asks the weasel-eyed silk worker who confronts me on the street that afternoon. I do not know his name, but I remember that he had been a Bilsky echo until the Hats killed Abe Becker, and then a few days later, choking on his own rage, he jumped one of the Hats who was simply walking down Seventh Avenue, jumped him and rode his back like a cowboy in a rodeo rides a steer. Two of the Hat's friends finally managed to pull him off, had left him with both eyes blackened and his left cheekbone fractured, and with a vision of himself that sent him strutting through the market from that time on.

We drew up the leaflets and posters. Gus took them to Kallen the Printer. "You want it in forty-eight hours, Gus. It's too big an order."

"You used to tell me you could get me anything in twenty-four hours. Now we give you forty-eight and you can't do it." Kallen shrugs, turns away. "Did they at least pay you? Or threats alone?"

"I don't want no trouble."

"Your life is your trouble. You'll never get a line from us again."

Even the firm that printed party pamphlets turned Gus down. Our sergeant, it turned out, had made a few visits. Barney telephones. An hour later three young printers picked up our sketches. They were back that night with the leaflets. "How much?" Gus asks.

They laugh. "We borrowed the presses. It's nothing."

We blanketed the garment center and the fur district, too. The Hats came in after the police had warned us against littering. We sent squads of our people through the streets with leaflets. The Hats melted away, puzzled by the obstinacy of men disowning their pasts.

The first Monday in October and the city air washes itself to come out clean, smelling of the salt and brine of the river a few blocks away. Mixed smells crash Seventh Avenue. Franks, knishes, omelets. The sun is a huge orange floating above us. The streets erupt with silk workers, tailors, furriers, pattern makers. At one o'clock, work in the market ceases. Workers turn off their machines. As they do in Montreal, in Toronto, in Milwaukee. The men gather. The October air is festive with homage to Abe Becker, homage to Bednarik, homage to themselves. Nostalgia filters through their minds until they have managed to convince themselves that this is how they have always been. Descending in twos and threes from their shops, they are amazed at their numbers, and they jostle each other for recognition.

Signs leap above their heads. "Down With Union Gangsterism!" "Our Martyrs—Becker and Bednarik." "All Workers United." Signs left over from other causes. "Free Tom Mooney!" Signs in Yiddish, in Greek, in Italian, in English. Words to assure each man's incipient majesty. They pour into Seventh Avenue from the side streets. The avenue has been closed off to traffic from Twenty-third Street to Thirty-fourth Street. Twin phalanxes of mounted police hem the people in. Hundreds of police on horses, big men, chosen for how they look mounted on horses. Their blue uniforms are speckled with shields, their medals are worn like amulets. They look like marionettes out of control as their horses move back and forth.

Barney had ordered the platform constructed in the middle of Twenty-seventh Street, across the street from the Carney Tower. From there we watch the sea of people rock back and forth. A procession ripe with the sense of its collective self. The cops draw their horses back on the fringes of the crowd, nervously draw themselves into the horses. Nervous, disdainful centaurs. A tough afternoon's work. The cops prepare for the brooding eruptions that latch on to all gatherings in this city. The cops and their masters are linked by their hatred of us.

At one-thirty, Barney steps forward to the microphone. His hands outstretched to the early October sun, he listens to the swell of anticipation from the crowd. The signs shift back and forth, although there is just a slight breeze. Barney begins in Yiddish. *"Brider arbeter."* And then in English. "Fellow workers." The words weren't language. The roar from the human sea overwhelms us on the wooden stage. He could have spoken in Chinese. Signs, portents, a declaration of independence from Minschin.

Barney's speech is short, a celebration of Abe Becker and Bednarik. Hands against the bright October sky, he introduces Old Becker, who has been pushed toward the platform from his place below, literally picked up by crowds milling beyond our range and half-carried, half-swept, like a sack of apples, toward the stage. Old Becker is trying to remember now just what the cause is, where he has buried his dead son, how he must speak to the living. The substance of their dreams is the reality of his pain. Old Becker has given for this human mass in front of him. Awed by his own presence, Old Becker resolves a *kaddish.* The dream, he has decided, outlasts sons anyway. Not like Isaac, burrowing deeper and deeper into his childish wants, the taste of a roll on the tongue, until he dies three months later. Besides, Isaac's son is among the living, here, standing alongside Old Becker, adjusting the microphone for him. Now Old Becker stands in the sweet Indian summer air. His arms reach out, as if toward that God he had long since forgotten except for the daily necessity of defying him. He tongues his dry lips in the effort to claim the correct words. But words do not come easily for Old Becker, not even in Yiddish. He clutches the lectern's sides, as if he is afraid he is going to fall. To speak is to become human. "Bednarik . . . " he begins, the Yiddish tremulo working against the crowd's anticipation. "Bednarik. . . ." His arms stretch out, as if to caress a body. Numberless bodies buried in equally numberless causes. The streets of the world flow with revolution, with causes. Old Becker clutches at the past, aware of all these eyes upon him. In the background, horses jostle against the crowds. Herdsmen herd.

"Bednarik . . . was a man. My Abe was a man. Only a man should not say *kaddish* for his son. I do not believe in their God, but I believe that the son should say *kaddish* for his father. But for Bednarik, I want to say a *kaddish*. Because what have they left us? What have they left you? Or me?" The silence is absolute. Old Becker is an orator, filling our legions with the promise of impending glory. Old Becker drifts into a sleepwalker's hatred. Everything has been designed to press us down, to separate Jew from Greek, man from man. His vision is halting, broken. "If I could say it in English, would that make it better? Nothing for us. . . ." Phrases caught in the air, snatched at. In the distance, the triumphant blast of an ocean liner. Is it making its way in or out of this New York? No one cares. History has caught each of us here, with this old man. Caught us, deposited us on Seventh Avenue.

A grasping eulogy. Old Becker wanted us to see ourselves as Bednarik must have seen us (I think of Bednarik's slow shuffle, ripples of fear corroding a man's ambition), as his Abe saw us, as Barney Kadish, president of the union, sees us. We were men. Not a motion of dispersal from the crowd. And then, on a signal known only to them, the blue phalanx at the borders of the crowd wavers, shifts, the horses clumping together. A few angry shouts, then bewildered screams. The distance collapses. Old Becker pauses before this mass. Wonders. Has the language finally betrayed him? Is it that he does not know how to say it clearly?

The horses and men press forward, loosen, clot together

immediately, press forward again. They are hemming us in, squeezing us from north and south. And then the sound of sirens from east to west. Barney's Tartar eye narrows as he squints into the distance. The crowd is being pushed together, the side streets cut off by cops on foot. The crowd sucks in, toward the stage upon which we are standing. The people are being forced to give ground, slowly, methodically. Old Becker looks at Barney. His eyes beg for time to finish. He does not understand what is happening. Callahan appears on stage and takes Old Becker by the hand. He leads him as if he were blind. The crowd pauses, the mass seems suspended. Then there is a sullen roar, as if there had been an explosion from the middle and it was forcing itself outwards in wave after wave. Suddenly, our people are charging the police, smashing the windows of the shops on Seventh Avenue. The police are both retreating and attacking, cops on horses riding down on the crowd now, brandishing their nightsticks as they lean low in their saddles like Hollywood cowboys. I watch fascinated as a lone horseman rides down on a running worker thirty feet away and I feel the sharp crack of the nightstick breaking the bridge of the nose, parodying the parody nature had already made.

I jump off the stage and find myself running alongside another man. I run toward the police. Sirens are wailing and more and more cops are flooding the avenue. A chain of demonstrators moves against the police, like an undulating giant snake, out of control. Cops, horses, workers crash against one another, nightsticks flying, sirens wailing. I grab for a nightstick rolling in the gutter at exactly the same moment that a cop slams against my shoulder and sends me spinning against the curb. I roll over, drive my knee into his balls. While his hands grab his scrotum, I reach for the nightstick and bring it crashing down on his head.

A hand grabs my elbow and I spin around, the nightstick already descending. It's Barney. He jumps aside, I slash the

empty air. Sirens blare all around us. Barney grabs my elbow
once again and points to the Carney Tower across the street.
The heavy plate glass of the bronze door has been splintered.
We run through the lobby, up the stairs. On the second floor we
stop. The gold lettering is neat and precise, as if it had been
carved into the plate glass by a jeweler: JACK LEFTWICH, INC.
FINE COATS, SILKS, FURS. Barney grabs my nightstick and slams
it against the plate glass. He laughs. "We've won, Marty. It's the
dumbest thing they could've done." We race up the stairs together, higher and higher until we stand breathlessly on the roof
of the Carney Tower, thirty stories above the cops and the
rioting workers and the horses and the broken windows. Barney
stands on the edge, panting from the long climb. Together, we
gaze down at these miniature people, like moving Dresden
porcelain figures battling each other. Barney shouts, to me, to
those below who cannot hear us, to *their* river, *their* ships, *their*
buildings, *their* streets. "We've won, you bastards! You'll never
beat us again! Because we've won! We've won!"

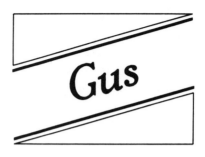

Gus

1

I sit here dying. Barney died three days ago. In New Mexico. Lisa telephoned. All you have to do is learn how. And dying is real, simple. So definite. A single paragraph in the *Times*. Three sentences. Homage to Comrade Kadish. In the *Future*, the body dressed out. A full page eulogy. Let us pray for the soul of Comrade Barney Kadish. Embalmed by one Robert Atwill, a "young black comrade." Deathless prose. Letters like snakes crawling across the past. Roginsky is now the editor. The *Future*. A new name for old ways. I can't understand his dying there, in Albuquerque. I always meant to visit him. He wrote. Until two years ago. Then stopped. Bitter memories, bitter man. Even bitter against the party by then. He wouldn't tell me why. But I could feel it. He just stopped writing and at first I kept on and then, a Sunday morning it was, a year or so back, I telephoned. And Lisa—she took him in all those years back, I don't remember what she called herself then —answered and I say, "Lisa. Lisa. This is Gus. Gus Constantinou."

"Yes, Gus. How are you, Gus? How are you?"

"I'm tired. I got cancer, Lisa. They say I should go live in a nursing home instead of my apartment. Only my niece, Sophie Korylas. I don't know if you ever met her. She says. . . ." Always drifting off. Memory shrivels. I loved Barney. Loved Lisa, too. But I had the cancer then, was dying. As Barney was dying. It takes a long time to die. I want to speak to Barney.

"No, Gus," she says, "he doesn't want to remember too much. Not now. You understand, Gus. You're a good man. He loves you. All the old ones. Only it is too difficult. Please understand."

Cells multiply. I understand that, too. "Lisa, I still love you. I always loved you."

Only she chose Barney. Or was it that he chose her? Because Barney was different. Barney Kadish did the choosing. Even in the name of the revolution. Perhaps even death. I'm not Itzik. I wanted what I wanted. Barney took. "Gus," he says, "if I should die, it's you who should run the union. But it can't be. You don't speak Yiddish. Still, one life to live." Laughing, punching the office air. I could run it now. Greeks. "One life to give the revolution. Gus, a man should be able to split himself in two. For the revolution." Sipping bootleg whiskey he keeps in the desk drawer.

But what good? Dead of a heart attack. In all that sun. In my gut, the cells bubble over. Eat this eater. Fat Gus grown thin. Fat Gus grows angry thinking of Barney dying in that western sun. In Pyros, the streets bend away from the wind and you feel protected. I don't know what it is like in New Mexico. California is figs and dates. When Sophie graduated from college, she goes to California. "Bring me back dates and figs, Sophie. And oranges."

"In the supermarket, Uncle Gus," she laughs. "The whole world." She brings me books. From California.

Memory is like cancer. The pieces of the past exist. They devour each other. Bubbles in the body, the cells stew. Hot deaths. Sophie's boyfriend explains it to me. An intern at Montefiore, where they probe me, photograph me, watch the cells and nod in amazement. *Remission. Prognosis.* I choke on time. Each moment stolen from the moment before. "You're a brave man, Uncle Gus," Sophie's boyfriend says. He explains the process.

"Tell me about heart attacks. How do they work? What is the difference between cancer and heart attacks?" Dead is dead. Sophie's boyfriend is a Jew. All my life I have been surrounded by Jews. In the movement. In the union.

"A real American," Barney says, when we come back from Flint. "John L. is a real American. Even on the *Mayflower*, there was steerage."

God fucks the daughters of the poor. If not God, then Barney. Will they speak of that at the memorial? The telephone rings. Itzik. Itzik is seventy-two, I am seventy, Barney is dead. Not yet sixty-nine. Itzik wants me to come for him. To Brooklyn. Itzik is the last white man in Brownsville, the last Jew in the world. He refuses to move. He can only hate their class. Poor Itzik. They do not let him out at night. But he refuses to move. "For Barney," he insists. The black faces peer at Itzik Perlin. "Brothers, you are men. Do not let the bosses make animals of you." The black faces laugh.

"Hey, man, this here ain't no Caddy Jew."

"Man, this here Jew be lucky he got fuckin' shoes on his feet."

On the telephone, he pleads. "Take me with you, Gus. Come to Brooklyn and we'll go together."

Itzik, I want to say, *the dead do not call each other. Soon, we too shall be dead.* All very simple. The cells bubble, multiply. Itzik weeps. My friend and comrade, Itzik Perlin, is alive in Brooklyn, weeps into the phone, wants to attend the memorial for Barney Kadish. "All right, Itzik," I say. "I will come to Brooklyn."

We will go together. I stare at the cradled telephone. I

remember Lisa's thighs. I dream of Barney parting them. "Like Moses at the Red Sea." Dolkin laughs. Flushed, Marty sits next to me. Did Dolkin know about Marty? Or about me? Whores in Odessa, whores in Pyros. We remember our lives away. In Pyros, Old Maria breaks me in. Lips like blubber. "Niggerlips!" the boys taunt. She is ageless, old. I am thirteen. Her taste is vinegar. I stare at the cradled phone, remember Lisa. I am going to Brooklyn for Itzik Perlin.

2

Brownsville destroyed. In the streets, the young drift, pack against one another. We liked the way they moved. Their music. A black man on a street corner plucks his guitar, sings in Spanish, Madrid in flames. Sings in Russian, in Yiddish, in English. Black bodies slouch, dart in and out, tease my slowness. A new white man. Victims.

They follow me up the stairs. I am not afraid. Cancer kills all other fears. "Hey, man," he says, not even thirteen yet, face like highly polished brass aged beyond its time, "you be comin' for the Jew?"

And the other, his friend, "He don't have, Roland. He don't have shit. What for we want to play with this here old white man?"

Before I reach the landing, they disappear. I ring the bell. Itzik is dressed, waiting. He slams the door behind him. He does not bother to lock it. Itzik will not betray his class.

On the street, no one stops us. They are used to Itzik, bored with this crazy old Jew. We are going into Manhattan together. Itzik holds my arm, still towering above me. As big as Leftwich he was. He wears a frayed dark blue suit. It is clean, pressed, the white shirt starched, the black wool tie carefully knotted. He even wears a red flower in the lapel. Like the American Legion used to sell on Memorial Day. In the country of the workers, red poppies in buttonholes. The earth yawns. Even the children disappear. They have lost interest. The streets are empty, burnt out. An old Greek and an old Jew walk arm in arm to the subway. In the train's explosion, we trail ourselves back to Manhattan. A memorial meeting in memory of Barney Kadish.

The meeting is in the Labor Lyceum. Itzik remembers. We drift through Union Square. The revolution floats in the breeze. We enter the auditorium. It is sparsely filled. "Where are they?" Itzik whispers. "The people." *Dead, Itzik,* I want to say. I cough, take his hand in mine. We are two old men for whom the future vanished. *It never came, Itzik. Dead. Like us.* But I do not speak. I recognize few faces. I close my eyes, think of Old Becker, of his son, of Callahan. And the ones we killed. Remorse for our triumphs? No, they were the enemy. Their dying mattered.

"They want us on the platform," Itzik says. A man of about thirty-five is standing in front of us. Obsequious little man, thin body carved into a gray turtleneck sweater and gray slacks. Even dead Communists deserve better. Party emissaries.

"If you'll permit me, comrades," he says, offering his hand, "Carl Grant. The people at *Future* particularly asked for you two. We want you on the stage."

Itzik smiles, pleased. He is delighted to discover that his life possesses significance. Itzik is loyal to the party, to Barney. He still hands out leaflets on street corners. "Barney taught us," he says, taking the little man's hand in his own huge paw. "Everything."

The little man smiles. His teeth are very even, as if they had been inserted in his mouth one by one, then clamped together in a vise. The little man in the turtleneck will not die of cancer. Or of a heart attack. Perhaps he will not die at all. "Comrade Constantinou," he says, turning to me, "we would like you to speak."

"I cannot speak." The little man makes me nervous. I do not like him. Itzik's grip on my shoulder tightens. "I do not know the language well enough."

"Even pattern makers understand English well enough by now," the little man says. He is still splendid. "It is no problem."

His teeth terrify me. My head aches. I wish I had not gone for Itzik. "I speak no English either." First I say it in English, then in Greek. His smile dies. Roginsky stands on the stage, sees me, waves. Kiss the language of the past. Roginsky once tried to teach me Yiddish. I taught him Greek. A worker's exchange. Roginsky learned quickly. I learned little. Words belong to others. The little man is trying to capture Roginsky's attention. "Roginsky!" I call loudly, amazed at the harsh clarity of my own voice. "He wants you." I point to the little man. "Him."

Roginsky limps toward us, leaning on an elaborately carved white cane. A revolutionary dandy. He embraces Itzik, turns to me, hugs me. There are tears in Roginsky's eyes. He ignores the little man whose smile grows wider because he is being ignored. "You two," Roginsky says, "you've come home. You're a real find, you two." Itzik mumbles something in Yiddish and Roginsky laughs. Itzik smiles. It takes little to please Itzik. He is happy. "Speak English!" Roginsky commands. "We have the Greek comrade with us."

The ache in my head lessens. But cancer bubbles away. "A death without meaning," I say. "You want something more. For Barney, anyway."

"For all of us," Roginsky says.

"Yes," I echo, "for all of us."

"It's the times," Roginsky says. "First the congressional

committee. Then the labor people. That was the hardest. To be bitten by your own."

"It didn't break him," Itzik says defiantly. The little man has disappeared. "He was living with Lisa Grumbach. Do you remember her, Roginsky?"

"I heard about her. After he left her, she went out to California. To become an actress. Isn't that it?"

"She left him," I say. "To marry a druggist."

Roginsky shrugs. He is not concerned with Lisa. "You'll say a few words, Gus? For Barney."

"I can't. Too much effort. I told the little one I can't."

"Doesn't want," Itzik says bitterly. "He didn't even want to come."

"That's true," I say. "I can't speak, Roginsky. I have cancer. I am dying and Barney is dead."

"Let me speak," Itzik begs. He thrusts his face down into Roginsky's. I smell his old man's breath, smell of death's approach. "Like Old Becker."

"In Yiddish?" Roginsky muses. He looks above the line of the stage. Itzik nods eagerly. "Not enough understand. Never mind, Itzik. You and Gus just sit on the stage. Others will speak." Less than half the seats have been filled. I can see Roginsky making a mental note as his eyes scan the Lyceum. Roginsky sighs.

"I can't," I say. "It's the cancer."

He shrugs, turns on his heel, and limps off, stabbing the floor with his fancy cane. "He didn't want me," Itzik whines. "He wanted you, Gus."

"Nevermind." I take Itzik's hand. It is as if Itzik and I are each other's children. A gavel descends, the air splits, time is sliced in half. Barney's ghost, heart in hand, walks alongside of us as Itzik and I move toward the stage. But Barney is still young, winking at the world. The heart he holds is green, embroidered at the edges with red poppies. "So much attention to the organs of necessity," Barney's ghost laughs. His single eye winks.

Itzik and I stand before the stage. The little man in the gray turtleneck stands in front of us. "Comrades!" Roginsky cries into the microphone. He pounds his gavel three times. "Comrades! Your attention. Please. We have come together in memory of Comrade Barney Kadish." Then the little man signals for Itzik and me to follow him onto the stage. We sit down and Roginsky starts to speak again and I look around for the rabbi because in the fifties they always brought a rabbi. Only there is no rabbi. There is Roginsky and Roginsky's words and there is nothing else. I close my eyes, tired beyond feeling. In my stomach, death bubbles away.

3

I first heard about Barney from the Jewish silk cutters. But Barney was distant, a figure in the world out there. Jews and Greeks kept apart, did little more than acknowledge each other's presence. Guarded conversations walled in each to his own. We were their strangers. For us, they were another reminder that life in America was upside down. More Jews in two blocks of the garment center than in all of Greece. Greeks are creatures of habit. Everything in its place.

Two men screaming at each other. We watch. I don't know what it is about. Arguing about fighters. In Pyros, too. Who is the strongest in the village? As if life can be salvaged by what you invest in another man's life. After the revolution, I used to tell Barney, no more heroes. No more gods either. That was before they made the dead Russians into gods.

He talked about the union and I knew I would follow him.

I had found nothing else here in America. But I didn't understand. Not in the beginning. In the books, the revolution was swift, sudden, a swooping eagle or a bursting dam. Power. Impetus. When Barney talked about the union we could build, I forgot that the revolution had to be total. We inched forward. And I wanted to run. Four years after the Bolsheviks came to power in the Soviet Union. Our revolution had to be just around the corner. Organize silk cutters. Garment workers. Furriers. Machinists. A step forward. "Good trade unionists make good revolutionaries." Always. Like a priest urging you on the catechism.

You learn to curb impatience. You stop having to believe that the promised land is just around the corner. You accept the need for lies, the illusions you help perpetuate. And you learn to sit at a desk and wait because you tell yourself there is something to sit and wait for. Lead a strike. Get rid of a hood. Organize a benefit. You keep the frustration inside. You know. No one else has to know.

Now an old man's dying. Well, the revolution never claimed it would end that. Not an end to dying. Am I doing it the way it is supposed to be done? Death claims all the things a man owes. Even his memories. Minschin killed Old Becker's son. I dream of time now. I remember everything, but it all slides together. I unscramble moments, clutch events to new sequences. The student Al was early. Ths shit deep in the belly. What kind of man takes from his own? My father used to brag about the rich Greeks on Pyros. Built themselves up. On the sweat of his ass. He admired them, he didn't know any better. Used like an animal. "I don't give a fart for such nonsense!" he screams. Slams me into the corner of the one-room house. Beats me while my mother stands in the other corner, hangs her head. Greek women do not question. Lives choke on their patterns. No cancer. Other ways to die on Pyros.

I am fourteen then. "Listen," I tell him, blood streaming

from my nose, "your son is dead. I am my own man now. Touch me again and I kill you." Endings.

Callahan cut his throat. Callahan was like me. Only he didn't understand. Callahan's hand coils in my stomach now. Dead is dead. Keep your eyes on the ceiling and Callahan does his job. Marty's face like a mask. "I wanted to do it myself," he insists. He wanted to be clean. Didn't join the party. Roginsky is still in the party, leans on his cane, talks. His life, his son's life—there is nothing Roginsky will not give.

"You Communists," Sophie laughs, "always figuring with words. So what is it you feel when they murder? What, Uncle Gus? In '56, what did you feel? Workers of the world. . . ." Roginsky would have argued, each convert a necessity. I stare at her face. Full lips. A body thicker than the bodies of American girls.

Pick your bones clean. White sand, hard peasant bodies, wind in the corners of their eyes. "Is America so bad then?" my brother-in-law asks as we watch Sophie accept her diploma. The smell of death fills my nostrils. Years back, already dying. "You with your European ideas. And your Jews. This Kadish, this leader of yours, where did the son of a bitch leave you? Where is he now? Florida? Miami? And you?"

Sophie, death is the true beginning. This wilderness, this America, it cannot conquer. Death is the true beginning. Listen.

4

Minschin sent the cops when Barney called the memorial for Bednarik and Old Becker's son. "Of course, there will be trouble," Barney says. "They have no choice."

"I'll have our people ready," I assure him.

"They won't come themselves. Understand?" The one eye measures me. "With you, Gus, there are no illusions."

"Let them come. We'll turn it to our advantage."

We didn't know it would be the cops. You don't expect the cops to be so open about it. The cops were usually brought in when the manufacturers had nothing else left. Barney figured Minschin had a lot more left. Maybe that was why he didn't move quickly when Minschin came back at us in 1930. It wasn't really like Barney to underestimate an enemy. In the office, he turns to me and Callahan. "It's Leftwich. He pays. The cop's name is Turley."

"My sergeant," Callahan says. "With his County Cork stories."

"Nothing personal," I laugh.

Callahan shrugs. "Do you think they get overtime for that, Barney?"

"Cops should be more subtle," I say.

Barney shakes his head. "Leftwich controls the payroll and Minschin plays with Leftwich. Does it matter who pays Turley?"

"It's not very nice being a target," I say.

"Especially for the cops," Callahan says.

"Especially for the cops," Barney echoes.

"Let me take care of the bastard, Barney," Callahan urges.

"No more revenge for you, Jimmy. One is enough."

"But we can't let it go," I insist. "If they think we won't fight them . . ."

"The question is how," Barney interrupts. "You can't fight every cop in New York. You can't hit them openly."

He kept his own counsel. It was the way he faced the world. And he enjoyed it. You watched him when it looked as if Minschin had him encircled and you saw the pleasure he took in not giving anything away. He was always pulling us together. Making us consolidate our strength. And always looking at the next move. You didn't matter, he didn't matter. Only the union mattered. And the revolution.

So concentrated that the flesh around the leather patch would bunch up as he questioned me about my Greeks. Everything I knew about owners and men laid out on the table of his mind. This man had a liking for sharp clothes; this other gave money to the church and had the priest bless the first load of cloth shipped him each season; this one was an incorrigible gambler; this other a lecher; yet another a dedicated family man whose children were his passion. Barney listens, questions. And sends me into the market. By 1927, the Greek shops have begun to break. The younger workers know me, trust me. A few join the union in secret. They aren't particularly happy with their bosses, Greek *landsmanshaft* and all. And that was when Barney sent me into the shop of Nikos Gargus.

Nikos was close to forty then. But he still dressed like a young man. He still tried to inspire the mistresses he gathered like a collector of antiques gathers old vases. "She's one of Nikos's women," you would hear. Bought, paid for, and kept out of the vanity of not wanting to surrender anything stamped "Property of Nikos Gargus."

By 1927, Nikos employed thirty people in his shop. He was the biggest of the Greek manufacturers. It was Nikos whom Leftwich sought out when the association decided it needed a Greek vice-president. Leftwich assumed Nikos was a Greek made in Leftwich's own Odessa image. At fifteen, Nikos had been the uncontested leader of a gang of Athenian street urchins who trailed English and American tourists around the ruins of the Parthenon and snatched purses or else placed themselves "in service." He was quick and he was tough and he was willing to fight to hold on to what he owned. Like most successful men who remember poverty, he was puffed up with a sense of destiny. The union defied that destiny by the very fact of its existence.

As bosses went, Nikos was decent. Even in poor times, he tried to carry his people. He was fair. Still, they were children to be led. Maybe a third of the men in his shop had run with him in Athens. Following him to the coat lining market was natural enough. "You have to understand," Barney says. "When workers don't see anything else, there's a certain solidity in that. The ground is under their feet."

So when I enter the shop of Nikos Gargus on that April morning, I am deliberate. Even when I spy the reflection in the mirror hanging from Nikos's ceiling, my face shows no emotion. Sergeant Turley has followed me inside, as if we were both paying a social call on Mr. Nikos Gargus. The shop is too warm, even though the April morning is still thick with winter. Nikos sits in his shirtsleeves in front of a cutting machine. His hand brushes the silk rolls softly. The steam hisses through the risers. Nikos does not look up when he speaks to me. "We don't need your kind here. Get out."

Turley is alongside me. He smiles, weathered Irish face lightened. "Away from your Jew friends?" he asks.

I do not answer. The workers are bent over their machines. They deliberately ignore me. Turley twirls his nightstick. "It won't do, Nikos," I say. Turley is going to hit me and even as I talk to Nikos I concentrate on accepting the pain I know is coming. "Your only chance is to sign with us. Our president, Barney Kadish, has sent me to. . . ."

I wake up draped across the hood of a car parked in front of Nikos's shop. In the hood's center, a winged A. It is the first thing I notice. Callahan is kneeling in front of me. Barney's one eye peers into my vision. I cannot understand what Callahan is saying. The pain in my head enlarges, my throat is dry, I want to scream. I am enraged at Barney. He sent me into Nikos's shop.

"Not dead," Barney grunts. "Hard Greek head."

Callahan snorts, giggles. My head spins, screams. "I'll help him back to the office," Callahan says. I want to tell him to leave me alone. But thinking about speaking makes my head hurt even more. Itzik appears out of nowhere and throws me across his shoulder. He carries me two blocks to the office. I do not remember it. Callahan describes it later. Sergeant Turley lifts his nightstick in mock salute when he sees Callahan.

"I see you've been busy protecting the citizens," Barney says as he and Callahan trail Itzik. Turley smiles, waves his nightstick, disappears down the street.

I lay in bed for a week. Alone in the small apartment on Tenth Avenue. Callahan and Itzik take turns staying with me, feeding me. My mind gropes for vengeance. The men in Nikos's shop would not listen to me until I had squared things with Nikos and with Turley. Short of killing them, I can imagine nothing that will satisfy me.

"You'll have to organize somewhere else for the time being," Barney tells me on my first morning back. "We can't do anything with the Greek shops. Not until we show them we're strong enough to handle Turley."

So I organize among the Jews. Few shops need me, all look at me with suspicion. I sulk, convinced my needs are being ignored. I am not acting like a revolutionary. But I am a man. Barney commands logic, embodies the calculations that haunt all of us. In Europe, the revolution shrinks. On Seventh Avenue, it waits. In dreams, I hear my father's voice. My father's voice mocks my anguished fury as I go into the market to organize Mannie Kaminsky, George Steinkohl, Herman Meyrowitz. A void separates me from Barney. I rage inwardly against Callahan and Itzik. I snap at Marty because I suspect him of laughing at me. "See," I imagine him saying, "blood is blood, Gus. You thought Barney would stand up for you."

One soft Saturday morning in the middle of June, I find myself sitting in the office. It is not yet eight, but I have spent a sleepless night, consumed by envy, frustration, and a growing sense of my own victimization. At five-thirty, as dawn has just begun to break, I walk down Tenth Avenue, past the deserted loading platforms and trucks sealed like sleeping dinosaurs in the morning air, past the Irish slums of Hell's Kitchen, until I find myself in Dolkin's Cafeteria. It is just after six and Dolkin himself is behind the counter. Free-thinker that he is, Dolkin makes it a point to work behind the counter on Saturday. Defiant gestures. He points to a table, brings over coffee and a sweet roll. Dolkin is my friend. But this morning his insistence on our casual brotherhood irritates me.

"The organizing goes well?"

"Not with my Greeks."

Dolkin nods sympathetically. I drink his coffee, hot and black and as sweet as syrup. Bite into the sweet roll. I examine Dolkin's solid, fleshy face. I feel as if Barney himself is sitting cross-legged in front of me. "Dolkin," I can hear him say, "take care of the Greek. He thinks we haven't paid enough attention to him. Don't let him grow bitter, Dolkin."

"Better not to think of Greeks and Jews," Dolkin says. The spiced warmth of his breath mixes with the coffee. I feel nauseous as the tuneless summer air floods my head. I swallow the dregs of the coffee down, take a last bite of the roll, shake Dolkin's hand and leave, his "remember what I've said" accompanying me into the morning streets. I rush to the office.

In the office, I stare across the street. Only occasional strollers. "Why do you sacrifice yourself?" my father's voice demands. Empty dreams. "You got enough in you to be a Greek? A man?" The telephone rings and the voice at the other end is not my father's, but Barney's.

"I figured you'd be there. We have him. Itzik and Callahan are on their way."

"Who?"

"Your sergeant. He's alone and drunk. Still in uniform. An all-night bender. Opatashu is following him. And Itzik.

They'll telephone." I close my eyes. My father disappears. "Are you there, Gus?"

"I'm here."

"He's yours. Only remember. The union is yours, too."

"Yes," I say, as I hang up, "I'll remember."

I take the bottle of Greek brandy out of the file cabinet. I fill a dirty coffee cup three-quarters full and drink it down in two long swallows. My stomach burns. I feel Turley next to me. I can't kill him. I must remember that. I do not permit myself to grow drunk and when the telephone rings again I am pleased at the steadiness of my voice. The voice on the other end is Itzik's. Itzik is so excited he is speaking Yiddish. "Speak English, damn you. I don't understand."

"They're on their way upstairs. Opatashu and Callahan. With Turley." He pauses, expecting a response. "Understand?"

"Don't get excited. Barney told me."

Turley's face is flushed. He is unable to hold his head up. He hangs limply on the shoulders of Callahan and Opatashu. He shrinks from Callahan, so that he seems to embrace Opatashu. His lips are withdrawn, bloodless. He begins to sob when he sees me. "Listen," he mumbles drunkenly, "listen. . . ." We listen. There is nothing else.

"It's for you to decide," Callahan says, freeing himself from Turley's retreating form.

"And you?"

"I'm trying to get it out of myself," he confesses. Barney is recreating him. Before he dies in 1942, Callahan will be credited with a party pamphlet on revolutionary self-control. Dedicated to Barney. "I want to kill him so much it hurts me to breathe." His small body screws into itself even tighter, as if he is about to spring through Turley's terror. "You know that, don't you?" Still sobbing, Turley nods. Callahan straightens up. "You better."

The telephone rings again. This time Itzik remembers to

speak English. Should he come upstairs to help me kill Turley? No, I tell him. I hang up. Then I take my present. I hit him without fear of retribution. Opatashu and Callahan hold him and I hit him in the stomach. Then I break his nose. I feel the mash of the break as he gurgles. It does not occur to me that Turley can have the entire police force down on me. Soon, it will not occur to Turley either. When we let him go an hour later, Turley is finished. He will continue as Leftwich's errand boy, but he is finished. "If you ever touch me again," I tell him, "I'll kill you. Obey your laws, you bastard. Your masters made them." We throw him out into the street and Callahan and I head for Dolkin's.

"He won't be back," Callahan says. Dolkin is puffed with pleasure. Callahan sips at his coffee. "Does it feel better?"

Dolkin smiles. "It was necessary," I say, irritated now at myself. "There was nothing else to do."

A week later and I am back in Nikos Gargus's shop. Opatashu and Itzik flank me. Arms folded, they stand at my sides. Dressed in suits and straw hats, they look like Minschin's Hats. Nikos is again at the machine in his undershirt. "How's your friend, Nikos? How is your friend with the police?"

Nikos doesn't answer. His people edge away from him. I am filled with contempt for my own. He sucks their blood and they are grateful. Now they run from him.

"You remember what Turley did to me, Nikos. He won't do that again. Not to me. Not to anyone in the union." Nikos continues to brush the silk with his hand. He refuses to show fear. Nikos Gargus. Out of nothing into America. I admire him. I do not want to hurt him. My eyes catch Poly Vastakos, a young cutter who secretly belongs to the union. Poly smiles. "Your shop will sign with us, Nikos. Automatic dues checkoff. Payday is every Friday at noon. There's a new wage schedule, a list of paid holidays. Anything done on weekends is time and a half. Workers must agree individually to work weekends. An immediate raise of three dollars for all cutters, four for dyers and silk workers."

"I can't afford it," he protests in Greek.

"As well as the Jewish shops," I answer in Greek. "No more free rides, Nikos."

"You'll break me," he says in English.

"It's only money. You'll survive. Get rid of your women, Nikos. You're too old."

Nikos glares at me, then resumes brushing the silk. He is beaten. The men in the shop seem to relax all at once. Barney has given me Sergeant Turley. And I have given him the Greek shops. "Until all workers in this shop can vote under joint union and management supervision, Poly Vastakos is appointed temporary shop steward. Are you willing, Poly?"

Poly stares at the gold and brown dyes that have stained the floor a rich mocha. "I am willing," he says quietly.

5

Language wakes the past. "Let us be human!" he cries. With Lisa, with Greta, with Comrade Rita, with a parade of women he barely knew. We sit in my apartment and Barney stares down at the traffic on Tenth Avenue. "Not enough, Gus. Let us be human! How make a revolution from this?" The party tests him. Always checking. To see whether he is loyal enough. Even his marriage. Itzik is their kind of creature. Itzik chokes on words. But when the party wants to protest allegations of anti-Semitism in the Soviet Union and calls for the signatures of Jewish workers in the *Times*, there is Itzik's name. The party never asked me to sign anything. I was never trusted. Except as a life for the union. In 1930, it is I who walk into the shop of

Nikos Gargus. Nikos is three years older, heavier. He has prospered in our triumph. Grown more American, his body swells, thickens, plunges into his pants. The rich are still buying silks. The poor are burrowing into their Hoovervilles. Nikos has given up his women. His oldest son, a young man of twenty, is with him now. His oldest son is like me. He is fat.

Barney laughs. "Gus, you defy logic." And laughs again. "Fat men make poor revolutionaries. But you are different." Yes, I am different. Even Mr. Hoover will hear of me. "Gus Constantinou. Linked to CP. Suspected of being agent. Possible incendiary. Deported to Greece, 1951. Wins appeal."

Ginott, the party lawyer, pleaded my case. They let me go. "They have to make exceptions, Gus. They chose you. I guess they figure you're not dangerous anymore." To hell with Ginott. Smart lawyer from the party yeshiva. Ginott puts Nikos Gargus on the stand. Nikos is to be my savior in 1951. Old and fat, like me, with a woman's dugs. Breathing heavily. Spent wars. Nothing lasts. Not even belief.

Minschin's absence didn't last either. He comes back into the market in 1930. The Depression frightens the association. Profits are no longer high. The smallest shops work two, three days a week. Barney tries to persuade the association to let us shift workers around. The association refuses. "You're not going to run our business for us," Leftwich says. "Take a back seat this time, Kadish."

"There are no unemployed in the Soviet Union, Leftwich."

We tax those who have work. Ten percent of their pay every Friday. Few complain. The ones who are political see it as the last gasp of capitalism. They smile as we take our assessment Friday at lunchtime, preparing to seize the kingdom of their sweat. The new age hurtling into our midst. Clean sheets and cigarettes. I can't remember a time when our people were happier than early on in the Depression. A giddiness seizes Seventh Avenue. Even Callahan laughs as we wait in Dolkin's and count the days until the revolution rids us of Leftwich and his kind.

"What'll you do, Dolkin?" Callahan asks. Winks.

"I'll make violins. I'll make violins and you can manage this crystal palace."

Minschin does not recognize the imminence of the revolution. He gives us no warning. "Hey boy!" a Hat calls out. Young Henry Felker who has been pulled out of the shops to become a full-time organizer looks up from the egg cream he is drinking inside the candy store on the northwest corner of Seventh and Twenty-eighth into the barrel of a sawed-off shotgun. Old Mr. Blauman, who has just finished serving Henry, finds himself staring down at the body lying on the floor. Where Henry's stomach had been there is now a huge hole. And the metal disk on the wall where the pay phones are has been blown loose from the black and white tiles. Everything lies in pieces, mixed with Henry's intestines. Tile, metal, blood, flesh.

And so, Minschin returns. Bankers jump from windows with their secretaries. Workers in the garment center cut and sew and wait expectantly in the streets for the impending revolution. Minschin will not wait. Barney believes Leftwich has brought him back. Marty argues. Leftwich does not need him. There is not enough business for the association to pay him. "A dollar is a dollar," Barney insists. "What else?" Minschin is practical. Minschin is a gangster for the same reason Leftwich is a manufacturer.

"We beat him," Marty insists. "And he remembers. He wants *us* to pay this time."

Barney seems uncertain, nervous. "He never met the devil," Callahan says. Barney drifts, content to let me and Marty handle union affairs. We work well together. Marty understands. Minschin wants his own back. He has not forgotten.

He was already branching out. He was deeply involved in

trucking. There were rumors that his Hats were muscling into the bakery workers' union, too. Minschin's wife's cousin has been given that assignment. Minschin invests in the labor movement. A matter of percentage. But when it comes to expensive clothes, it is a matter of wiping out a past failure, too. Minschin wants to correct the past. A mistake *can* be erased. In August 1930, he sends four of his Hats to Lake Excelsior in the Catskills.

It was a farm Barney had bought at a foreclosure sale two years earlier. The main barn had been converted into a social hall. Small cabins were now scattered throughout the grounds and a communal dining hall had been erected. Any union member as well as any member of his family was eligible to take a week at Lakeside for ten dollars. We loved it, maybe because we helped build it. Callahan and Itzik and I went up there for the first time a few weeks after Barney bought it. The world kissed by sun, Itzik rolls down among the grasses, as if making love to a woman. Itzik is a child of the streets—first Warsaw, now New York. He knows nothing of life in the earth. That night, in the barn, where the three of us have been working on roof beams all day, Callahan gets drunk. He does not turn mean or sentimental. But the crippled hand seems to loosen up, to uncramp, as if Callahan's happiness had brought it back to life. We three sit and drink bootleg rye. Through the opening in the roof, we eye the stars.

I think of Lakeside as I first knew it that summer weekend, a haven for Itzik's ignorance and Callahan's drinking and my loneliness. Revolutionary eunuchs, so in love with the working class that we are able to ignore its daughters. Barney could take care of that for us. He could take care of everything. We sought skeletons, he sought flesh. Callahan has not touched a woman since six months before the patriots turned that hand into a claw. Not even whores. Itzik stands like a big-footed fumbling animal before the women who move through union headquarters. And me?

I wait to die. It is the sole expectation remaining. Maybe it would have been better to have died with Callahan and Itzik staring through the broken roof at the star-filled sky. Lakeside is gone now. Sentimental memory. It is all gone—the barn, the resort, the union. Sucked into our American emptiness. Butcher, baker, candlestick maker. One has adopted the United Garment Workers of America. I cannot even remember which one took the union over. I do not allow myself to remember. Bought and sold. Like the prostitutes I sought out on Union Square. Or the rotting projects in which poor Itzik's soul is squeezed dry by the black children of the dead who do not understand that there are ways of dying, yes, and of living, too, that they cannot imagine. Let them look at Itzik Perlin almost forty years ago, face pressed to the matted grass, as if he too were fucking the daughters of the poor.

I close my eyes, concentrate on Roginsky's words extolling the dead Barney Kadish.

Scrub memory clean. We spring like lions out of the deaths we die. The past is dry. I want to take Itzik in my arms. Here, now. I want to beg his pardon for never having allowed him that grass he bought with his mute aspirations. Poor Itzik. Disinherited Itzik. Brave Itzik. Because it wasn't Barney Kadish that second time with Minschin. No, and it wasn't me or Marty either. But this dumb clod, so simple that Roginsky cannot let him speak for the embarrassment he will cause. A man in whom order and self are transformed into history's burden. Itzik is like Callahan. Others do his thinking for him. He does what is asked by the party, by the union, by whatever the in-evitability of history has authorized to do the asking. And that is enough for such as Itzik Perlin. Kiss the matted grass.

How could Minschin's Hats have known that for the third summer in a row Itzik had come to make love in secret to the smell of grass? The rich loam of earth is God's only gift to him, for God has long since taken his leave from poor Itzik's life. For Minschin, Itzik does not exist, not even as a cipher. Sam

Minschin is smart. From Minschin's life, you can construct an idea of what this country is about. From Itzik's, nothing more profound than a minor embarrassment, a fly tickling your nose. "Cheap shot, Uncle Gus," I can hear Sophie insist. "This country has its faults. But it's not Minschin. And your Itzik, he only did what he was told."

Sophie's father, my brother-in-law Andreas Korylas, drives a Chrysler Imperial, keeps the keys to St. Minas's Greek Orthodox Church in Astoria, contributes enough to the Blessed Society of the Sons and Daughters of Hercules so that he has three times been named presiding regent. His daughter and her Jewish boyfriend believe that love is enough to change the world. How would any of them understand what it is that makes a man like Itzik Perlin rise up from the matted grass, an insane angel of vengeance coming at Minschin's killers, pitchfork in hand, bellowing like some maddened bull? The shotgun discharged, Itzik realizes that what his dry-humping the earth has been interrupted by are Hats shooting up Lakeside as if they were competing for stuffed animals in a Coney Island arcade.

In the first cabin, they caught two men in bathing suits playing pinochle on the front porch. The car stops. Two Hats jump out. Two cutters killed. I forget the names. Lovemaking interrupted, Itzik rises above his fantasies. The pitchfork lies under the tree. "Like I was still dreaming," he explains the next day at breakfast. "I didn't want to give it up. It was nice lying there. The smell and everything. You know how quiet it is when it's warm. You even breathe different, more relaxed. Two more blasts from the shotgun and I hear screaming. They blew out the sign above the social hall. I hear people yelling. 'They're back! It's them!' I see two of them running toward the barn. One is screaming, 'Kadish! Where's Kadish!' If I understood about the guns, I wouldn't do a thing. But all I know is they took my sleep. And they're after Barney. I didn't even know it was the Hats. Only they're still taking from us, the bastards. They don't even leave my dreams alone.

"So I grab the first thing I see. The pitchfork's lying under that tree outside the barn. I never held one before. But I feel the way the handle's been gouged. I like it, Gus. That's when I see the one with the machine gun. The gun is pointed down at his foot and he's staring at me. Like a baby. He just stands there, like he's expecting the pitchfork to go through him. The right hand got the gun and his mouth is open and when I hit his stomach it's like the body is going to stop the pitchfork and then I hear him grunt, like a man throwing up, and then it's like his body is being held up by the air. And then he just buckles down to the ground.

"I should've picked up the gun. Because the other two come running out of the barn and all I can think is I'm going to kill them, too. They owe me. Like I'm better than they are, stronger. Nothing can hurt me. I'm going to shove that pitchfork right up their asses. It's not like I'm killing a person. It's all the bastards who stick us in a box and close the lid. 'Come back!' I scream. Only they manage to get to the car and the driver takes off like a bat out of hell. Brownsville bums. Then the wind comes up, a nice soft summer wind, and I hear our people screaming for me to come back. It's over. They got two of us. I killed one of them."

Under the yellow spotlight, Roginsky turns pale. He pauses, wipes his sweating brow. He is in pain. I hear his heart. In my mind. I tap Itzik's shoulder. "Does Roginsky have a heart condition?" I whisper. Itzik does not understand. He smiles through his tear-stained eyes, like an idiot awaiting benediction. "His heart," I repeat. I point a shaking finger at Roginsky. Roginsky begins to speak again. The light in the auditorium sags. I wonder what people are here. Do the young ones know who Barney was? What we did? Or are they here because the party told them to come? Itzik smiles his idiot smile at the audience, fingers his frayed shirt collar, fiddles with the knot of his tie. "Roginsky," I whisper again, desperately wanting Itzik to understand. "His heart?" But Itzik hears only the past now. He lives where Brownsville housing projects disappear, where the revolution is still just around the corner. In his head, he screams at gangsters. A vision of payment.

"In the city, it was you and Marty organized us that time. Remember, Gus? You got to give Marty credit. He wasn't really with us anymore. He hated the party. But he organized us to fight back." I remember Marty that fall. Addicted to protecting the union. Tough, strong. Itzik is pressed down to the past, the way he once pressed himself to the grass. He wants to rid himself of the image of black children who scold his sense of justice like stray lumps of coal lying in front of a chute. "There was something different about Barney then. I never went against him. Him and Marty, they were still working together then. Barney said we needed more time when they come against us again. The Hats used to collar our people and beat them in the streets. Always knew our people, who they were. Barney says the manufacturers told them. Marty says no, it costs too much for them to give in to Minschin then. You remember, Gus?"

I remember. Marty and Callahan training our people again. And Barney talking about the law this time. "I'll go see John Hudson," he says. But what can Hudson do? Even the other gangsters aren't strong enough to hold Minschin in line by 1930, Minschin wants us. It's not money. It's not even really Barney. It's what Minschin owes himself. He remembered, too.

The shadows in the middle of the auditorium collapse. I am staring into the set smile of the little man with the gray turtleneck. The little man is an arranger. He has been sent to make certain that Barney's death is properly certified. Roginsky's job is to make Barney acceptable in death. On my other side, Itzik sits with his wet eyes. Sobbing clown. There will be no eulogies when Itzik Perlin dies. Neither Itzik nor I are successful enough for the party. There is little that can be done with us. They do not understand what we achieved. Marty understood. So did Minschin.

"You and Marty, you two did the organizing that winter. Like Barney the time before." Yes, Itzik. Marty and me. We took the ones who fought the Hats eight years earlier. We made them the leaders. We hammered out a system for constant patrols in the district.

And Barney wonders. "Perhaps you're right. Maybe it's not the manufacturers." And then disappears to make love to the world. The sun glances across the Palisades as it sets, the women are everywhere. In the world beyond, revolutionaries are fashionable among the rich. Insurance policies. Not to be murdered in your sleep. Barney is invited to a party on Fifth Avenue for the widows of murdered southern textile workers. Barney laughs. But he goes. Marty and I organize our street patrols. Envy like a worm.

"There's Minschin now," Marty mumbles. And the richest of women crouch in anticipation in each of our imaginations. Every failure is of the same order. Love or politics. Once performed, the next time out of habit. "To hell with him. We'll survive. There's always Minschin."

Puppets choke on envy. Imagination betrays the past. I close my eyes, see what I never saw. Barney stands in the houses I never entered. Once a week, I walk down to Union Square to negotiate with one of the two-dollar-a-throw whores who strut their too-fleshed bodies for a working class clientele. Once a week, when the pressure grows too great to bear. Barney Kadish mixes with the sleek bodies who have come over to our side. Insurance. "They cover their bets well," Marty says. I am silent. But I imagined it then, too. In unknown apartments, music from some hidden Victrola descends on the blessed couplings. Illegal drinks cool in slender white hands. Clear eyes absorb the world from a face that is not only unlined now, but that will remain unlined forever, for its promise is of the world without aging. Barney Kadish stands poised at the edge of expectation. Parties for the party. For the workers, this world, too, will dance. In darkened corners, acquiescence is fate. The woman tosses her long blond hair. All through the long night, he strokes the blond mane, rides the ponies of the rich. Such expectations as the Fat Greek does not permit himself.

"Listen, Barney," the mind's voice insists, "I tried not to envy you. But I failed. Do you understand the cost? Not to feel envy? The desire to question, to ask you what it was like?" I am like a shopgirl who reads only movie magazines, drifts into her own fantasies so perfumed by dreams as not to need flesh. And Barney? Breathing passion from his inevitable triumph, Barney reins her in, lies with his hands on her hair. The flesh his, the motions his, the need his. In the houses of the masters, Barney Kadish proves himself master. I see the vision of my friend Barney Kadish stroking her on the bed and I remember how once a week I bargain on Union Square. I still want what Barney had. Even now. Even dying.

6

At the turn of the year, he was back. It was as if he had never left us. Follow thou me! Our wandering leader, cock between his legs once again, intimacies of flesh lingering in the memories of golden women. What does sex with the rich do? It made Barney Kadish quieter, drew him into himself, so that he came back to us like a man who wakes up in the middle of the night with a sour taste on his tongue and sweat on his brow but who knows that he can finally get out of bed, that his fever has broken. Not that his life changed. A stream of women still haunted the office, like messengers waiting to be dispatched. Only now they were again the daughters of the poor.

Minschin's hoods had disappeared from Seventh Avenue after Marty sent our people into the streets. Both sides spent a few weeks eying the other. Even Marty and I began to wonder whether Minschin had decided that there really was no future for him in the garment industry. He had other unions to play with by now. "Maybe it's his nature," Marty speculates one cold afternoon late in January. The three of us are sitting in Dolkin's, more relaxed than we have been together for some time.

"I don't believe it," I say.

"Neither do I," Marty confesses. "Minschin is the kind who'll scratch his ass, send chocolates to his momma, contribute to the Fireman's Ball. Only every time he thinks he's got the world by the short hairs, he'll remember what this union did to him. A man like that doesn't know how to fail."

"So he failed," Barney says, chewing on a Swiss cheese sandwich stuffed with tomatoes and coleslaw. "He's still the biggest fish in this ocean."

"He owns New York," I say. "But he doesn't own us. And he remembers. Like Marty says."

"He'll hit us, Barney," Marty says.

Barney's one eye holds his sandwich in focus as if he were studying it. His mind is no longer with the women on Fifth Avenue. He is a man playing with possibilities. Should we hit Minschin first? He weighs alternatives. What will the decision cost him? What will it cost the union? He is an American now, and he has learned enough, even in the party, to trust only that which works. What works explains itself. "So the question is how to do it best. But even if we beat him now, does he simply quit? Does he sit back and think he has everything but he has to choke on our people? Does it come down to our giving in to him or his giving in to us? If it does, can we figure that Minschin will give in?"

"Something decisive," I say. "Something he'll never forget."

"Can't forget," Marty says. "Hit him hard enough so that he sweats every time he thinks of us. So that when he remembers this union, he'll wet his pants even if he doesn't piss." In Dolkin's overheated cafeteria, Marty's swarthy face seems to grow darker. A light band of sweat touches his brow. His face tightens until he looks a good ten years older than twenty-six. There is no fat on him. "You can kick a Minschin in the ass. But the only way to be certain he isn't going to come after you is to kill him. We can't kill him. We'd have every gangster in the country down on us if we did. You don't touch their big people. But we can hit him hard enough so that he gives up the idea of getting even. Writes us off to experience. It's a permanent settlement we want with him. Nothing else."

"Kick Minschin in the ass," Barney muses, "and we're on top of the world."

"It's the only way," I insist. Marty nods. Barney eats.

It is Barney who suggests Lisa. Lisa is twenty-four now. For the past two years, she has been working as an organizer in the taxi industry. But the union never manages to get off the ground. Lisa grows tired of her lack of success, of the bickering among the AFL people behind the union. Barney telephones. One morning, on the last day of December 1930, Lisa Grumbach walks into my office, takes her coat off, and sits down. She is distant, uncommunicative. She eyes me up and down, then walks over to the battered desk I use and shakes my hand. Her handshake is firm, like the grip of an adolescent boy. She is not so much tall as slender, erect. Her legs are shapely. The lines of her body seem to curve into the contours of the air itself. Watching her, I remember again how much I love her.

The rumor is that she has dropped out of the party. Simply stopped paying her dues. But I will not hear about that from her. She has turned into herself, like the women in Pyros waiting at night for the fishing boats. Her silence is captured by her hands, the fingers strong and slender. She shapes the air. Marty enters my office. He sees Lisa and his face flattens into the distance she demands. Barney enters, bends to kiss her. She turns her face away. An awkward pause. He takes her hand, shakes it, as if still considering the unspent kiss. "We'll talk," he says. "You must be careful. Subtlety."

Her face immune to command, the lips part. "If women allowed what men demand, that would show you our subtlety."

Barney turns his head. He is irritated. The conversation is not of his choosing. He will not make the impression he wants to make. Still, the problems with Minschin remain. I watch him. I have never asked him what happened between him and Lisa. "Your work, too," he admits. "We have never denied that."

"We?" she mocks.

Barney's face flushes. "Not I."

"And not the party," she adds.

"No, not the party." Barney pauses, clears his throat. "There is no profit in this, Lisa. We are together again. The way it was." Lisa's hand softens, her fists unclench. "We will do it the way you suggested. But there is danger."

"What have I done to free myself from danger?" She touches Barney's shoulder. "Anything for our blessed workers. And the revolution."

"Be serious," Barney persists. Her moods play with his irritation. He is aware that Marty and I are still in the office.

"I am serious," Lisa says, her voice now businesslike. "I see little profit in my work. It turns out I'm not a very good organizer. I ask too much of people. And taxi drivers are not like garment workers. They think of nothing but today. No sense of solidarity. Being a woman makes it worse."

"How?" I ask.

"All are lovers. Or so they tell each other. Some believe it.

They insist on demonstrating for me. I spend my time pushing them off."

"Not particularly appealing, those encounters."

"I'm not ready to die for the United Taxi Drivers of America. Not for their virility. I'd rather take my chances with Mr. Sam Minschin's Hats."

"You've spoken to the others?" Barney asks.

"I've asked Malka. You remember her? There are four others I've spoken to. Labor people. I'll choose two. The only problem should be if they sense why we're with them."

"Marty says we have to kill them. Our Greek friend, too." He points to me. Marty still lingers in the corner.

"Dear Gus," Lisa says.

"I'm glad you're back, Lisa."

"You're the only one who can smell blood without getting sick, Gus."

"I didn't know such talents attracted you," Barney says.

"Only when necessary," Lisa answers.

"And with Minschin, it's necessary. Stamped and certified."

Callahan enters my office. Marty leaves. Callahan embraces Lisa, takes her hand in his crippled claw. Lisa laughs, kisses him on the forehead.

7

Invisible ropes scrape against the walls of the stomach. Death's grating measure sings in Roginsky's voice. I dream of Lisa. The only time she permitted me. When she was going after Minschin's Hats. Alone in the office. A Friday night. I touch her cheek, ask her, "Are you sleeping with him? I want to know." Now I know why she will live beyond any of us. She is our witness. Like a fool, I cry in front of the woman I love. I feel ashamed of the wetness on my cheeks. But I am unable to stop.

"Poor Gus," she whispers, taking my hand in hers. "Poor lonely man." We leave the union office together. We walk into the cold winter night. A light snow brushes against us. Lisa huddles into me and we walk downtown together until we stop in front of a brownstone across the street from a Catholic school on Sixteenth Street. Lisa does not ask whether I want to come upstairs. She pushes me through the door and we climb the two flights of stairs, hand in hand. I feel her presence. I want to push myself through the walls of the staircase. I want to disappear.

Ashamed of my needs, I stop. Lisa pushes me on. At the door to her apartment, I think of the prostitutes a block away on Union Square. "Lisa," I say, "I do not . . ." Finger to her lips, she stills the child in me.

The apartment is warm. The lamp glows against the winter night outside until Lisa pulls the shade down. She turns me into the bed neatly folded against the corner wall. She unbuttons my shirt. She leans against me. I can hardly hear her breathe. With the women in Union Square, I do not feel shame. With Lisa, the shame is mixed with everything else I feel. I want to be handsome, like an actor. I am ashamed of my body. I want to make love to her. I want to be gentle.

The bed is narrow. She turns off the lamp. Darkness envelopes us. I feel her moving through the darkness, across my body. I reach out, touch her legs, breast, stomach, the suppleness of her. I feel old, my chest heavy. Barney's face looms in my mind. I push it away, struggle against it. Enveloped by darkness and Lisa, I pull myself through my history. Cradled at birth in Pyros. The walls reach out, Lisa's hands stroke my cock, her lips cross into the wetness. Faces in Pyros. The old, like stained glass. So old that the color has been rubbed away, leaving the glass purer, softer. I do not want what Lisa gives. I want her, but not this way. I do not want to be given charity. Her body slides into mine. Like drowning into yourself. With the prostitutes, always quick, always business. The children of necessity. Perform their tasks, exit into their own lives.

Lisa defines the secrets. She knows more than I do. I feel myself swelling, the warmth of wet, fight to hold in, to force each of us to work for the pleasure. Her legs wrap around me. My cock in her, we press body to body. Caught by our needs, we grind against each other, until I feel her shudder, the snake shedding its skin, and I know that I can let go. And do. This time, tears for both of us and the voice through her tears touches deep inside me, holding to itself that which is most vulnerable, where the moist gathers and the fear buries itself beneath the moist. Like discovering a cave. Suddenly, it is there in front of you. And you know the next step will be your last. But there is no help for it. Nothing to do but plunge to the bottom, all the way down. "Poor Gus," she says. "Poor lonely man."

I lie in the arms of Lisa Grumbach, whom I love and who knows what I have paid. "Lisa, I do not. . . ." Words dwindle. My tongue lies dead in my mouth and I know with that certainty of the past, the thickness of truth, that this is a mere interruption to my weekly excursions to Union Square. A woman's charity. Gifts offered and fearfully accepted. Lisa touches me, moves deeply into me. Her touch will float inside me until I die.

"Poor Gus."

Now cancer battles to pity poor Gus. When I walk out of her apartment, I am angry. Never have I envied Barney more, hated him so much. Her breath fast in my mind, the way she touched me under the blanket, an explosion in which I lose all fear of self. Only for a moment. Dying, her hands still stroke me, not to bring me back but to meld our bodies, to create a touch in darkness that reassures, soothes, speaks of familiar memories. The memory of her shapes a curious afterthought. God, let me die. Smell of her like rain sweeping the sands of Pyros. A single evening and I am trapped for life. Once given, desire grows more powerful. Fat Greek accepting the charity of the woman he loves. Let me die in the memory. Smooth limbs, hands like the play of water on my back. Finished for others. Any chance of getting beyond the prostitutes of Union Square disappears into Lisa's moment.

We sit on the bed. She holds my hand in hers, rubs the knuckles softly. For years afterward, I wake up in the night, the feel of her fingers stroking my knuckles. The dark encloses us. "I love you, Lisa." I feel her beside me, but I cannot look at the shadow she presents in the dark. Her hands withdraw. I touch her back, the lingering damp of sweat. "I do not expect anything," I explain. "Please. It is only that we are together again. All love you, Lisa. You know that. If only—"

"Dear Gus," she laughs. And pushes me face down on the bed. She rubs my back. I feel as if I can afford to keep silent, can live in the moment. Silence absorbs.

It is to be the only time. Acts of charity. Acts of faith. Lisa gives because Gus needs. A revolutionary syllogism. Gus is tied into the eruptions of his own fat body. Lisa is learning to be gentle with herself. "Dear Gus. Do not make so much of it. We have had this together. The pleasure is not just yours." She pulls me to her. In the narrow bed, alone in the darkness of each other, I am gentle. The world drifts away. I beg to linger in Lisa Grumbach's memory.

8

A simple plan. Practical women. They frequent the Lower East Side cafeteria where Minschin's Hats drift in and out. Trotsky ate here. Actors played here. Poets lied here. Lisa has an eye for propriety. She chooses with care. Each woman understands exactly what the purpose is. They do not go out together. In the cafeteria, they avoid each other. And they play to the sentimentality that drifts through the lives of such men. Minschin loved his mother; his men love their images of women. Gallants of the closed fist.

We do not ask how she plans to do it. Need embarrasses us. How far will charity extend? In a rush of shame, I think of the one she chooses for her own, lying alongside of her, touching the damp flesh of her back. Pictures of Lisa loving her stranger slide through the center of my rage. Her hands caress the small of his back. Hatred blooms like a rose.

In my office, Callahan eyes me uncomfortably. "What is it, Gus?"

"Nothing. I was thinking of how it was. Becker's son."

Callahan knows I am lying. He nods, leaves the office. I am his friend. Alone, I envision Lisa in every possible position with Minschin's man. He is young, tight-muscled. But faceless. Murder is the commerce of sex. Sitting at my desk, I whimper, "Lisa. Lisa."

I leave. Callahan is waiting for me outside. We walk together through the hard cold of Seventh Avenue. The darkness is cut only by the streetlamps and the lights from restaurants. "Gus," Callahan says softly, "don't tear yourself apart. We all love her, Gus. Only—"

"Only she is not for me," I finish, as he expects me to. Callahan shrugs. "It's our revolution and it's Barney's game. Right?"

Callahan halts. "Be fair, Gus. Without Barney, we're nothing. He made everything possible."

His ferret-eyes shift back and forth. I think yet again of the vise closing on his hand. He is right. Barney made the union possible. Barney will help create the future. We are mere soldiers in the ranks. "All right, Jimmy. No individual is that important. Not Barney. Not you or me. Not even Lisa." I, too, need to believe.

In the apartment Lisa rents, life dances. One by one, Lisa's women bring their men there. Different nights for each. Perfume wafts over the rooftops of Greenwich Village. We dare not ask what happens. Barney pays the price silently. Afraid she may be spotted, Lisa stops coming to the union. I sit in my office, locked into my own inadequacies.

And now I listen to Roginsky's voice and I wait to die fleshed out in the very certainties of that time. Once again, I feel myself wanting as I have never wanted before. Other cancers. Older. Perpetual reminders. Fate is injustice. But in the mind's true kingdom, a body to bring tears of envy to Apollo himself. For Gus. Over and over, I create her performance with the gangster, whose face is now Howard's. And with Barney. It is not for the revolution that never comes that I want vengeance. It is for me. Not Minschin alone. Not Leftwich alone. Not Barney Kadish either. No, and not the bastards who buy and sell the world until they assume the sun itself is open season for their hawking. Clear murder in the heart. No need to think I hated because of the union. No, hatred for me went down to that fat boy in Pyros, snot running from his nose, and his belly already splashing over his belt as he runs down to the wharf to greet the ships coming home each evening, and to eye the whores, old Niggerlips and the three or four companions who trail after her, whore chaperones to other whores. A boy who wonders what it will take to rid his soul of its emptiness. A boy who knows even then that he is doomed to buy his pleasures.

Relentless dialogues in the imagination. She brings him to the apartment, speaks to him softly. A party, she tells him. He frowns. Not what he had in mind. But he does not protest. He should be suspicious. But he had grown used to her in these three weeks. She urges him to enjoy the evening. She wants him to feel comfortable. He rises from his chair, goes to the bathroom. He splashes cold water on his face. Refreshed, he thinks of the woman waiting for him in the other room, smiles into the mirror above the sink. His teeth are even, well-spaced. He holds his nails in front of him, examines them for cleanliness, the way the Irish schoolteachers at P.S. 114 used to do. He prides himself on neatness. Again, he scans his teeth. Satisfied with the inspection, refreshed by the cold water, he adjusts his tie and returns to the living room. He looks at the woman, enjoys the neatness of her. She is a beautiful woman, a clean-looking woman. He considers the possibility that he is in love. The prospect pleases him. He likes talking to her, likes making love to her. She is comfortable. The thought surprises him. But she holds back. Does she think she is too good for him?

"Lisa," he says, dropping into the club chair and fingering the rye and ginger ale she has left on the side table, "do you think you're too good for me?"

She is curled catlike against the huge blue hassock next to the couch, her legs drawn beneath her. She does not answer immediately. Instead, she stretches, yawns. Her face bursts into a smile. He can relax with her, she is an easy woman to relax with. Her laziness drifts into him. He dreams of coming home to a nice apartment, like this one. She is waiting for him at the door. Many of Minschin's people are married. Minschin himself approves of marriage. It would not be a bad life. "Lisa. I asked."

"No one is too good for you, Howard." She is the only woman who calls him Howard. Others call him Howie. He likes her formality. She is proper, like his youngest sister who understands the motions of this American spirit. He wonders whether he will propose to her tonight. The thought frightens him just a bit. He will hold off. He will temper his needs tonight. "No one is too good for anybody else. We're all just people."

"Don't be annoyed," he says. "You can count on me. But I've got a lot to learn. Still, I've got to ask you. Does it bother you?"

"Does what bother me?"

"What I do for a living."

She shrugs. He wants to get up from the blue club chair, to go over to her curled like a cat into itself and touch her. He wants what he cannot understand wanting and he is frightened of wanting it. "A man does what he has to do," she says. "I'm surprised you ask."

"You know who I work for?" he asks.

"What does that have to do with us? I'm not your conscience, Howard. Anyway, you're not at all evil."

"I'm reliable," he tells her. "I'm the reliable type."

"Howard, are you proposing?"

"There's no one else I could ask, Lisa." He feels cheated. The words hollow out. Not the romantic moment he had envisioned.

"We'll talk about it another time," she says, springing to her feet almost before the doorbell's ring can be heard. Irritated, he gets to his feet. But as she glides past him she playfully pushes him back into the overstuffed club chair. He sprawls, hears laughter, voices. He takes a cigarette from the pack in his shirt pocket. He feels for the short-barreled .38 he carries in a shoulder holster. Usually, the feel of the .38 reassures him. Tonight, it is irritating. He wants another calling. Respectability is what he wants. He closes his eyes, leans back into the club chair, and drags on the cigarette. Lisa returns to the living room, followed by another couple. He recognizes Frank Vitelli, who drifts between Capone and Lepke and Minschin. His irritation grows. He knows Frank, has worked with him.

"Hey!" Frank calls, stalking across the living room with hand outstretched. "It's Howie. How are you, Howie?"

They shake hands. He tries to catch Lisa's eyes, to tell her there has been a mistake. He wants to get away from this. From Capone, from Lepke, from all the Frank Vitellis he knows. Even from Minschin. But Lisa is talking to the other girl, whom she introduces as Malka. A funny name, he thinks, for a girl with Frank Vitelli. Lisa picks his half-empty glass from the lamp table and returns a few minutes later with a fresh drink. She winks at him. The wink reassures.

By the time the others arrive, he is no longer resentful. One he knows only peripherally: a shark named Manny Eisenberg. Manny is on loan to Sam Minschin. Manny is a special. Manny is married. He works for Lepke. Lepke does not like his people to play around. Lepke considers marriage sacred. It is rumored that his brother is a rabbi. Still, it is not his problem. It is for Minschin and Lepke to work out. After a few minutes, they are all laughing together. Howard drinks. His mind fogs over. He loosens his tie. He will take the evening as it comes.

9

Callahan waits at the subway exit. I see him as I climb the last flight of stairs. He is standing next to an Italian shoeshine boy. The boy hops from one foot to the next, rubbing his hands together to fight the cold. Callahan's shoes have been shined. His sentimentality irritates me. I scarcely acknowledge his greeting.

"Hey, mister, you want—?"

"No!" The word jumps out of my mouth. The boy jerks out of my way, as if I had hit him. Callahan and I walk to the corner, turn east on Eighth Street. We walk in silence. At University, we turn north, then walk around Ninth and Tenth Streets. Ninth Street is filled with brownstones except for the new apartment building on the corner of University. As we walk toward Broadway, Callahan nods at the doorman. The doorman is an old drinking buddy who makes the proper noises about the Wobblies. Callahan trusts him. It is Callahan Lisa sends to rent the apartment.

Barney and Itzik emerge from the shadows of Grace Church. In the clear winter night, they seem ripe and full. Each is dressed neatly, in a business suit. Callahan and I turn west and continue to walk. As we again near the apartment building on University, we separate. Callahan enters. I wait at the corner. Then I walk to a drugstore halfway down the block to buy a pack of cough drops. Anticipation grows. In the street a woman in a short white mink jacket emerges from the building Callahan has entered leading a Russian wolfhound leashed to her wrist. The woman wears no hat. Her face is young. Her hair is silver white. She ignores me as she passes.

The doorman has conveniently disappeared when I walk inside the building. I count to thirty. I ring for the elevator. The bronze elevator arrow is at nine. I walk up the stairs. At the third floor I pause, count another thirty, then walk slowly up the next two flights. Callahan waits for me in the stairwell. He lights a cigarette. I take it from his mouth and grind it into the concrete floor. The stairwell floors are painted dead battleship gray, but the hallways in front of the apartments have alternating light and dark oak wood squares. "I forgot," Callahan whispers defensively. His ferret eyes dart at me. In the enclosed shadows, I examine his familiar face once again. Tight, ravaged by the need for vengeance, as if some Renaissance cardinal had tried to obscure his own sins by commissioning a portrait in which all the faces of his subjects would be made visible. Callahan is each of us.

"I got a gun, Gus. You?" I nod. Two figures move up the stairs. Barney's face is boyish, although he is thirty by now. Itzik seems removed, somber in the gray coat he wears like a shoe salesman visiting some strange city. He hulks over the three of us.

The dialogue I have constructed between Lisa and her gangster lover spins through my head, even here, no more than ten feet from the apartment. (The only time she comes to the union offices after the killings, she says, "There is nothing to do with a corpse but bury it. I did what had to be done. Why do you need details?" Malka and the other two girls kept silent, too. When they left the apartment that night, they disappeared from our lives.) I rage. Still rage with the thought of it. Nights betray. *She enjoyed him!* So simple a taking. His life and her pleasure.

In the stairwell, I feel for the gun. In a few minutes I will discover that mine is the very same blunt-barreled .38 that Howard carries in his shoulder holster. Sick or nervous, dead or dying, a certain professionalism.

Standing in front of the apartment, key in hand once again, I hear the soft swell of Itzik's blubbering sorrow. Barney is dead. Inside the door, a man's voice. "And another!" Then laughter. Voices swim together, embrace each other's time, until I can no longer distinguish. Now is then. Enough.

"Open the door," Barney whispers. I slide the key into the lock, cautiously turn to the right. The door opens soundlessly. It has been oiled, the hinges like velvet. The voices are louder as the four of us step inside. I close the door soundlessly behind us.

Lisa is in the blue club chair. Walnut strips center the arms. Malka sits cross-legged on a small Persian rug triangularly set in front of the modestly upholstered sofa. The sofa is also blue. The two other girls are sitting on the sofa. One of the gangsters is drunkenly sprawled across a wooden kitchen chair that has been moved into the living room. He is sleeping. Two others sit cross-legged on the floor to the right of Malka. They have a deck of cards in front of them but they do not seem to be playing. With Malka, they seem part of a seance. The fourth Hat is in the bathroom. Only the drunk in the chair has a gun visible. It juts out of the shoulder holster he is still wearing. The two others are without their jackets. When she sees us, Malka quietly gets up from the floor and drifts to the side. Lisa smoothes her skirt. The Hat in the bathroom appears at the door. No more than four feet from him, Callahan holds his gun to the Hat's face.

"Christ," the Hat says. "Jesus Christ."

The two men with the deck of cards between them look up. One jumps to his feet, turns to face my drawn .38, then sits down on the floor again. "We're had," his companion says softly.

The drunk gets up from the chair, sees us, staggers to the couch and falls across it. The women get up. The drunk is trapped by the softness of the sofa. He begins to giggle. Lisa and the three other women leave the room. Barney goes with them. Lisa's boyfriend is still standing in the doorway leading to the bathroom. His hair is disheveled, but his face is clean-looking, the kind of face you expect on a billboard. He closes his eyes, as if he were going to wish our presence away. He moves toward the couch and then lunges for the gun in the drunk's shoulder holster but Itzik's hand doubles him over. He grasps his stomach. Itzik pulls the gun from the drunk's holster. Itzik examines the gun. "A .38," he says. "All of them carry it."

Barney reappears. The gangsters with the cards examine

his glass eye. "It won't bleed," Barney says. Itzik snorts, as if Barney had said something very funny. Barney sits down near Lisa's boyfriend, who is still doubled over, white-faced, on the floor.

"You don't have to kill us," the boyfriend gasps. If he was drunk, he has sobered up quickly. "Minschin will pay."

"For such as you? Anyway, killing is your trade."

"I know more about you than you think," Lisa's boyfriend says. Itzik slaps him across the mouth, almost gently.

"Leave him alone!" Barney snaps. The drunken one on the couch is now whimpering. The other two are trying to brave it out. Howie is their spokesman. "What do you know?"

"You're Kadish." He pauses. "I wish it was me took that eye."

Barney laughs. "A lion. Maybe you'll have a chance at the other."

"Minschin will pay."

"We'll just take off," says one of the two sitting on the floor. "Leave the business for good."

"Minschin kills you then," Barney says.

"All those girls," Howie says, as if he were talking to himself. "A setup." The drunk's sniveling irritates him. "Shut up, Manny!"

"I don't want to die, Howie. I got a kid."

"Shut up! You're not dead yet." He turns his attention back to Barney. "That's some girl you got there, Kadish. Here she's setting me up like stuffed derma in a deli window and I'm wondering whether to marry her."

I hold the .38 on Lisa's boyfriend. I notice the clock on the table next to the couch. I wonder whether Lisa chose the furnishings. The clock reads eleven-thirty. The drunk is still whimpering. He still doesn't want to die.

"Make the call," Lisa's boyfriend demands. "There's money in it for you."

"You killed two at the resort," Itzik insists. "Two." Barney signals. Itzik pulls Howie to his feet. The two sitting with the deck of cards stand up. Callahan helps the drunk whose smell—whiskey, cigarettes, sour sweat of fear—irritates. My gun is still pointed at Lisa's boyfriend. I fantasize about pulling the trigger.

There is a knock at the door. Callahan edges it open. Then he smiles. Four of our people stand outside. The Shapiro twins, a young furrier named Al Bliss who has a reputation as a tough union man, and Poly Vastakos. Poly smiles at me. "Hello, Gus." We shove the gangsters out into the hall. The drunk is still sniffling. Lisa's Howie is quiet. Poly and one of the Shapiros grab Howie's arms and push him into the elevator. I focus on Howie's neck. Above the line of his jacket, a peculiarly jagged scar, shaped like concentric Vs, runs markedly into the neck, disappearing into the thick chestnut hair.

Callahan leads the drunk into the elevator. Poly and one of the Shapiro twins push Lisa's Howie inside. On the way down, the drunk's sniffling grows louder. When we reach the lobby, Howie tries to jump free through the door. But the other Shapiro twin has positioned himself right outside the elevator. He hits him in the stomach and Howie pulls up short, grunts. "You fool," the other Shapiro says. "Waste time like that, I'll kill you here."

Even the drunk quiets now. We push him through the door into the cold night. Two cars are waiting, their motors running. Al Bliss shoves the drunk into the first car, then gets in next to him. The drunk is propped between Al and another figure I cannot make out. Howie is pulled into the second car, between the other Shapiro and Poly. "Barney says you can sit up front," Poly says.

The driver is Mitch Kessel, a minor union official. He slips the clutch and we drive away. On Fifth, we turn up the avenue, north toward the garment district. The streets are empty, except for a few trucks lining up in front of the flower market. The car pulls to the curb in front of union headquarters.

We take the elevator to the seventh floor. A large shop that the building owner cannot rent. We pay a nominal monthly fee for it until he can find a tenant. Property is theft, Proudhon wrote. In the recesses of his soul, our landlord agrees.

We push Howie through the door. The Shapiro twins straddle him between two chairs, one leg tied to each chair. The drunk is gagged, his feet tied together. He looks like a fetus curving into his mother's womb. The two cardplayers have already been tied back to back. They, too, are gagged. The shades have been drawn and the entire shop is lit by three naked bulbs in the ceiling. In the center of the room, Marty and Barney huddle. Marty points toward Lisa's Hat. I want to tell him Howie is the one who has been bedding Lisa. I want to see what his reaction will be.

"All four," I hear Marty. "Leave one and there's trouble."

"Minschin will know anyway."

"Let him know. He may also know he's got too much to lose if he hits us. We're not lying down for him."

"You hear, Gus?" I nod. "Well?"

"Kill them all."

"All?"

"Either Minschin quits or else he stays and fights. If he stays, there are four less. And the rest are a bit more frightened. If nothing else, it's getting rid of some of the roaches."

Barney nods. "Okay. But not here."

"They'll know anyway," Marty says.

"There are different kinds of knowing. I don't want him to feel that he has to come after us."

"What is it you want us to do?" Marty asks.

Barney's single eye measures Howie, who is staring down at the floor. For a moment, I think he is going to kill Howie himself. But I am wrong. His eye catches mine. He knows I want to kill Howie. "How is it you want to do it?"

"Each one in a different place," I suggest. "So that Min-schin can never be certain."

Marty nods. We are united in this common purpose. "If they're found in separate places, he won't know that it was us alone," Marty says. "We've got to remember, Barney, he's got a lot of other business. Laundry workers. Bakers. The cutters in women's wear." Barney listens. Marty points to Lisa's Howie. "I want him," he announces. Marty knows. But he will not speak of it to me. I shake my head. "All right then," he says. "The two of us." I nod. Barney turns away.

10

A simple retribution. Men die. None deserved it more. All terror comes home in subtle reminders. Proper endings. Those you remember are proper. Stalin's terror. Lenin's mummy. Kennedy with a bullet through the head. Trotsky with the pickax. Deaths. A swollen bubble in the soul. Poor Itzik sobs for Barney's memory, for the reality of the black lumpen burning the Brownsville streets. But for me, time freezes.

I never talked to Marty about it. Not really. Hints of what each of us wanted. Barney insisted that Mitch Kessel go with us. Mitch was dependable. Mitch is not interested in Howie or his end. He is interested only in the way to the warehouse in Long Island City. Near the Macy's warehouse. "Tap city on the town's dead," Howie laughs. He sits between me and Marty, his hands bound behind his back. "Never lend a buck from me. I fucked her."

Marty's fingers press the sides of his temple. Howie screams. "Dead is dead. But that's pain."

"Christ, I'll die anyway," Howie gasps. "You and this greaseball. In the backroom with my sweet lady, I touch her lovely—" Marty's fist splits his lip. Blood gushes. Howie spits out a tooth. "You and this greaseball, you got the hots for that lady. Sweet body." Marty hits him again. "Jesus, I wanted to marry her. And she sets me up. Tell her how sweet she is. Like Cossack shit in winter."

In the warehouse, the smell of rotting fish. Howie's face like a bloodied piece of carved wax. Blood caked to his lips and cheeks. Owners and beggars. He was the owner. After he was killed, I used to try to envision him walking through the streets with Lisa on his arm. A possession as stamped with a signature as a letter. "This woman is mine. A man gets what he takes. Ask Minschin." A cool distance. Even in death.

Gagged, he waits for us. "You're a mind reader," Marty says to him. "But you're no big deal, Howie. Just one more East Side *boytschik*. Minschin won't even remember your name. Nothing."

I say nothing. I want him to tell us the details. I want to sit in a darkened theater and watch their two bodies. I study his face. The chin, blood-stained and bruised, pulls forcefully from the mouth as if it were seeking a greater share of existence. The eyes level at me. Quiet blue. A priest's eyes.

"Want me to stay outside?" Mitch asks.

Marty shrugs. "It doesn't matter," I say. Mitch walks to the door, changes his mind, walks back to the wooden barrel he has been sitting on. Now he leans across its top, lights a cigarette. In the dim light, I can see his hand twitch. We drove across the railroad tracks, past the noise of loading platforms at night. Long Island City. I claim indifference. Death is not a place. Not Albuquerque. Not Long Island City. His eyes laugh at me. I want to know him better. Mitch shrugs again, kisses the barrel with his head, closes his eyes.

"What're we waiting for?" Marty asks.

"Nothing," I say. I close my eyes.

"Damn you, Gus. Another intellectual in Barney's revolution. At least look!" I see through my closed eyes. I want to crush whatever hurts him. Howie's head jerks up. Even dying, his eyes fight to meet mine. I hear the silencer kissing death with a pop, watch blood break the meeting of mouth and nose while the blue-green sea smiles beneath the sun of Pyros.

In the blurring of his needs, Marty Alschuler avenges Lisa Grumbach, who has no desire for revenge. Howie is dead. A bullet in his temple. The hole neater than I would have expected. The eyes still refusing to plead. On the ride back over the Queensboro Bridge, Mitch Kessel spits out the window. In the back, Marty sleeps. A knight in the armor of his shining.

All that spring, cold shadows the sun. Old men sitting on park benches nod off, sniffing the final dead ends of lives confirmed in meaninglessness. Our rhetoric then. Expendable lives. Pressed like grapes in a winery. Meanwhile, working people divide their dollars, stare at the solid figure of Barney Kadish as he moves through the garment center. Four Hats are found murdered. So ends one winter. The new world at hand. One body found floating in the Hudson; one jammed into an elevator shaft in a newly completed building on Lexington Avenue; one discovered with a bullet through his head in an unused warehouse in Long Island City; one with his neck broken found stuffed in an ashcan under a pier on the outskirts of Far Rockaway. The newspaper speculate about gang wars. In Dolkin's, a cutter says to his friend, "We did it!" Murder, too, is collective.

We wait to see whether Minschin will respond. Marty broods. He waits in his restlessness, not even pretending to work on union affairs. He roams the streets, a prisoner of circumstance. To leave while Minschin's intentions are still not clear is cowardice. Marty needs his self-esteem. But when he is in the same room as Barney, the air seems to freeze with their struggle. He has done what Barney did not do. What I did not do.

One April morning, I see him in his office cleaning out his

desk. I enter his office. "I'm quitting," he announces. He does not look up. Papers are piled on the desk, the wastepaper basket is full, he holds a large cardboard file in his right hand.

"And Minschin?" I ask.

"He's finished with us," he snarls. "We've beaten him. You know that as well as I do. It's been almost two months. He can't afford to do anything to us."

"He won't always be finished."

"He will with us. We're small potatoes to Minschin. He's lost to us. Before that, the furriers beat him. We're not worth the price of Alka-Seltzer." He turns, looks directly at me, his body tense. "You're a prize mourner, Gus. You manipulate. Then you stand by and tell yourself that. . . ." He pauses. "What? What the hell is it you tell yourself? That the bastard didn't need killing? That there were other ways to do it? You make it mysterious. Gus the philosopher, who lives in Athens with Socrates and Plato. Is that it? Listen, the way it turned out, it was as if you weren't even there."

"Because Lisa—"

"No!" he roars. "Lisa did what she had to do. She's not a fucking philosopher." He grabs me by the jacket, shakes me, my body goes slack in his hands. He is talking in spurts, like a wild man suddenly given the power of speech who has no idea of where to begin. "Lisa never . . . for . . . us . . . these pleasures. . . ." Words tumble out of his mouth. He gasps for coherence. Then he lets go of me. His lungs fill with air. "You've followed him for so long, Gus. Like me. You define yourself through his eyes. My god, we both know why you couldn't kill."

"I'm sorry." I can say nothing else.

"Killing," he says, shaking his head. "It's like anything else in this world. You and Barney, you still haven't learned. Ask that bastard with the mustache. Don't you know by now we're not in the business of saving souls?"

"I'm sorry," I repeat. "I didn't mean to make it tougher for you."

"Forget it," he says. He turns away from me, returns to his desk. He removes the papers from the cardboard file and jams them haphazardly into a large leather satchel. The satchel is frayed, the black leather cracked and peeling. He closes the satchel, slams the desk drawer shut, and walks out of the office.

11

On a crisp October day in 1931, Barney Kadish—president of the United Garment Workers of America; recent victor over Samuel Minschin in a struggle for control of the garment industry; even more recently appointed to the Labor Executive Committee of the Communist Party of America; in a few years to be numbered among the founders of the CIO; friend of such as Costa Nassos Constantinou, James Timothy Callahan, Itzik Perlin, and ex-friend of Martin Altschuler—took as his bride one Greta Hedwig Edmundson of Albert Lea, Minnesota, a handsome woman whose silence inevitably suggested the mystery of what might have been. Official witnesses to the wedding were James Timothy Callahan and Costa Nassos Constantinou, himself recently appointed vice-president of the union.

Not a wedding to be celebrated in song and story. But in the chambers of Judge Michael Horton, Barney smiles like a Hapsburg prince. Callahan and I flank him and his bride. Behind us, his mother and two sisters stand uncomfortably peering at the walnut-paneled walls, waiting for the judge to make official what neither they nor Odessa would ever understand.

Look on love, too, as a record the past demands. Odessa

was right. There was something wrong about it. He should have married one of his own. Greta was distant beyond Barney's understanding. She never fit in, not even after she gave him three sons during the early years of their marriage. Not that the children changed anything. They were never part of his life. Just accessories to be displayed. Commodities. How many ambulances were purchased with those three smiling faces posed beneath huge blowups of Roosevelt and Stalin dropped from Madison Square Garden's ceiling?

How account for Barney's affections? A beautiful woman. Yes. But not Barney's. Barney was the revolution's actor. And Greta was the woman the gods had sent to annoint his stage. Beautiful and shy and virginal, even after the three children. Distant, too. Strange and distant. As their marriage is strange and distant. A joining of strict forms and proprieties, as proper a union as anyone could imagine. And yet, he loved her. Or so he always claimed.

In the well-appointed but modest apartment on Sixteenth Street, on the corner of Seventh Avenue, little more than a city block away from where Lisa lived before she abandoned New York, Barney Kadish turns to his wife, Greta. Barney hints. Gus imagines. Greta retreats into her quiet Scandinavian self-assurance. Even lovemaking defines a kind of justice. It is easy to imagine without envy. I see her. She lies quietly, absorbs his being. The children come, the union demands, politics takes his time. But there are moments to be tasted. He watches his body make love to her. She absorbs his sense of himself. She waits for him quietly, like an animal pushing herself backwards. There is nothing he asks her to do that she questions. She sees herself as he sees her, a reflection of his need.

I return from a membership meeting at the Labor Lyceum. The meeting has been called to protest the destruction of Hoovervilles in Central Park. Greta opens the door. I remember how I imagine their lovemaking, am suddenly filled with loneliness. But it is not like Lisa. I do not envy Barney this time. Her presence, like her voice, is a distant music.

"Good evening, Mr. Constantinou," she says, taking my coat. From the other room, a baby's cry. She ignores it. Her gaze remains on her husband.

"Call him Gus," Barney urges, kissing her politely. Dutifully, she smiles.

"Good evening, Gus. Will you join us for dinner?" The long lovely face is framed by the thick blond braids which are tied like a peasant's golden crown around her head. The face is softened to gentleness.

"Good evening," I say.

"Greta," Barney insists.

"Greta then," I say.

"And dinner?" Greta asks.

"Thank you," I say.

Like a page from a novel, we relive the myths of our pasts. Greta Hedwig Edmundson Kadish laughs into time.

12

We were never more convinced of winning than during the Depression. And we never needed less from the party we had sworn allegiance to. We had a job to do. To organize working people. And it wasn't just garment workers we were interested in. There was a sense of a labor movement —not unified, but singular, able to combat a common enemy. Even our cutters and silk workers saw themselves as part of a larger movement. By 1937, it was a sense they shared with working people throughout the country.

In December 1936, having negotiated a new contract that

outlined the wage pattern for the industry for the next two years, having spent a week in Montreal attending the funeral of Simplon LaTour and giving his official blessings to Albert Magnum, the new president of the Canadian local, Barney Kadish asked for and received, from the executive council whose commands were his wishes, a six month leave from the presidency of the United Garment Workers of America. He did not ask for, but received nonetheless, leave from his wife of five years, Greta Hedwig Edmundson Kadish, from his three young sons, and from the city and state of New York, to follow John L. Lewis out to Flint, Michigan. And it was Costa Nassos Constantinou who, not being Jewish and not particularly wanting to run a machine that had been oiled for him in advance, insisted that the temporary presidency of the union be thrust on other shoulders so that he could follow Barney Kadish out to Flint. The irony of James Timothy Callahan leading a union of largely Jewish workers implied little enough to me—except that I wanted to be in Flint.

That was when the messiahs of the labor movement seemed to flood out of every bottled-up dam in the country— Swedes from the Northwest, old Wobblies whose memories were still long enough to want any chance whatsoever for getting even, hill people from Kentucky, Russian Jews from New York, Irish drifters, Germans from Ohio. "Sitdown" they called it. And Lewis loomed over it, like some gigantic Welsh beetle stinking of the bituminous pits of his past. You took one look at a man like Lewis and the first thing you figured was that he was in the wrong profession. He stared at you out of the depths of an existence that seemed to move back into itself even when he talked about the future. He should have been a preacher. Or else a party man, like me or Barney. Instead, he was one more practical American. He would run with the devil himself to get what he needed. I never met a union man who wasn't afraid Lewis might see him as less of a man than he was. And so, when he crooked his little finger, they came from everywhere. For those cold winter weeks in Flint, we were the heart of America.

Flint was different. Not a shop hiring two or three workers. Not even as large as Leftwich had grown, with fifty workers. But a plant that went on and on, a stadium filled with cars that hung racked like beef on a meat trolley. Men angry; men waiting. Sitting down, taking turns to drift to the windows. Cops staring up at us, uncomfortable, more puzzled than angry. Barney and I are quiet. It is too American a scene for us, too big. The world is not this simple. On Seventh Avenue, personality remains. In Flint, there is only mass. When the talk drifts from one topic meant to relieve boredom to another—baseball, how to repair radios, boxing—we listen. Bottled-up energy poured into childish disputes, unreal meanings hammered out of hours. In the cold of Flint's winter, the cars hang suspended, like giant insects waiting to be buried. Outside, the world gathers momentum. "Not our world, Gus," Barney says to me sadly. He touches his chin, puzzled. He looks like a one-eyed school master. "Americans. A difficult people to understand."

But like the sitdowners, we understand the significance of the cars hanging above us on the line and the cars lined up outside the plant gates like oversized animals. Dead without people who have enough money to buy them. Silks, jewels, gold are for the rich. Cars are for everyone. Our union and Gold's furriers were the two most successful left-wing unions in the United States—and the work we both performed went to shield the bodies of the rich. In Flint, we listened to the talk of men who sat down to create the one big union that would give them the leverage they needed. The talk was in many languages: The tone was American.

After the first three days, Barney was sent for by John L. Lewis. Lewis had come to the Statler in Detroit to end the strike and seal the success of the CIO. From the moment the CIO had been a mote in the corner of Lewis's eye, Barney had thrown in with Lewis. He had never been comfortable in the AFL. Whatever might have been lacking in John L., he took you for what you were. No priests waiting in the wings to convert you to his way. No redbaiting. And Barney leaves the plant for the Statler with a certain hard pride. It is a reward earned.

CIO. A name in books now. Dead letters for dead men. Magical incantations. Well, maybe not. Still, no better note for Barney Kadish. Or for me. I sit here, dying, listening to sounds. In memoriam. Old charms to ward off devils. CIO. Muffled now in the voice of the skinny one in the gray turtleneck. "Brave and faithful comrade . . . fighter for the rights of the people . . . hero of the revolution . . . worker of the world in the world of the workers of the world. . . ." Hall of mirrors reflecting not Barney's past but what the party can now make of that past. Barney is dead. The one thing the party can still use. I close my eyes. I dream myself behind the little one. Itzik and Roginsky stand with me. As he speaks, we chant in unison, "CIO, CIO, CIO, CIO." His voice drowned out, we lead ourselves home.

Maybe we didn't even have a real role there. But we were union people. Acts of solidarity. Ordered from above. From John L? From the party? Who knows? All those weeks in Flint and then, later, when Lewis sent him through the Midwest to solidify support from the unions that still had large contingents of members who were not yet comfortable in English, or the two of us a year later in Pittsburgh to work with Lewis's lawyers and search out any party people among them—not conspiracy, not anything more than looking for a way to cut through to the sacred yet unbloodied heart of this America. Like penitents being told in advance of the trials awaiting them. Kiss the memory of it. So that if it wasn't our finest moment, it *was* a time when we called the turn, when we didn't have to prove that we were American enough to speak for Americans because who could be more American than John L. himself?

I sit with all the others and I listen. If this is what I have been given in place of belief, then it is as much as I deserve. There is nothing else. All right. A different time. Different people. But they stoke their own fear like firemen stoking a boiler. "Tough times," the companies cry. And then step up the pace at each plant. Tough times, hard knocks, kick ass. Old tricks. Depression is language, too. To make a man afraid—of a machine, of another man.

"You finish with the line," Pop tells me as he sits drinking a bottle of milk, "and you feel like your own body don't even belong to you. Like you're dead. At least, the way I figure dead is going to be. It's all empty. Marie tells me at night, when I'm sleeping, she can feel my body shake. They drill their rhythm into your soul. And you figure you got to go along. Because it isn't even your body anymore. It's not even what they tell you. Not a voice. Not a man. How the hell is a man going to fight a rhythm, Gus? Answer me that."

The back of his hand is scarred and ridged. He takes another swallow of milk, offers the bottle to me. I shake my head. "Younger ones, they think they can take it. Sooner or later, though, it catches them, too. A speedup is an aching thing. Makes you doubt yourself even while you're hating what they do to you."

We are sitting in one of the racked car bodies ten feet above the concrete floor of Fisher Body Plant Number 2. Barney is now in Fisher Body 1. He has returned from Detroit but I have not seen him. The UAW people decide that all outside union people should be separated. It is their strike. I have been thrown together with Pop Myers. We are taking a break from sweeping out the toilets. We must keep Fisher Body Plant Number 2 impeccably clean, as if the only thing that stands between the cops rushing us and our keeping the plant is a suds and brush demonstration of our respect for property. Workers of the world, unite! Clean the walls! Wash the toilets! Kneel to the power of property!

Ordinary Americans. Pop Myers drinks milk. In his flat Oklahoma drawl, he spreads his life before me. Sharecropping with his father on thirty acres outside Chickasaw. Running away from home at the age of fourteen. "My pa was a socialist. Read those little blue books. Except when it come to us kids. Used to get drunk nights, lay out in the fields, and then come back to the cabin and beat hell out of whichever one he could find." I remember my own father on Pyros. No socialist he. I understand. Mining in Kentucky at the age of fifteen. "Women better than what you got in New York. Whores put their muscle and flesh into the work." Only now he is married, two kids of his own, a boy who is already working at Fischer, in Number 3 plant, and a daughter who, Pop insists, will finish high school. "So she can wind up smelling like a woman instead of a truck."

Pop is a union man. Had been union from his time in the mines. Didn't know whether or not he trusted Lewis. General Motors had more damn finks than any company he'd ever worked for. But they never caught him, he was too damn smart for them, he would bust his ass to stay a union man. "Would've pleased my old man. Might've made him sorry for those beatings he gave me. Poor bastard. He sure could lay it on you though. You know, Gus," and he pauses to finish the last of the milk, "it's a shame, what the working class does to its own. That's not the least we owe the bastards."

Another member of our plant family whistles for our attention. He points to a tray he is carrying. "White paper wrapping is ham and cheese. Wax paper is just plain cheese." I am not hungry but I ask for a ham and cheese sandwich anyway. The men know that Barney is a New York union man who has been sent for by Lewis. And they know that I am Barney's vice-president. And they know about Minschin. The first day I work the toilets with Pop Myers, I hear a voice from behind me say, "Minschin." After that, silence. My stock goes up. Minschin's name is enough to cement a man's reputation even here. An aisle parts for me when Pop and I head for the makeshift recreation area at the entrance to Fisher Body 2. To have fought Minschin is to be known. To have beaten him is money in the bank.

"You and that Kadish," Pop Myers asks as we chew on our sandwiches inside the car body, "you're Communists. Ain't that it?" I nod. He eyes me as if I were behind a display counter. "I don't trust Communists. But you're all right. You and that Jew, you took on Minschin."

"Minschin's not GM."

Pop grunts. We move out of the auto body and climb the ladder to the floor. It is time to scrub the toilets once again.

On my knees, scrubbing the rims of the toilet bowls, meticulously wiping them clean, I am a fat and happy Greek. Not a speck escapes my eye. Pop Myers is telling me about the summer of 1936, when the speedup sent hundreds to the hospital and you could hear the ambulances all day long. "You just wait. You know it's going to get you or someone you know. Sooner or later. All right. Men die. But the way they tried to kennel us—like goddamn dogs. Must've been the hottest July in hell. Heat touching you everywhere, like fire poured down your throat. That's when parties unknown broke one of the line belts. The speedup ended." I scrub the bowl. Pop smiles. "And you a man what's fought Minschin." I wipe the tile clean. The fat rolls on my gut. The sweat pours. I want the approval of Pop Myers.

They shut off the heat. We turned back into the cars. Butterflies returning to their cocoons. I never felt cold like that. When word reached us that the company police were planning to hit us, we armed ourselves with steel rods stripped from the transmissions. One afternoon, the company police tried to stop us from getting food. Property was still property. The company decided to cut the pulleys that sent hot meals to the second story of the plant. The guards locked the front gates. Twenty or so of our people, on orders from the Reuthers, took the steel billies from the car in which they were stored and went downstairs. "Want to go, Gus?" Pop asks me.

"No," I answer. It is what Pop and the men want me to say. It is their strike.

We watch from the window. The cold air rushes against us. Bitter Flint. Dead stones striking one another. We stand at the window, like a crowd waiting for a fight to begin. The men with the billies position themselves directly in front of the plant police with their guns. Luke Beech, a younger worker who is a friend of Pop's son, Johnny, splits the line of guards by simply walking right through it. "Hold it!" the captain cries out. "Hold it, you son of a bitch!"

Luke turns. "Open the gate," he says.

"One more step and I blow your head off."

From beyond the gate, a voice from a loudspeaker mounted to a Chevy truck. "Don't start anything. But if they touch one of our people, get every mother's son." A Reuther voice. The men at the window whistle, clap. Groups of other workers have begun to assemble in front of the plant. They collect, hesitate, surge up against the gate. Then they drift back. The tips of lit cigarettes are like scattered fireflies in the cold afternoon dark. Luke Beech shrugs. He had been standing facing the captain.

"You still going to blow my head off?"

The captain, a big man wearing a white steel helmet, says nothing. The other company police look to him for their cue, shift from foot to foot to keep warm. From the women's washroom at the furthest end of the plant, yet other guards call out encouragement. "Don't let the bastard bluff you, Moose." We howl derisively. The war at Fisher Body 2 has come down to epithets hurled against each other and against the cold dark. Luke Beech turns on his heel and walks to the gate. He brings his steel billy down on the padlock, a stroke so sharp that sparks fly from the friction of metal against metal. While the company police stand in formation, staring at their captain, Luke continues to hammer away at the padlocked gate.

"What're we waiting for?" one of the other strikers cries. They surge forward, push past the guards, who try to stand their ground until one of them is rocked back on his heels and falls to the ground. He is pulled to his feet by the captain, whose eyes shift to the gate.

"Join your buddies in the ladies' toilet, finks!" one of our number yells from the window. Applause. The cold seems less fierce now. We are jumping up and down. "CIO!" a voice calls out. Laughter. "CIO! CIO! CIO!" The company police retreat into the ladies' washroom. Pop Myers and I cleaned that washroom yesterday. I slap Pop on the back, point to the washroom, laugh. Victor Reuther's voice comes over the loudspeaker. I cannot make out what he is saying. The billies have done their work, the locks at the gate have been smashed. Hundreds of workers stream through the gate inside the plant grounds. In the distance, down Chevrolet Avenue, we can hear the first high-pitched wail of sirens. And then the squad cars loom up before the gate.

Heavy wooden stanchions are dropped from the second floor window. Striking workers form a defense line, the stanchions held as if they were oversized spears. Reuther's voice is clearer now. "Aim the water low." The cops congregate in front of the squad cars. Now they are moving forward, dozens of them. The air smells of the sweetness of tear gas. Then the first stream of water cascades down. The line of advancing cops falters, retreats. The water freezes to their bodies and they seem to crack apart from each other, like icicles broken from their moorings by a fierce wind. As the cops retreat to the gate, the wind shifts, the tear gas rolls like a feathery silver ball back into the faces of the cops. Our people cheer. "God's for the CIO!" a voice cries.

"And his mother, too!" from another voice.

Urged on by the Reuthers, we become a force. The next charge of the police is met by pop bottles, the road that narrows into the plant is strewn with nails and shards of broken glass. Tires pop like firecrackers on the Fourth of July. The cold assists us. The tires are tight. Our people go to work on the cars. They spot the sheriff's car first. They rock the car back and forth, back and forth, while the sheriff and the two officers with him try to climb up the window. Finally, the car is flipped over on its back and Sheriff Walcott and the two others crawl out, their heads cut and their uniforms wet from the cannonading water. The cops retreat, beaten, cold, wet. Three of them are to come down with pneumonia.

We're still cheering at the window when we hear the first sounds of gunfire, sporadic popping noises. "Christ," Pop says to me, "they're shooting."

"They wouldn't," I say. "Not here."

"What do we do if they come at us with guns?"

"They won't," I insist. "But if they do, you follow your leaders."

Reuther's voice again from the sound truck. "General Motors chose war. Give it to them!"

"Christ! I'm hit," a man at the next window says. He does not cry out. He speaks matter-of-factly, too unbelieving to accept the idea of actually being shot. The man next to him grabs him around the shoulders, and holds him up against the wall, in a half-sitting half-standing position.

"Get him into a washroom. Away from the window," I tell him. "Keep away from the windows."

The man is pulled away while the rest of us retreat from the windows. From the Chevy plant, we can hear the sound of gunfire. The man is bleeding from his thigh. His face, as they pull him away, is still amazed. The company police are now firing buckshot, which rakes across Fisher Body 2. Windows have been blown out. Two other strikers have been hit, one of them lies in pain under the car conveyer belt, his right femur shattered. After fifteen minutes, the firing grows sporadic.

The sound truck has disappeared. "I hope Victor is okay," Pop says.

"He's in the plant," an unidentified voice calls out. "Near the entrance."

The firing now punctuates its absence. Occasionally, a shot is followed by a yelp, like a dog startled. But it is impossible to tell whether someone has been hit by buckshot or is jumping to avoid flying glass. The soft drone, expectant and falling to something resembling a number of people whispering together and then rising again, folds like a blanket across Fisher Body 2. A voice cries out, "They're coming again!" and the Flint police and company police come charging across the iced-over quadrangle between the plants. The water is turned on again and the police retreat back into the Chevy plant much more quickly than they charged.

They hit us one final time. In a wave, a line of company and Flint police uniforms. This time we came piling out of the factory and met them in the yard between the plants. The Battle of Bulls' Run, the Detroit papers called it. It was nice to see the cops doing the running. Even in that cold it was nice. They came at us, the lines of police and strikers met, and each cop seemed to go down beneath a mass of strikers.

A few days later, Knudson of General Motors insisted that the company had never intended to shut off the heat in the plant. General Motors was not inhumane. It was perfectly willing to sit down and reason calmly with its employees. Lewis had won. The union was here to stay. And the CIO would carry out its industry-wide organizing. Almost forty cops had been sent to the hospital. Fourteen of our people had been wounded. We spent a final night in the plant. Quiet celebrations.

"You going back to New York?" Pop asks me as we stand early that morning in the winter sun outside the plant gate. The ground is still caked with ice, thick patches, some more than a foot thick, from where the hoses cascaded water.

"Where else?" He nods. A fine moment. Listen to the little one in the turtleneck and you figure anyone can be a good union man. But it isn't like that. Not really. First you pay, then you know what union means.

"I figure Minschin ain't tougher. You and that Jew took him. He lights a cigarette, taps the head of the pack, offers one to me. I take the cigarette, leave it unpuffed, dangling from my mouth. "Minschin is Minschin. But this is General Motors."

"Sure," I agree. "They're legal."

"You done well for us, Gus. You and that Kadish. I heard about him. A lot." He offers me his hand, just a touch embarrassed. I shake it. I feel reluctant to let go, scold myself for being sentimental. Pop makes me forget that what I believe in is process. "I wish you could've known my old man. When he wasn't drunk. When he wasn't beating the hell out of us kids." He turns on his heel and walks away, carefully maneuvering his way between patches of ice.

"So long, Pop," I call out after him. He doesn't turn around. His hand raises in a backward salute and then he disappears in the milling throngs of workers. Leaning on everlasting departures, I search for Barney's face among the masses. In Flint, we have won.

13

The people in the auditorium file out. Itzik's head is cradled in his two hands. The hands are veined and spotted with brown age-drops. Itzik sobs for Barney's memory, for past grandeurs. We walk with no sound but Itzik's intermittent tearfulness down to Astor Place where Itzik is to take the subway back to Brownsville. He takes my hand in his and for a moment I think he is going to kiss it. Instead, he holds it between his hands, and pushes the words out of his mouth. "They were good days, Gus. Weren't they good?"

I touch his shoulder and pull him to me. I embrace my friend Itzik for the last time. The old-man smell of his breath mingles with my own dying.

I walk back toward Fourteenth Street as Itzik disappears into the subway. The last I see of Roginsky, he is walking with the smiling little functionary toward Fifth Avenue. The gray turtleneck is like a beacon. Bureaucrat of the revolution that has never come, that will never come, that the little bureaucrat does not want to come because the hope of such as he is in the *possibility* alone—and where he feels brave is in the rigors of his time. I can hear my heart pounding as I get to Fourteenth Street. I hail a cab.

Inside, I lean against the vinyl seat. The cab smells of cigarettes. I swim against the skyline. Eyes closed, I twist away from these bustling streets. Evil rots like grace in my stomach. Let me die, I pray. And then remember to remember defiance. In God, neither grace nor failure. In such as Stalin, changing twists. Truth for the making. I imagine myself screaming all night long, tearing at the locked doors of the cab while the driver's Puerto Rican anger looms above my efforts. Witnesses without understanding. The lies we told, the errors we committed. And the demand to believe.

Anchored to the solidity of Greta's kitchen, the children sleeping down the hall. His single eye brittle, his face smudged by disbelief, he shifts his weight from one side of the chair to the other. "Telephone Roginsky," I suggest. He shakes his head. Greta brings a bottle of retsina. They stock it for me. "Someone on the executive committee. Someone who knows."

Again, he shakes his head, lips still tightly pressed together. Greta's hands soothe his neck. They have already drifted apart. But she soothes him, the way women have always soothed Barney Kadish. That very morning, his secretary slides past me, face flushed, like a hunted animal. Barney shrugs.

"It will be explained," I tell him. "Have faith."

On Seventh Avenue, shocked faces search other faces. We have paid with our time, our dollars, the pieces of our belief that scatter down the street like confetti. In the beginning, the revolution. In the end, whispers of discontent. "Gus," the voices call, as I push into union headquarters. "The truth. There's something to it we don't understand. No?"

Another voice: "You think it'll be different for you Greeks? You, Comrade Gus. Do you think they'll let you go?"

Like cripples at Lourdes, we bathe in possibilities. We can accept the trials, the dark brooding discontent. Not as difficult as it seemed for Zinoviev, Bukharin, one after the other to sell his soul to the devil. Necessity is the mother of belief. Time reigns in the truths we learn about our comrades. After Trotsky, anything is possible. We tap our skulls as we assent to the trials. "It's not impossible," Callahan offers. Then blushes. Belief, too, is a question of practice.

"But this!" Barney howls. "Hitler. How much can they demand? And there is nothing else."

Jews at their mourning. Headlines in *Der Royter Morgn*. Roginsky's passion. I read without knowing the alphabet, the heavy black letters oppressive in the lies they force upon us. Believers believe. It is their nature. No different in Greek. Words for the party's time.

Lying is a discipline like any other. Barney learns to do it with energy, embracing the very largeness of each new turn in the party dogma as if he were plugging up his heart's desire. The puzzled faces approach. "Is it some kind of strategy we don't understand?" Eyes furtively search Seventh Avenue as if even here Hitler's spies are to be discovered. Barney smiles, assures, explains, develops arguments he memorizes like prayer from Roginsky's pages. One can settle for habit. And what else is belief but the habit of knowing? Minschin was easier, a known enemy. The measure was out for him as well as for us.

Already forty then. And the women like a steady stream. I imagine it, a joyless relentless grinding of bodies. Nothing gentle. Nothing of the woman allowed inside. Even with Greta. If he was still doing it with her by that time. Bodies matched against each other. To make love is transformed into the politics that lifts one from politics.

But only for a moment. In whispers, we reclaim our myths. If a man is willing to give his life for an idea, he should be willing to give his conscience for it, too. I did not have to read Yiddish to know how shrill the voice could be. Truth, too, had its drainage system. We could give our language and our lives. Conscience remained a magician in the wings.

Drunk on retsina, I giggle, "To hell with Stalin."

Drunker even than I, Barney answers, "And Ribbentrop. Don't forget him."

Women lighten the betrayals. A millionaire of his own sexual imagination, Barney seeks to lose not his fidelity to party dictates but his knowledge of that fidelity. White-faced, one-eyed, sober or drunk, he wants to lash out at something. Women are a means toward forgetting. He knows that Greta knows, is aware of her silence, just as he is aware of the party's deep-seated prudery. He would welcome her accusations, her reproaches, even a lover hurled into the face of his own unfaithfulness. She greets his wanderings with distance. She has given him three sons, and even in 1940, the oldest no more than eight, they are preparing to orphan themselves into respectability. Part-Jewish, part-Scandinavian, the three smiling handsome faces study the ascendency they already know they deserve. Each has already taken leave of his father. Is it their children who are to be the final test for radicals here in America?

Did he think of them when he died? Three strangers. He didn't think of them then. He had been lied to, hoodwinked, taken. But how protest? How question a belief whose very power was that it insisted on one truth above all others—that we would be lied to, hoodwinked, taken? And so, the women behind the closed door of his office. In the next room, brooding against this latest betrayal piled upon the darkening record of the past, clenching and unclenching his crooked claw, Jimmy Callahan tests the faith of his most Catholic Marxist soul. Christ or Marx, what difference for Jimmy? Whosoever shall knit these bones is savior enough. Brooding in the office beyond mine, I hear his high-pitched Irish toughness, amazement like a scroll of language quickly unfurled. Early warnings. Jimmy in the outer office. Our own radar.

We should have known it was Marty. There was no one else who might have guessed what it was we were going through. Minschin would not haunt us again. By 1940, he languished in jail awaiting execution. No manufacturer could possibly understand a grievance that had nothing to do with cash and carry, not even Leftwich, who had at least greater paranoia than his peers. Never a question of justice when the chic products of imagination and design are being marketed.

Nine years since he walked out of this very office. I haven't seen him in all that time. Neither has Barney. In Flint, we hear about him. He is on the CIO's payroll, rumored to be one of its most effective organizers. When Barney is about to take his leave of John L. Lewis at the Statler, Lewis says, his voice as casual as if he were asking about the weather, "That fellow who used to be with you in New York, Barney. That fellow Altschuler." And pausing then to read Barney's face, which freezes. Not to hide, simply freezes, because it is what Barney himself feels.

"What about him?" Barney will not try to disguise that the subject is painful. Lewis understands. Lewis has lost enough of his own.

Lewis coughs, still sick with fever. Barney stands up from the plush armchair across from the bed. "It doesn't matter what there was came between you. What I want to know—"

"Is whether he's a good union man," Barney finishes.

"Precisely, Barney. Is he a good union man?"

"None better."

"The Reuther boys tell me he can be trusted."

"He doesn't go through the motions," Barney admits. "He goes straight for the bastards."

"You taught him that, did you?"

"We taught each other," Barney says.

And now we're in the office and Marty's face slides past Jimmy Callahan. He stands in the doorway, a bit stockier than I remember him. But not heavy. It is only as if his body has been banged around more. "I was passing through," he says. "I grew curious."

Barney sits behind his desk. He stands, smiles, offers his hand. Marty advances, takes Barney's hand, shakes it. Then he shakes hands with me and with Callahan.

"We'll celebrate the return of the prodigal," Barney says.

"Depends which of us has been away," Marty offers. He drops into one of the desk chairs and kicks against the file cabinet so that he rolls to the window. "All in the line of work. It looks like it did when I left."

"What we had," Callahan says, a lingering touch of bitterness in his voice. Callahan took Marty's leaving hardest. It was his way. His Irish longing for love.

"Like dropping into an interrupted dream."

"We missed you at Flint," Barney notes. "Gus and I. You know we were there, don't you?"

"Christ, Barney," I snap, "we don't have to explain."

"Of course not," Marty says. "Where else would you two be?" Still, he was judge now. Stalin had given him that present, and he grabbed it like a child filching a candy bar. "And the party gave its permission?"

Cancer gurgles in my stomach. Death is soft, like a baby. Up front, the Puerto Rican driver whines his way through Sunday New York traffic. Gus fat; Gus thin. Gus eats air. Only memory keeps him alive. And soon to be done with that.

"You'd judge your mother," Barney says. "You still have your virtue, Marty. A man couldn't ask for more."

"We work with all sorts in our business. All kinds of politics. Did you know, Barney, that there were a number of Christian fundamentalists in the organizing at Flint? Think old Mr. Knudson is going to lead us straight to Jesus. He's the devil. Which makes John L. and you and me and Gus here . . . ." He laughs, leans back into the chair. "What does it makes us? I could use a drink."

Barney goes to the desk and pulls a bottle from the drawer. Marty didn't drink at two in the afternoon before he left us. I wonder what else he learned. Organizes. Town to town, plant to plant. A scar now bridges cheek to mouth, a light scar, a thin white line that disappears into the darker hues of his face. It adds interest to what he looks like. A badge, like Barney's eye. Later, in a conversation with John L. over the telephone, Barney asks about it. A gift from a group of heavies working for Studebaker in South Bend. That is all John L. tells him. But we can fill in the rest. Pulled into a truck, driven across the state border into Michigan, maybe Niles, maybe as far away as Eau Claire, worked over, dumped, the scar one last furious raking by the youngest of the heavies who has to show his fellows that if Jew means union and union means less work for them from the powers that are at Studebaker, he, at least, will turn in a professional performance. And how well Marty took it. Where fear and pride mingle, kiss each other's ass. Like with the killing.

"Anyway," he continues, "Gus is right. You got nothing to explain. For John L. that kind of thing doesn't matter. Communist or Republican dowager, he'd shit pickles if it would let the labor movement go where it has to go. You know that, Barney. Better than me. Maybe better than John L." He takes a swallow of the whiskey.

I eye him ceaselessly. God knows where he is. The reflection in the driver's mirror is the Puerto Rican face. Banked rows of mirrors, slanting everywhere. Distorting the past. Why wasn't Marty there? With me and Itzik and Roginsky. I am in the bind of death. Marty was in other binds. The party. I choke on the little one with the gray turtleneck. Marty would have choked him. Belief is long since gone. Does it matter?

"With my kind," the voice in the mind continues, "what's important is that there be no master's voice. You and Gus here, you've packed in your souls for the party. Gus is right. You don't have to explain."

Barney walks over to where Marty is sitting, refills his glass. Then he goes back to the desk and pours three more shot glasses. Callahan and I each take a glass. Barney drinks. So do the rest of us.

"Do we smash glasses?" Marty snorts. "Like Jews who marry."

"I'll answer your questions now," Barney says.

"There's no need for that!" I shout angrily. Comrade Rita, the secretary sent to us by the party, opens the door and stands in the doorway, her prim face snapping at each of us in turn.

"It's all right, Rita," Barney says. "Gus is a bit excited."

"I'm not sensitive," she says, her voice as spiky as her face.

"Gus," Barney says, after she closes the door behind her,

"you and Jimmy had better go, too. This is for me and Marty."

"We've got the right to stay," I insist, still angry.

"Between us," Barney says. "It's not at your expense. I have to give him that." Marty's face is clear triumph.

"Nothing to fear, Gus," Marty says. "A private conversation. About what might have been."

Callahan leaves. So do I. I say nothing to Marty.

14

The cab pulls up in front of the gray tenement on Tenth Avenue. Graffiti crusted to walls and door. A barking dog slithers across the street as I pay the driver. Three white boys, between eleven and fourteen, sit on the step leading into the entrance. The boys challenge me. Like Itzik's blacks. Two of them are the remnants of Hell's Kitchen Irish. The other drifts through ethnic couplings, a butterfly not quite willing to leave the cocoon—part Greek, part Croatian, a drop or two of Spanish conquistador via Mexican Indians. The boys jam together to block my way. I stand before them. *He don't have, Roland. He don't have shit.*

The three boys do not move. An old Irish woman who lives in the apartment below mine and who walks her dog every day at exactly this time appears. She is framed in the doorway. Her eyes flicker green fear, her reddish hair is sparse, brushed to the side to disguise the wreckage. Vanity observed. You learn to look at your own passage through as a series of circles and then you learn to watch yourself moving down and down until you touch bottom. The dog jumps against the thick glass pane of the cast iron door. The oldest boy turns to the old Irish woman, his face flushed. He is embarrassed. He roughly pushes the boy sitting next to him to the side. That one, in turn, shoves the mixed breed, who is the youngest. The entrance is unblocked. The old woman pulls her dog to the side and waits for me to enter.

A series of circles, spiraling down and down into the bottom. Where it is empty. I am almost touching the bottom now. I am dying. I am happy to be dying. I think of Sophie as I turn the key to my apartment. Three locks. But I have a key only for the bottom. I do not bother with the other locks. They have broken into the apartment often enough. There is nothing left to steal. But they have allowed me the small radio in the kitchen. I do not know why. Perhaps it is worthless. And they never bother with the bathroom, which is dirt-stained, the tiles lined with mildew from which the entire apartment smells on damp days. The last time they robbed me was a few weeks ago. Neat. They took only the electric clock. And they made themselves coffee, the dishes in the sink a testimony to their neatness. Left a note on the kitchen table. "NO shotage of shit in this world, gramps. Next time, maybe we'll leave you. Something, gramps. Anything is better. Die, old man." Underneath, a curlicue of ornate signatures. Artists claiming their time.

We shall be all! Remembering Callahan. In the narrow kitchen with the high ceiling, a dented tin coffee pot, four unmatched spoons, neatly laid out on the porcelain sliding counter that tops the washtub sink. A half-filled bottle of Nescafé instant, and an old blue candy dish filled with tea bags. A life's possessions. I fill the pot with water. Pain balloons throughout my body now. I want to eat. Fat Gus now wasting into time's bone. Fat Gus is thin. The circles near bottom. God could have made me a poet. Instead, he made me a trade unionist, a Communist. And I, in turn, unmade him. An even exchange. Rest for ambition, too. In the cupboard, an almost-full box of Ritz Crackers. I take the chunk of feta cheese from the refrigerator and coat some crackers. I sit by the window.

Unspoken whispers. Did he try to use Barney as a lever to acknowledge me? Dim possibilities. The past wrestles with the pain. An exchange of equals. I am never exactly certain of the way it was. But I imagine it, the words between them. Itzik's old man's face laughs at memories of what we were in our strength. No ebb tide for decay. And I know with the cold surety with which such things are known that I will die this very night, dreaming of Marty, of Itzik, of Callahan. Dreaming my memories of Barney Kadish. I close my eyes. I see them.

Barney sits behind his desk. The desk is cluttered with papers, pencils, old newspaper clippings, an empty cardboard shirtbox. Marty sits in the chair with rollers. His fingers are spread apart as if he were a blind man preparing to single objects out by feel. It is Barney who speaks first after Callahan and I have left the office.

"At least we're in the same trade."

"What is it I came for? I don't know."

"Of course you do," Barney says derisively. "You don't have to lie to yourself."

"Victor says the problem with people like you isn't that we can't trust you. People like you would give their lives for the movement."

"My enemy's praise is better than my friend's. What else did Victor say?"

"He's a Reuther. He talks union. He analyzes the things others don't look for."

"And you?" Barney questions.

Marty laughs. "It's not your life that worries me. You'd give that." He pauses, measures Barney. "I hear you're married. Children, too."

The verities of bourgeois life," Barney says. "We party people manage to get around. In the long run, it's just a question of which system you live under."

"And your system provides its own truth?"

"Even you and the Reuthers have a system. You take what there is. Still, what good is it if that's the end in itself? Are you really willing to give your soul for twenty cents an hour? Do you really think you can achieve socialism without us? Without our kind? You all hate the party so much that you measure your lives by the virtue you muster against it. Who do you think made the victory at Flint possible?"

"Hitler-Stalin. The trials. It's a mockery of belief, Barney, this system of yours." He stands up from his chair. "And you think you're immune."

"I've never thought that's important. Remember when we met? The forces of history. Remember? You can fight only one enemy at a time. I have no illusions, Marty. Do you think I don't know it's a sellout?"

"Then why stay? It's not enough to tell me. Tell the world. You're a prize for them, Barney."

"There's no other place to go," Barney says, shaking his head. "I've thought about leaving but there's no place to go. I'm not you, Marty. The labor movement isn't enough."

Marty bends down across Barney's desk, trying to convince himself that his arguments have begun to win the day. "I'm a socialist. It's possisble to remain a socialist. You don't have to lie to yourself. You don't have to eat the party's shit and pretend it's ice cream. Look at yourself, Barney. Look at what they've made of you."

A knock at the door. Without waiting for an invitation, Comrade Rita Ginsberg, the bun of hair beginning to disintegrate but the lips set as narrowly and firmly as before, enters the office. She is here to rescue Barney. Lovers and comrades. She is carrying a tray on which there are two glasses of steaming tea. She does not smile when she speaks. "I thought you might like some tea."

"My God, her, too. They've made you a child, Barney."

Flushed, Barney protests. "Don't be a fool."

Comrade Rita is angry. "We do not have to pay for your sins, Mr. Altschuler. You know nothing about us."

"I know enough," Marty says. His eyes turn to Barney. "She talks. You don't even have to wind her up."

"That'll do, Marty," Barney answers angrily. "Rita, leave the tray. Close the door behind you." Comrade Rita does as she is told. "You didn't have to do that," Barney says, after she leaves.

"Do you make love to that one, too?"

Barney swivels in his chair until he is looking away from Marty at the wall. "From you, Marty, I might have expected understanding. We went through a lot together." He turns again in his chair to face Marty. "A man shouldn't be a slave to his own will. But he gives a lot to circumstance. You don't understand that? Then understand this. The party is my vengeance. I've left everything else. Mother, sisters, a father who died like a vegetable. My wife and I live in an armed truce. My children see me from a distance. If I've given all of that, do you think I'm afraid of what the party can do to me?"

"But you stay."

"Because I *want* to stay. And believe. Someday, lies won't be necessary. No more trials, no more Trotskyite conspiracies, no more obscenities like the Hitler-Stalin pact. But that's a long way off. Now I follow. If the party says the moon is made of green shit, then, damnit, the moon is made of green shit. If the party wants to re-order time, to restructure history, then I'm willing to follow that, too. What's your virtue to me?" He pauses, walks around to the other side of the desk so that he is standing directly in front of Marty. "You know why we won at Flint? Because Lewis decided what to do. Not you, not me, not the Reuthers, not Homer Martin. Lewis was the heart and mind of the men in the plant. You've said it yourself. Do you think Lewis gives a damn what your politics are? Or what mine are? Stalin licks Hitler's ass to buy time. All right, we all vomit. But you know what's coming. We all know what's coming."

"You'll stay then?"

"Stay?" Barney echoes. "I'd give the other eye, Marty. There's nothing else."

The wind slips through the open kitchen window and rustles the wax paper in which I have wrapped the rest of the feta cheese. In Pyros, the boats turn into the wind, boats against the evening sky. A long time before memory goes. Itzik with his black child thieves. Barney dead. Kaddish for Comrade Kadish. The mourning of Jews. And my mourning, too. The nose swollen, but he does not cry out. The one good eye half closed, the nose ballooning into the distance. Marty standing over him while Comrade Rita splits the air with screams.

"What happened?" I cry, pushing through the door. Jimmy tears at Marty. Marty turns into him, tries to press him against the desk. Odessa smiles. The ships of Pyros gleam in the sun. Not a sound from Barney. Marty turning from Jimmy to me, like a madman. And Jimmy, himself enraged, coming off the desk again and again. Marty hated what he was once part of. He comes to us now without restraint, and Jimmy and I smash against him, until Comrade Rita pushes three organizers into the office and the five of us pin Marty face down to the floor. Comrade Rita helps Barney to his feet. When Barney leaves the office, Marty's rage slackens. We can feel his body collapse. "Let him go," I say.

Marty does not speak. He picks up his leather jacket, puts it on, leaves. I follow him to the elevator. When I return to the union office, Barney is groping his way out of the washroom. He is leaning on Comrade Rita and on one of the file clerks. The patch has slipped down across the bridge of his swollen nose, so that the still-red flesh of the empty socket shows as the swollen cheek rushes to embrace it. Comrade Rita bravely looks on, as if she wants nothing more than to embrace the leper in his leprosy. Barney gasps as he sucks in the office air.

15

In pain, memory waits for the darkness to break and for dawn to flood. The last time. In Pyros, the sea ran dark blue with the dawn's coming, tinged with yellow, sparkling as if the departing moon had given the world some subtle secret that would weigh us down with its presence. All day long, the fishing wives wait for the secret to be revealed. And then in the evening the boats return and the secret is known to everyone. There is nothing out there, no secret, the sea is a liar, too. Folds of flesh in a fat man. Cancer kisses memory. I am now like one of the survivors from the camps who filled us all with such horror after the war. Death is never impersonal. In with the dawn, touch of fingers. Warm is how I imagine it. Every death is of the same order. An ending. A finish. Life is where the difference lies. With me, with Barney, with the crumbs poor Itzik will leave to memory. Dredged beyond the reach of his black urchins, his lumpen attending the streets and scattering the sun. Faces in the sun, faces squashed together, like melons dumped on a wharf. Pyros, Brownsville, the cold dawn on Tenth Avenue.

Kaddish for Comrade Kadish. Kaddish for Costa Nassos Constantinou. What is left to remember? The women I envied him? The sons stamped out of the blending of Barney Kadish and Greta Hedwig Edmundson? Abstractions. Barney was neither lover nor father. I know that now. Departures steady our dreams, anchor our envy. Death waits at the door to enter. Old Niggerlips sucks at the time before and the time before that. Memory burns. Kaddish for the king. No sign of agony in the flesh. The spirit whimpers its assent. The next day, returning to the deserted office to discover— What was it I looked for? Charts? Manuals for the coming revolution? How many organized in Milwaukee? In Toronto? How many delinquent in their dues?

And saw the face still swollen, the one eye opened wide but the cheek below still puffed, so that he looks like some landed fish struggling to breathe. Not in his office but in the outer office, where Comrade Rita works. On the wall, a blown-up photograph of Barney standing alongside Lewis at the CIO convention. Barney holds John L.'s right hand in the air. John L. sternly looks straight ahead, his face already jowled into the future. Barney is smiling. Even his single eye seems to smile into the camera, his face broken by a wide-toothed smile. And now the swollen face shadows the bottom of the photograph, the smile smiling into the smile, grimace of discovery and pain. On her knees, Comrade Rita, dark hair hanging loose now, kneels with his cock in hand and stares, gasping, into my face. Above them, John L. Lewis gazes off into the distance. Comrade Rita blushes, cries out like a wounded bird, turns her face to the wall, cock still in hand.

The dawn is breaking. The revolution ascends.

Greta

1

I hold the photograph in my outstretched right hand. I study it, as if being able to re-create its composition guarantees the precise emotion of that time. Barney stands to my left. His right hand enfolds my shoulder. The hand promises to caress me in the future, as it has already done in the weeks past. As I stare at the photograph, I feel no grief. His death is of little consequence. For me, for his sons, Barney Kadish died long ago. And yet, memory's insistence remains strong. Reminders are everywhere. The photograph taken the day after we were married. A clear day in October. Barney takes off from work with the union. A day's vacation. We take the subway to Coney Island. The amusement park is still open. It will close two weeks later for the winter months. Barney insists we ride the Ferris wheel. In the picture, his leather eyepatch seems soft in a face itself softened by wonder. We are in love at Coney Island. The world is kissed by proletarian splendor. We laugh, walk hand in hand across the boardwalk, take our shoes and socks off and trample the beach. Remembering is like being pressed to sleep between giant blankets. Peeping out from the past, Barney's leather-patched eye smothers the anguished nights that wait for us in the future. Barney's time is here again.

I wasn't there to see him die. It is more than seventeen years since he last wrote me. In defense of lovers abandoned. Daughter, wife, mother, stranger. Three sons I never shared with him. He claimed he loved them. Perhaps he did. At least Isaac. Barney Kadish's youngest is now the Republican councilman-at-large from New York's silk-stocking district. A long journey to meet an ironic fate. Isaac chose. All of our sons chose.

In an hour, I will stand before Isaac's door. Isaac himself will answer the bell, loom before me like a Renaissance prince of the realm. The apartment stands in cut-stone splendor across the street from the museum. Isaac smokes a pipe, is interviewed by the *Times*, offers the substantial world view of a solid Republican lawyer. A world of form and proportion. Isaac peers out of the window to examine the mobs of students and strollers who ogle each other on the sea of steps. Isaac is comfortable in his Fifth Avenue apartment filled with proprietors and owners. Solid afternoons in the sun, exhibition banners kissed by the wind. Police on their horses. "Cossacks!" Barney used to call them, laughing his contempt. Now the Cossacks protect the halls of culture. And they listen respectfully to the voice of Isaac Kadish, Barney's son.

Barney's son and Barney's ex-wife speak of him. Isaac stands before me, as handsome, dignified, and clean-cut as the brown herringbone English tweed jacket he wears. No pious little socialist watchmaker is this Isaac of ours. "Your father," I insist. "At least acknowledge him as your father."

He puffs his pipe, eyes the baby daughter sitting wide-eyed in her playpen on the living room floor. Isaac and his wife have placed the baby here for her grandmother's cool enjoyment. Isaac's wife and daughter are blond. Isaac's mother is still blond, too.

I watch my granddaughter struggle to her feet. "No, mother," Isaac says to me, sucking on his pipe the way his great-grandfather in Malmo or his grandfather in Odessa might have sucked on a fishbone. "No. I'll feel no guilt for him. Tell me when Barney Kadish was alive for his sons. Tell Frederick and Olaf, too. He died for us when we were children. Was Barney Kadish ever alive for his family? Acknowledge what father?"

Subtle truths are expensive, like the English weave of the cloth. I walk to the playpen to pick up my granddaughter. Holding her is like holding time. Sculpted emotions. I hold the three-year-old Frederick by the hand, push the carriage in which the five-month-old Isaac sits facing his sixteen-month-old brother, Olaf. On Sixth Avenue, the Greek florists dress their vases in the bright morning sun, carefully placing them down on the wet-hosed sidewalk as if they were nubile young girls curved to the form of each man's fantasy. From across the street, Barney casually observes us. He is walking with Itzik Perlin and Gus Constantinou. "See my sons!" Barney shouts. Waves. Laughs. A man's possessions—lineage and laughter. Barney laughing. Barney laughs at night when we make love. Discoveries embarrass me, but not him. An absurdity of love during those early years. The questing girls are still unknown to me, still in the future. Barney grunts on our new bed, springs fastened to expectation. His hands soothe the small of my back. Seasons of living—winter, spring, summer, fall. A time for exchanges.

Before Barney, how hard it was. The long cold nights in Albert Lea where I stare into the faces that mirror my own. Outside, horses still riddle the mud-splattered streets like dutiful missionaries of approaching spring. Thick farm horses, their plodding ugliness as solid as the heavy blond men who maneuver them. As the town slips to its boundaries, the flat landscape calls to us. All sky and sun, the snow on the ground promises that it, too, will soon be a memory. Lonely telegraph poles string the roadside to measure space. Barney loved to hear me talk about it. Lone eye closed, he marries his vision to my past. "All that space," he whispers. "Land. And then more land." Rocks Frederick on his knee, rocks in the yellow rocker. Presses his life to the shape of mine. *"Mayn eyntsiker,"* he coos, the eyepatch suspended in the brittle kitchen light. He stands, smiles, cradles his sleeping infant son, affection momentarily confused with need. Even Communists are entitled to pride in possession. Flesh of his flesh, blood of his blood. "Poor Lenin," he laughs, after we make love later that night. "So much he didn't know." In the next room, Frederick sleeps in the crib. The night is simpler now. I lie quietly, filled with the long pleasure of waiting for nothing at all. My needs have been served.

"Eyntsiker. Balibter." In the lingering smell of *his* son, words caress darkness. We drift through the welcome respites. Never have I been more content. The window is open, the cold enters. Twelve stories below, Seventh Avenue is frozen, an occasional night bus moving up or down its length. I touch my husband's face, feel the leather blindness. The kindest eye can see no more. I feel the high-boned cheeks, feel the Kirghiz eye staring into my own emptiness. His hands stroke my flesh, shape the relentless gathering of movement in me. Dying Minnesota light streaks the northern flatland with the promise of one more cold tomorrow. Collectives dot the towns. Grain elevators, freight trains, water towers. Farmers give themselves over to American needs, American opportunities. The land gives itself over to its own breeding. Long winters mean an emptiness of will. Wobblies, Communists, casual hobos—itinerants drift through Albert Lea. No different from the peddlers who sell us pants, knives, pots and pans.

In bed, Barney takes what we create together. I take pleasure in his taking. With the others, I worked the passage through town to the small empty shacks on the edge of prairie space. Deserted rendezvous in winter. He is inside me. Neither regret nor pain. Only the hunger to get beyond words. Barney

wants what all of my lovers have wanted. Barney takes. In the
cold dying light, the first one touched my expectations. It is
1927. I am sixteen. The revolution is yet to descend. My Uncle
Paul who waited for it with the pain of its birth indented on his
skull had been dead for three weeks. I believe in the new world
coming. I believe in the destruction of capitalism. I believe in
the workers' millennium. I believe in these motions of the body.
I welcome the lovers into me.

As I still welcome Barney seven years later in the apartment on Sixteenth Street. In the lobby below, the doorman
awaits the future as we do. Cold Depression winds sweep the
city dry. I remember the long sunsets of Minnesota. The colors
fill in. It is after the birth of the third son. Isaac is a love child,
a needed reminder of the future. History is the glass of water,
not sex. Lenin had it wrong. Barney is inside me now. Dead, I
want him, remember wanting him in the past. I dream of distant places, afraid of wanting once again. The world grows
beneath us. Sex is working past each of our needs into time. At
home, we could watch the animals on the farm. No other
teachers were needed.

And yet, he felt little for any of them. Only words to
suggest what he should have felt, as if the suggestion brought
him home to the way it might have been. Poor Barney. The
attraction always lies elsewhere. I push Isaac through the street,
Frederick and Olaf struggling along hand in hand at my side.
But Barney is caught up in the demands of his people. He
ignores our presence, pretends he does not see us. Workers
greet us, puffing the two walking boys up with their importance. They do not know what their father does, but they know
that here, at least, it makes them more important than children
should be. At Barney's heels, Gus waves, interrupting his own
urging of the people to close ranks behind Barney Kadish, to
recognize what Barney had brought into this world. Barney
speaks, the phrases already so well known that the response is
as automatic as the language. This animal is political.

Sometimes, when he sees me with his sons, he does not know what to do. There are no suitable myths, no examples absorbed into the party's stories, like Hector's father seeking out Achilles' tent. We are an intrusion in these cluttered streets —like Odessa, like memories of the sisters I have not seen since the wedding and will not see for the rest of my life (except the youngest, during the war, her face plastered across a billboard that juts into the searchlight-speared night of the Lower East Side, her giant teeth embracing the Yiddish lettering urging all of Delancey Street to some indecipherable effort), like the mother-in-law so weathered by fear that she shrinks into the walls of the kitchen on those three or four times her revolutionary son permits me to invite her (and to teach the three grandchildren to shriek "Baba!" as the soul fades back into the haunted distances of her eyes, madness speaking out of the blue-green depths of those eyes which understand neither sons nor grandsons nor daughters nor daughter-in-law, eyes that whimper into oblivion, huddle into the reserves of timidity and fear she carries with her like the musty smell of her flesh, carries, finally, into the series of nameless institutions her son and daughters, who themselves do not even speak, bequeath her to). For Barney Kadish must be cut loose from his own past. It is the future that demands. Only men whom I have never known can be permitted to live in memory. Old Isaac, Avram, Moishe—faces that loom before his eyes while his people pledge themselves to Barney Kadish. And to Barney Kadish's vision. In the beginning was the word and the word was with Marx and Lenin and the word sought out Barney Kadish.

Still, the years act themselves out. Barney's politics, Barney's needs. In our apartment, the soft beagle eyes of Gus Constantinou seek me out. Ask and you shall be answered. Gus does not ask. It is 1937. Rumors of Barney's girls float through my life. Beggars for his favor. I examine Gus. Neither youth nor age, but a man who wants to matter. Gus dreams. Greek music hidden in an excess of flesh. Fat Plato. Lean Jew. Did I dream of other lovers then? I do not remember. Is Gus alive or dead now? Was he with Barney at the end? Along with Lisa, my sister in mourning? The quiet deaths are the ones mourned by those who remain. Who will mourn Gus Constantinou?

Was it that I knew by 1939—after eight years of marriage and three sons and the trials and confessions in Moscow and the strangling death of Spain and the Hitler-Stalin pact—that to leave Barney was to leave my own past? Was it that which held me back as he stacked his infidelities before me like a child parading a collection of toy cars? I despise him for the need to display his conquests. Lover, my revolutionary lover. Eager Jewish virgins from Hunter College seek him out. A few words, sex and politics, moist passion in the glance, all quotations are proper and recorded. A silence in which everything is pledged. A second-rate actor strutting his sexual needs.

Gus follows, trails behind him. On Seventh Avenue, in Flint. Gus would have been honored, fat frog in the fairy tale. But Gus needs permission. Barney has frozen him to the revolution, the way a child shapes a snowball and leaves it in a corner of the freezer, until weeks later he comes upon the rock-hard mass and is surprised to discover its hardness, the way it had clung to the form he gave it. Gus was always frightened of Barney's pleasures and pains. Barney returns to the apartment after one of his trysts. Gus is in tow, like a hesitant but obedient stranger who is careful to wipe his feet on the straw entrance mat in the hallway. After dinner, the three of us put the children to bed. Each of them dutifully kisses Uncle Gus. Then we adjourn to the living room, where we crack walnuts, mix them with raisins, and drink the retsina we now keep on hand for Gus's visits. I can feel Gus studying the distance separating his presence from my own, as silent as some carrion bird circling its dying prey above the plains. We talk into the void. Gus is intent on keeping his fantasies a secret from all. He circles overhead, cunning in his need.

I study Gus. His body retreats into itself. I remember how the bodies of the farm boys back in Minnesota shrunk back into their very bigness, split the emerging man from the child who refuses to die. Gus is different. He seems to have been put together but never quite finished. He sits on the couch, nervously twists hand against hand. Minschin is beaten, the union is secure, the two of them have recently returned from Flint in triumph. He speaks to Barney and me about the party, what must be done about the trials, the situation in the CIO, the war in Spain. Meanwhile, on some deeper level known only to himself, he takes his fantasies as the measure of the real. Gus remains the victim of the myths he has been willed.

Barney and I are victims also. What had I myself given at sixteen, as I took the weight of that first one in the shack in Albert Lea? I was so intent on fusing romance and revolution that I willingly bound myself to his need for the lie. A face I cannot even remember. Not that I thought of it as lying. Even then, played the game well enough. And years later, with Barney, when all passion is spent we are disciplined enough so that we hug our illusions to sleep. When the ax descends into Trotsky's head, Barneys hugs illusions even more tightly. By that time, he cannot hug me. I do not number myself among the gifts our time offers. Barney and I lie in separate beds, apart. The children sleep in the next room, like soldiers in a barracks. Discipline descends, touches us like the Holy Ghost. When all else is lost, we remain faithful to the need for discipline.

Why was it so difficult to reach across that empty space, to hold each other in an embrace that would have enabled him to deny what they demanded he give? Was it my failing, I wonder? "Listen," I might have said to him, "we have each other. We have our boys. Solid possessions. The children, a mahogany coffee table, the leather-bound set of James Fenimore Cooper in Swedish which you gave me one birthday morning, the bed that creaked when we used to make love. Bourgeois bargains. All right. But it is of such bargains that lives are constructed. The revolution will not change that. There is life beyond the party. Us, Barney. Us."

I never said it. Not to Barney.

The afternoons slant into the nights. Barney sits at the breakfast table. He stirs the bowl of oatmeal I make for him each morning. He stares with his one eye at the three sons sitting around the table. Even pride of possession withers in what his mind tells him makes no sense—not for a man who had willingly pledged body and soul to the revolution, who assigned to the party the self he never quite believed was his, with all the care of a dying widow assigning her possessions. Arbitrary legacies deeded to the future. Three sons are not among the bargains he has made with himself.

Other legacies are equally arbitrary. Stirring his oatmeal, what is it Barney Kadish senses? That there is nothing left—neither wife nor children—that can be conceived of before the demands of the future. And the party is the voice of the future. Sons that are his, known because his wife speaks of them. Is this, he wonders, the way life was meant to be? Eying the future out of a solitary vision, he sees the dead end of our love. Still, he hangs on. The revolutionist, too, demands respectability. He brings the cereal to his lips, stares across the table at his dutiful children. Does he push them through their childhood catechism? Possessions. Had the party demanded, he would have surrendered them as easily as he took me in. Abraham with his Isaac. And his Frederick. And his Olaf. But the party did not demand.

Not then, anyway.

2

Israel Albin's dark pensive eyes are set in a strikingly handsome face, so handsome that when I meet him I cannot quite believe that he is the man whose name has been given me in Albert Lea. Israel looks to all the world like a concert pianist rather than the man who has by 1930 already evolved into the American party's most orthodox theologian. Israel is no more than a year older than Barney, but already he is called upon to render judgment. And only when those to be judged are important. It was Israel Albin who brought Barney and Greta together.

His name had been given me by one of those itinerant party organizers who found his way to our house in Albert Lea. The organizer had dinner with me and my father. My mother was dead by then, dead five years past. My father's own revolutionary fervor was already crumbling to indifference. He was tired. "I'm leaving for New York," I announce, as I clear the dishes from the table. My father glances at the itinerant organizer. His white-stubbled face registers no emotion. It is 1930, I am nineteen, he does not know what to do with me. I have just heard rumors of a new woman he is seeing, the widow of a farmer some fifteen miles south of town. I am a barrier to his desire to remarry. Or so he thinks. Not knowing what to say, my father says nothing.

Our guest takes out pencil and pad from his jacket pocket. He scratches out a name and telephone number and hands me the paper. We are standing in the small curtained-off parlor where my Uncle Paul slept during the last years of his life. "It would be better for the cause if you were content to remain here," our guest offers. "But I understand. There is work in New York, too. And for a young woman. . . ." He slides his hand against the air, as if that were finish enough to the sentence. "Here is the name and phone number of a comrade in New York. He is well-known in the party. And he will see to it that you are given work that is proper." He wipes at his furrowed brow with a handkerchief, although it is cool and he is not sweating.

He follows me outside into the star-blotted Minnesota night. In his mind, the address he has given me and the work he is doing are payment enough. He takes my shoulders in his hands. "No," I say, annoyed at the flash of surprise in his eyes. "Only with those I choose." I haven't chosen him.

"Nothing," he insists, pressing hip to hip, grinding against me in the dark. His clothes are shabby, but he is clean. "Please, Comrade Greta. It has been so long since I have been with a woman. Please. Organizing is lonely work. You have no idea how alone I feel." No, I have no idea. I want no idea. I want only to be left alone in this quiet house I must leave. I want to breathe. I shake my head. When I push him away and run back into the house, I hear him suck in his breath, like a man in sudden pain.

It is a half year later that I contact Israel Albin in New York. I remember how he looked that first time. He took me to the Automat for coffee and sat across from me, dark liquid Jewish eyes, brooding handsome face slashing with dissatisfaction against the future. A displacement of time—so certain is Israel of the future's imminent descent that he can afford to refuse the opportunities of the present. He ignores the nineteen-year-old woman whose uncomplicated self-interest demands his allegiance. For Israel, I am simply a young party member. He asks me about what he calls "our situation" in Minnesota. I answer as best as I can. A week later and Israel escorts me to a cell meeting on West Fourth Street in Greenwich Village. It is a cell composed of sailors, most of them drifting in from Sweden or Norway. I have, I discover, been sent to help the party understand what is on the minds of the sailors from overseas. The owner of the book-lined cramped apartment is a tall slender man with a markedly Southern accent. He hops nervously from spot to spot, as if he were about to beg our pardon for intruding in his own apartment. He eyes the dour Swedes and Norwegians sitting on the floor in front of the living room's closed-off fireplace. I smile at him. "I'm from Georgia," he offers and giggles, as if the idea that he was from Georgia explained everything. Or perhaps he was proudly telling me that the revolution's net was spread wide.

Not knowing how else to respond, I translate what he has said into Swedish. The sailors sitting on the floor nod approvingly. A few applaud. A big blond man with a large forelock hanging almost to his eyes rises from the floor, and says in Swedish that Georgia has produced Comrade Stalin. Our comrade host should be proud. I nod, thank him, decide not to translate what he has said to our comrade host. An hour later, Israel Albin takes my hand and we leave the apartment. The meeting has broken up. There is a lot of handshaking among the sailors and with the comrade from Georgia. I smile my good-by to him. He seems visibly relieved at our departure.

In the bright New York late-summer twilight, Israel Albin and I walk up Sixth Avenue. We head for the subway at Fourteenth Street. "You did well, Greta," Israel says. And then, in the same tone I imagine he would use to reward a child who has done its lessons, he adds, "I want you to meet Barney Kadish."

"And who is Barney Kadish?" I ask. I have read Barney's name often enough in the *Future*. But I feign ignorance. I don't know why.

"A trade union leader. Absolutely devoted to the party." For the first time since I have known him, Israel Albin squeezes my hand. A gesture of emotion so surprising that I stop walking and stare at him. But Israel is oblivious. He continues walking. "A man of action," he says. "You'll see."

For the next six weeks Israel talks about Barney Kadish every time we are together, as if admiration for Barney were what had brought us together in the first place. And since the party has given me over to Israel as a kind of amanuensis, we are together often. Barney brings out Israel's sense of expectation. When he speaks about him, he sounds like a boy of twelve talking about an older brother he worships. He has, I soon suspect, decided to play party Cupid. It is safer for Israel that way. And so, in September 1931, about two weeks after Labor Day, Israel Albin escorts me up a flight of stairs to a Mexican restaurant near Eighth Avenue on Fourteenth Street. On one side of the restaurant stands a pawnshop, its windows filled with unredeemed treasures. On the other, the John Bunyan Christian Publishers, Inc. Black leather bibles are scattered throughout the unkempt display window with a casual insolence. I am nervous, irritable, like a farm girl on her first date in the city. I have never eaten Mexican food before. I frown as Israel Albin, eagerly anticipating introducing me to his friend, pushes me through the heavy wooden doors of the restaurant and guides me through the large hot room. I am surprised to see so many people laughing and eating in the restaurant. Men and women starve in the streets, fight one another for space in Hoovervilles. And yet here I am, being escorted to a revolutionary tryst by this handsome, sensitive Jew who refuses to notice me.

We halt before a corner table to the right of the swinging kitchen doors at the rear of the restaurant. Barney Kadish sits as straight as a prisoner about to be interrogated. He is pressed against the wall, as if he were guarding himself from some potential eruption. A man of medium height, in the shadowed corner of the Mexican restaurant he looks taller than he turns out to be. Israel's hand thrusts against Barney's shoulder. "I want you to meet a beautiful comrade from out West, Barney. This is Greta Edmundson. From Minnesota." It is the first time Israel has spoken of me as beautiful. The word is striking in his mouth. Then he laughs, as if only a fellow Jew in New York could appreciate a hunger so plebian that it makes a Swedish girl from Minnesota the bearer of revolutionary sweets. I join in Israel's laughter, only to discover myself staring down into a leather patch drawn across the socket like a badge. Barney does not get up at first. His face is high-cheekboned, slightly Oriental, more open and relaxed than I had expected. Even the leather patch speaks of openness. His smile slips free, like a quick clearing in the sky. It is a smile presented to me alone, as if Israel had disappeared into the smoky shadows. A New York smile, it takes my full measure, tells me I am the last woman in the world.

Abruptly, Barney stands. He takes my hand in the warmth of his own. For a brief moment, I think he is going to kiss it, as if he were a Viennese baron in the nineteenth century. Instead, he shakes it vigorously. "A pleasure, Greta." Then he pulls the chair next to the one he is sitting on out from under the table and guides me into it. He smiles again, this time like a young man who is surprised at the adroit manners he has picked up. This smile invites me inside, tells me that I need not be wary of Barney Kadish.

I sit down. Across from us, Israel Albin, his mission already assured of success, seats himself, his handsome sensitive face lit now by a smile of its own. Israel is relaxed. He takes a peculiar pleasure from the thought that Barney possesses powers he himself does not possess. Turning first to me and then to Barney, he looks like one of those mechanical wind-up toys that decorate department store windows at Christmastime. "You two," he gushes. "I've wanted you two to meet for so long."

Even then, I remember thinking that Barney and I have somehow been trapped in a play staged by Israel Albin. And the party is our angel. I don't know why I believed that. It is an idea I am never to free myself of, even after Israel is purged from the party. And yet, it makes little sense. What reason did the party then have to bring Barney and me together? The party was never quite that efficient. Nor that diabolical. But in 1931, I am not yet twenty. I am alone, creeping beneath cold sheets at night. The imagination of terror, like the imagination of omnipotence, must be served. And I am prepared, in 1931, to serve it faithfully.

We made love that first night. In Barney's arms, I feel as if I have come home to myself. We eat Mexican food, walk hand in hand to the small cellar apartment I have rented on Third Avenue and Thirty-sixth Street. Israel disappears. Three weeks later, Barney and I stand before the judge. I become his wife. In reality, we each recognize that we have become the property of our mutual performance. I feel terribly isolated without Barney. I have never felt this way before, not even when my mother was alive.

While workers starved and cops walked heavily through the streets, Barney and I made love. All that fall and winter, we make love. When it is over, the political animal folds into his pillow, holds me to him. We talk. He tells me of Minschin, of the evils of capitalism, of how it had once been Marty alone whom he trusted. But Marty is gone now. And Barney asks himself, asks me, what went wrong. For he had loved his friend with all the fervor that he needed to embrace the tortuous logic willed to him. There could be no such thing as the truth of the individual. I understood that, didn't I? The party was correct in what it demanded—planning and patience and dedication to specific ends.

Marty had not understood. I do not know Marty but I love Barney Kadish—therefore, I understand. A revolutionary syllogism. Clinging to my body as if it alone guarantees the faith he needs, Barney reassures himself. Together, we struggle with his need to convince and his need to act. With a lover's zeal, he smashes his own doubts. He had created Marty. Or so he told me then. But it was Marxism that had created him. "I'm the party's child, Greta. I used to boast of that to Marty. He thought I would leave the party if he was only able to convince me it's dishonest." He flattens back against the pillow. He shakes himself, like an animal emerging from water. "Who knows better than I what I've given? I know the lies I've told, the lies I've forced myself to accept. Only I've never been able to convince Marty that I would lie again and again, ten thousand times over, if my lying might help our triumph. You understand, don't you?" Yes, I understood. It was absorbed into our lives, into our lovemaking, as if every action served to push us to the edge of belief. Others might divide their lives, compartmentalize their beliefs. For us, those first few years of marriage were in themselves a political act.

We are neither lighthearted nor flippant. Life is rich, as it can be rich only to those who feel they have a stake in that future they talk so much about. We believe in the ultimate arrival of a world that will trail our happiness in its wake. Barney moves into me hungrily, eager to lock us into the future we seek. In his wiry, knotted body, I discover not only his sex but his need to right the balance. Sex, too, is a form of vengeance. His dead father shares our bed with us. I do not mind. I bring in my dead Uncle Paul, head split open on a dark night in South Dakota just after the war, so that for the next seven years he wanders in and out of my life, for the last three silent in the curtained-off parlor, feeding me his death in small daily doses. The revolutionary bride strips self and bed. "Our way!" Barney cries, blocking out the hot afternoons. The windows are open to catch the noise from Seventh Avenue—buses honking like geese flying south, cars nuzzled like dogs in heat. Never more intimate, more eager to uncover my needs. Were there others then? Even today, I do not know. And if I had known, would it have been our love he was betraying? Our bodies are grafted together, our minds feed on the future. Below, on Seventh Avenue, the world continues.

3

I sit in the darkened theater with my two sons. We are in the Loew's Sheridan, across from the Catholic hospital. It is Saturday afternoon and I have taken the boys to the movies. It is the first time I have taken all three of them. Frederick is seven and a half, Olaf is six, Isaac is five. In the darkness I spy Olaf waving his arms as if he were reaching out to embrace the screen. On screen, Mickey Mouse runs as Olaf's arms plead. The two young boys laugh nervously. They look not to me but to Frederick to see whether laughter is called for. Frederick giggles. Relieved, his two brothers imitate him.

Barney refused to come. There is to be a meeting tomorrow, he must work on plans for it. He is to announce that the union is to purchase one more ambulance for the Lincoln Brigade. But the Lincoln Brigade has been destroyed, the war in Spain is over. Everyone knows that the remaining Loyalist troops are fleeing across the border into France. Barney shrugs. He does not even attempt to explain. Hitler and Stalin have signed their pact. Barney weeps. The world spins like a top to its wobbly destruction.

"I'm taking the children to the movies," I tell him. "The children asked that you come with us. Please, Barney. They asked."

Barney shakes his head. "I can't," he shrugs.

In the candied darkness, I float in silence. On screen, horses pound across the world. The children edge to the front of their seats, eye me nervously for permission to enjoy what they see. I smile at them. Beyond the space of darkness is the space of my girlhood. The horses rolling across the empty plains remind me of home. But these horses are sleek, graceful. Eyes closed, I once again see the flat land. The love-grunting blends into all other noises. I do not awaken until the newsreel comes on. On screen, the war replaces the horses. Dive bombers sweep into pictures of a smiling Hitler standing on a balcony, flanked by Goering and Goebbels. The announcer's voice turns somber. He senses that the world is burning and we shall burn with it. Spain dying, Russia neutralized, Poland teetering. The future is a closed fist. The boys shift in their seats, bored now that mouse and cowboys and horses have been swallowed up by the strutting men on the balcony, equally fidgety when smiling mannequins modeling gowns walk across the screen while the announcer's relief pierces the movie darkness. Isaac shifts uncomfortably in his seat next to mine. His head drops against my hand and I curl him into the crook of my elbow. I tell myself that this is what I have been put on earth to feel, that all the injustices we protest against do not matter in the face of this. But I feel the lie even if my mind voices it. I am horrified by my sentimentality. I feel trapped between sentimentality and politics—Barney with his "people," Gus's incessant talk about the inevitability of Marxism in America. The voices in my head are like the shrieking of idiots in a family that has learned to take idiocy, too, for granted. I believe in none of it any more than I believe in the smiling mannequins strolling across the screen like giant dolls brought to life.

I am encased by my own presence in this darkness. I love my sons, am enraged at my husband. Isaac's lovely high-cheekboned face floats against my arm, clusters of silken hair probing the abstractions of motherhood. Once I wanted Barney to feel their presence, too. Now I am indifferent. He pledges amazement to their existence. Enough has been given for Barney Kadish. For him, the union is child enough. The revolution guards the future. Immortality is in the making, while Old Isaac molders in his grave.

Before the children, we remain polite, courteous to each other, as if we were viewing ourselves in a film about a solid American family at the turn of the century. We are a family photograph enmeshed by a fantasy. Real life exists elsewhere. For Barney, in party meetings, exhorting his people into the streets, in slogans scrawled across the walls of his mind. Wives and lovers and children to the rear! Revolutionary women swarm to the barricades built by their husbands and lovers. Clean the floors! Wipe the baby's ass! Purify the revolution so that none will be afraid of it. And always, we are faced with the demand that we yield, that we surrender even the vision of revolution for the obligations we have been taught are forever ours.

The darkness tightens, the images collide. We drift through our own dreams, waiting for reality to surface. That at least part of the promised future should emerge as the youngest Republican city councilman in New York ("friend of Nelson Rockefeller," the papers report, and show him strolling through that same East Side to which his grandfather brought his hard rage), was no more than one of the minor ironies that call attention to the original dream, like a falsetto voice on an athletic young man. But he is only five now and I take him into my warmth and let him drift through the darkness, satiated with dreams and images. Sleep, my child. And if I had known then, what difference would it have made? By that time, I had lost my own politics, wanted no more than some simple, essential truths that would enable me to walk into the corner grocery devoid of a sense of history as plot. Wherever it was he ended his days in New Mexico, wherever Albuquerque is, what was it he actually felt? Was Lisa herself stripped of the children she had borne? Did one of hers stand around puffing on a pipe and denying the reality she surrendered herself to? Did Barney Kadish finally voice his disapproval of the official myths? Did he deny not his own past but what he had insisted others make of that past?

Drifting was easy enough. There were other theaters, other dark places. Casual watchings measure our disintegration. As the world plunges to its burning, Barney and Greta purge themselves by sputtering out. It was as if we had mutually decided to release each other from the most respectable of middle-class arrangements. Had we sat down together and divided the furniture and silverware, we could not have behaved more conventionally. All through the war, we smile. And we sleep apart. Already separated in spirit, we move out from each other's world. But we remain in the apartment on Sixteenth Street. He does not leave. I do not insist that he leave. By April 1944, as the world waits for the Allies to strike across the Channel, we continue to circle each other, like two antagonists who have learned after a lifetime of fighting to avoid deliberately treading on each other's toes. Even our scenes are sufficiently domestic.

The children are in their room listening to the radio. The April sun has descended into chill. The days are shorter. During the war, there is no daylight saving time, for as even the children know, the enemy has eyes as well as ears. From the children's room, the radio blares loudly. It is five minutes past six. The children have finished their dinner. I am washing the dishes. I hear the key turn in the front door and Barney walks past the kitchen. In a minute, he has returned, his jacket off, his tie loosened.

"Do you want something to eat?" I ask. I am surprised to see him home so early.

"Do they have to listen to so much of it?" he asks irritably. "So much of what?" I ask. I am always taken off guard when Barney speaks of the habits of the boys, as if he had forced himself to notice the dirty socks lying around the living room couch.

"Those stories."

"What stories?"

"That garbage you allow them to hear. Remember, I complained about it the other day." I do not remember. I cannot remember even seeing him the other day. I am not even sure of which day the other day might be. "I came home early," he continues. "And there they were, listening to this 'Terry and the Pirates.' Imperialist junk. They were excited. I thought they were feverish. Flushed and everything."

His one eye glares. He will be forty-four in another three months. But he looks ten years younger. His hair is still full, a rich chestnut, imperiously straight. Where, I wonder, did the boys get their curls? "Do you know what that junk teaches them, Greta?" I sigh. I am not in the mood to discuss "Terry and the Pirates." "Imperialism. Racism. It trains them to accept such evils." He shakes his forefinger at me, the lecture fronted.

"Your sons will not become imperialists from listening to stories on the radio, Barney. Not from Shakespeare. Not from 'Terry and the Pirates' either." I return to the dishes, wipe them carefully.

"I didn't say anything about Shakespeare. We're not barbarians, Greta." He pauses. The one eye moves slowly up and down my body. Once I was centered by his vision, loved to feel his eyes roving over me. Now I want to disappear. His voice softens, the anger mutes itself. "You are still lovely, Greta. Sometimes, I forget."

There is nothing left. I feel neither tenderness nor desire. I feel abstracted from myself, like a nun watching a film of her pre-cloistered past. I remember the rally at the Garden less than a year ago. Nineteen thousand screaming faithful urging the nation on to a Second Front. That was the time I met Marty, while Barney remained away from the apartment for two weeks, sleeping in the suite of rooms the union now permanently rented at the Penn Hotel. Proletarian splendor for Barney Kadish. I remember the ringing doorbell, the note of impatience grafted onto its nervous repetitions. And knowing it was Marty standing before me, the way you sometimes know a face without even knowing.

"It's a bit late for that, Barney," I say, surprised at the bitterness in my voice. I thought I was beyond bitterness by now.

"Do you want me to leave?" he asks, hesitantly. It is not a question. It is a line he has mulled over, a scene he has set in his mind, but now that he has finally said it he is surprised.

"What does it matter? Yes. No. You left a long time ago."

"The children . . ." he begins. He shrugs.

"They'll survive," I say. "With you or without you. It's a funny time to think about them. Frederick will be twelve in August. And what are you to him? A man who sometimes eats here." He raises his right hand, as if to protest, then drops it to his side. He does not really want to argue his case. There is no case to argue. Barney retreats. It is an ending that has been a long time coming. "Barney, there's no need to pretend family feeling."

"I feel for my family," he insists. I do not respond. The lone eye retreats from my face. For a moment, Barney Kadish looks old. His shoulders slump, his trim body sags in the middle. Then he straightens up, as if he were aware of what I was thinking. "You don't believe me when I say that. You think such lives as we lead divorce us from everything else. When we first married, Greta—"

"I was your life raft," I interrupt.

"Is that so awful? Isn't *that* family feeling?"

"Your sons, Barney. They've existed for years. Even anger would be better than indifference."

"Indifference? Is that what you think?"

"And self-pity. Listen to yourself, Barney. What is it you *feel*? Under all the words, your need is to worship. You don't even know those boys. Your feelings for them, a man of undigested sentiments."

"I never lied to you," he insists. "I told you in the beginning that I am a creature of the party." I stand and watch him. Do I imagine the tear streaking down his face from the one eye? There is no tear. "Do you think it has been easy? Without cost?"

"You chose," I say. "You chose the lies you listened to."

"Yes," he admits. "And the lies I repeated. As well as the lies I obeyed. That changes nothing."

"What does the cost matter?" I insist, my voice deliberately controlled so that the children will not hear. "*You* chose. Of course, you've paid. But there's a point where even a one-eyed man sees."

"Like you?" he mocks. And yet, he is trying to hold on. "Like all the virtuous people. Politically moral."

"Not exactly."

"What then? What, if not moral?"

"Just not lying. Not feeling *that* obligation."

"Your truth then?" I nod. "Today's truth. Bourgeois truth." He draws himself erect, like a prosecuting attorney about to lunge for the kill. "A sandwich for Leftwich. A truth sandwich. Or what Minschin tried to do to us."

"Minschin is dead. The bourgeoisie you despise so killed him. And your Stalin?"

"What do you want me to say?" he snarls. "That he hasn't murdered. All right. He's murdered. He's murdered, he's lied, he's stolen. For all I know, he cheats at cards and raped his mother. Stick him next to Attila and he'll still drip blood. So what? No one man—no, not even Stalin—is the movement. No individual matters as the movement matters. And the party is the mind and heart of the movement. Once you understood that, Stalin is a face on a banner. No more."

"And what are you?"

"All right!" he shouts. We are both oblivious to the boys and their blaring radio by now. "What do you want me to say?"

"For the people," I mock. "Barney Kadish sings for the people and the people love Barney Kadish. You're sick of your people by now."

"You don't know when to stop, Greta."

"That's my trouble then. A lack of proportion."

"Of propriety," he corrects. "I don't expect you to understand any longer."

"But you still expect me to feel a great deal when you talk of the movement," I answer bitterly. I examine his features—a face made familiar through time's passing, like the face of a celebrity seen over and over again in the newspaper. I do not think of him as a man whose life I have shared. How distant Barney Kadish seems. How distant the slogans I once taught myself to hurl against the world's darkness.

"The woman I married," he says. "I expected her to feel for the movement."

"You grow melodramatic, Barney."

"I'll tell the children after I've left. Agreed?"

"I've been explaining all these years. I'll tell them. It will be easier." I close my eyes. "Anyway, they expect us apart. In their hearts, they do. It is what they have always known."

Barney moves out the next day. How easy for the mind to conceive its nightmares transformed into farce. There is finally honesty between us. And we have, I believe, burned ourselves out of each other.

4

But to remember the nightmare is still what I seek. "I love our children," Barney insists. "For the promises they allow me to make to my own future." He is asking that they accompany him to the rally at the Garden. He is speaking to me on the telephone. I will give them to him. Marty's presence burdens me with guilt. And they are, I tell myself, Barney's sons.

Meat for the lions. Barney is the impressario. In the arena, the Romans scream. Not for blood but for a Second Front. He parades the children on stage. The children are embraced by the president's beautiful daughter-in-law. Spotlights illuminate their faces like electronic halos pointing the way for the worshipers. Overhead, two giant banners drop into the smoke-filled air of Madison Square Garden. The giant faces of Roosevelt and Stalin stare side by side into the audience. He asked me to sit with him on the stage. "Please, Greta. You understand the necessity." In 1943, as in the past, necessity justifies all. I refuse. But I give him the children for the night.

Unknown to Barney, I sit in the farthest corner of the Garden, my hand tightly wrapped in Marty's. The figures on the stage seem to loom larger because of the very distance between us. The faces of the children push like some ectoplasmic horror out of the stained canvas stage that looks like an unroped fight ring. I close my eyes, trying to shake off the vision. Marty's grip on my hand tightens. I do not look at him. I do not open my eyes again until I hear a fresh burst of cheering from the crowd.

Barney has picked Isaac up on his shoulders and is walking slowly around the stage with him, like a boxer claiming victory to the cheers of his audience. Isaac's face disappears into his laughter. He is delighted. Nineteen thousand people have come together to purchase three ambulances for the Soviet Union. Barney and the party have commanded. This year the ambulances are for the Soviets. In the past, rallies for ambulances for Kentucky miners, ambulances for the fruit pickers of the Salinas Valley, ambulances for all the blessed mergers of causes throughout the world. The faces surrounding us are holiday-like with anticipation. Even the speeches have not succeeded in boring them. The lights scorching the Garden haze filter through my children on the stage. The other two boys clap their hands. They are not envious of their brother Isaac. Sitting two rows behind them I spy the face of Margaret Selencourt, daughter of an apple farmer in Washington. Margaret Selencourt has come to New York to be a writer. And here she has discovered Barney and the revolution. Talents cling to the lives of the people. The parade continues. Olive-complexioned daughters of the poor, intent on escaping their parents' drab lives, yet loyal to their revolutionary visions. Dreams of romance on the barricades. This latest a writer from Washington, her high northwestern color testifying to the same anticipation I myself brought to this city some thirteen years earlier. Barney was willing to serve both of us.

Now he stands on the raised platform in Madison Square Garden, backed by the huge hanging pictures of Roosevelt and Stalin, and holds his beautiful Swede-Jew son high in the air. He smiles, catching the full blast of the crowd's approval in the cheers that sweep up and down the Garden. Marty presses my hand.

I look around. My eyes absorb the massive facelessness that fills the Garden. There is something frightening about it. Isaac sits like a pet monkey perched on his father's shoulders. He looks back at his two brothers sitting on the stage. He waves. They applaud him. They share their father's pride. The illusion of self depends upon the self, even for children. I can wish them nothing more than childhood's drowning. Marty's arm loops around my shoulder. He hugs me to him. I am crying. In the noise of the crowd, no one but Marty notices. In the beginning, man emerges. The father commands. My sons will bitterly come to terms with their father's presence, just as they come to terms with his absence. Frederick, Olaf, Isaac—each is celebrated in the chanting of Barney Kadish's minions. Father Stalin beams. Father Roosevelt sets square jaw against the world. I choke, cough. I feel as if I am living inside a world passing into the dust of its own illusions. I want to strip Barney and Margaret Selencourt naked, here, in this war-crazed Madison Square Garden. We are buying ambulances. We are urging the Allies to open a Second Front. We are praising the brave sons of Mother Russia. We are embracing the beautiful sons of Barney Kadish. With Isaac still on his shoulders, Barney beams like a drum major about to high-step into a parade. He loves himself for winning, anticipates what still may be seized from the future. I imagine a naked Margaret and my naked husband, her consort, making love on the stage before all these witnesses. Triumph of a wife's imagination.

When the rally is over, I leave Marty. I meet Barney on Eighth Avenue. He says nothing when he hands the children over to me. He stands and stares at them, then turns on his heel and walks off with Gus and Itzik Perlin. I watch them pile into a taxi. Barney deliberately keeps his face turned from me and his children. He will not be home this night.

5

And yet, in a curious way we continue to mix our needs, even after he leaves the apartment for good a year later. He still wants to be loved, to be acknowledged. "Tell me you love me!" he demands, on one of his visits. He is here to see the children, obligated to do his duty by his sons. But I am alone on this afternoon. The children have gone off to the library on West Eleventh Street. The performance is to be for my benefit, not for theirs. He has been gone scarcely ten months now. The war in Europe is flaming to its end. America waits to see the *Götterdämmerung* embrace Hitler and his legions. Barney Kadish is one of the most important trade unionists in the party, his star rising as he is quoted—almost daily—in the *Future*. He enters my kitchen.

I take two glasses from one of the cupboards and pour wine. I must allow the proprieties. I do not miss Barney, and yet, on this gray February afternoon in 1945, I permit myself a touch of the past, a feeling of love—although I claim to despise the word. I want to take care of myself. I do not want to surrender to Barney's needs. Still, I stand before him, again awaiting the arousal of expectation.

Where did Barney fail me then? Was it that the parade of lovers had already marched through my expectations? Or was it the staleness of what we were? If he had simply taken me then and there, an even exchange of bodies, I think I could have kissed the very emptiness he offered. Instead, he must go through his obligatory rituals, must pretend that it is me alone he desires. What he wants is to possess, to blot out a single failure by an act of will. Barney Kadish still wants the world, revolution and all, to descend through the closed holes. Barney's dead eye given to the cause. My love hole given to Barney Kadish.

"Tell me you love me!" he repeats. The voice is the voice of a beggar. Barney Kadish no longer believes that the self he offers is enough. One-eyed lover on the precipice of doubt. He circles me with words. "Greta. Remember."

Suddenly, I despise his needs. I despise the simplicity of what he wants. I despise the words, "I love you," which I watch him mouth. He wants not me but some token he can pocket for his pride. He wants a language capable of denying the errors of the past. Perhaps he wants to wipe the past out. He is pressed now by his loyalty to the party, by his need for the vision. And yet, he is determined not to give too much there either. Barney Kadish has learned to keep even the party off balance. (Yes, he had told me about Leftwich, again and again, as if so clear and simple a heroism could explain all that followed. Barney Kadish knew simple clear solutions then. And he cannot believe they are gone.) He is a child in his eagerness, a child crying, "Look at me!" He is like his son Isaac, laughing on Barney's shoulder in the Garden, laughing not with his own fantasies but with those bestowed upon him by this mysterious figure he has been told is his father, this man who absents himself from whatever reality Isaac has known. What is Leftwich to Isaac? Or to Frederick and Olaf? Will any of them have even a hint of recognition years later when they drive down Seventh Avenue and see the name strung across on a banner? Leftwich is an event that structures the life of their father. For his sons, Leftwich is not even a name from the past.

"I love you, Greta." In words, he spreads the human in himself against my body, which he imagines is pliant and willing. He is offering his need to me, unwilling to believe that I have grown tired of the past we shared. I now want to throw off the mistakes we made in trying to hold onto one another. I now take lovers—not like Barney, but quietly, each rendezvous marked off by a simple assumption of satisfaction. Barney seeks from the estranged love the passion of his ex-wife. He waits to service her as she once serviced him.

And were the lovers I took so different from the husband I pushed away? Men who were always asking permission. Brave in everything but the obligations to the self. How terrifying such dreams of solidarity. They were careful men, so proper in the liaisons they permitted themselves. So much quaint virtue paraded in fear of Stalin's madness. Our own Caligula sets the style for all.

Israel Albin enters my bed like a defrocked priest. Israel Albin has discovered that he is in trouble with the party as the war approaches its end. Browder's loving embrace of East and West is now anathema. The smiling posters with pictures of Soviet and American children disappear as the party prepares to pluck poor Browder clean. Not even permitting him the *mea culpa*, the formularized contrition voiced with the acceptable tears. Israel has been close to Browder, is under suspicion. The clutch of memory must ultimately destroy itself. Righteousness splits the sides of hesitation. Israel is doomed. Theoretician now of cold empty nights, a deserted shell of a man roaming his own mind like the last buffalo in America roaming the plains.

My body lies as cool as a spring night beneath the nervous stroking of his hands. He is feverish, not with excitement but with fear. Like a child reciting his catechism, he transforms desire into ritual. The party has left him with no room in his heart for acts of personal charity. In the *Future*, in *Emerging Mankind*, in party cell meetings, Israel discovers he is under fire. His judgment is questioned. He is reprimanded, attacked, ultimately he is demonized. His unknown Trotskyite sympathies are uncovered. He is thrown before the party wolves like some heretical theologian. Another party Faust. His soul whimpers. Nervous hands. Israel wants to restore himself to the good graces of the revolution. Even as he pushes into me, I know that he will give up this nervous lovemaking with Comrade Kadish's estranged wife if only he can once again be restored in the eyes of the party. "I love you," he mumbles, drifting off to sleep while cradled in my arms. I press my lips together to keep the laughter smothered. Always the need to justify. Never the mere pleasure in another's body. Or in your own. Never as simple as it is with animals. Never to know those moments where you can feel yourself thicken right inside the landscape. Even the Swedish farmboys could push aside their Lutheran consciences for those summer moments when grunt and groan were for simple pleasures.

Was it that I deliberately set about to avenge myself on Barney? I don't know. I was capable of it. If we measure our lives in what we deserve from our parners, then I was simply paying back a long string of injuries. I will not mourn Barney out of sexual guilt. "I love you," mumbles the defrocked priest. And wakes hours later, blushes as he pulls his pants up and I push him out of the apartment before the children can return from school. No further words of love, as he looks over his shoulder and I imagine him wondering whether the party has planted its moral censors behind these walls, too. His flesh must be punished for such unlooked-for pleasures.

He returns three months later, his haunted musician's face framed in the balance of his announced excommunication. His sins have been this very day paraded before the *Future*'s readers. The party faithful can now witness the rabbi twisted on his own doctrines. Sex is a break in the tension of belief. But no apologies are necessary. Not for me. Nor does it matter that I know that in Israel's eyes Greta Hedwig Edmundson Kadish, once loyal daughter of the party, who sat with him on the living room floor of a Greenwich Village queer, might so easily be sacrificed for his own absolution—if only the party would agree to such mundane exchanges. Like Stalin, Israel knows what is and is not important. All party accountants of the flesh measure propriety. Not even puritanical rage can be allowed to hinder the revolution's coming. Only Stalin had the true cut of it. The rest make love like clergymen. Israel is no exception. Nervous, apprehensive, looking around himself like a fugitive adolescent about to enter a whorehouse, he rings the bell to my apartment. Ten in the morning, the children again off in school. He stands at the front door as if he were not convinced I would let him in.

"Do you need the naked lady?" I ask, smiling.

But Israel is in no mood for humor. To be denied the party, I remember, is like being denied the sacraments. He will never grow used to it. "Please, Greta," he whispers. And enters the apartment, the beggar in his eyes not even at ease with himself. "They refused to listen. There was a hearing a week ago. A lifetime of work gone." He takes his jacket off, drops it on a chair in the foyer. "And for what? For a few mistakes. I didn't understand, Greta. All that work for nothing. For a lack of understanding." He drifts into the living room, where he wearily drops to the couch. His head is in his hands. He is weeping. Seductive revolutionary torment. Part of me pities him. Part of me wants to laugh. I take his head in my arms. Israel turns into me like a child who has run away from home only to discover that his mother has followed.

Later, as I shift out from under the surprisingly solid weight of Israel Albin, I must remind myself that it is only surfaces I want. I no longer want to please. I try not to think of Marty, who loves me. Israel will claim that he loves me, too. Barney loves me. They all love me.

Sex replaces belief. All are disillusioned, all lives anchored to the party's excommunication. And each knows Barney. It is, I discover, among my more profound attractions for my lovers. I learn to distinguish between this new, profligate self and the self Barney Kadish sought refuge in. I think back to the itinerant radicals passing through Albert Lea, remember what each demanded of women. I can no longer feel contempt for them. Poor hungry mouths. Minds swollen with expectation. And who was I? As the party compounded our illusions with its lies, I listened as eagerly as anyone else. The need for truth, I was to insist to Barney. Was it the need for truth I offered to Barney? His loyalties were elsewhere. He followed each new twist of party logic, each new dictum sent like a papal bull from Moscow, for he knew that his sanity ultimately rested upon acts of faith. He would give whatever was demanded. "One must believe, Greta," he says to me before we split apart. "Otherwise, there is mere chaos." Barney Kadish could not love where there was chaos.

I am never to escape him. Not even my promiscuous rush through lives that have touched his own will stop Barney Kadish from haunting me. In the streets, as I walk away from the fresh impression of pillow and head, testimony to my stubborn endurance with one or another lover, I watch him push through his days. "Facts are the worker's poetry," he used to insist. And I observe the facts of Barney Kadish's life. It is 1948. He stands in front of the building that houses the *Future*. He is waiting. I am on the other side of the street, in front of the German Evangelical Church with the red roof. Hands plunged into his pockets, he spies me. He is startled. He looks like an angry refugee. He stands with neither wife nor mistress. He stands without his children. He waits for instructions.

No reason is enough to create doubt in the future. A stream of men are exiled from themselves. Peculiar devils touch their faces, like nervous tics. Stories drift through all of radical New York. Giuseppe Marazzo spends spring and summer in the Fire Island cottage of his wealthy socialite wife. What the party demands, Giuseppe gives. It is all that he knows. In between, he touches the pubescent daughters of his neighbors who pass him by summer after summer. And then, one warm summer day, the whispers of his neighbors growing louder and louder, he reaches into the serenity of that long-promised future and walks into the Fire Island water while the whispers kiss his ears, "Something must be done about that man." Walks and walks and keeps on walking until there is neither water nor land but an end acceptable to him and to the party, which has, by 1948, grown conscious enough of its tenu-

ous relationship to this America so that it will take its martyrs
where it finds them.

Across the street, Barney stands. He no longer pretends to
ignore me. He waits. Barney Kadish is alone. Barney Kadish is
a rock, a man to be considered. I fight the urge to cross the
street, to embrace this man I loved. Quite suddenly, Barney
Kadish is surrounded by his own. I spy Gus a few feet behind
him. I spy Roginsky, who emerges from the building like a
proprietor. Gus sees me, turns his head away. Gus is embarrassed. Gus is as much the party's creature as Barney is. Voices
hail each other. Voices slap the sultry afternoon like pistol
shots. Waiting for the future in America isolates one comrade
from the next.

I see Barney's finger pointing at me. I see his face cloud
over, the one eye glow like an incandescent ruby. Ghosts
crowd the streets. *Free Tom Mooney!* the ghosts cry out. Other
ghosts answer, *Free Sacco and Vanzetti! Free the Scottsboro
Boys!* Barney's finger is like a gun at my breast. Gus reaches
across, grabs his outstretched hand. I disappear into the German Evangelical Church. *"Gottesdienst"* the bulletin board at
the rear says. Times of services are listed. The Sunday sermon
is to be given by Dr. Hugo Wolf, who will instruct the faithful
on "The True Meaning of Calvary." I seat myself in a small
pew at the rear, to the side. I like the musty stone smell. Surprisingly, I do not feel uncomfortable. I can never remember
being in a church before. Barney's lone eye cuts through this
air, too. Dreams are currency. I think of Barney peering down
into Isaac's crib one winter evening, as if he were measuring
this strangeness he had conceived with me. In my mind, a voice
cries out, "Free Barney Kadish!"

6

In the bar, drinks are served working-class style, the shotglass pushed like a bocci ball across the beer-stained mahogany. I sit with Marty at a table in front of the bar itself. I feel out of place, as if I were staring through the keyhole of a stranger's apartment. I do not know why. "You're a daughter of the working class," Barney used to say. But this is 1951. And bars snap illusions. They leave no room for the myths of your past. Only for the defiance of what you are afraid to become.

"When does Barney get called?" Marty asks.

"I'm not altogether certain. I telephoned Gerstein. He works for John Hudson's son. I telephoned him long distance."

"And what did he say?"

"It's a disease," I say. "This sense of suspicion that lingers on every word you hear. Sooner or later, you begin to hear it even in what you yourself say. Gerstein was very tight-lipped. I'm not even certain he believes there is any such person as Greta Kadish."

"You should have spoken to Hudson's son," Marty suggests. "He would remember." He sighs his exasperation. "We're in the kind of situation that justifies anything. You figure all the party people are paranoid. Then you discover that the reality is even worse than they can conceive. Beyond even their paranoia. A hell of a victory for truth. We may choke on it yet, we virtuous ones." He takes a sip of his Scotch. "Why did you want to watch it here?"

I take his hand in my own. "I've made you unhappy?" I ask.

"Of course not," Marty assures me. "It's just that I

haven't heard from you in . . . how long is it now, Greta? Three, four years. That last time in New York, when we agreed not to see each other."

"Five years," I correct gently.

"Five years then. At least, you decided we agreed. And then you telephone me Saturday out of nowhere and you fly out here yesterday. A union bar in Detroit. Which is fine with me, Greta. I'd meet you anywhere." He looks directly into my face, takes his hand from mine, and brushes the hair that has fallen across my right eye. "You're still splendid-looking."

"I'm too old to be splendid-looking. In two months, I'll be forty. Did you know that Frederick, my oldest, is in his second year at Dartmouth?"

"Dartmouth," Marty repeats, uncomprehending.

"If you look closely, you'll notice the crow's feet in the corners of my eyes. There's a touch of silver in my hair now. I dye it weekly. That's the way it is with Swedes. They go bit by bit. A matter of erosion." Marty laughs. "You laugh so pleasantly, Marty."

"Like Barney?"

No embarrassment in his question. We are two old lovers who no longer need even the affirmations their bodies once provided each other. But we can afford to be gentle now. "With Barney, even laughter was a political thing." Marty slaps his thigh, as if I had said something particularly clever. "Still, you know, he enjoyed laughter. When we were first married he did. It's simply that after a while there wasn't much room for it. Not with Barney."

Marty signals the bartender, who brings another Scotch straight up, water on the side. The bartender takes the empty glasses. Marty observes me observing him. He shrugs. "The life of an organizer. There's nothing for it that's better."

I touch the glass of wine that has been standing in front of me. "Will they watch the hearings?"

"This used to be a political bar. Used to be a lot of talk. Union talk." He takes another sip of the Scotch, puts the glass back on the table, stares at it, then picks it up again and empties it. "To hell with it," he mutters. "You're not drinking, Greta."

"I saw enough of it with my father. Even my uncle. Drink really is the curse of our class. It's not just one of their stories."

"To hell with that, too," Marty says. "It's a world without virtue. If there was a game this afternoon, they'd tune that in. But there is no game. And I asked Tommy." He rubs his hands together, as if he were cold. "So we'll get the hearing. But what's the difference? Even politically? We're in-between, Greta. For people like us, there was a time when resistance could be what we stood against. Like trying to create a Left independent of the party. So what's Left now? The party's an obscenity. But what's able to take its place? The Right's never been happier. They couldn't have dreamed of a comeback like this."

"Will they make a martyr of Barney?"

He waves his right hand in the air. "Who's he going to be a martyr for? The party is such a Charlie McCarthy, even its heroes become jokes. Still, if he does as well as Gold of the furriers, he'll be all right. Just the truth. That's all." He shakes his head. Sighs. "Look at our choices. The people who've made careers out of following every twist in the party's line because they can't envision living without it. And these congressional bastards on the other side. What kind of martyrdom is that? It's a hell of a country, Greta. Eats your heart out, then winks like a Mississippi whore to let you know it's one more game to be played. And we're all supposed to be in on it.

"But what will happen to Barney?"

"Technically," Marty answers, "there's not much they can do to him. He left the party when they passed Taft-Hartley. Like some other party labor people. He wanted to remain head of the union and the law said he couldn't do that and remain in the party. He makes no bones about where he stands. After he resigned from the party, he testified in Washington in favor of a change in the law. Only our conservatives in Congress, they're getting smarter. They let him talk. 'At heart,' he tells them, 'I'm still a Communist. I've quit the party because the laws you've made say it's illegal for a trade union leader to belong to the Communist party. It's a slave-labor law. But it's the law you gentlemen made. So I quit. In my heart and mind, I'm still part of the struggle of the American working class for emancipation.' If they'd given him a script, they couldn't have asked for better."

"You've memorized his words."

"It's not difficult, Greta. The same speech all of them make. Charlie McCarthy." He pushes up from the table. "I've got to go to the john." He moves away from the table and disappears into the back.

I want to cry. But not for Barney Kadish, lost husband, long-ago lover. I am not worried about Barney Kadish. And I am not worried about the only one I can remember loving after Barney. Marty and I read each other's needs too well by now. It is good that we never married.

I balance my life out. What I want is to cry for myself. But I am beyond that now. You look back and you judge your relationships to memories that burn like fireflies in your mind. Burn and then burn out and then burn again. A professional onlooker. Greta Hedwig Edmundson Kadish. Age: 40. Race: Caucasian. Religion: Atheist. Politics: Compassion for her own past. Lovers: Taken from the Left. Or the ex-Left. Or the Left that is by now so choked on itself that it defines what it is by insisting what it wasn't. If I could weep for Barney Kadish, that, too, would be a lie. Marty might not know which side he was on. I knew. I could see Barney and the congressmen who would pull at his life like jackals as, finally, each embodying that same self-seeking that went to the heart of all politics. Whatever compassion his life evoked would burn itself off in my growing rage at what he had permitted them to make of that life. Barney Kadish, whose courage would inevitably check him up short, force him back to the party's orthodoxy for his schooling; Barney Kadish, in whom the prophetic vision came down to a seminarian ransacking biblical texts in the hope of countering his own growing disbelief; Barney Kadish, who still believed that repetition of the proper words was like a magical incantation, that he could defend himself as a child recites his ABCs and thrust heart and mind and soul into the dead center of belief. Defeat and victory blend, tied to the question of how long Barney Kadish could refuse to give in.

And be satisfied to define himself in negatives? *Not* to be a sellout. *Not* to be excommunicated from their holy center. *Not* to give in to those who wanted to buy him, who wanted to deny him the self-respect that comes from knowing you have defied your inquisitors, so that even loyalty to class could be reduced to the need to hold on to the self he cherished. And to triumph in the midst of his own righteousness, like some old-fashioned preacher whose life is tempered by the idea of martyrdom. The last gift of the party—a sense of how strong you had been in resistance.

Marty is back at the bar now. The bartender leans over the bar, listens to him as men listen to other men they respect. He wipes the mahogany with the dishcloth in his right hand, ear cocked to Marty's whispering. I cannot take my eyes from the hand going round and round, rubbing the beer-stained mahogany down to the grain. Then he turns, switches on the television set, nods to Marty. At the bar, there are four solitary drinkers. Their backs are to me, but I can see their passive faces in the mirror.

"It's due in five minutes," Marty explains, when he returns to our table.

"You told me it was a union bar. Why did he need urging?"

"It's 1951, Greta," Marty answers. "Not 1937. These men are politically homeless. Like you and me."

"I'm not homeless."

"You've got no place to go. None of us has any place to go. At least, Barney has his fight."

"I'm not homeless," I insist.

"Watch the screen," he commands. "The Holy Ghost himself in a minute. And all the struggling devils."

"I'm not homeless," I repeat again, aware now of the salt of tears, strangely unashamed, as I fold my hands on the table before me.

Marty takes my hand, like a gypsy fortune-teller. "Okay," he says. "You're not homeless. He'll be all right. He has his discipline. What do those congressional bastards have?"

"I want another drink."

"You haven't touched your last one," he says. I pick the glass of wine up with my free hand and drink it down. I cannot taste it. Marty signals the bartender, who glides over to our table without seeming to move. "You'll hate yourself if you got sick."

"I won't get sick," I say.

On the screen, a picture of the Federal Building in New York City. The announcer's voice locates the audience. The camera pans the room. It stops to close in on Barney, sitting in the center of a long table with five or six chairs around it. Flanking Barney are John Hudson's son, John Hudson III, who has now taken over the running of union legal affairs from his aging but still-living father, and Gus Constantinou, who is still Barney's lieutenant. Behind them sits another battery of lawyers and union officials. I catch brief glimpses of the aging faces of Itzik Perlin and the Shapiro twins. Men in their fifties now. The camera shifts to the faces of the congressmen, who have just taken their seats. Self-consciously serious faces, determined to reflect the weight of their mission—to save the republic. They look like a group being instructed in how to pose for a portrait. At this moment in history, they are defenders of the national virtue.

Suddenly, I am swept up in a wave of pity for Barney, like the rush of nausea after too much drinking. He deserves better. These men exist for each other and for the cameras. They seat themselves stiffly, awkwardly, as if the very roles they were called upon to play fill them with dread. Performances are not to be hurried. It takes a full five minutes for the committee members to sit down. How much more appealing if in the middle of panning their stiff faces the camera were to capture a wink, a smile, some simple recognition that even in 1951 there are more important ways to save the nation's virtue. Instead, their faces reflect the gravity of the threat facing the republic.

"The Reds are coming!" one of the men at the bar calls out. Even the bartender laughs.

"God," Marty says, "look at those faces and you'd think it's a convention of undertakers."

"Yeah," another voice from the bar cries. "And each one of the bastards is trying to become a funeral director."

The chief counsel to the head of the Congressional Subcommittee Investigating Subversive Influences in the American Labor Movement leans over and says something in the ear of his congressional superior. The congressman nods, then bangs his gavel on the table like a Bourbon judge. "Call to order!" he cries out.

"Call to order!" an aide echoes.

"I hope Barney's enjoying it," Marty says to me. He deserves something out of this." His hand covers my own on the table. He seems suddenly happy, as if he were sharing a place with Barney, a place I am no longer able to share. I stare at the screen. Shots of one congressman or another interspersed with shots of Barney Kadish, the eyepatch like a mask designed to reflect the voices of the congressmen. Congressman Carter of Tennessee, the committee chairman, takes a glass of water, then clears his throat. The bar quiets, except for a newcomer who takes a seat and claps.

"We all know what it is we're here for?" Congressman Carter says. His voice is soft and Southern. "Mr. Kadish, are you ready to testify?"

"I have a statement to read first, Congressman," Barney says. I am surprised at the sound of his voice. It is as if he were trying to imitate Congressman Carter.

"We don't want any statements right now, Mr. Kadish. This committee's taking up enough tax money as it is."

"It's my right to read my statement into the record. I've been informed it's my right by counsel."

"This is not a trial, Congressman Carter," John Hudson III interrupts. "And I respectfully submit that you're not a presiding judge."

Congressman Carter's flat dry features seem to grow smaller as he peers through his glasses at John Hudson III. "That doesn't seem to have prevented Mr. Kadish from bringing you along, has it?" he says, voice still soft and civilized.

"My client has the right to counsel. Particularly since this hearing is a form of political intimidation contrary both to American law and to American political tradition. You know that as well as I do. Mr. Kadish's only sin is—"

"No one's accused your client of sin, Mr. Hudson," bellows a skinny Republican congressman from Indiana, Herb Borkum. Borkum's voice quivers in the air, like taut rubber, so that I expect it to break in midsentence. "But I admit," he continues, "that I'm surprised to hear one of your client's kind invoke the idea of sin." A nervous giggle drifts through the hearing. Encouraged by what he takes to be approval, Congressman Borkum turns to Barney. "I am correct in believing that your kind don't accept the existence of the Lord, Mr. Kadish?"

"My kind," Barney responds, "are free to believe what we want to believe. Just like congressmen. But we've been cautioned about God. Not to expect him to do our work."

Annoyed, Congressman Borkum replies, "In Indiana, Mr. Kadish, we know just what to do with your kind."

"Congressman Carter," John Hudson III says, his right forefinger pointing at Borkum's chest, "in a court of law you would be obligated to disqualify the gentleman from Indiana as obviously prejudicial to the interests of my client."

A murmur of approval from the men sitting at the bar. Congressman Carter wipes his glasses. "This isn't a court of law, Mr. Hudson," He sighs. "As you know. It's simply an investigation."

"Then perhaps you would be good enough to tell us exactly what my client stands accused of."

"Your client isn't really *accused* of anything, Mr. Hudson. By his own admission, Mr. Kadish is sympathetic to the aims of the American Communist party. The task of our subcommittee is to probe the influence that party has had upon the organized labor movement in this country." From the bar, one of the men holds his fingers to his nose and farts with his tongue. "Isn't it true, Mr. Hudson, that Mr. Kadish has had considerable influence upon the labor movement in this country? Particularly upon the formation of the CIO?"

"Why don't we let Mr. Kadish address himself to that?" Congressman Jencks of Massachusetts suggests. Jencks is a rangy man, whose face is as cragged and attractively ugly as the face on the Lincoln penny. He has a reputation as a defender of civil liberties, an old-fashioned Republican conservative in whom John Hudson III's father would have recognized a friend. He sits purposefully distant from his fellows, as if he were intent on establishing a separate identity.

"If Barney's still got the brains God gave him, he'll mark that Jencks down. He'll try to get him both ways," Marty whispers to me.

"I'll be happy to tell you what I can," Barney responds. John Hudson III whispers something in his ear. Barney frowns. "Only I'm not certain of exactly what point it is you want me to address."

"Well, I suppose we might as well begin with your telling us whether or not you are a Communist. And then I suppose we can take it from there."

Barney pauses, eyes Congressman Jencks for a half minute or so before he continues. "My counsel tells me that I have the right to take the Fifth Amendment on that. I'm tempted, Congressman Jencks. I don't think you really should ask me that. But I'm not going to take the Fifth."

"Admirable, Mr. Kadish."

"I'm no longer a member of the party. But I am sympathetic to its aims. When the Taft-Hartley Act was passed, I left the party. But only because I couldn't remain as president of the union if I didn't leave. Gold of the furriers did the same thing. So did . . ."

"By that, Mr. Kadish," Congressman Carter interrupts (eager to return to command of the hearing), "are we to assume that you are still, ahhh, philosophically, a Communist?"

"I'm still part of that movement which calls for the liberation of the working class."

"Which makes you a Communist," chirps Congressman Borkum. Barney doesn't answer, other than to examine Borkum as though he were an insect mounted on a slide. "Doesn't it? Doesn't it make you a Communist?"

"It makes me sympathetic to the aims of the party which is in the vanguard of the struggle of the working class. In this country. In all countries. If that is how you choose to phrase it, Mr. Congressman, I have no substantial objections."

"Is it fair," interrupts Congressman Jencks, his voice dripping with distaste for Borkum, "to say that you would have remained a member of the Communist party of the United States but for the requirements set down by enactment of the Taft-Hartley Act?"

"Congressman Jencks," John Hudson III angrily snaps, "you're experienced enough in the law to know that my client cannot be expected to incriminate himself."

Barney's hand clamps viselike but gently across his lawyer's forearm. The camera catches the gesture. Barney smiles. "Do you want a confession, Congressman Jencks? Or is a simple statement of opinion sufficient?"

Jencks smiles, as if he is enjoying himself. "Either way, Mr. Kadish. I'm not really particular. But you have to recognize that this committee has its function, too. I don't want anyone to think that you're being railroaded. But I suppose we do have some legitimate interests here."

Borkum leans forward in his chair, the glasses folded in his right hand thrust forward like a teacher's pointer. "You may not understand the mandate of this committee, Mr. Kadish. That doesn't mean that those of us serving on it have to call its validity into question." His voice is even tighter than it was earlier.

A pause. "I never assumed that was the case, Congressman," Barney answers. "You've certainly established your validity, haven't you?"

"Without permission from you, Mr. Kadish."

"Or my kind," Barney adds.

"I didn't say that," Borkum objects.

"No, you didn't," Barney admits. "But I don't know how valid you are for me. Or for any other trade unionist whose interests are the interests of the working class."

I could have invented them. They are two strays sniffing around each other. Barney is defiant, like a wounded animal.

His time is passing. Marty's hand holds my arm pressed to the table. Marty wants to protect me, to keep me from harm's way. To love me. Barney, too, once loved me. In my mind, I wake up. Early morning. Frederick's cry identifies the morning and the warmth of my husband's body reinforces the warmth of the sun falling across the bed. Quiet affirmations linger in memories of the night before. I move toward the memories, the luxury of half-remembered sleep, the sex distant, absorbed.

In distance, the mind seduces itself. On the screen above the bar, a fifty-one-year-old man reflects contempt for what has by now already defeated him. Barney Kadish knows this. As I know it. As Marty knows it. As the men sitting at the bar know it. For them, too, Flint may strike the curled wick of memory. But their memories are passive now, an acquiescence to fate. They sit at the bar and nurse their drinks and eye the habits of loyalty and virtue paraded before them on the screen. The committee is interested in their loyalty to America, although it is Barney the committee questions. The men at the bar can only surface like dying fish into old wants and older memories. Reality demands of them, too. When was the last time they could assume that to be a working man was important? It is important now. Barney must face down a middle-aged congressman from Tennessee, a blustering congressman from Indiana, a shrewd and amused congressman from Massachusetts. Barney's quests. To prove that he is American enough to face those whom he must despise.

"Kick the sons of bitches in the ass!" cries the oldest worker sitting at the bar. But this is 1951. And in 1951 it is difficult to tell exactly who the sons of bitches are. Yes, he has his memories, perhaps of Barney himself standing alongside him in Flint. And yet, the moment recedes, embalmed in a different time, when men were braver and life was simpler and their wives wrapped sandwiches in letters from their fellow workers urging them to stand, hold, so that for one single moment at least they might know themselves as men. All of them. And Barney Kadish, my husband then, had helped teach them that. "In the ass!" the man at the bar repeats. "Hoosier fuck."

And if Barney is the braver monkey, he is, like the congressmen who sit opposite him, still only one monkey among many. Barney Kadish, ex-husband, one-time lover, whose life now seems to have shrunk to the limits of a show of defiance. Barney wants the worker at the bar to know he is a hero. Marty has guessed right there. Were Barney and the congressmen on the committee acting out an agreed-upon script, they could not have been more predictable. Each monkey to its stance. Each mind brushes itself off for the camera, rehearses for posterity, for that future which will judge the past.

"Easy, Greta." To the sound of Marty's voice, I taste my tears again. All of my life, I have despised exactly that, the idea instilled by birth. As if politics, too, were no more than a way of robbing biology. Marty wants to protect me. Instinct prevails. The warning bell goes off in my imagination. Alarms in a Detroit bar. The congressman from Tennessee is talking now, but I feel myself slipping back into darkness. I do not understand the words, do not understand what my involvement is with these people in the bar, with these pictures on the screen. I try to think of my sons, grown to manhood. Even Isaac is seventeen now. But then the mind blacks out. I want simply to trade places with an animal in its lair. I despise the human. Marty sits next to me, protective, tender. Noting my tears as if each suspended his past over this American void. "Easy, Greta. My poor darling."

I want to scream at him. I fight the urge to cry out, to tell him I do not want to be loved. I do not want compassion, I do not want protection. All that is human repels me. All words seem patent, predictable, hurled into the emptiness. Sponge and softness. For the first time in my life, I want desperately to destroy. I pull my hand from Marty's. I dry my eyes with a handkerchief, stare once again at the screen. Barney speaks. "You want me to admit to your record. All right. Gladly. Whatever my life claims of value is a product of everything you gentlemen want to destroy. You want to know what the influence of the Communist party was on the founding of the CIO. I can't answer that. But I can speak about what the CIO meant to me. You want to make us out to be conspirators. But conspiracies exist in your minds alone."

"Are you trying to tell this committee, Mr. Kadish, that the Communist party in America doesn't take its orders direct and straight from its overlords in Moscow?" Congressman Borkum seizes the monkey's ladder. He swings on the ladder. At the bar, the oldest of the men snorts again. He sips at his drink.

"Fucking Hoosiers," he says to no one in particular. "Salt of the fucking earth. American Legion. Shit in red, white, and blue." His head drops into his hands and his lips kiss the mahogany bar. But he is not really drunk.

I am slipping back into myself once again. I try for the moment to block the voices out, as if I can anchor myself to a world beyond the television set. But I have come here to watch the hearing. The world's definition in a cathode tube. Marty is saying something. But I cannot hear him. On the screen, Barney pulls his breath in, like a swimmer about to plunge into a race. "You listen to your own propaganda, Congressman Borkum. I have no overlords in Moscow. No one I know has an overlord in Moscow."

"Has there ever been a time when American Communists have been permitted to disagree with their superiors in Moscow?" Barney sighs, closes his eyes. "Was there? Just tell me."

"If you could listen to—" Barney begins.

"Nevermind *my* being able to listen, Mr. Kadish. Or maybe I should say *Comrade* Kadish." Thin as he is, Congressman Borkum sweats beneath the klieg lights. The anger in his voice seems surprisingly genuine.

"Mr. Chairman," interrupts Jencks of Massachusetts. "I must ask that Mr. Kadish be allowed to answer my distinguished Indiana colleague's questions. There is such a thing as the dignity of this Congress to consider."

"And I'd like to remind my distinguished colleague from the great state of Massachusetts," angrily declares Borkum, "that this witness is part of a worldwide conspiracy which has nothing but contempt for anyone's right to speak."

"All the more reason, Congressman Borkum," says Jencks patiently, without a shade of irony touching his voice, "that we permit this witness to answer the questions." Borkum is caught by the camera, his face drawn into a theatrical sneer. Jencks smiles, then adds, "Who knows? Being part of the democratic process may convert him."

At the hearing, laughter. Even Borkum is forced by the camera to acknowledge Jencks with a smile. From the bar, the oldest of the men says, "Not bad for a Yankee son of a bitch."

"Where's he on Taft-Hartley?"

"In hell. With all the rest."

Congressman Carter from Tennessee bangs his gavel on the desk. "Mr. Kadish does have the right to answer. I must remind my distinguished colleague from Indiana that as long as I'm chairing this hearing, everyone is going to have the right to speak his piece. Now I suggest we get moving along."

"With all due haste, Mr. Chairman," Jencks laconically adds. Borkum is silent. His hands fold into each other as he stares at the ceiling. The camera follows him.

"Continue, Mr. Kadish," Carter says.

"I was trying to say, Mr. Chairman, that I've never known anyone who was sent by Moscow to infiltrate the American trade union movement."

"But you admire the Soviet Union?" Borkum asks. "And

you've known plenty of people who share that admiration with you."

Barney sighs. "I certainly do. The Soviet Union, the People's Democratic Republic of China, the socialist countries that have emerged since the war in Eastern Europe, I believe all these countries promise more to working men and women than a system such as capitalism."

"Are you calling for the destruction of the United States?" Borkum snarls.

"I'm calling for change in the United States," Barney answers. "I live here. No matter what you may believe, I'm not ungrateful to the United States. But I want a country in which the working class gets a better shake. I want a socialist country because socialism is justice for the workers. I don't expect you to understand that. But it's what I want."

"He'll ignore death itself," Marty says. "So long as he can score points for the party."

The screen flickers. I think of Barney's needs. Marty is right. Barney will do anything to prove himself worthy. The need is sucked into his rage. Admiration engulfs him, even at this remote electronic distance. A socialist hero. Does he feel the pulsations in this Detroit bar from the older half-drunk man chortling to the screen. "Tell the bastards, Barney. Give all of them a what for." The admiration of working people has come down, for Barney Kadish, to lone drunks in bars like this. Well, neither Marty nor I can deny him such affirmations. He is on display, along with the congressmen. There is neither drama nor tension, and the question of whether or not Barney Kadish will come through has been answered. The self will remain intact. Barney will survive. It is among the things he knows how to do.

I stand up. "I want to leave," I tell Marty.

"It'll be going on for a while, Greta."

"To your place, Marty." I am crying again. "I want to get

out of here and I don't want to go back to the hotel. Please."

Marty stands. He takes my arm, acknowledges the bartender with an abbreviated wave of his hand. As we leave the bar, the last thing I see is the face of my ex-husband, Barney Kadish, once again bending his mind to the task before him with all the fervor of a trapped man who knows he has nothing left to lose. Barney talks, talks into the camera, into the future he so desperately wants. At the bar, the drunk union man listens.

7

Marty sleeps. We have finished making love, a silent, harsh, open taking of each other. Habits dictate to our bodies. There is neither joy nor passion. Still, we acknowledge what time we possess. We must make love. We have made love. The pressure has eased. Marty does not own a television set. His radio is broken. I am grateful for the silence. The shades are drawn. I no longer know whether it is night or day.

A small clean apartment in a Polish section of Detroit. A place away from places. Marty's place. The bed narrower than it should be for two, as if I had to adjust to Marty's definition of himself even as we make love. Marty is a loner. It is good that we didn't marry, that I refused him those six years past.

I sit in a wooden armchair across from the bed. I am wearing Marty's dark brown bathrobe. I am sitting on Marty's pants, which he has thrown across the chair. Marty breathes deeply. He does not snore. Barney did not snore. My father snored. I remember little enough about my father. I remember how he looked. And I remember that he snored.

I close my eyes. I imagine a harvest moon outside. Like

in Minnesota. The times when sex was juiciest, when the Swedes managed to drown their inhibitions, their mechanical struttings, in the fleeting recognition that time was, indeed, far shorter than even good Lutherans might believe. Live for the moment. A lesson never learned.

"He's a vain man," Marty said, as we sat in the taxi driving home. Yes, a vain man. And a bit pompous, too. "I want a socialist country because socialism is justice for the workers." As neat as a puff of smoke in a movie. The father fathered. Or fathering himself.

Marty sleeps. Does he dream of me? Or of the days when he and Barney were young, before I knew them? When the enemy took the names of Heinrich and Bilsky and Minschin and the woman loved was Lisa and good and evil must have seemed clear and simple, yes, even to Marty, a glowing geometry of the emotions. This for the future, this for the past, here future and past and present joined together. So that men might envision the future beyond the future. A justice. So available then. For each of us.

What did we need, Barney and I? To steal a different fate for ourselves? Was there really a time when my own need for the party's approval matched his? Or was it merely the way I searched for a place for Greta Hedwig Edmundson? At the end, my Uncle Paul wanted nothing more than to obliterate the memories of those beatings. "I am not a brave man, Greta." Sobbing in my arms. Barney would not have broken so. Not with a witness in front of him. Not in private either.

Still, he could be gentle with those who were broken. Was gentle. Was. Even Marty admits that. You marry out of your own expectations and then you wake up one morning and you discover that you must defend the bargain, learn about this stranger.

The lines strengthen. And strengthen. The enemy grows bolder. Barney's past still pursues me, even as I sit in this chair, the touch of Marty lingering on my body. I am pressed to the very edge of memory. I open my eyes. I want something to happen. I want something to drive Barney Kadish from my mind. My mind battles, races, seeks connections. Twists of the possible. Like a drugged zombie, I search.

In bed, in the light cast from the lamp above me, Marty's face is content. Light and all, Marty sleeps. A clear conscience. That first night, when Barney came into me and I found myself staring into the black leather patch and did not see and yet saw what there was and took the weight of him in the absence of choice. How I loved him then. My body reaching for whatever he was able to offer. In the hollow of his shoulders, nestled into protection, I push past the touch of him, past our two bodies struggling to get beyond the memory of the self. Before sons. Before the self that ascended its own summit and cried out for the world, "Listen to me! I'm Barney Kadish."

In memory then. Barney in the flesh. And Greta in the flesh. Each searching for the other. And still loving him now. Mixed with all that enrages me, a part remains. And I want to tell you, Barney, to carry us once again past that edge of disbelief. I want you to remember that first time. And the good times after. Drive inside me, Barney. Again.

Marty sleeps.

Lisa

1

As dusk falls, I take the leather box from its resting place on the window ledge above the corner table and leave the trailer. Saandia has already been sucked into twilight, a massive darkening purple clarity, the way Barney loved it all through those final years. Dinner ended, I would walk behind him from the trailer to the dusty patch of dirt and grass fat Mildred Clayhorn insisted on calling "the garden" every time I stopped in the office to ask why the water pumps worked so spasmodically between ten and twelve each morning.

"Low pressure, missus," says fat Mildred Clayhorn. Her chins bubble into each other. Mildred Clayhorn and her husband own and operate the Saandia Shangri-La Trailer Park, where Barney Kadish and I live during the final four years of his life.

"I'm the sociable one," fat Mildred tells the delivery boy, "the one what keeps it all going. Buck, he don't know diddlie about how to treat folks. I always liked to be sociable. Even back in high school in Grants. All them boys." Fat Mildred laughs.

"Low pressure's the problem we folks got here in New

Mexico. Back East, you people got too many folks, too much water. Here, we ain't got enough of either." Having drawn me into a conspiracy of understanding, Mildred Clayhorn winks. Her chins wobble. "How's the garden?" I smile, retreat back to Barney sitting in the dirt patch. I am amazed once again at the depths of illusion we will each other.

Broken like a reed, Barney waited. But not for death. Just for time to pass. He was never impatient where death was concerned. It would take him soon enough. A hard, methodical mind, each arrangement in its proper place. Even the past was a contract of sorts. And Barney Kadish sat in the chair in the garden and reviewed the past. Staring up at Saandia, he controls his own floating, reviews sequences of glory lost. Memories march past his review with military precision.

He sits on the folding gun-metal bridge chair he prefers to the plastic-roped yellow and green lounger I offer him. "Do you remember that time you set Minschin's Hats up? Just before you left New York. A woman like you were then. . . . You could do anything." Eye closed, drifting back into ordered remembering, he frightens me. All through the last years, Barney Kadish balances accounts. Withered body drawn in, husbanding its resources as he struggles with death's imminence. The attacks a ceaseless ten-year war, so that by 1968, as he waits for the final one, he has come to look upon each attack as a personal enemy, a witness to his obligations. "It's war, Lisa. You plan for it, like you plan for a strike. Only I've got to plan correctly. Not like the last time with Leftwich." I brew a cup of tea in the trailer, bring it outside so that he can drink in the sun. He smiles, sweats the sweat of the sick and dying, laughs sparingly. Resources must be held back for when they are needed. The final lesson in the radical's catechism.

As his body breaks down, his mind commands discipline. He is like an army general poring over maps pinned to the canvas walls of his tent. But this is Barney Kadish's mind and memory. So little instinct in a life to be measured out. In the sun, Barney Kadish sits and sweats and drinks tea. And remembers.

2

And now, refined down to a small sack of ashes inside a leather Florentine jewel box given to me by Michelle, the daughter I left in Los Angeles when Barney Kadish emerged out of his need and my obligations on a sun-drenched afternoon in October 1953. Bourgeois spoils brought back in 1963 from a Smith junior-year-abroad in Rome. My lovely Michelle with the straight black hair sits with me and Barney in the small pink adobe house we are renting in a box canyon outside of Gallup. My Michelle has absorbed her manners with her view of civilization. "It's splendid country," she says eagerly, as she stares into the endless dead space broken only by the baked mesas where the red clay has dried out to the rattle of time. She is still young enough so that she can tell herself that country can be splendid only if it is empty. On Saturday night, she sits next to me in the Plymouth as we drive into Gallup. Barney sits in the rear. The streets are thick with drunken Indians and their equally drunken white caretakers and howling college boys from New York and Boston who eye Michelle as if she were the rush of danger they traveled west for. My life now provides my daughter with enough romance so that her imagination thinks she forgives me for getting up and walking out. "A week after my tenth birthday," she says with wistful pride. "It took guts, Mom, for you to leave like that." Empty space. Cruel sun baking the world from overhead. 102°, 103°, 104°—like tokens of endurance the natives bequeath themselves. "It's dry heat," she says. "Like in Los Angeles." College girl wisdom. Barney sits in the back, in silence. His own sons are mere names. By 1963, he cannot even visualize them—not even Isaac, the one he talked about in the beginning.

Florentine craftsmen ply their wares for the tourist dollar. "I bought it in a little shop off the Ponte Vecchio," Michelle explains, pointing out the gold-leaf tooling in the design. The leather has been dyed deep blue, a series of evenly spaced gold fleurs-de-lis covering its strategic face. "Hand-tooled, Mother. They do such splendid work."

Michelle turns in the old Plymouth to stare at Barney who sits in his silence and sweat in the back seat. I am angry with Barney. He hates my past without him. And Michelle is living proof of that past. What did he suppose? That I had come back to him out of need? He had no right to expect so much. And yet, I *had* come back—because Barney Kadish expected to be taken in, needed to be helped.

"What do I call you, Mr. Kadish?" Michelle asks softly. Barney stares at her, wets his lips. I see him in the rear-view mirror. Years ago, he stared at so many others like that. I am not offended.

"Barney," I interrupt. "Just call him Barney."

"Is that acceptable?" Michelle says to him.

"It's all right," Barney says hoarsely. "If it's all right with your mother. Call me Barney."

The leather box is the gift of a daughter forgiving her mother. Arthur's daughter. Not Barney's. Even as her generation drifts out of its boredom to resurrect our dreams, my Michelle holds the proprieties at her fingertips. She has obligations—to herself, to her father, to her two brothers. And to the woman her father married four years after I left him, the woman she later tells me, embarrassed at so intimate a confession, she calls, "Mother Kate."

And I once again remember Arthur, whom I loved enough to leave. I wonder whether he still puzzles over the Lisa he took as his wife off the Metro-Goldwyn-Mayer lot in 1935. (No eager starlet for Arthur Pankow, just a twenty-nine-year-old seamstress with a certain reputation for competence and craft on the studio back lots.) An achievement. The dark serious face, so markedly out of place as it searches the studio back lots. All sin and energy and talk in the back lots. Grubby little egos seeking their twins. The up-and-coming young actor who insists that we lunch together—nevermind that he has just signed a seven-year contract with the studio, is rumored to be the next western box-office draw, the deep voice back in the throat, the promise of timing and expectation. How bored I am as he explains studio politics, discusses salaries, diagrams his relationship to Louis B. himself in the studio commissary as if I were incapable of understanding so complex a magic without benefit of maps drawn on white paper tablecloths. He asks about left-wing politics in New York, pretends interest in the party when all he is really interested in is translating the Left to the world in which he lives so intensely. Who is X sleeping with? What do party people think of love?

"When will I see you again?" the actor asks from the seat of his white sports roadster. He holds my hand in his. His immaculately handsome face centers itself on me.

"Hopefully, never," I say. And disappear into the small house I share with three other women from New York.

Ultimately, I choose Arthur Pankow. Or at least give in to being chosen by him. A serious dignified pharmacist who has landed, quite by accident, in Los Angeles, Arthur is struggling to rid himself of the memory of the woman he had married seven years earlier only to discover that he could be little more to her than a companion, watching her drift away as the disease for which the doctors do not even have a name captures her, seals her in bed. "Anne was delicate. Even before she grew sick. I tried to be good to her. When she died, there was nothing to hold me in Philadelphia. I picked up and came out here. Bought a drugstore on Fairfax Avenue. There's been no one since Anne, Lisa. A few women for sex. But no one really." The flush of embarrassment mars the seriousness of the confession. Years later, I will see it once again, when Michelle hands me the leather box with the gold fleurs-de-lis and her face darkens, only to break into a smile almost beatific as it touches the absent mother.

And yet, I ran from Arthur. Was I doomed always to run from those I loved? Not wanting the siege, the relentlessness of his pursuit. I spend three months fighting with a thirty-year-old lawyer who insists he is a Communist and who supports himself by milking the studios for contracts, assuring me as we dine at the Brown Derby that it is simply a matter of picking capitalist pockets to provide the party with what it needs.

"And what does it need?" I ask, tasting the mixture of his assurance and my skepticism with each mouthful of baked Colorado baby trout.

"That we recognize necessity. Money breeds the possibility of truth, Lisa. Even for a Marxist. Do you understand?"

And I am almost past the hatcheck girl as I parry, "I understand. All too well."

3

I put the box down carefully on the seat next to the driver's. I turn the key in the ignition and the Mustang responds with its customary roar. "Money breeds the possibility of truth, Lisa. Even for a Marxist." Well, Barney Kadish would have understood that. I understand it, too. On the seventh of every month, without fail, a money order in my mailbox. No matter where we are living—Gallup, Albuquerque, the six months in Tucson, I open the mailbox and discover Arthur's reminder of my desertion. Except when the seventh is a Sunday, when the money order arrives a day earlier. For the first five years, there is no word from my children, not even a note, until Michelle sends me a birthday card in 1958. By the following year, Daniel and Ezra, grown men now, write to me. They each visit me, dutifully distant but forgiving to their mother, so that I sense their father behind their pilgrimages. To create what is right, to do the decent thing. "The human obligation," Arthur used to call it. Distant even from his sympathies. No lover of the working class or of the future was Arthur Pankow. He asks for little more than decency, competence, a grasp of what is possible in this world.

The darkness has overwhelmed the twilight now. The purple is absorbed in a solid deep blue curtain exploding with stars. Instinctively, I slide off Route 66 to 14 North. I am heading in the direction of the mountain itself. Just before the intersection that leads up to Saandia, I turn right and drop down into the winding road. The road is jutted by rocks and broken paving, but I head toward the darker mountains. The moon-ripped landscape is precipitous, but I take it in drive and press down on the gas as soon as the level stretch of road comes up. The dark smothers 14 South and I drive by instinct, the high beams of the Mustang's lights slicing the world.

I feel no fear. These are the places Barney loved. I know the small Chicano towns lit by a single streetlamp outside the church even without seeing them. I drive through Chillili, past Monzano, Tesuque, Ysiddro, the pressing silence broken only by the whinny of a lone horse. I smell the bursting piñon cones. As I sweep past it, the tin roof of the Catholic church in Tesuque reflects the word's leveling. I remember how Barney loved that roof. I loved it, too, for what it gave him. We would picnic in the mountains and he would lie on the grass, studying the Rocky Mountain jays that would strut right past us, breathing deeply of the piñon-scented air. Barney would invariably fall asleep on the grass and later I would wake him up and the two of us would get back into the car and drive through Chillili, past the Catholic church in Tesuque, the tin roof shining in the sun, drive all the way to Preston to eat pie and homemade ice cream in the restaurant where nobody spoke. It was new for Barney. It was new for me, too. It amazed him to discover that there existed an America that stood light years removed from the problems of garment workers in New York. Maybe that was why we remained in New Mexico. The government was more or less willing to leave Barney Kadish alone by that time. And the mountains pulled at something in him he had never known existed. As close to peace as a man like Barney was allowed to come, even with the heart attacks at two year intervals.

In Preston, I pull up at the restaurant. There is a hitching rail directly in front of it, a piece of leftover Americana that has failed to make of this quiet cattle town one more tourist attraction in a country in which movement guarantees the absence of history. I have been driving for two hours on 14 South. The Saandia Shangri-La is more than sixty miles of difficult road north of here. I take the leather box from its seat beside me and place it under my arm. Memory quickens. Quite suddenly, I am in bed with Howard. The pain is too pungent, a spicy guilt that fills me to the point of choking and then passes to leave me empty. I never spoke to Barney about it. After he returned, he wouldn't ask me either. One death as easy as another. There is a discipline to it all. And I have discipline, I remind myself, as I walk up the two steps to the wooden sidewalk and turn to eye the Mustang standing in lifeless darkness in front of the hitching rail.

Would Howard have been as amused by it all as Barney

was? Stroking the rail as if it were a young girl, searching for connections to what he called "this giant America." And insisting on loving the smoky, wood-stained light of the Gran Arriola Bar and Restaurant, Glen Higgens, Prop. In all the time we have been coming here, Glen Higgens has never acknowledged our existence other than by a brief nod of his head when we enter. As I walk into the restaurant this time, with the leather box under my arm, Mr. Glen Higgens does not ask me Barney's whereabouts. He nods his head, continues counting at the cash register to the left of the bar. The bartender nods as I pass him and make my way to a table in the corner. I don't know whether or not he links me to Barney, but he, too, does not ask about him. Above the bartender's head, tacked to the shellacked knotty pine wall, a calendar stands out from a drawing which links a pitchfork and a spoked wagon wheel. The calendar is a gift of the local blacksmith shop, which now repairs both tractors and automobiles. Next to that, nailed into the knotty pine wall, is a wooden plaque into which has been burned:

DON'T LET YOUR PARENTS DOWN—
THEY BROUGHT YOU UP!

The bulletin board above the men's room contains two notices, one about a rodeo in Durvale that occurred a month earlier and another about the polio-immunization program jointly sponsored by the Preston School Board and the Preston United Church of Christ Women's Auxiliary.

I sit down in front of a table shaped like a barrel covered by a red-and-white checkered oilcloth. I remember how much Barney loved these tables. I place the leather box on the chair next to my own. The waiter comes out from behind the bar and asks for my order. A glass of beer and a slice of the homemade pie. The waiter nods, retreats. There are no more than ten other customers scattered throughout the Gran Arriola Bar and Restaurant. Most of them sit at the bar. No one speaks. Conversation is an intrusion here. Only the television set above the bar speaks. The news is being broadcast throughout New Mexico, but I ignore it. The bartender brings my pie and beer to the table. The pie is apricot. I eat a forkful. I remember how Barney's anticipation would rise during the final five miles before 14 entered Preston. Wondering what flavor the pie would be. Not really a man for pleasure in food. And yet, he took such pleasure here. "There's never been a revolution in this country by the workers, Lisa. It's the pie. Lenin once said that Beethoven made him forget the Revolution. What can you do in a country where it's homemade pie makes you forget?"

I finish the pie, drain the schooner of Mexican beer, and walk to the register to pay Mr. Higgens. Mr. Higgens takes my money in silence, hands me my change in silence. The newscaster on television is still the only voice I hear as I leave. Outside, the night stillness is broken by the high-pitched searing whistling of the cicadas whose nightly cacophony orders the New Mexican blackness. Despite the moon, the darkness is deep, impregnable, enfolding everything in luxurious waves. I walk past the parked Mustang, the leather box still crooked in my right elbow. At the intersection where I left 14 South, I cross the street and cut over the railroad trestle in the direction of the arroyo that corners town's ending. The mountains in the distance are a darker note against the dark. I halt just before I come to the arroyo. I close my eyes. I want to remember it the way Barney and I first saw it four years ago, when we moved to Albuquerque from Gallup and drove into the Monzanos to picnic. Pop Kagle was still alive then. After the pie and ice cream, Barney and I wander through the town. Tensions evaporate. Death is not imminent for the moment. He takes my hand in his and we explore Preston, as we used to explore each other, filled with sharp expectancy. Hand in hand, we drift past the railroad trestle, eye the feedlot and farm equipment depot knotted with clumps of farmers and ranchers who have driven in from Durvale and Willard. Preston is an Anglo town, but we do not understand that in 1964. We are strangers in the land, and the silence that greets our presence is as natural as the two hawks circling high above the feedlot.

At the arroyo, the shimmering mountains in the distance signal town's end with a starkness that bursts upon us. First it is not there and then it is there. The wooden sign above the door as neat and clean as the day it had been first hung back in 1929: KAGLE HOTEL. The white paint on the adobe front is fresh and bright, as is the green wooden latticework decorating the windows and the arch above the door. Everything seems new. Except for the chained padlock strung through the double lock on the door and twined over and over itself.

On each side of the hotel entrance, the carved wooden totems post like surrealist sentries in their green and yellow and red. The design is unlike anything else we are to discover in the pueblos of New Mexico. Three stone cabins stand behind the hotel. In front of it a stone fence. On one side of the fence there is a picture of a running deer, followed by a buckboard tied to a hitching post. On the other side, faces that seem part gargoyle, part angel, beauty and beast inextricably mixed, so that a perfectly aquiline nose is set beneath a wall eye that explodes into the very center of our wonder. And running on each side of the fence, the carefully spaced pebbles that spell out: BUILT BY POP KAGLE, 1929.

"Amazing," Barney offers, breaking the sleepy afternoon heat of Preston.

"I've never seen anything like it. Curious."

"Beautiful," he insists.

"It looks like wildflowers. As if someone had planted it here by accident. In the middle of nowhere. Where it doesn't really belong."

"It belongs," he assures me.

"I wonder who built it."

"Pop Kagle built it. Pop Kagle. Don't you see?"

"Who's Pop Kagle?"

We spend the rest of that afternoon trying to find out. First we go back to the feedlot. A few noncommittal shrugs from the clumps of men. And then someone offers, "I heard tell about him. Built it way the hell back. Then he moved somewhere's nearby." Why? Shoulders shrug. "Fellow like that Pop Kagle, you can't tell nothing." Was he still alive? "Fixes the place up still. Him or his ghost."

Pop Kagle still owns his hotel. We discover that in the real estate agent's office. The real estate agent is named Wally Faulk. As we approach his office, he stands in the doorway, smiling. Wally Faulk is a big man who wears a robin's-egg blue jacket and checked blue and white slacks and a black string tie that falls loosely down his pink western shirt with the bright brass buttons. His office is on Main Street, directly across from the bank. "Have to keep an eye on them," he laughs, winking into the hot afternoon sun. "Can't let them get away with all my money." Wally Faulk laughs again, pleased with what he has said. He rubs his hands together, eyes us as if we were emissaries of God sent to pull him from the wilderness. But when Barney asks him about the Kagle Hotel he slumps despondently against the desk. "I should've figured," he sighs. "You don't talk like folks who want to buy here in Preston."

"Not for money," Barney says, failing to understand. Barney does not like to think about money. He draws his small pension from the union, along with the social security disability benefit the government agrees to give him after the first heart attack in 1958. The social security payment is the government's way of telling him that it is no longer interested in Barney Kadish. I have Arthur's monthly check along with a small income from some investments he has made for me over the years.

We are rich enough. An ironic fate for Barney Kadish. No less
ironic for his Lisa.

"Of course, you're interested in the Kagle Hotel," Wally
Faulk says. His voice is like a horse's whinnying, as if he had
just enough breath left to push the words through. He lights a
cigar, hand held steadily. "All you people are interested in Pop
Kagle's place. Had a fella coming through here last year. Jew
fella from New York." He eyes Barney up and down, not even
pausing at the eyepatch. "Like you." It is said without hostility,
as if he were observing the similarity of their sunglasses.
"Must've took a million photographs of the place. Tells me he
wants to buy. Price ain't an object. Claims he's willing to go
high as seventy-five. Mr. Baron, that was his name. Price ain't
an object. There ain't a house or a hotel in all of Torrance
County worth that kind of money. You think Pop Kagle'll
listen?" He snorts. "Fat chance."

"He's alive then," I say.

"Biggest alive you ever did see. Lives in Chillili. Know
where that is?"

"North," I say. "One of the first towns you hit coming
down from Albuquerque."

"You got it. Chicano town." He eyes Barney once again.
"Not that I'm talking against them, mind. But Lipman Kagle's
the only genuine white man living in that town." He pauses. "If
you can call him a white man."

"Who pays the upkeep?" I ask. "The taxes?"

"Lipman takes care of everything," he says, dejectedly. "I
could've sold that place a hundred times. Made old Lipman
goddamn rich, too. But he ain't interested. I drove all the way
to Chillili for that Jewish fella last year. Dragged Lipman to
one of them fancy new places in Albuquerque. I could've cried.
He got to scrape blood for taxes. But he pays. And he comes
down here every five, six months or so, touches up the place.
Paint. The works. Like he was a goddamn caretaker in a

museum." He puffs at the cigar. "I don't understand. A dollar is a dollar."

Barney has been struggling to control himself all the time Wally Faulk has been speaking. He has even managed not to react to Lipman Kagle's being the only genuine white man in Chillili. "Is there some way we can get in touch with him?" he asks.

"Figuring to buy without an agent?" Wally Faulk snaps. "Hell, think I'm trying to keep you from it? I make my living giving folks honest value. Ask anyone in Preston. Just go ahead and ask."

"We weren't questioning you," I explain.

"Your husband is sure as hell implying."

"No," Barney says. "I just want to meet him. I don't want to buy it. Even if it was for sale."

The real estate agent's eyes hold mine for a few seconds. "You got to understand," he says soothingly, "how frustrating it is to deal with a man like Lipman Kagle." I nod my head, trying to be sympathetic. He tears a piece of yellow notepaper from a pad on his desk, draws on it, then hands it to me. It is a crude map of the route, an X marking the church in Chillili, another X marking the turnoff from 14 North that leads into a switchback. A third X signifies where Lipman Kagle now lives. "It's a cabin. He built that one, too. The cutoff's a few yards down from the social hall. Kagle's two miles or so back. He don't have a phone."

But we don't try to find Lipman Kagle that same day. We drive back to the trailer park in Albuquerque to spend a speculative, restless night. Why had Lipman Kagle built so lovingly and then signed his name and left? Was it simply to create what he alone could create? Not for his fellowman. Not for endurance against time. Not for anything that had given meaning to the life of such as Barney Kadish. Not for anything Barney knew. But for something he recognized in the signature. All that next morning, I feel Barney's impatience. He eats little, says nothing, ignores the two-day-old *New York Times* that Mildred Clayhorn leaves at the trailer door. He sips at his tea in silence.

"We'll clean up when we get back," I say.

We walk outside. "I don't understand it," he blurts out. "All my life, I've struggled against this system. Leftwich, Leftwich, and then more Leftwich. Whether they sell scrap iron and talk like they just got off the boat or send their kids to Harvard and eat lunch at the Union League. But this isn't for money. Or for power. Lisa, I knew men who couldn't help but sew their souls into the coats they made. All right, a thing is beautiful in its way. But that wasn't why. They were selling the one thing they had to sell, their work. They sold to eat. That's all. But why build like that? It makes no sense."

"Because he didn't make his dollar out of it?"

"Yes," Barney insists. He frowns. "Being out of fashion, it's almost a relief. The revenge I've wanted, maybe it doesn't even matter anymore. But this Kagle, what he's done makes no sense at all."

We do not speak on the drive to Chillili. When we turn past Escobosa, Barney pulls out the real estate agent's drawing. In Chillili, we have no trouble finding the switchback. It is past a large barnlike building. A sign over the door says in red paint: CHILLILI SOCIAL CLUB—MEMBERS ONLY! Below that, someone has chalked against the barn: "ANGLOS—KEEP OUT!"

The road is deeply pitted. On the left is what looks like a prosperous ranch. Beyond that, the mound of rusted bodies that has been absorbed into the landscape, an automobile graveyard with a few horses grazing around it. I wonder how a craftsman as obsessed with his work as Lipman Kagle is responds to the mountain of junk and ravaged metal. Armageddon's morning after. A single Chicano boy rail-sits in sullen torpor. He does not look up as we slowly drive past him. He is the first person we have seen since we left Albuquerque. Only the silent buildings and the grazing horses testify to the human-ness of the world.

"I keep thinking I should be helping out more," Barney says. "With the driving." He has never learned to drive.

"Are you uncomfortable?"

"Just guilty," he answers.

I laugh. A smell of dry grass and manure fills the air and I am, quite suddenly, buoyantly happy. "Well, you never wanted to learn before. And you don't have the patience now." I do not mention his heart.

"No," he admits, "I suppose I don't. Anyway, it's no dis-grace for a cutter of fine silks not to drive, is it?" He checks the piece of paper Wally Faulk gave us.

"Does it indicate how far up the road?" I ask.

"He wrote it on the side. Two miles."

I snake the car slowly between boulders and ruts that seem to have been deliberately placed in the most awkward spots. "This Kagle is a true American," I sigh. "Either that or he's a hermit."

About a hundred yards ahead of the next right turn, across from a fenced-in part of the range which ascends dra-matically into sloping Monzano Mountain itself, is a small neat cabin with a sun deck cornering one side of the roof, like a New England widow's peak. An old man sits on the sun deck against the back of what looks like a settee that has been hewn out of one of the huge ponderosa pines that sweep up into the mountains. Barney waves out of the open window of the Mus-tang. The old man is looking directly down at us. He doesn't acknowledge the greeting.

"What does he do there?" Barney wonders aloud, still waving. "What is it he does?"

"He survives," I suggest. "Like us. He's a survivor. The twentieth century's gift to civilization."

"Don't make jokes."

"I'm not," I answer, as I maneuver the Mustang into a clearing to the right of the house. Trees bower the clearing so that it is like maneuvering into a narrow garage space. "Whatever I'm doing, I'm not joking."

Barney gets out of the Mustang and approaches the cabin. He stands next to the wooden staircase on the side that leads to the sundeck. "Are you Lipman Kagle?" he shouts.

"That's me," the man on the sun deck says. He looks down at Barney, pointing the unlit pipe in his hand as if he were a teacher with a ruler. "What do you want here?"

"You're the man built that hotel in Preston?" Lipman Kagle doesn't answer. "You *are* that man, aren't you?" Lipman Kagle sucks on the unlit pipe. "I came to talk to you. From Albuquerque."

"I'm not selling." The voice is surprisingly deep, each word carefully pronounced. "I told that real estate fellow Faulk. I got no reason to sell."

Barney climbs the wooden stairs. He moves cautiously, guarding his resources. I follow close behind him. "I didn't come to buy," he says. "I want to talk to you."

"I'm not selling," Lipman Kagle repeats. "Not to you. Not to Faulk either."

"We know that," I say.

"We're glad you're not selling," Barney says. He wipes his brow. The stairs have taken more out of him than he wants to admit. The stairs and his excitement.

"Glad?"

"Glad," Barney and I echo.

"You're here already," Lipman Kagle grunts. "I suppose I might as well ask you to sit."

There is no other place to sit, so Barney drops to the sun deck. I stand. It is very dry and already hot. But Lipman Kagle seems cool enough. He is tall and lean, his face a mask of ridges and lines. I guess his age is anything between seventy and eighty-five. It is a weathered face, a western face. He wears blue dungarees from which most of the color has already been washed out. The open-necked, long-sleeved red shirt is too large for his lean chest. His face is clean-shaven. Even his hands, which are knotted and scarred like pieces of wood that have been dried in the sun for a long time, are clean. He stares at us for a full minute. Then he grunts.

"It's a beautiful wall," I offer. In the distance, the Monzanos already shimmer with the waves of heat.

"That's why we came," Barney says eagerly. "Because we understand how much it must've taken out of you to build. The craft of it. Anyone can see that. I understand about not selling it. I'm not sure I understand why you don't use it as a hotel. But at least I think I do. What I don't understand is that you don't even live there."

"No," Lipman Kagle agrees, "I don't live there."

"Did you?"

"Only when I was working on it. Lived in the smallest of the cabins then. The left side of the hotel. It's about a foot narrower because the sump made the side ground too soft." He sucks on the empty pipe. For the first time, he looks directly at Barney. "I built that first. Right after I bought the land. A single room and a kind of outhouse. Then I ripped down the outhouse and built a fireplace." Listening to him, I feel guilty because I cannot remember ever having built anything. I remember my Uncle Frank. A carpenter. A different kind of worker. I remember how he shows me the slide rule he carries. My Uncle Frank is very proud of that slide rule.

"And then?" Barney urges. His eyes are fastened on Lipman Kagle's face and he seems unaware of my presence. Something is happening inside Barney. It frightens me. It makes me wonder whether I want Barney to live.

"Then what?"

"What happened after you built the fireplace?"

Lipman Kagle looks at us suspiciously. "That's what that Faulk couldn't understand. At first, I figure I'll just live there. Preston's good enough. Like it is today. Nothing's really changed."

"But you didn't stay."

"No," he admits, "I didn't. I kept building. First them other two cabins. I paid Johnny Raton to take stone from the old mission. Back in the twenties, no one paid much attention to them things. Johnny lived in a wood shack between Willard and Preston. Give me a cheap price. Nice man, Johnny. Had a Navaho wife. I remember her, too. After I finished all three of them cabins, Johnny and his wife come into Albuquerque with me and the three of us, we got drunker than you would Jesus Christ believe."

"But then you built the hotel," Barney insists.

"Of course I did. I built it."

"Why?" I ask.

"That's what Johnny asked when I told him I was going to build it." He shakes his head from side to side. " 'Why, Lip?' he asks me. 'You ain't no hotel man.' And that Navaho wife of his laughing like she's going to split a gut. Well, I wasn't a hotel man. And I guess I knew even then I'd never run the damn thing." His eyes turn to me, ask for understanding. "It just seemed like that was what I had to do. Like when I was shipping out of Seattle in '21. We smuggle this Chink into the ship coming back from Shanghai. Me and this fella Newberry. Didn't take a penny that Chink offered. Why? Because it was the right thing to do. Some things you don't take money for." He waves the pipe in the air, his lean frame bending into the horizon. "I tried to explain it to that Faulk. Only all he can think is money. Offers me more than the place is worth. Even if I wanted money, I can go out and make it. Can't I? But the hotel. I built that!"

"But you don't use it," Barney insists.

"No, I don't. But I built it. And it's not mine to sell. It's only mine not to sell. Is that clear?" He doesn't wait for an answer. "I was thinking of staying there when I built it. And when I finished, I knew I wasn't going to stay there. It didn't seem meant to live in. That's when I added the wall."

"The wall is the thing that catches you," I interrupt.

"Yes," Lipman Kagle says. "Not from anywhere here, carvings like those. I copied them from what I seen up past Seattle when I used to ship from there. Coast Indians is a better class of people. More handsome. Cleaner."

"But why did you build the wall?" Barney asks.

"When in doubt."

"When in doubt?" I repeat.

"To celebrate," he explains. "I didn't know what else to do."

"Celebration of what?" Barney asks.

"Of me, damnit. I built it. Didn't I build it?" Barney and I nod. "All right, then. That wall stamped it mine. Tells them who built it. Pop Kagle, 1929. That's when I finished. Only I never rented. Not even the spring of '34, when the rodeo got burned out in Durvale and they come and asked me to put folks up. They moved the rodeo to the big pasture that used to be outside where McLaren's Feedlot is now. Put up a tent for shade and built these wooden stands. After, they turned it into a ball field for the kids in Preston. But when they asked me to put the rodeo people up, I told them it wasn't no hotel. 'Goddamn, Pop, you got a sign says Hotel. Is that goddamn sign a liar? It's your sign.' Okay, it was my sign. Only it wasn't no hotel. Didn't feel like a hotel when it was finished. And I wasn't going to put up every cowboy bum from Durvale."

"Does anyone ever stay there?" Barney asks.

Lipman Kagle shrugs. "What I don't know don't hurt me. I clean up every few months, touch up the paint. Keep it look-

ing good. Sometimes I find a few scraps of food in the kitchen."
He laughs suddenly, a bright opening to the world. "Once I
found a five dollar bill on the kitchen sink. Funny, you think
them Mountainair kids would just tear through the place. Only
they don't. Nothing's ever been broke. Not deliberate anyway.
People, they respect . . ." He catches himself. "Anyway, nothing's been broke. You two, you understand. I can tell."

"I think we understand," Barney answers. "I think so."

"It's mine because I built it. Only it's not mine. Because it
stands there."

"I understand that," Barney says, his voice quivering
slightly.

"Maybe you two want to stay there sometime?" he offers.

"We'd like that," I answer. "We'd like that very much."

"I got an extra set of keys. You two, you understand."

4

And so we became Pop Kagle's guests in a home Pop Kagle
himself rarely visited—except to clean and paint and
give it a shape that had never been necessary. During the
final four years, when even Albuquerque's slow pace became
too much and Barney Kadish, the child of Odessa, would stand
in awe on the edge of the world, the two of us would get into
the Mustang and take off for a few days or even a week in
Preston. First we would turn off at the social hall in Chillili to visit the only white man in town. Pop would be sitting in
the sun on his roof, a tattered old blanket at his feet in all sorts
of weather—in winter, when a light dusting of snow would
coat the automobile graveyard and the horses would nuzzle
each other looking for a little more to eat; in summer, when the

sun would bake the heaviness into the mountains and Chillili would appear burnt-out and drab, its emptiness scorched and submissive; in spring, when the roadside burst into color with red and purple and yellow wildflowers clinging tenaciously to each other in scattered clumps of growth; and in fall, the best season, when the heat was gone and before the cold had come and with the sure, clean breeze spinning right off Manzano itself. Pop only joined us once on our excursions to Preston and his hotel, but he took pleasure in our visits—and he took even greater pleasure in the use to which we put what he had built. I guess Pop came to think of us as the people who had been sent by fate to justify the decision he had made more than thirty-six years back. Kagle's Hotel was his—he had built it and he had declared for all the world his right to leave it standing empty.

And then, one spring day in 1967, it was ours. For when Lipman Kagle died we discovered that in the will filed in the state repository in Sante Fe, the hotel and three stone cabins and property in Preston had been deeded to Barney Kadish and Lisa Pankow, on the sole condition that they accept the gift in the spirit in which it was offered. Nothing more than that. But we both understood he meant it for an occasional refuge. And no more.

And that was how we used it, spending weeks at a time in the trailer park in Albuquerque and then driving to the hotel in Preston for a few days. "I want to be buried here," Barney says to me one sharp October day. "I've never felt this way about a place before."

"Buried?"

"Cremated. I just want to be. . . ." He shakes his head.

"Part of a place," I finish. He nods. "Not even Odessa?"

"No," he admits. "Not Odessa either. It's not a question of where you belong. Everywhere else you go, it's a question of which side claims you. There are sides here, too." He laughs.

"That real estate agent was right, you know. Pop was the only white man in Chillili."

"If you call him a white man," I add.

"Yes," he laughs again. He leans back into the scooped out tree trunk that Pop also willed us and which we have added to the overstuffed furniture in the hotel living room that must have originally been intended as the guest parlor. "Still, that's accident, not choice."

"Unless you make it your choice."

He shakes his head. "I'm no Zionist, Lisa. I've caught myself sometimes wishing I had been. But I'm not. Pop was different. The only man I ever met who really was beyond politics. Remember that time he claimed to have run with Wobblies. Like Jimmy. But he really had no idea of politics. He could've run with the Boy Scouts. People standing up for each other. Just a helping hand. That's all."

"And there's Pop," I say.

"There's Pop shooting the working class right out the window. And the owning class, too. It's not as if knowing Pop changed my beliefs. I know how little movement there's been in my life. We Marxists, you know, we're children of our fathers." He closes his eyes, as if he were meditating. "Sometimes I wish I could get past that. I'm sixty-eight. And I still wake in the middle of the night and you're sleeping, Lisa, and it's as if I can feel Old Isaac scolding me. Like when I was a boy. 'Avram and Moishe,' I hear him say, 'no consciousness. You're pledged to the future. There is no other way.' I wouldn't have had it any other way. But that's because no other way appealed to me. In Odessa, you were either a worker or a bourgeois. The lines were always clear. At least they seemed clear then. But Pop, where do I fit him in?"

"Pop's way was natural enough."

"For him, yes. But not for me. And not for you either. Not even what you had with Arthur." He pauses, measures me with his lone eye. I can feel his hesitation. Barney Kadish does not usually speak to me about Arthur. "I don't mean that Arthur wasn't capable, Lisa," he adds, softly.

There are still moments when I think of myself as the comfortable wife of the owner of six drugstores in Los Angeles. I taste the big house in Sherman Oaks, the garden, the movement into the world in the assurance of clothes I make myself out of the richest fabrics I can find. I cannot speak to Barney about it. I catch a glimpse of the black leather patch, close my eyes, try to remember what Barney looked like before Minschin took his eye. I cannot remember. I can no longer imagine him without the patch. I think, painfully, of Arthur, rich despite the loss of a wife never his to begin with. I have apologies to make, explanations to offer. But I feel little regret. I tried with Arthur. Failed in the very need to have my own being needed, affirmed. What's mine is mine. I ask for no more.

Barney is uncomfortable. Barney Kadish is not quite certain of how to handle the silence of his aging inamorata. I thrust my silence before him as I once thrust my devotion, when I was sixteen. Barney sighs, explains. "There's a way of immersing yourself into something. I had it with the movement. That's all I meant. Pop had it with this. But Arthur was too measured, too careful. Arthur wasn't Leftwich. The business was money. And the things money could buy. But that was nothing for Pop."

"And you know what it was to Arthur?" I say. I can feel my body quivering with a kind of hard rage, the way I used to feel it when I was fifteen and the thought of sex ran so deep that it was like living with a boil, a boil so embedded in your soul that to lance it is fruitless. My rage is for Barney. Barney. Life eats away at him so that he must measure it in every breath he draws—and yet, the ego still demands that he put distance between himself and others. With Pop Kagle he can share a universe, for he can pretend that each in his own way was an outlaw. But Arthur is proper in Barney's eyes, and propriety must be arranged in its bourgeois conspiratorial order.

For a moment, it is as if I am suddenly faced with a stranger. The face is still recognizably the face of the man I have loved since he made love to me on the pile of foxes in the rear of a Seventh Avenue showroom. Barely fifteen then, alternately loving him, hating him, feigning indifference to him, running from him after I set Howard up because the idea of anyone's commanding such power over me filled me with a fear so intense as to turn me to quivering rage. It wasn't Howard's murder that sent me fleeing to California. I could kill as easily as the rest of them. Perhaps easier. No, it was the cause that demanded and Barney that insisted and Lisa—Lisa performed. And then drilled all the anger deep within her soul during the years in California. And then, twenty-two years later, leaves husband and children and maybe life itself because the past catches up with her. The lone eye stands in her home. Reality blinks and the past again thrusts home. I am a cornered animal who suddenly discovers that the cave it has burrowed for itself is not deep enough.

But I will not give him more than I must. I will not give him Arthur, too. Enough that I have given myself.

He stands up from the tree chair. "All right," he says. His face flushes. "Arthur was a good husband. A good provider."

"A good man," I insist.

"A good man," he admits weakly. "He supported you, even when I . . . took you away." He turns from me, I want him to confess shame, to reduce the dimensions of the revolutionary self he huddles to his memories as death approaches.

"You make it sound as if you triumphed over him."

"Whatever the word," he says defensively. "It's the reality that counts." I taste his dying. "Like it or not, you chose me. Over Arthur. Over Marty, too."

"You were my destiny," I say, my voice dipped in as much irony as I can muster. "Is that it?" He doesn't answer. "Old men flatter themselves."

"I'm surprised you don't say 'dying men,' " he says angrily.

"Don't talk about Arthur. I don't want you treading everywhere. It's no good. Not for either of us."

He breathes deeply, gasps. For a moment, I think it is the last attack. But I steel myself not to give in. I cannot give in. What's mine is mine. I do not want Barney taking it all with him. I will not be sentimental. But I will not give him the right to trample on what belongs to me either. Barney sits down once again. His one eye begs. I turn away.

The next day we return to the Saandia Shangri-La Trailer Park. The weeks drift into each other. Winter bends to spring. In April, about the time Marty comes to visit us, the sun is soft, pleasant. Barney spends his days sitting in the garden, staring up at Saandia. Or else just sleeping. After Marty's visit, we spend a final weekend at Pop's Hotel. It is to be our last weekend away together. Barney senses it. So do I. Neither of us tries to deny it. On the first of June, the heart attack comes. For the next three weeks, Barney Kadish struggles, is moved from a ward to intensive care and then back to the ward again and when the young intern tells me that there is real hope for him, I know that Barney Kadish will soon die. And he dies that night. The day before the summer solstice. In the dry heat of Albuquerque, New Mexico.

While Barney is being cremated, I telephone Gus in New York. "He's dead, Gus," I say. I hear Gus's sharp intake of breath, as if he had been hit in the stomach.

"Did he suffer, Lisa?"

"He died, Gus. That's all." I am happy that I cannot see Gus.

"Shall I tell the party people, Lisa?"

I am pulled up short by Gus's question. I no longer think

of the party. Not even when I spoke of it to Barney. Still, Barney died a Communist. A politics in which one affirms the past by not leaving. How peripheral it all seems now. Even Barney began to think of it as something that belonged elsewhere, a sense of history's erosion. And yet, he remained. "We must understand. We must admit mistakes. We cannot throw away what is good about the Revolution while we destroy the habits of the past." We. Our. Us. Barney's need for collective man. A principle. The party itself an abstraction by now. Belief fades. But Stalin is his legacy. Time buttresses all obligations. He has remained loyal to the demands Old Isaac made.

"Lisa?" Gus's voice again. He has been waiting on the line, confusing silence with grief. "Shall I tell the party people, Lisa?"

"Do you still believe, Gus?"

"It doesn't matter," I hear him say. "What does it matter whether I believe? I'm dying, too. I told you the last time."

"Tell whoever you want."

"He never allowed me to visit him, Lisa. Why?"

"He grew old, Gus. And then, you have to understand, here all such things are distant. What mattered for him was simply getting through the days."

"I love you, Lisa."

I laugh. "I'm sixty-three, Gus. And you? How old are you, Gus?"

"Seventy."

"Seventy," I repeat. And laugh again to the salt of my own tears. Barney is dead. "Goodby, Gus."

"Goodby, Lisa."

I hang up the telephone.

That was yesterday. And this morning I stand in the yard between the hotel and the three stone cabins with the twisted piñon tree that hangs on butting against the stone fence he admired. I hold the bag with the ashes of Barney Kadish. The

Florentine jewel box is on the ground. I whirl around and heave the bag like a discus thrower. It empties itself of ashes and then plops against the wall of the center cabin. I pick the bag up. I shake it, turn it inside out. The remains of Barney Kadish have been strewn across the ground. I pick up the leather jewel box, walk back to the restaurant where the Mustang waits for me in window-closed silence. The clock above the bank says 7:38. The morning sun is bright and sharp, but there is no heat yet. Mr. Higgens stands in front of the door, a pail of water in his hand. He is wearing the same short-sleeved, green-and-white checked shirt and the same khaki pants he wore last night, his midriff partially covered by a short apron that drops to his thighs. He throws the water into the street. Some water splashes against the Mustang. "Sorry," Mr. Higgens says, face creased into a frown. It is the first time I remember hearing him speak. I smile, shake my head to assure him, and get into the car. The Mustang's ignition responds to the key, I throw it into reverse, spin back, then barrel down Main Street to the intersection with 14 North. The last person I see in Preston is Mr. Higgens, standing on the front porch of his restaurant with an empty pail in his hand.

I drive silently. And I drive fast. Hawks circle the horizon. Past Tajique, I turn east toward Durvale. Then I turn north. At Moriarty, I find the cutoff for 66. I ease the Mustang onto the highway. Sandwiched between two large trailer trucks, I head east. Away from what I have left in Los Angeles, away from the trailer park in Albuquerque, away from Barney's ashes resting beneath Lipman Kagle's craft. I am going home. I drive through Santa Rosa, through Tucamcari, into the dead Panhandle heat of Texas.

5

Across the highway from the motel in Amarillo is a billboard that blinks its neon message into the flat hot night. I do not draw the shades. Shadows jump across each other into the carpeted room. "HAVE A BREW, TEXAS! DRINK SONORA DOWN!"

I feel surprisingly tranquil, as if I myself have just emerged from a long illness. The blinking neon fits my mood. The first night without Barney since he showed up on that sun-filled Los Angeles afternoon in 1953. Except, of course, for the times he spent in the hospitals. I am happy to be alone. I know that I will wake up tomorrow or the day after tomorrow or the day after that and discover that I have been caught in this elongated America, this landscape that presses down on my mind so that its sheer emptiness is a box, a trap. And I know that then I will realize that Barney is no longer alive, no longer here to comfort, to do battle with, to absorb my joy and my pain.

Would I have felt so tranquil, I wonder, if I had buried Arthur? The question brings an involuntary smile to my lips. I giggle, embarrassed, slightly ashamed, focus on the play of neon and carpet. Arthur was still alive, undoubtedly in as good health as a man of seventy-five could be. Arthur took his health seriously, as he took the other aspects of his life. He insisted on his time, gentle, but firm, content enough to squeeze a sense of himself out of circumstance. Not like Barney. The future did not beckon to Arthur.

Remembering Arthur, I close my eyes. I play with images of each of their faces. Arthur and Barney, Barney and Arthur.

Their faces split apart, like a jigsaw puzzle that has fallen off a table. I unscramble the pieces in my mind, jam them together. The face that peers out at me is Barney's, but the patch is gone, the other eye has been filled in. Arthur's eye in Barney's face.

Later, lying in bed, I feel the channels of my mind dredging themselves. Barney's need for justification balances Arthur's need for ambition. Solid ambition. Bourgeois ambition. Superseded ambition, doomed ambition—so we had been taught. For the bourgeoisie were neither brave enough nor perceptive enough to understand the inevitability of their doom. An article of faith as easily adopted as the need for vaccination. The word *bourgeoisie*, like a signature which reassures in the familiarity of its curves. I form the word in my mouth: "Boor—geee—waah—zee." I laugh. "Have a Brew, Texas! Drink Sonora Down!" I laugh again. I feel lightheaded, drunk.

To hold yourself accountable for the injustices committed by others. Barney's way. Not Arthur's. Where Barney first agonized over Khrushchev's speech to the Twentieth Party Congress and then claimed the repudiation itself was proof of the revolution's devotion to truth, Arthur would simply have shrugged his shoulders. "Thugs," I can hear him say to our children. "What do you expect of gangsters except that they behave like gangsters?" And then continues to read his paper, armed with the certitude that a man must dig into his own resources to salvage whatever this life enables him to salvage. I was living with Barney then, listening to his tirades against Khrushchev, against the party, against Old Isaac's molding of him, listening to him shake with rumors about old associates in the party, the ones who had gotten past McCarthy with honor, gotten past the congressional packs hunting them throughout the forties and fifties, gotten past being ostracized by the very labor movement they had helped to build—only to break in the face of the one betrayal they had refused to imagine because to imagine it was to create a portion of hell for themselves.

We were living in Phoenix then. The front doorbell rings and I open the door. The face like some shrouded Christian emblem, as haunting as it is distant. He asks for Barney. His name is Harry Karlin and he has not seen Barney since 1950. But he sits in the small kitchen in Phoenix, his face as white as a fish's belly, his shoulders slumped, like a man who has come through a long illness. He stares at the cup of tea in front of him.

"We knew back then he was a sick bastard, didn't we, Barney?"

Barney shrugs. He is nervous. He has been reading the *Times,* voraciously devouring the sections of Khrushchev's speech that have been printed. Stalin's crimes weigh him down with confusion, indecision. Speaking to Harry Karlin, he speaks to himself. "The world is what it is, Harry. We Communists didn't create it."

"We were supposed to change it, Barney. Don't you remember? His madness became our truth. Like they've been accusing us of all these years."

All over America, all over the world, the faithful are shaken. I want to say to Harry Karlin, whom I do not know, to Barney Kadish, whom I know too well, "It's too late for regret. Either accept whatever the party offers or else begin again. Cast the party outside and create a new movement." But by 1956, Barney is two years away from his first heart attack, as old as the century. Harry Karlin is ten years older.

"We're not to blame, Harry," Barney insists. "At least understand that. We're not to blame."

"Why? Because we didn't sell out to capitalism? We sold out to them, to ours. Doesn't that count? What kind of society were we fighting for?" He taps his teacup with a forefinger. His face probes the edges of madness. In the mind of orthodoxy crushed, possibilities war against each other. "What are we left with? We're like children, Barney. Ridiculed by our own beliefs. Remember how you once laughed when anyone mentioned anti-Semitism in the Soviet Union? Do you laugh now? Or do you just say, it could be worse, he wasn't as bad as Hitler."

"It'll die. A vestige of the past. You can't build a new society in a few years, Harry."

"What about thirty-nine years? Can you build a new society in thirty-nine years?"

Barney sighs. "There's no other place for you or me. We're doomed to acceptance."

Harry Karlin stands up, wearily circles the kitchen. "I'm too old," he says from the doorway. "I can't pretend anymore. Black isn't white. It's black."

Fifteen minutes later, Harry Karlin leaves. In a month, he is dead. Gus's letter mentions "possibly suicidal circumstances." The "possibly suicidal circumstances" turn out to be a fall from the twelfth floor terrace of Harry's apartment in a housing project on the Lower East Side.

But Harry Karlin's leap into the future is itself still in the future when he leaves Barney Kadish sitting alone at the kitchen table in Phoenix. Barney weighs the evidence he has been called upon to weigh all his life. Only this time, he has been called upon by one of his own. For weeks, he barely speaks to me. Barney Kadish thinks, broods upon a life that he holds up for judgment. In the summer of 1957, having thought about his situation for close to an entire year, Barney Kadish sits down to write a letter to the party in New York. He asks that his membership, which he had been forced to give up because of the Taft-Hartley Act, be reinstated.

"Choices," I say, when he tells me.

"There was no choice."

"It isn't necessary now," I say.

"Then when?" he asks. "When?"

We never again speak of his rejoining the party. But until his death eleven years later, Barney Kadish faithfully pays his dues each quarter, when the bill from the party arrives.

6

Together with the blinking neon sign advertising Sonora beer, the moon floods the motel room with light. Almost as bright as day. The moon reassures. It jars memory loose from the secret alleys in which memory hides. Reminders spring from everywhere. A kiss of moon and neon on the carpet and I am once again caught inside the glow of a soft California twilight. Arthur is at my side. We have just finished dinner. The children have gone their separate ways. The woman who cleans up—Arthur calls her "the maid," but I am so embarrassed by the thought of someone in *my* service that I manage to call her nothing at all—has already removed the coffee cups and silverware. Solid possessions in the very fragility we have purchased.

The ranch house in Sherman Oaks is not palatial, but neither is it modest. Like Arthur himself, it stands fixed in a certain quiet self-assurance. The Southern California mountains in twilight have been created as much to provide a suitable background for this scene of domestic tranquility as for anything else. Arthur carefully pours a snifter of Grand Marnier. He tilts the bottle in my direction. I shake my head. I feel curiously restless, irritable. I feel smothered by the perfection of the California scene and by my husband's courtesy, his unfailing attention to my needs. I am forty-eight years old, and for the past eighteen years I have fought to preserve Lisa Grumbach's self in Lisa Pankow. And yet, I love Arthur, I admire him. He is fair, he is just.

I turn to the garden outside the sliding patio door. An ordered attempt to create Southern California spontaneity. The colors bloom against one another—red, yellow, white, purple. An exotic dryness. Red clay bricks stamped into the garden walk. I feel stranded, as if the twilight were taking place in some foreign country. Arthur touches my elbow, turns me around, kisses my lips. Arthur is already sixty. But he is lean, remarkably strong, the flesh lined but firm and his arms hard to the bone and muscle. It is as if Arthur's aging were a form of resurrection. He is all angles and surprises, even in bed, a lover who still, after eighteen years, studies my needs with the quiet assurance of a man who wants nothing in the world so much as to please the woman he loves. In everything observable, Arthur stands apart. And yet, I still run from him. I resent it when my body obeys his impulses, his vanities, rather than my own. His roughness descends with the touch. I do not want that now. I feel older than he. I want the self he has taken returned.

Arthur's mouth forms the words, "I love you." As he is about to take what he will not, for all his consideration, allow me to deny him, the telephone in the foyer rings. A slight grimace crosses Arthur's face, but I find myself relieved when the ringing is followed by a knock at the door. "Come in," Arthur says.

The maid enters. She looks at Arthur. "A phone call for Mrs. Pankow," she announces.

"Who is it, Helga?" Arthur asks.

"A gentleman named Barney Kadish. That was the name he gave. Barney Kadish."

I free myself from Arthur's arms and leave the sliding door with the Southern California twilight deepening against the mountains. Arthur does not turn around. He sips Grand Marnier, eyes fixed on the distance.

"Hello," I say into the telephone. My voice is deliberately steady. "Barney? Is it really you?" I am appalled at the innocuous sound of my own voice.

"It's me, Lisa." There is a long pause. "They've thrown me out, Lisa. Of the union leadership. I had to come, Lisa. I had to come."

On the telephone, Barney Kadish chokes on pity for himself. I invite him for breakfast the next day. I assure him, reassure him. Over the telephone. When I return to the enclosed patio, my husband is no longer in sight.

7

I sleep. Sleep fuses with memory. Dreams fuse with fact. Blinking neon anchors memory's rhythms. Flash fires of neon. Flash fires of memory. Barney staring into my eyes. His lone eye is ringed with fear, his shoulders slumped. He looks older than Arthur, but he is fifty-three. His face shadows into pain, his chin is ridden with stubble.

"Leftwich," he offers.

I do not respond. But I do not have to respond. Barney continues.

"All my life I'd dealt with Leftwich. And then, when it counts, I forget about him." It is desert night, cool outside, and the car, the gray Plymouth coupe, which Arthur bought me for my birthday six months ago and which I will drive for the next eleven years, moves effortlessly through the moon-strafed emptiness. The back seat and trunk are loaded with suitcases, most of them mine, two of them Barney's. In my pocketbook is a wallet with a check drawn to myself for $5,000. I know that Arthur will not protest, although it is to be another month before I discover that Arthur will continue to support me. "Leftwich. Getting his own back."

"Not the government?" I ask. I want to keep Barney talking.

"That's the funny thing. We were in a strong position to strike. The war in Korea."

"You must've known they would attack you as unpatriotic."

"They've been attacking me for that ever since I can remember." Barney stares out the window at the desert emptiness. He is aware of the space, a grudging frightened awareness in 1953. "Leftwich," he muses again, as if to break his concentration on the passing landscape. "He finally got even."

As I drive, I feel as if I am the last woman in the world and Barney the last man. With our deaths, the world will end. I can scarcely remember the three children I have suddenly left behind in Los Angeles. I want to curl up inside my own fantasies, empty my mind of memory the way one empties a pitcher of water. To ring hollow. No questions of right and wrong. I feel distant from everything but the 3 A.M. smell of the morning, the isolated desert cold gathering for the daily assault of heat.

"I'm afraid," Barney confesses. His right hand clenches the side-window post of the Plymouth. "I know it's ended, Lisa. But I don't know how to end it for myself. And I keep wondering how I could forget about Leftwich." The voice chokes. I can feel the hand clench and unclench. I touch Barney's shoulder. A comfort. A silence.

"How could they turn against me, Lisa? *My* people." The rejection relived, again and again. Memory, fresh and urgent, catches him on its rise and chokes him with its treachery. *His* people. Don't blame them, I want to say. They were never brave. Never as good as you thought you had made them. But I say nothing. I listen to the steady roar of the Plymouth cutting through the Mojave. Places caught on the bounce back into one's own past.

"They had me up before one of their committees." I drive into Los Angeles, rent a hotel room for the day, so that I can watch the hearing without having to explain it to my children or meet the quiet frown of Arthur. "I gave them nothing. I left the party, yes. Because of their Taft-Hartley. Did you hear me, Lisa?"

"Yes," I say. Indian country in darkness. A record of exterminations. Jews. Indians. Death like a spider's web, incessant, embracing all. I pick up speed, my foot almost to the floor of the Plymouth now. The car roars through the empty desert, seventy, eighty miles an hour. We have been driving for three hours, the moon like a beacon hanging in the star-ridden spaces above us.

And then Barney again: "The day after I testified I'm back in the garment center. Like it was always. 'You did well,' they tell me. 'You stood up to them.' So I wait. I figure the government'll do something. Nothing happens. Maybe with Korea, with all the others they're going after, they decide they don't need Barney Kadish. I'll tell you, Lisa, I almost regretted it. I had it coming." He laughs. "Still, I'm home free. I have the union."

The smell of the desert's emptiness overwhelms. Like cold velvet shaped to your body. "But why a strike?" I ask, surprised to hear two voices, mine and Barney's. "Why did we strike?"

But he doesn't notice that sharing. It is *his* strike, *his* failure. And it is *he* who has stood up to them, *he* who has paid the price. Mere ego? No, something far stronger than wanting to be loved by his people. Yes, there was that, too. But the obligations Old Isaac insisted upon were never in the past. In the mind, rows of reflecting mirrors transform past into present. There could be no past when everything was the past.

"Our time," he explains. "They were parceling out the work before Korea. Slow and then slower in the market. They never give up. Always dream of a time when the union will disappear. If I could prove to them that *they* benefit when their workers are content, it still wouldn't change things. It's not just dollars and cents. It's their need to make workers feel they're worms." He sniffs the night air, tastes the cold. "Do you enjoy this, Lisa?" The first personal note he has struck.

"What?"

"Driving in the desert. Do you do it often?"

Barney Kadish is worried that he has taken me away from my family. He is feeling guilty. "I love it," I laugh. "I've never crossed the desert at night before. Two years ago, Arthur and I drove to Lake Tahoe. Arthur did the driving."

At the mention of Arthur's name, Barney retreats into silence. On the drive to Arizona, I must, I discover, learn to fall back on old habits. Once again, Barney speaks: "After the hearing, the government left me alone. Maybe they were going after others. I had the union pretty much under control. By 1952, I figured the manufacturers were smart enough to settle without a fight. In '46, '48, even '50 when conditions in the industry weren't too good, they'd pretty much agreed to what we'd asked. A lot of government money around by '52. Only I made one mistake."

"Leftwich," I say.

"I'd forgotten how much he hated me. The funny thing, Lisa, is that I tried to be conciliatory. I should've gone straight for their throats." He sighs, exasperatedly. "You're always trying to be smarter than the situation calls for "

"You study the world, Barney. Maybe you study it too much. Most people try to do less."

"I understood something. Then I forgot it. And then I was in trouble. A union leader shouldn't think too much about the world. You're right there, Lisa. Even if he's a Marxist. It's there to be acted upon. Once he understands that, he's safe."

"Safe?" I ask.

"Safe," he repeats. "It cost me, Lisa. Losing control of the union like that. Do you know what it was like when I learned the people wouldn't stand by me? Like a child you've brought up and trained. Then one morning he slaps you on the back, says, 'Thanks for nothing,' and leaves. *The people* "

"But you're not them. You didn't make that mistake, did you?"

"What if I did?" he asks. "Who else? Gus? Itzik? Jimmy when he was alive? The man in the street? They followed because they didn't have enough"—he drums the dashboard with his right hand—"nerve, courage, whatever you want to call it. The word doesn't make it any more real, does it?" His voice races the engine, a high-pitched buzz that seems to breathe new energy into the desert chill. "Did they expect me to look for peace? Nevermind the old wives' tales we tell ourselves. In this country, the working class is no more than its leaders. Without them, it's nothing. Nothing."

"You used to think differently."

"I used to think I could depend upon them. *The* people. *My* people. Lobnick. Marty understood. Lobnick is not you or me. Lobnick is never braver than the day he's born. Courage is a brief spasm And after he's shivered, he's back sucking on self-abnegation. To follow him is humiliation." He is shouting now. "Does that make sense?"

"I'm here, Barney."

"I'm sorry, Lisa," he says, his voice beginning to quiet. "And I'm scared."

"Of what?"

"Of being useless." He pauses. "What's the word in English. Supernumerary. Big word."

A wounded animal, I remember, is autonomous. In rage, dispossession. "And Leftwich?" I ask.

"We built up a strike fund. I always insisted on that. Only I never expected Leftwich to convince them to hold out for three months. I never thought they could afford it. Patterns had been cut already. The manufacturers held. It cost them. But Leftwich made them hold. Tells them all their troubles will end as soon as they liberate themselves from Barney Kadish."

"And the government?"

"They weren't interested in me. Except Leftwich has become a substantial contributor to the Democratic party. 'What could be better?' he asks. The party that's always accused of being soft on communism going after a labor leader who's a famous Communist. The Republicans are going to take power anyway. Truman is finished. So, they have nothing to lose."

"Didn't you have a plan to fight them?"

"They outsmarted me. Refused to negotiate as long as I was under investigation. And then made sure no one was in a hurry to finish investigating."

"And the people left you?"

"For a contract, they'd leave their mothers."

"And did you," I ask, my eyes glued to the desert road, hating myself for tampering with Barney's need to believe what he wants so desperately to believe, "go to them? To the people? Did you ask them to back you?"

"Yes," he says quietly. "And they turned away from me, Lisa."

On the borders of my mind, pity. A sense of justice never given Barney Kadish. Whatever his faults, he would never have betrayed them. A brave man made useless by fears plaguing others. Timid generations. Barney's need is to be needed. How different from Arthur. I listen to Barney Kadish sob. He shrinks into himself, a one-eyed man who weeps because he is superfluous. "Maybe I asked too much of them, Lisa. Still, I always used to insist that working people never deserted their leaders unless their leaders deserted them first." He takes a handkerchief from his jacket, wipes his eye. "Did I ever serve them less loyally because I was a party member? Did they ever find me wanting?"

"No," I assure him, "I'm certain they never did."

"I fought as hard as I could, Lisa."

"Yes, Barney. I know you did."

Survivors together, we drive on, into the desert.

8

Imagination demands. As he slips into the decline of years and powers, Barney Kadish searches for himself. The way a man ends. Reconstruct the past, pay homage to the melding of cause and self. In slippers and bathrobe, he putters around one house or another: a small two-bedroom garden apartment in Phoenix, the pink stucco house in Gallup, the high-rise apartment in Tucson, the trailer in Albuquerque—each a stage upon which Barney Kadish reenacts his history. Artificial New Yorks drawn to memory's play.

An evening in Tucson. We stand at the window of the living room, the city's sweep below us. Barney is eating a banana. In his other hand, a glass of milk. It is 1958, a week before the first heart attack. No warnings for the party veteran. Returned to the party, he has shed his qualms about the Stalin revelations. Contemplative, firm, he yields to no man in his willingness to admit past errors. But the vision remains, if not untarnished then at least ascendant. I do not argue with him. I do not try to convince him that the history that he claims is the very history he must betray. And that must betray him.

If we stand apart politically, we are together in the distance we place between ourselves and the world. Barney and I are like bones found in an archeological dig that mesh so closely they cannot be broken apart. There is no space between us. Together, we look upon his life as if it were a journey undertaken by a stranger. Nothing needs changing, Barney insists. And changes all. "I'm ashamed of nothing," he brags, taking a swallow of milk. "Nothing."

The heart dictates and realities fall into place. I protect

Barney Kadish now, protect him from his own inquiries. Like a child restructuring a world of make-believe, he drifts back, wars with the monsters. Barney's gift to his own history—to embalm it. Leftwich grows more and more calculating, more manipulative than even Barney knew him. "All my life, I've been looking for faith where it can't exist. Marx was right. Class molds the man. Expect decency and you forget origins. A manufacturer. A man with his hand out. To spend a lifetime counting profits. And then, at the end, to want to shape events and men. 'I involve myself, Kadish,' he says to me. 'That's what I learned from you.' To involve yourself. My God." He finishes the milk, discards the banana peel.

"Nothing from the party either. 'You're beaten, Barney,' Levitt says when I go to see him. 'Learn to ride with it. You can still be of use. A man doesn't have to run a union. There are other ways to serve.' Just like that." Anguish relived is no less anguish. His throat burns. His hand shakes, scolds the Tucson evening.

"Was there anything they asked of me that I refused? I *was* the party's creature. And I offered myself. I was good enough. Conscious enough. If they'd asked me to walk on water, I would have done that, too. To be in history. That was the party's gift."

His fingers close on the empty glass, and he puts it down on the window sill. "But what are the forces of history," he continues, "when I meet the sheep in the market? 'I'm sorry, Barney. I got to make a living. I got a family.' You get sick with it." Bitter mimic surfaces in the stage Yiddish accent. " 'I got to make a living,' " he repeats. Workers of the world, you have nothing to lose but your pasts. "One Communist more or less. What did it matter?"

"One Communist more," I say.

"All right," he says. "I never denied it."

"No more tonight, Barney. Let's go for a walk."

"You don't want to hear?"

"Not this evening," I confess.

But he must re-order experience. He must shape the story of his downfall, like a structured nightmare. Leftwich one villain, the government another. In exchange for a small raise, Leftwich insists that Barney and all Communist sympathizers on the joint council—Gus, all but three members of the council whom Leftwich deems acceptable to the manufacturers—be stripped of their positions in the union. "Pension them off," Leftwich insists. "We'll even contribute to a farewell dinner." No government contracts for unions controlled by subversive elements. A letter from the attorney general:

> It is not the policy of this government to support, in any manner whatsoever, those groups which consistently advocate the violent overthrow of this republic by revolutionary means. While this government cannot ban an ex-Communist such as Mr. Barney Kadish from being elected to the presidency of a trade union— despite our knowledge that Mr. Kadish has repeated, time and time again, that he remains loyal to the principles guiding the worldwide Communist conspiracy, principles which include the revolutionary overthrow of legitimate governments—it can do everything in its power to discourage support of such an individual on the part of trade union membership. A democratically elected government is not obligated to cooperate in its destruction. Suicide may be the prerogative of individuals, but it is not something to which the republican form of government can subscribe.

In the market, the people waver. A rich country awaits Eisenhower, shuts itself in the bedroom of its mind. "I would've died for the man!" shouts one Bernie Rednick. "But a no is a no. We're not fighting for Barney Kadish. We're fighting for what we as workers deserve." Bernie Rednick is of the Left, one of those who can greet Barney Kadish out of political affection. He would die for Barney. But neither he nor the mass of workers in the garment center want to live for him. There are other things to live for.

Besides, one man's disaster is another man's newspaper headline. Barney is remembered as a creature of the party. "How many times you seen him at the *Future?* Is that where he fought for us?" It is time for all of America to strike a positive balance. Barney Kadish is out of step. "Changing times, changing people. I'm not saying he didn't do good. But this ain't Minschin he's fighting now."

And so it turns out that Barney Kadish is the problem, not the solution. "Suddenly, I'm the enemy," he explains. "In the flesh. One day, I walk down Seventh Avenue and I watch them turn from me. I'm an embarrassment. It's over. Barney Kadish isn't going to run the union anymore."

Leftwich sends for him. Leftwich's firm now occupies five stories of the Carney Tower, and it is rumored that Leftwich has purchased the building for his son, who is already making a name for himself in real estate. Barney Kadish sits in the marble cool, air-conditioned offices of Jack Leftwich—Fine Coats, Silks, Furs, Inc. It is June 1952. Barney wears a sports jacket and a pair of light-blue summer slacks. Before he enters Leftwich's offices, he spits on the tiled floor. But it is only a gesture. Barney knows it is only a gesture.

"You've lost, Barney," Leftwich announces. He himself leads Barney into his office, past the unsmiling secretary who remains head-down at her typewriter, afraid of contamination by the virus Barney carries.

"Is that supposed to be generosity in victory?"

"I don't have to be generous to you. There's nothing you can give me. Even beaten."

Barney smiles. "Bolshie scum! You owe nothing to Bolshie scum. That's it, isn't it, Leftwich?"

"Owe nothing to anyone. Let others owe me. That's my philosophy."

"Like with Minschin. Or your friends in the Democratic party."

"Why not?" Leftwich asks. "Democrats. Republicans. Minschin. You live with what you buy and you buy what you live with. You think you're different, Barney? My father came from Odessa and your father came from Odessa. So where did they end up? Your father played with toys and mine played with expensive coats."

"Yours was a manufacturer," Barney corrects.

"What the hell does "manufacturer" mean? You know the way the industry operated then. He farmed out the work he contracted for. Took in a couple of greenies to work with him and my mother and me in the shop."

Leftwich leans back in his chair, lights a cigar. He does not offer a cigar to Barney. Leftwich looks old and thick and powerful. "Not fat exactly," Barney explains to me. "But the way the rich get when they grow older. As if the power of the money has spread into their bodies. Like the body he had before this became cramped, inhospitable. It was the body of an . . . What's the word? *Expansive.* The body of an expansive man."

Sitting back against the leather desk chair, the cigar between his teeth, the gold pinky ring as bulbous as his pitted nose, Leftwich testifies to the success he has pursued so relentlessly. Men feed on the act of getting even. Leftwich remembers. His jaw still throbs with the memory of that one time, in 1919, when Barney sent him to the floor in front of his own workers. Leftwich still twitches with the memory. Humiliation demands acts of private vengeance. In 1952, he is sixty-three years old. In another two years, he will leave the moneymaking and the buying and selling to the son who is bigger than Leftwich himself—taller, heavier, richer, known as the "boy wonder of Manhattan" in New York City real estate circles—and retire to Miami to spend the final thirteen years of his life in sun and splendor. A success. But for now, Leftwich focuses on Barney Kadish. He *has* Barney Kadish. Memory dictates need. "It can be arranged, Barney. Don't think your life is more important than another man's. Or more honorable."

"What can be arranged?"

"My son inherited a start in life. You inherited your politics."

"*That's* the mistake?"

"My son is now thirty. American-born. You have sons, too, I hear." Barney smiles. "American boys. No politics.'"

"You're correct there, Leftwich. No politics."

"No left-wing politics," Leftwich insists. "If they do something with their lives, well, then—"

"Buying and selling."

"Call it whatever you want to call it," Leftwich laughs. "For me, it's more a kind of realism." He blows smoke in the air. "A word is a word."

"You brought me up here to tell me that?"

"I brought you here to talk. There are things a man don't forget."

"I hit you? More than thirty years ago. And now, you're going to do . . . what? What is it you're going to do?"

"What would you do? Nothing." He blows more smoke. He is being cautious. After all the years as the voice of the Pattern and Silk Manufacturers' Association, Leftwich has been transformed: a cautious man waiting to cut loose. "Me? I'll wait. Like selling coats. You stick with what's dependable. And then one day you see something different. And you *know* that everyone is going to want one. You don't even have to go after the rich ladies on Park Avenue. They'll come breathing like twenty-year-old bimbos getting their first. Understand?"

"You're afraid to hit me. You want to, but you're afraid,"
Barney says.

Leftwich shakes his head. "I'm sixty-three, for Chrissake.
I'm not even in good shape. I got this here emphysema. My
doctors tell me, 'Don't smoke.'" He laughs, waves the lit
cigar. "So I smoke the best Havanas. I have them shipped from
Havana special. Live once and live well. Anyway, how the hell
I'm going to hit you? I'm soft, fat."

"Then you'll let your goons have the pleasure."

"What good? If I want, I don't need goons. The government of the United States is my friend, Barney. You and your
kind, you spit on the flag. On patriotism. I got no use for
people who shit on this country. Take its bread and shit on it.
Especially people like us."

"Like us?"

"From the other side. What did my old man come here
for? To be better than he was. In a country where a man can
breathe and he don't have to suck the czar's ass. Or Stalin's
ass. Understand?"

"It's not difficult to understand you, Leftwich."

"You want more complexity, Barney?" This time Barney
shrugs. Leftwich hunches forward, raises his head like a
whale's hump out of water. "You think like a schmuck. What
good are you to them? What?"

"You're trying to buy me."

"Buy you! Barney, you got nothing to sell. N-O-T-H-
I-N-G. Children's games you want to play? This is big. Countries are involved. The United States. Yes, the richest, best
country in this world. You and me, Barney, our kind ought to
thank God for putting us in such a sweet country. Buy you? You
ought to cry tears of joy you live here. What do you think
would've happened to you or your union in Russia? With your
fucking Soviets." There are real tears in Leftwich's eyes as he
crushes his cigar in the sculpted glass ashtray on his desk. He
closes in on Barney. "Goddamnit, this is America!" He coughs.

Suddenly, Barney feels admiration for the man. Leftwich believes. And Barney Kadish knows such joys intimately. "You're terrific, Leftwich. A really great patriot."

Leftwich flushes. "You make me sick, Barney. If it was up to me, I'd run you out of this world. Only some government people, they want you to renounce your Commie friends. I told them you're too stubborn. You don't have the sense God give you in Odessa when you was born. But they think you're an important man, The government people want you. So I told them I'd try."

"When his country calls, Leftwich listens."

"To you and the bastards around you, that's funny?"

"It's not funny."

"So why don't you listen, Barney?" Leftwich pleads. "All right, you don't want to be rich. You want to represent your workers." Leftwich bends his massive body across the desk, shares the intimacy of space with Barney. "I understand. I'm even a bit jealous. Your people love you. My employees, they're simply afraid of me. Your people depend upon you to make them feel like men." Leftwich drops back into his chair. He breathes heavily. He opens the bottom drawer of his desk. For a moment, Barney suspects Leftwich is going to pull out a gun. But Leftwich touches a button and a cut-glass decanter of golden Scotch resting on a black marble slab rises to desk level. An expensive set of six matching tumblers surrounds the decanter. Leftwich removes the stopper and pours two large glasses. He hands one to Barney, who looks hesitant. "It's not poisoned."

"Never occurred to me it was."

"So I'm not good enough you should drink with? Listen, a few more years you'll also grow to sentimentalize your old enemies. Like me. A simple world is decent. Fighting me and Minschin was easier than today." He drinks the entire tumbler of Scotch. "*L'Chaim*, Barney." Barney takes a sip of his drink. "Good stuff. Nothing but the best for memories of Odessa."

"Nothing but the best for money."

"And for other things." Leftwich pauses. "You remember that boy worked for me? The one you killed."

"Minschin's hood. The one who claimed to be his nephew. Al, his name was."

"Is that what he said?" Leftwich smiles. "Nephew?"

"I've seen others die. Remember Becker's son?"

"He didn't know how to take care of himself, that one. Shoved himself right in front of Minschin. That's how I heard it, Barney. A man like Minschin was, with so many interests, you don't really want a man like that should notice you." A glint of tears in Leftwich's eyes. "You know something, he was *my* nephew."

"You're lying."

"Oh, not by blood," Leftwich admits. "Not by blood. We was no no more related than you and me. Less. Your father and my father, they were *landslayt*. But a fine boy. You know how a boy can appeal to you. A promising boy. A college student, too. Used to work a full day at the shop, then go to college at night. Always shoulder to the wheel. I felt guilty about him. It was me sent him to Minschin, you know?"

"I didn't know. But I figured."

"He began as a stock clerk. And I seen how strong he was. A young bull. He could take a hell of a physical punishment, that Alvin. And trustworthy. In this business, they steal you blind. But him. Tells me, 'You been good to me, Mr. Leftwich. I'd cut my throat before I steal from you.' That's character. When you killed him, it hurt."

"It's crazy," Barney says to me. "Here I'd fought the son of a bitch all my life. And now I feel sorry for him. Not sorry I killed his Alvin. But sorry for him."

"I was going to sponsor him to law school," Leftwich continues. "He was good to his mother. Some people don't think that's important no more. It's important. A young man like that, he got his whole life ahead of him. I'll tell you something, Barney. I sent his mother a check every month. She just died six years ago. A woman in her eighties. I took care of her and I took care of his sisters. Until they married. That boy *was* like a nephew to me."

"He was a traitor to his class. Becker's son wasn't a traitor. He didn't take for himself."

"I didn't kill Becker's son!" Leftwich says loudly. "You killed Alvin Gestetler. A lesson for me."

"A lesson for Minschin. I didn't know he was your creature then."

"And if you had?"

"I would've wanted him just as much." Leftwich leans across the desk once again, as if he wants to be certain he hears Barney's every word. "I had the union. If we hadn't beaten Minschin then, we were through. For good. A life for the cause. We fixed it so that your boy served his class anyway."

"And now?"

"What?"

"Why do you think I sent for you?"

"Because you don't have the nerve to kill me. But you think you can buy me."

Leftwich shakes his head. "I got this craziness in my head. Know what I figure?"

"That if you buy me now, you've avenged him."

"You could've been a smart politician, Barney."

"Like your son. Courted by Rockefeller."

Leftwich waves his hand in the air as if he were dismissing Barney. "You think you melt everything down and Odessa disappears? My Aaron don't speak like me. For him, Odessa is a place on the map. No more. But he understands he can shake Rockefeller's hand, call him Nelson, fuck his daughter even. Only he's still Odessa. Harvard and all, he's Odessa. His shit and theirs don't lie together. You're a little nervous, Barney. All this crap about the working class and international brotherhood. But somewhere in the back of your head, you wonder what'll really happen when they find out."

"Find out what?"

"That you're scared shitless of this working class of yours. That if they ever *do* triumph, the first knock on the door will be for the owners. And the second for the Jews."

"I didn't know you'd turned religious, Leftwich."

"Odessa is my religion. Odessa. Where people like us once learned to survive. Where between Jews and the world, there was an entire record. Czars instead of Stalins. Or Rockefellers. You think it don't matter. You're a fool, Barney."

"A fool you want to buy."

"Yeah. To watch your balls sweat."

"How much are you offering?"

"As much as you'll need," Leftwich says. "The government don't need you."

"I get off clean. Is that it?"

"Cheap enough so that it bothers you."

"I don't have to give you anything."

"You don't have to," Leftwich agrees. "But I'm betting you will. It's like someone who's been constipated and then he takes a laxative and he can't stop shitting. No muscle. I promise you. Just what you want to give. You yourself. What you can't afford to leave in Odessa. I can even arrange it, you'll shake Rockefeller's hand." Leftwich laughs. "Like that mummy they keep of Lenin. In the Kremlin. What is it? An image. Truth to yourself. That's all you need."

"You'll teach me to tell the truth?"

Leftwich shakes his head vigorously. "No, I don't have to teach you. Not even to eat shit because of that boy you killed. I don't care if you've forgotten."

"You're a charitable man, Leftwich."

"You don't listen, you lose the union, Barney. Guaranteed. As sure as God made apples. Listen, you're not like me.

You can't retire to Miami. You got no life outside the union and the party. Give one and you keep the other."

Barney turns his eyes upwards, to the ceiling. "A dark blue ceiling. You know the way they build today with these acoustic tiles. And I stare up at the ceiling and I remember what I'd done to him all those years back. Only this time, I figure maybe he's right. I was tempted, Lisa. I was. The party had told me to go my own way. The union slipping from my grasp. And if I stayed there one more minute, I would've bought what he was selling."

"And so?" I ask.

"I hit him."

As much a slap as a fist. Leftwich absorbs it, as if a fly had landed on his mouth. He is not in pain on the floor this time, bellowing like some stricken bull. Only he does not understand. What he has offered he has offered out of sentiment. He and Barney are bound together. They have butchered each other's pasts.

"Hitting him," Barney continues, "it was a form of self-protection. He was offering me the union back. And he knew how much I wanted the union. It was like hitting himself. My truer instincts." Barney sighs. "Even Marxism comes down to a choice of humiliations, doesn't it? I walk out and I turn to look at him when I get to the door. He's sitting in that desk chair, smiling. Smiling." He sighs again, wipes his brow which is stamped with beads of sweat. Remembering has cost him. "After all, he was right, wasn't he. I was the one chose to kill Alvin."

"Were you?" I ask.

"You don't leave yourself anything in this world. Not a damn thing. Not even your own past."

9

Every ghost creates its own shapes. For me, the moment of speaking is the touch of recognition. A kiss on the cheek. But there is nothing to feel. As prim and proper as Victorian gentry. Barney is dying. Marty telephones. Ageless romantic. Fat Mildred Clayhorn calls me to the office. "Telephone, missus."

Barney is outside, sleeping in the gun-metal bridge chair in the late afternoon dryness of sun and the whisper of a clean April breeze off Saandia's crest. The voice scratches at the past. But all voices do that. Sudden intrusions on the life we lead.

"Who?" I ask. "Who did you say it is?"

Laughter. Nervous, groping, adolescent. "It's me, Marty. For Christ's sake, Lisa. It's Marty Altschuler."

I listen to the voice. I remember Marty as I last saw him. When Howard died. How old then? Twenty-seven. Twenty-eight. And earlier, the three of us running down Seventh Avenue. Illusion to the wind. The world out of shape. Age is not a protector. It simply steals the past, shapes it to the demands of the present. Barney dreaming of his own importance. Me. Greta. The half-remembered organizers, secretaries, party camp followers. Not even names any longer. Gestures. Hungry, thin, voracious, clinging. Gestures.

Marty wants to see us. He is driving through Albuquerque, on his way to Los Angeles. A conference on the future of the labor movement in America. Lovely eager girls, like my Michelle, with long raven hair and open faces listening to the history of the labor wars during the nation's midcentury sleep. Dead in Vietnam. Dead in River Rouge.

"I want to see him, Lisa. And you."

"That world's finished, Marty. Dead and gone."

"Because it's finished then." The voice over the telephone is eager. "We're the survivors. And I'm still trying to understand what our survival means."

"That's what Leftwich said. Because they survived Odessa together." In Mildred Clayhorn's garden, Barney sits, asleep, face to the sun. It is the face of a child who has been whipped into submission. But only while he sleeps.

"Leftwich?" Marty questions. "Again?"

"Nevermind," I say. I do not want to explain. "Barney's dying."

"I thought so," he says. "I telephoned Gus. He gave me your address. I was surprised." The operator interrupts. She wants another dime. I listen to the *cling* of the coin being deposited.

"You never liked Gus." Mildred Clayhorn moves around the office, pretending not to listen.

"No," he admits, "I never liked him. If there ever was a revolution, he was Barney's chosen executioner."

"Did you think Barney would execute his friends?"

"Before anyone else, Lisa. You, too. I was his student. And you. . . ."

I can almost feel the shrug of his shoulders through the telephone. "What was I?"

"The woman he loved." He pauses. "And who loved him."

I am suddenly enjoying myself, enjoying the conversation, as I remember Marty in the old days. "I thought you were going to say mistress," I laugh.

"No. You created too many conditions."

"I never made him sign a contract."

Another pause. This one signifies an end to flirtation. "Is he in pain?" Marty asks.

"An occasional spasm from the angina. People live with worse. But the next attack will finish him. There isn't very much left." I hesitate, eye Mildred Clayhorn who is self-consciously reading the paper. "I take good care of him, Marty."

"I'm sure, Lisa."

"It's obligation. What else is left for us?"

"Love isn't obligation. Not even at our age." I deliberately do not respond. "Can I come?"

"You won't tire him?"

"Does it matter?"

"Not to him," I admit. "It matters to me."

When Barney wakes from his afternoon's sleep, I tell him that Marty telephoned. "He'll be here for dinner this evening."

He greets the news silently. Then he goes inside the trailer and changes his shirt. As he putters around the trailer, waiting for Marty's arrival, he is uncommunicative. He answers my questions with short grunting sounds, like an animal unwilling to destroy its own concentration. Saying little, he speaks of everything. About a half hour before Marty is to arrive for dinner, I clear the drop table of papers and the usual mess that decorates its surface. I open a bottle of California wine and let it stand in the dry New Mexico twilight. "To love Germany is not to love Hitler," Barney blurts out suddenly. Then he sits down in the wooden armchair and studies his two-day-old copy of the *Times*.

The three of us are awkward together. But we get through dinner. After dinner, Barney pours three cups of wine. He takes them around with a tray. He and Marty eye each other, each of them holding the plastic cup of wine. Marty's index finger moves mechanically up and down the cup. "*L'Chaim*, Barney," he says. He does not drink. I watch the index finger moving up and down the cup.

"Why?" Barney asks. "Why now? After all these years."

Marty shakes his head. "I wanted to see you again. That's all."

"And the reason."

"I don't need a reason, do I?"

"Of course you do. And not sentiment."

"Curiosity then. Curiosity is better." Having waited for Barney to respond to the toast, Marty now takes a sip of the wine. "I like curiosity. It's more accurate."

"How about pity?"

"Pity?"

"Confess it, Marty. A certain nice shading to it. The student who passes the teacher in the middle of the road. You're a success, Marty. I'll drink to you." He raises the plastic cup, drinks the wine down.

"Me? A success?" Marty laughs. "What the hell does that mean?"

"It means that you're still part of the labor movement," Barney answers. "You're a success at what you do. That's more than I can say."

"I don't know what you mean, Barney."

"Yes, you do," Barney responds. "You've done well, Marty."

They stand like that, matched against each other. Barney's face is hollowed out beneath the lone seeing eye. The patch seems to have grown into the skin, a discoloration tight against the dying flesh. Beads of sweat touch his brow. It is dry and cool but Barney Kadish is dying. All three of us know he is dying. The voice grows hoarser. The old and dying must measure each word they utter. A man is apportioned a certain number of words in a lifetime, the Apaches claim. Barney Kadish comes down to his last alloted words. He is struggling to maintain the past. Even in this dry, highway-scented, trailer camp, he must continue to view Marty as the threatening brother. Gus served him, Jimmy worshiped him. But Marty insisted on seeing the world for himself. "There is depth and dimension out there," Marty's appearance tells him. But Marty does not speak the words. "You don't see that, Barney, you with your one eye. Minschin took the one and the party took the other." But the judgment is not voiced.

Marty judges in silence. Barney coughs, flushes. A spasm. Embarrassed, Marty looks down at the floor of the trailer. He pretends he does not hear. *Dignity.* Workers of the world will die in dignity. They are like children about dignity, wizened tough old children, daring to be dared. Defiance reduced by remembering.

Barney's hoarse voice again. Out of the dry air. I look out the door of the trailer as the dark rolls down from Saandia. I listen to Barney's voice, each note dryer than the note before. Touch the imminence of death in a man and you touch his voice. "No one forced you, Marty. Or me either."

In the distance, the swooshing emergence of jets from the Kirtland Air Force Base. "The party betrayed you, Barney," Marty says. "No use for you."

"You're sixty-four, Marty," Barney says hoarsely. "Sixty-four. And if you think it's that easy you're a fool. Betrayed me? The party never looked at me, never saw me. Never saw any of us."

"The party of the workers does not see the workers? For you, that's its strength, isn't it?"

"Did you think because I'm dying, I would have a revelation? A conversion? Maybe become a Catholic? Or a *tsadik?*" Angrily, he crushes the plastic cup he is still holding in his hand, throws it weakly against the drop table. The hand he holds up to scold Marty with is stained with red wine. "Don't think it. Two kinds of us and two kinds of them. The forces of history. That's what you never understood. No man is worth a damn. Of course, the party doesn't care about me. That *is* its glory, its strength. It uses what it can use. Then discards it.

Like an old shoe." He stumbles to the chair, sits down again. His face is white, even in the encroaching twilight and the dimly lit trailer. Neither Marty nor I make any attempt to stop him. "Most people, they let the forces of history rain down on them. I didn't. That's what the party gave me."

"You killed Alvin. That student. Didn't you?" The question is so sudden, it takes me off balance.

Barney clears his throat. "Jimmy killed him."

"You ordered him to."

"I suggested it. No, it wasn't the party told me to have it done. The party people didn't give a damn. They didn't even know who he was."

"Why then?"

"Leftwich said he was a nephew. What was he to you, Marty?"

"It wasn't a necessary murder."

"Yes it was."

"Why?"

"Because people like you sit and weigh each moment, each decision, as if the war between us and them is temporary. There is no morality in our business. You can't choose sides every day. Either the working class or those who shit on them." As he speaks, the eyepatch seems to grow, to encompass more and more of his face, like a ballooning nightmare about to swallow up the rest of Barney Kadish. "You still want virtue. Only it's not clean, this world we live in."

"But the killing. That was a choice."

Barney sighs. "Yes," he admits, "a choice. I made it. I made it for both of us. And for Gus and Jimmy and the others, too." He pauses, searching for the words to explain the past. Marty stands in front of him. "When I was before those congressmen, Marty, it was you I was talking to. I knew you were listening." Marty nods, but Barney ignores that, too. "Whether you did or not, what difference? I was talking to you, Marty. You were always trying to figure out how you might act if this happened or if that happened. Hypothetical situations. They burn at you, Marty. At your insides. You wanted to be moral and it made you less than what you were. A radical learns. First he learns there is no God and then he learns there is no people either and finally he learns that there's nothing but the self he's already given to the cause."

"So that he can believe," Marty interrupts.

Barney coughs again. His breath is coming hard now. I will not interrupt. I stand above the small sink and wipe the dishes. I feel transformed. To die into yourself. I can scarcely hear Barney's voice as he says, "'All right, so that he can believe.'" An interminable pause. "But not in his fellowman. The loneliest of trades, this radicalism business. These college children you're going to speak to, what do they want you to tell them?"

"Whatever I can teach them, Barney."

"That all their logic is nonsense," Barney gasps. "Lenin's mummy would howl if he could hear them. Solidarity! Solidarity with us! With their illusions of what we were! With what? But you don't want to seem pompous. Or heroic. You want to encourage them. To be modest, to affirm their illusions."

"And you, Barney? If you were going in my place?"

"I would tell them it's not difficult to kill. The difficulty is when you try to understand what it was made you kill." He sucks in air. "The hardest part is to be tireless in pursuit of what is laid down for you."

"To follow orders," Marty suggests.

"To follow orders," Barney agrees.

"And you still believe."

The good eye closed, Barney speaks into darkness. "I would have killed a hundred like him. But take your triumph. I had my doubts. I didn't go back into the party until 1957. I stayed out for a long time."

"But never dissented publicly."

"No." Barney's breathing is deep and even now, as if he were trying to hold on to his portion of the universe. "Not in public. Because that would have given the victory to them. To the government and to the party, too. Don't you see? My life *belongs* to me. The party took it for a time. The government tried to buy it. But in the long run, it's mine. And that matters."

"Why *did* you leave, Barney?"

"You mean, why didn't I go back right away. As soon as they threw me out of the union." Marty's face blends into the orange-painted wall of the trailer. "Because the forces of history explain it just so far. A man has to justify his life. Even a radical. Do you think any of what we did really matters? A footnote in somebody's history of American labor. You, me, the Reuthers, even John L. Lewis."

"And trying to prove yourself? To whom?"

Then Barney's voice again, softer, as if the hoarseness had finally disappeared in the need for resignation. "I didn't have a choice," he pleads. "Not the party. Not the cause. Not the union even. It was myself. I couldn't sell Barney Kadish."

"But you're still lying to yourself," Marty insists. He ignores my raised hand. "You're still their creature."

Barney's lone eye opens. "Am I? Well, what of it? A man is permitted to show up late for his own funeral."

The air vibrates with Marty's need to embrace Barney. " 'Barney Kadish,' Walter says whenever we're talking, 'you're lucky to have known Barney Kadish.' "

"And you?" Barney asks.

I chain my eyes to Marty's face. He smiles and stands before us, the young man who ran down Seventh Avenue with us, a little absurd, the parts tightened into one another, a handsome young Jew from the Lower East Side. That was when Barney had both his eyes, when the world seemed paused on the brink of its own rebirth and belief was not complicated by reality.

"I was your student," Marty answers. "No Reuther ever had to tell me. I knew how lucky I was."

"I'm tired," Barney says. "You wouldn't believe how tired I am."

"I'll be leaving, Barney." Marty nods to me. I point to the darkness outside and hold up the five fingers of my right hand. He nods, presses his lips together. The final assignation with Barney's girl. Marty walks over to where Barney sits in the chair. His fingers reach out, touch the leather patch. "Goodby, teacher," I hear him say.

10

Beneath our feet, the gravel seems to move, as if we were swimming through quiet pools of water. We walk toward where the moon lights up the road. A ribbon of concrete moves toward the mountain. The sides of 66 are frosted like the sides of an elongated ponderosa standing in the snow: gas stations, drive-in restaurants, taco stands, souvenir shops featuring genuine Navaho jewelry at rock-bottom prices, used television sets, neon signs flashing their unbeatable prices to passing drivers. Marty does not speak. As we crunch across the trailer park, he takes my hand in his. Gestures. I do not remove my hand.

"Always it's his," Marty says. We turn to the exit of the trailer camp. A single floodlight illuminates the gold-lettered sign: SAANDIA SHANGRI-LA. Outside, twisted dirt boundaries fade away into broken sidewalks and fallen curbstones.

"What's always his?" Marty still walks the way he did when we were young, slightly pigeon-toed, jumping off the instep of his foot as if he were prepared to run for his life at any second. I must force myself to keep up with him.

"Women, for one thing. The ones I love anyway. First you. Then Greta. Now I'm seeing you again and he's in there dying. And we're talking about Barney."

"Do you see Greta still?"

"Not in years. All silence in the distant years."

"I didn't know you quoted poetry."

"It's my line."

"Why didn't the two of you marry?"

Marty lets go of my hand. The cars whistle past, sixty, seventy, eighty miles an hour. "She didn't want to marry again. Then she didn't want to see me."

"Why?"

"Maybe it's Barney's effect upon women," he laughs. "One-eyed martyr. Doth not a Jew bleed? Ask Barney Kadish. I guess it's simple enough. Barney appeals. For me, it's acceptance or despair."

"You never married," I announce, as if I were offering Marty some information he had not known before.

"A remarkable lack of virtue. Marty the bachelor. Organizing auto workers. When I could have been fathering children."

"Where is Greta now?"

"You leave me nothing, Lisa," he sighs. "The last I heard, she was living on the Upper East Side. Near her son, who is apparently intent upon becoming mayor of New York. Greta may someday find herself the mother of the mayor. Not an overwhelmingly significant role in life."

"Why does it seem so unnatural that we've never met?"

"You ride a gale in this world, Lisa. All your life. Then you complain that it's not natural. You know, I never understood how modern you are."

We have come to the end of the sidewalk, where it peters

out into the foothills that rise into Saandia some eight miles away and five thousand feet above us. Marty halts. He takes my hand in his again. He stares up at the dark cut of the mountain, solid against the moonlit sky. "What will you do when he dies?" he asks.

"Go back East," I answer. "It doesn't seem very important. Our lives are finished."

"I had to see you again, Lisa. You and Barney."

"To say a proper goodby?" I can feel my smile. "We're too old to live our lives again, Marty."

He drops my hand. "I suppose so," he says. "Maybe that's what I'll tell them in California." Then his arms embrace me and he reaches down and kisses my forehead.

I close my eyes. Once again, I see myself running with Marty, with Barney. The world fresh and open and promising. And we are young enough to change it. I feel the night deepening. The past enfolds us, traps us, tears us away even from the futures we once willed ourselves. I hear Marty's footsteps walking away from me. I do not open my eyes. I want no more beginnings. To have come this far is enough—for me, for Marty. Even for Barney Kadish.